CW00677294

KENDRELL
PUBLISHING

THE BLANCHARD WITCHES

PRODIGAL DAUGHTERS

MICAH HOUSE

This is a work of fiction. All of the characters, organizations and events portrayed in this novel are either products of the author's imagination or used fictitiously.

The Blanchard Witches: Prodigal Daughters

First published 2021

Published by Kendrell Publishing, Birmingham, Alabama

Edited by Crystal Castle

Cover design by Paul Palmer-Edwards

ISBN: 979-8-9887296-1-7

Dedicated to my late grandmothers,
"Mama House" and "Big Mama",
the Olympias of my life...

And to my late Great-Aunts Virgie and Agnes.
Thanks for being my Zeldas.

CONTENTS

CHAPTER ONE

The Patient

There was a fractured sense of calm in the midst of the hysteria floating through her mind as she lay in the bed. She could hear screams resounding from behind the stone walls of her room. She could not be sure if it came from the corridors or if there even were corridors. But she heard them all the same, echoing through the dark spaces. The screams were eerie and unsettling, like the cries of mad people.

Psychiatric, she thought. *Is that where they have placed me?* It appeared to be more like a mausoleum—cold and frightening and haunted. Her eyes made their way across the room to take in her bleak surroundings. The walls were made of cinderblock, painted a light gray as if to shut out any ideas of joy or peace. A greenish-brown mold creeped across some of the blocks, and above the mold were streaks of water stains—proving the roof most definitely leaked. The only piece of furniture other than her bed, with its musty mattress and aluminum side-rails, was a thin metal cabinet with one door ajar to reveal the contents of tubes, cotton swabs, and catheter bags. There was a systematic beeping coming from one of the many machines she was hooked to. She wondered which one it was and which of the many tubes and wires stemming from her body connected to it.

The door to her room opened, and a woman walked inside. She was dressed like a nurse, but her demeanor was anything but pleasant. She could faintly recall having seen the nurse before, but her mind was still so groggy. *Have I been conscious before?* The only thing she really could remember was that she did not like the nurse. In fact, she found herself quite afraid of her.

"I see you are still awake," the nurse said approaching the bed to unfasten the urine bag from one of the many tubes. "Don't try to speak," the nurse instructed. "You wouldn't be able to anyway."

The nurse connected a fresh bag to the catheter tube and grabbed the patient's wrist with her cold, clammy hand. She told the patient, "Your pulse is good. You are definitely making progress." Yet she never made any notation in the chart hanging on the door.

"I-I...uh..I.." The patient tried to speak, but it was no use. The voice would not come forth. Her throat felt like hardened cement, and her tongue was so weak it could barely move. Each attempt at communication made her throat feel like a knee scraping concrete.

The nurse looked angry, almost like she wanted to strike the patient. "I told you not to try to speak!" she scolded. "You are not yet capable of forming words. Do not disobey me again! I am all you have around here. You'd be wise not to upset me."

The nurse removed a small bottle and a needle wrapped in plastic from her pocket. She tore off the plastic and plunged the needle into the bottle, withdrawing its contents. Grabbing one of the tubes hanging from the IV stand, she injected the medication into the tube.

"You'll be more relaxed very soon," she said to the patient before walking out and locking the door behind her.

The patient lay in bed staring up at the grimy, water-stained tiles of the drop ceiling. *The roof leaks*, she reminded herself. She was remembering now. She had been awake before. Many times. She could recall now what it felt like when water dripped onto her from those stains above. How long had she lain there with rain dripping on her face in the past? Did that awful nurse ever try to move her bed out of the path of water? What was in the bottle she injected her with? Was it the reason why she felt so sleepy all of the time? Was this why thinking was such a struggle for her?

There was so much she did not know. She had been in this room for so long, yet she had no memory of it. Would she ever manage to speak again? Or walk? And where exactly would she walk to if she could? Certainly not out there in that corridor. Not where all those horrible screams were coming from. She wondered just what they were doing to the poor person who was out there screaming. She wanted to cry. She was at the mercy of this cruel nurse. *Does anyone even know I am here?* The nurse was the only person she had seen since she had been here. Would anyone else ever come? Didn't this place have other staff?

The patient wanted to cry but stopped herself. It might anger the nurse when she came back. If she came back. Sometimes she didn't. Even though she was a terrible caretaker, the nurse was all she had after all. She did not want to anger her. She was quite sure that the tender place on her cheek which still stung a little, had come from angering the nurse—although she couldn't quite remember. She could not remember anything. All she could think about now was sleep.

CHAPTER TWO

Thanksgiving Day

November in Alabama was never predictable. One day might be a balmy 70 degrees and another could run as low as 35. Flowers which bloomed in late summer might very well hold their blooms until mid-November if the frost held off until the last possible moment. However, this November was proving to be a very cold and very wet one. It might have been borrowed from January. An early frost had killed the flowers surrounding Blanchard House, but nothing could disrupt the picturesque beauty which was Blanchard House itself. The large twenty-three room country mansion sat peacefully amid the sprawling acres. It was one of the largest homes in Daihmler County, Alabama, but its wooden façade calmed any pretentiousness. The house was decorated in the truest of harvest traditions. Corn stalks were tied to the porch railings and picket fence. Pumpkins in clustered arrangements lined the porch steps. Indian corn and hanging gourds stretched over the doorway.

It was Thanksgiving Day, and the entire house was bustling with cheer and excitement. It wasn't only the day which brought a smile to 85-year-old Olympia Blanchard; it was also that today her granddaughter Salem and Salem's half-sister Arielle were driving in from Atlanta to spend the weekend. The old woman sat impatiently in the living room waiting for their arrival as her two daughters, Artemis and Demitra, busied themselves in the kitchen preparing the feast. Olympia had spent a lifetime in that kitchen, but those days now seemed so long ago. Artemis took over the job of cook in the family many years ago, but now that she had opened her own restaurant in town, most of the day-to-day meals were prepared by Olympia's granddaughter Yasmine. Today being Thanksgiving and Yasmine being rather new to cooking, the family unanimously agreed to let Artemis and Demitra tackle the holiday meal this year.

The two sisters busied themselves happily in the large family kitchen. They worked well together, moving in a unison only years of experience together could teach. The sisters looked very much alike. Both were slender, with pale porcelain-like skin and raven hair cascading behind them—Artemis' down to her waist, Demitra's stopping at the shoulder. The small counter television was tuned to the Macy's Thanksgiving Day parade, although if truth be told neither of them had watched a minute of it. But it was tradition to have it on.

Olympia learned long ago to stay out of their way in the kitchen and had settled herself in her winged-back chair beside the living room fireplace as she anxiously waited for Salem and Arielle to arrive. Olympia was dressed in a matronly-styled pale blue dress which balanced nicely against her brilliantly white hair which had been rolled, set, and teased out the day before by her hairdresser. For a moment she thought she'd heard footsteps on the front porch, but it was only Yasmine stomping angrily down the foyer stairs.

"There's no use in trying!" her youngest granddaughter exclaimed joining her in the living room as she puffed the bangs of her long brown hair out of her face.

"What's that, dear?"

"Your grandson," Yasmine snarled. "Seth won't even look at me while that damn football game is on."

"It's the big game, I expect," Olympia sighed.

"Aren't they all, *the big game*? Cotton Bowl. Sugar Bowl. Orange Bowl. 'Alabama this, Crimson Tide that!" Yasmine scoffed. "This is our first Thanksgiving as husband and wife, and all he wants to do is watch sports."

Yasmine was Olympia's step-granddaughter, yet she was also the new bride of Olympia's grandson. She had grown up in Blanchard House after the crash which orphaned her at six years old. Yasmine had always been in love with Seth, but it had taken him his childhood, teenage years, and early 20s to realize he had always been in love with her as well. They were married a month ago on Halloween.

"I could run around buck naked in the upstairs den, and he wouldn't even notice me."

"Now, child," Olympia smiled. "Your bedroom is right above my own, and you have the squeakiest bed springs I've ever heard. I hardly think you're being ignored."

The front door burst open with the force of a train as Madame Zelda bounded inside shivering. Zelda, Olympia's lifelong friend, was always a sight to behold. She too had been to the beauty parlor this week, replacing her maroon-colored hair with a newer, burnt orange dye job. Her make-up always looked clown-school inspired, and her penchant for gaudy hair color only accentuated it. Today she was wearing her flowy, flowery, fuchsia and yellow muumuu dress. Zelda made her living telling fortunes to the townspeople of Daihmler. She told it like it was—often providing information her clients might not necessarily want to hear—but she was never wrong, and that made her as indispensable to the wives and businessmen of the town as their hairdresser or general practitioner.

"It is cold as hell out there!" Zelda cried rushing in.

"I believe Hell probably isn't that cold," Yasmine pointed out.

"Hell is probably diff'ernt for everybody," replied Zelda. "For me, being cold all the time is more a hell than any blame fire'd be. Had a cousin once who could walk through fire. He wouldn't been bothered a bit by Christian Hell."

"I remember that cousin," Olympia recalled. "Didn't he work with a circus for a while?"

"'Till he bought a pig farm in Mississippi. I think he died in a tornado back in 1982. Now that's a new take on the expression 'when pigs fly'. I'm sure he went to Hell, though. He was a mean feller."

Zelda's ability to cast snide remarks about nearly everyone she'd ever met was always a source of amusement for the Blanchard family. Zelda knew everyone in town and had a story about them all, which she never shied away from telling.

"I don't know if I believe in Heaven or Hell," Yasmine noted. "I'd like to believe my parents and Granddaddy are in Heaven and I will see them one day. But I just don't know if I actually believe in something like that or if I just want to believe all that's out there."

"Oh, there's a Hell," Zelda said. "Lympy and I went there once. Long time ago. Back in '68 wasn't it, Lympy? Remember that demon we stopped on that trip to Los Angeles?" Zelda was staring at Olympia now—not exactly *at* her, but at something below her chin line as she made a disapproving face. Olympia paid it no attention.

"That wasn't a demon, Zelda. He was just an average everyday psychopath."

Zelda walked over to her friend as she continued to speak, "'Naw Lympy, I remember quite clearly us going into Hell to stop him." Zelda reached her fingers toward her old friend's neck and lifted the thin gold necklace up with a finger. She shook her head at Olympia.

Olympia continued to pay little heed to Zelda's silent commentary on her jewelry and continued with the conversation at hand, reminding Zelda, "That was a nightclub in the Boyle Heights area, and you were on a lot of acid."

"What!?" Yasmine cried. "Zelda did drugs? Oh my God! Grandmother!"

"Girl, we wasn't born old, you know!" Zelda declared as she unfastened the gold necklace from around Olympia and pulled it free. "It was the 60s."

"I can't believe what I'm hearing!" Yasmine exclaimed.

"Well, let's not spend too much time worrying about it today," Olympia smiled, dismissively. "Zelda, what are you doing?"

"Getting' this tacky ass thing off 'a you. You already got pearls on. Why you insist on wearin' this junk every year I'll never know. Just cause your dumb old second husband, Martin, gave it to you on Thanksgiving 40 something years ago."

Olympia watched her best friend sling the necklace into an end table drawer and slam it shut. Zelda never did like Martin Caswell. And—if truth be told—Olympia hadn't been exactly crazy about him herself. She had only married him because he was a nice man with a decent income who was willing to take on the role of stepfather to three adolescent witches. Then he had the audacity to die two years later.

"No negativity today, Zelda. This is Thanksgiving." Olympia pressed her hand to her chest. Her heart was beating a little fast, probably from the excitement of the day. "Today we will have no bickering. It is a happy, calm family day."

"Speakin' of family," Zelda remarked. "Where's that husband of your'n, Yaz?"

"Upstairs watching the game."

Zelda turned around and started up the stairs. "That's where I'll be then. Call me when dinner's ready. Seth and me got a bet goin'."

In the kitchen, Demitra was stirring a bowl of macaroni and cheese while Artemis had the rather large turkey out of the oven, basting it with one of her special sauces. The aromas from the many pots, pans, and bread baskets filled the kitchen.

"I cannot believe you are making instant macaroni," Artemis said.

"The kids won't notice the difference. Seth will eat anything, and Fable only likes Kraft mac and cheese anyway. Beryl will skip the macaroni and gobble up your mashed potatoes with the clumps in them, and Salem is going to just cover whatever she eats with gravy—even her cornbread."

"It's funny how you still think of them as they were when they were children," Artemis laughed. "I doubt Salem still covers everything with gravy—not with her tiny little figure."

"I guess I do still think of things the way they used to be," Demitra smiled, still stirring the cheese mix in. "Like right now, I halfway expect to see them all playing in the yard."

"I know what you mean," Artemis agreed. "At Seth and Yasmine's wedding I realized all our babies are grown up now. I hadn't really put that together before."

Demitra checked her watch. "I wish the rest of our guests would get here. And I have no idea what's keeping Salem and Arielle."

"You know Salem, she's always late. And Howard said he would be here by noon. Of course, the one you're really concerned with is Jerry."

Demitra blushed and elbowed her older sister. "Jerry will be here shortly."

Artemis raised an eyebrow to Demitra and said, "Moving kind of fast, aren't you? You met him less than a month ago and already he's coming to Thanksgiving dinner."

"Thanksgiving just happens to fall a few weeks after we started dating. We see each other often, so I see no particular reason why he shouldn't be invited to Thanksgiving dinner," Demitra defended. "Besides, he's special." *Very special*, she said to herself as she placed the macaroni on the dining table in the connecting room.

Artemis and Demitra heard commotion in the living room and went to see who or what it was. Salem and Arielle had just entered amid a laughing frenzy. It took Salem a moment to recover herself to tell the story.

"You guys will never believe what just happened."

"Salem!" Olympia cried rushing from her chair to embrace her granddaughter. "I was worried. You're over an hour late."

"Just wait till you hear, Hecate."

"Arielle," said Olympia, ignoring Salem's urgency to tell her funny tale. "You look as lovely as ever. I'm so glad you're joining us for Thanksgiving."

"Thank you, Ms. Blanchard."

"Come now, child," Olympia replied. "I've told you to call me Olympia."

"Sorry, I keep forgetting."

"Will somebody listen to me?!" Salem exclaimed. "I'm trying to tell a story here."

"Then tell it," Yasmine said.

"We had a flat tire on our way here," Salem excitedly began. "When we stopped to change it, we saw that the spare tire was flat too because Arielle drives like a fool and didn't tell me she'd blown out a tire last week and the spare was already on the car. So anyway, a man stopped to help us change it."

"That was nice of him," Yasmine remarked to her sisters-in-law.

"Well, Arielle here tells him we don't require any assistance. Then she levitates the car so that the three tires are carrying the load and the flat tire is just hovering in place keeping the car level. We drove off leaving that poor confused man standing in the dust."

Everyone stared blankly at Salem.

"Okay, maybe you just had to be there."

"Oh, I'm sure it was hilarious, dear," Olympia carefully chose her words. "But Arielle, sweetheart, I'd caution you from demonstrating your powers so publicly."

Arielle felt a little ashamed. "I'm sorry. I guess I'm used to Charleston. Witches there don't really hide that much."

Olympia gave her a loving smile to ease any admonishment she may have felt. "I understand. But you'll find Alabama and Charleston are very different environments."

A sudden thud resounded as the front door slammed shut and the heavy stomp of a broad, six-foot man with graying black hair appeared in the entry hall.

"Is this where the all-you-can-eat turkey buffet is?" shouted Howard. Howard Caldwell was Olympia's financial advisor, lawyer, and man for everything. He had been a friend to the Blanchard family since birth—his father having been a childhood friend of Olympia and Zelda.

Howard made the round of hugs before tossing his coat over the staircase rail and following Artemis back into the kitchen. The second the kitchen door swung shut behind them, he grabbed a Coke out of the refrigerator and popped the top. "So, Arielle is still buddies with Salem, huh?"

"Of course," Artemis replied. "Why?"

"I just figured that was too weird a situation to last once they got to know each other. I mean, meeting your half-sister after all these years...it's strange they've bonded so much."

"They are practically inseparable," Artemis noted. "I told you about Arielle's homelife. Her mother is a terrible person. She treated Arielle horrendously all her life. Since she and Salem met, I think they've both been the missing link each other needed."

"Yeah," Howard said. "It's gotta be rough for Salem this Thanksgiving. Losing her husband and baby earlier this year."

"Arielle's addition to her life has really helped Salem move on and step out of her grief. And don't forget what I told you about that final battle with Patric. Arielle really came through for us. Had she not aligned her powers with Seth and Salem, I'm afraid Patric might have won."

"I still don't know about that werewolf story..." Howard said with a smirk. "Wish I'd been able to see something like that."

"Believe me, Howard," Artemis stated. "You don't. We all almost died last month. Thankfully those three siblings' powers united was enough to take Patric out."

There was a knock on the kitchen door. Artemis tried to peer through the window to see who it could be but had to wipe her hand over the foggy glass from all the heat of the cooking. She did not recognize the man standing on the back porch.

"Yes?" she said opening the door.

"Artemis!" he exclaimed. "It's me—uh, Jerry. Jerry Miller."

"So, you are Jerry!" Artemis said letting him inside. "Demitra has been so excited to have you meet the family." She paused momentarily—all at once it seemed peculiar to her that this man would come around to the back door. "Why didn't you ring the bell on the front porch?"

"Oh. I—I just wanted to take a look at your garden," he answered clumsily. "Demitra has told me all about how you guys grow everything yourselves."

Howard introduced himself and led Jerry into the living room where Demitra was waiting to introduce him to the family. Demitra's daughters, Beryl and Fable, shook Jerry's hand politely albeit reluctantly—neither too keen on seeing their mother with another man. Before too much awkwardness had time to set in, Artemis announced dinner was ready and everyone who had not previously met made introductions while filling the seats at the table.

As Fable took her usual seat, she noticed Zelda's new hair color for the first time. Her mouth hung open at first, mesmerized by the orangey glow atop the old woman's head. Finally realizing she was staring, she commented, "Zelda, I see you changed your hair color."

Proudly Zelda gave her round old lady bob a pat and beamed. "Yeah, gotta keep up with the times. You know what they say—your hair is tha' first thing people notice about you...unless you have bad teeth."

Attentions turned away from her pumpkin-colored hair and focused upon the spread before them. The long dining table was brimming over with the delicacies of the holiday. Two large, savory turkeys sat steaming on each end of the table. Cornbread dressing, cranberry sauce, an assortment of peas and beans, mashed potatoes, macaroni and cheese, fried okra, and steamed veggies sent their combined aromas up and through the room making the very air itself good enough to eat.

Seth began carving the turkey nearest him while Beryl started slicing the one nearest her. "You always slice it up better than me," Seth pointed out to his cousin. "Then again, you get paid to slice things up neatly."

"Beryl is a doctor," Artemis politely explained to Jerry. Jerry nodded. Artemis then felt a little foolish. Jerry was dating Beryl's mother—obviously he already knew she was a doctor.

"I always wanted to be a doctor," Jerry told Beryl. "But turns out I can't stand the sight of blood."

"I'm the opposite," Beryl said, using the opportunity to make conversation with the new man in her mother's life. She hoped perhaps by pretending she was okay with the situation, she might become okay with the situation. "I can take the big stuff, but if someone falls and scrapes their knee, I get lightheaded."

Artemis laughed. "I remember when you were a kid and fell off that tire swing we used to have in the oak tree. You split your chin open. Demitra fainted, and Larry and I had to take you in for stitches."

"I forgot about that," Beryl smiled. "I cried all the way, but Daddy said if I were going to be a doctor like I said I wanted to be, I'd better stop crying and be a little professional. Of course, that was before I knew how to..." She was about to say *heal myself* until she remembered there was a stranger dining with the family.

"Uncle Larry used to tell me whenever I got hurt that the girls would make fun of me if I cried," Seth said. "He said us boys have to stick together around here so we don't give those mean girls anything to hold over us."

Jerry looked a little pensive. Artemis noticed.

"I'm sorry," Artemis said, glancing at him. The epitome of a gracious hostess, Artemis never wanted anyone to be ill at ease in their home. "I hope we aren't making you uncomfortable mentioning Demitra's late husband. Let us change the subject."

"Not at all," Jerry replied. "He is a very lucky man to be remembered so fondly after all these years."

"You know, Beryl," Yasmine called from the other end of the table, spreading cranberry sauce over her dressing. "That swing didn't really break."

"What are you talking about?" Beryl replied. "The rope snapped in two."

"Actually, it didn't," Fable admitted. "Seth was being mean to me and Yaz, and we thought we'd get even with him. We cut the rope. We thought he would be the one swinging. He was always in that swing."

"I should give you all a spanking," Demitra quipped.

"*My wife*," Seth grinned as he elbowed Yasmine sharply in the ribs. "Trying to kill me at 10 years old."

Yasmine blushed and tucked her head into her shoulders. She leaned in to kiss him, and he met her lips midway. Then he gave her hair a sharp yank of revenge before returning to his turkey.

"So, Jerry," Howard asked, biting off a piece of overly buttered cornbread with a curious expression. "What do you do for a living?"

"I'm an accountant."

"Really?" Fable remarked. "My father was an accountant."

Demitra's eyes darted toward Jerry, who replied, "Yes, I know. I actually knew your father."

"Really? You did?!" Beryl exclaimed. The revelation was a surprise.

"Yes," Demitra told her eldest. "Jerry was a friend of your father's and mine."

Artemis gave a quizzical look at her sister which Demitra ignored.

"Did our father ever tell you about us?" Fable asked.

Jerry smiled kindly toward Fable and replied, "You two girls were the apple of Larry Mariner's eye. He talked a lot about his *little monkeys*." He looked at Salem, Yasmine, and Seth next and added, "He also spoke of his nieces and nephew quite often. He was very proud of all you kids. I think he'd be pretty proud of how you all turned out, too."

"Demitra," Artemis said suddenly. "Will you help me get the pies out of the oven?"

The sisters went into the kitchen alone. Demitra removed the two apple pies from the top oven while Artemis took the two pecan pies from the lower. They set the pies to cool on the counter before Artemis gently tugged her sister's arm.

"Just what are you doing?"

"Helping you in the kitchen," Demitra remarked, a little taken aback.

"You know what I mean," Artemis said with an eye roll. "Why is that man here?"

"Do you mean Jerry...my boyfriend?"

Artemis puffed a strand of hair out of her eyes in frustration. "That's the point, Dee. You are not only dating a man just like your late husband—he was even a friend of his!"

"So what?" Demitra asked. "I like Jerry. He's very nice. Larry liked him, too."

Artemis wrung her hands together in exasperation. She took her younger sister by the shoulders and looked her directly in the eye so that Demitra could see her concern was genuine. "We have been down this road before, Dee. You must get over Larry. He was a terrific guy—the best—but he is dead! You cannot recreate that part of your life with a similar man. It's not fair to you, and it's not fair to that man out there."

"I like Jerry for Jerry," Demitra said, pulling free of her sister's hold. "He is kind. He is handsome. Witty. Successful. I see no reason to stop seeing him just because he reminds *you* of *my* dead husband."

"No," Artemis corrected. "I think he reminds *you* of your dead husband. How much of this affection for Jerry is really just leftover love for Larry? Hell, their names are even similar. Jerry Miller. Larry Mariner. You lost your mind once because of grief for Larry. Please don't do that again."

Tossing the oven mitts to the counter, Demitra whirled around exasperatedly. "What do you know about love?!" she shouted. "You've never been in love—except with Howard, but even then, you didn't fight to keep him. You just let it go. Larry and I enjoy each other. I'm not going to stop seeing him."

Artemis' eyes teared up. "Honey, you just said *Larry*. You said *Larry* and I. Dee, his name is Jerry. Honey, this is not healthy. Don't you remember last time, how hard it was? You couldn't do anything for the longest time but stay in your room and cry. You half destroyed yourself grieving once. Jerry can't take Larry's place."

Demitra faced her sister angrily. In no uncertain terms she replied, "Stay out of it!"

CHAPTER THREE

The Gray Kiss

With the dishes all washed and put away and the kitchen in reasonable order, Salem stepped outside the door to the back yard. The chilly air made her shiver, even with the heavy coat. She walked along the sleeping brown grass to the little worn trail at the yard's edge. The yard had no discernable end, only a vague distinction between where professionally planted lawn met with age-old, regular grasses, weeds, and dirt which began the field behind the house. The Blanchard property consisted of many fields, meadows, woods, trails, a stream, and even an apple orchard. Salem took the trail through the meadow to the fork where she veered right. She continued walking down to the iron fence which cordoned off the family cemetery just before the trail entered the woods.

The squeaky gate pushed open on its rusty hinges as she went inside. Generations of Blanchard relatives were lain to rest here, but not all Blanchards were there. Most of the more powerful Blanchard witches' remains were too valuable for burial. Their remains—crushed after cremation—were stored in jars elsewhere...for other uses. No, the bodies resting in the Blanchard cemetery were typically periphery relations. Such as Salem's husband, David.

David's headstone was not weathered and worn like many of the others. Shiny, new, bright gray—David Lane was new to this graveyard. Salem gently stroked the smooth top of the marble headstone and traced the letters of his name beneath her fingertips.

"Did you hear all of us in there around the table?" she asked her unseen husband. "You always loved coming here with all of us chattering away over absolutely nothing. You never got to have a big crazy family 'till me. I was split over coming here today or not. I felt like maybe I should be at your aunt and uncle's with them. I invited them here, but they wanted a quiet Thanksgiving."

Salem pulled a little iron chair from the fence rail and placed it beside the grave where she could sit a while. She pulled one of the roses from the little vase sitting on the grave. It was kind of the aunts to keep putting flowers out here regularly for her. Salem clutched the pink rose in her hand. The wind blew her long auburn hair into her face as she smelled the rose. Sweeping her hair back behind her ear, she gave a short chuckle.

"I almost cut my hair last week. Got all the way to the salon before I changed my mind. I said, *David would be furious if I cut this hair.* You used to play with it at night while we'd watch TV. I don't watch as much TV as we used to. Arielle and I have some shows we watch together, but I can't watch the things you and I did. Those were ours. I don't do a lot of things I used to do.

"I don't make the bed much anymore. Remember how I could never leave for work unless the bed was made? I just don't care now. I don't eat the way we used to. Remember Wednesday night fried chicken, Monday meatloaf, country fried steak Sundays? Now Arielle and I just grab something or order in. Eating is functional now. It's not the at-the-table-how-was-your-day kind of thing anymore."

She replaced the rose in the vase and hugged her arms around herself to brace against another chilling breeze. The wind made her cheeks raw. It felt cold just under nose where her tears had collected. She could taste a bit of saltiness on her lips before she wiped it away on her sleeve.

"This is big," she said, shuddering back a sob. "The first Thanksgiving without you. These firsts are so hard. So hard. I don't know how I'll make it through Christmas. Arielle being around helps."

Suddenly it occurred to her she had never officially told him about Arielle. That alone felt strange. How could something so big happen in her life and she had not shared that with the man she shared everything with?

"Oh God, David, you don't know about Arielle! She is my sister. Can you believe it? I have a sister. She lives in Atlanta with me in our old house. She has saved my life in a number of ways. You'd really like her. She already likes you. Lord knows she's heard every David story there is under the sun. I met my father, too, earlier this year. You know how touchy that subject has always been for me. He was nice. I liked him. He even showed up for Seth's wedding—kind of. Oh, God, David—Seth and Yasmine got married! You always told me Yaz had a thing for him, but I never really believed it. Turns out you were right. And Aunt Demitra is dating. Demitra!

Dating! Can you picture that? She has been such the grieving widow for so long it's crazy. He came over today. He seems all right."

Salem looked across the meadow toward the chicken houses in the distance, but she wasn't looking at them. She wasn't looking at anything. Perhaps she was looking down the road of her life, wondering about her own future and where it was going to end up.

"And before you even say it..." she said to David's invisible voice in her mind as she looked to his headstone, "I have no intention of dating right now. I don't know if I ever want to try. How can a person expect to find love when they've already had the greatest love of all time? Nobody can be like you. Thoughtful. Kind. Funny—although not always as funny as you thought you were. And sexy. Damn, David, why did you have to be so damn sexy to me? And our fights! Boy, we had some doozies, didn't we? You always did know how to push me back down to earth whenever I got too high and mighty. No one else can do that. I miss you so much. I miss *us* so much. Sometimes I think I might just die from the hole in my heart. Losing Michael was the worst, I admit. But you're the only one who could ever understand what I lost with that, which makes losing you even harder."

Tears were streaming now. The ache she spoke of was hitting her gut hard as she shivered in the cold. "All our years together are now solely my memories. The running jokes. Our playful made-up words for things. Our sweet memories of our son and the years of our marriage. I am alone with memories no one else shares. No one else to reminisce about it all with. There is only me."

Salem was about to lose control of her emotions, something she would never forgive herself for doing. Quickly she wiped her face and braced her heart, hardening her demeanor and throwing up her inner walls. "People probably think I'm a little cold. I don't break in front of them. Maybe that's a flaw of mine. Maybe it's a strength. But I don't break down with people. I lost the only place I felt safe breaking down. But thanks for letting me do it one more time here with you. Now it's time to go back inside. I am really freezing out here. I just wanted to have a minute with you. Tell you that no matter how many times you see me laugh, whatever words I say to people, the face I show—inside I still hurt. I will never not love you. Happy Thanksgiving, my love."

CHAPTER FOUR

What Freedom Brings

There was nothing to do but try to remember. The patient could have watched the slow steady drip of some type of moisture running down the stained cinderblock on the wall. She could have tried to listen more closely to the agonized screams echoing down the corridor behind her door. But she used her ample time in better ways...and it worked. She reclaimed some of her memories that morning. Why shouldn't she? When she found herself awake, there was nothing but time to do so. Hour after hour laying in that uncomfortable bed thinking, straining, to recall her life finally ended her perpetual amnesia.

It was all coming back to her and she was remembering home. Home. The smell, the sounds, the faces. It became her focus and her strength to endure that horrible place, for she knew what was awaiting her...if she could just get out. But how? She could barely move, much less get out of her bed. She was so tired, so lethargic. Why wasn't she beyond this? Why did it seem she was regressing instead of progressing? Though her nurse had come back again several times that day, she was beginning to think of the nurse more as a warden checking on a prisoner, than a caregiver.

The nurse was silent as she came into the room this time. Holding a small brown box in her hand as she came into the room, she walked to the little metal cabinet on the blank wall facing the bed. She began restocking supplies. Tubes, wires, stained white towels that could have been any number of years old. As the nurse closed the cabinet door and the scratchy metal sound of the latch screeched, she finally faced her patient with that same grim expression on her face. One of disinterest or perhaps one of hatred, it was hard to tell.

"H-h-h-ho-me," stuttered the patient with much effort.

The nurse took an aggressive step forward towards the bed. Her furious eyes widened as her cheeks reddened. "I have told you repeatedly not to attempt speaking.

We must take things as they come."

"Wh-who a-a-are y-you?"

"Do you not hear a word I say!" the nurse scolded. "Your throat is not yet ready for speech. It will be painful until we exercise it with various sounds first."

The nurse was right. Her throat did hurt. Every time she attempted to speak it only felt worse. It had been so many years without a sound from it, but all she wanted was a simple name. A name to connect with this stern woman's face. If she could only know her name, she might not feel so alone.

"W-who..."

"I have told you before, you just don't remember." The nurse said. "I am Cassie. I take care of you."

"H-ho-home."

"You are home Nacaria." Cassie explained. "This is home now. This is your home until we can get you back on your feet. Your spirit may have been back at home with your family all these years, but your physical form has been here. It takes some time for your body and your soul to reconnect after being parted so long. You have not spoken, eaten, or walked for two decades. Just be happy your curse has been lifted and be patient while we get you ready to go home."

Home, Nacaria thought. Home with her children. With her mother and sisters. Salem and Seth needed their mother. They were so little, so helpless. *No, they are grown now. I remember. I watched them grow up from the walls.* The haze of the life she remembered being a part of mixed with the life she had merely witnessed go by from her time in the shadows. Nacaria was not sure anymore what was real, what was imagined. She tried to force her mind to reconcile her past—to make sense of her fractured life. But as always when she tried to remember it was cut short by the nurse.

The nurse removed a needle from her skirt pocket. Nacaria vaguely remembered she had seen her do this before, maybe every day. She could not remember. But she recognized the sting in her veins as the serum was injected into her bloodstream. Within minutes Nacaria could not utter a sound, she could not think. She only laid there, half lifeless, until she felt fingertips on her eyelids, closing them. For a moment she thought she heard another voice. It was distant, miles away it seemed. Someone asking about her condition maybe. Unchanged, she thought she heard Cassie report. But she couldn't be sure. She was so tired now. Then the blackness came back, and she did not exist again.

CHAPTER FIVE

The Call

The Scrabble board was laid across the coffee table of the third-floor den with Seth, Yasmine, Fable, and Beryl on each side. As was usual whenever they played, Yasmine was spilling her letters everywhere as she struggled to shield them from Fable's curious eyes.

"There," Beryl announced, spreading her word on the board. "*Plasma*.'

"Typical, Dr. Blanchard," Fable remarked, writing down her sister's score.

It was Yasmine's turn. Giddily she sprawled out her letters, connecting with another word on the board to spell out the word *pregnant*. Seth's eyes grew huge, and Beryl raised an inquisitive brow. Fable sat mute, cringing from the very thought of babies and pregnancy—still protecting her secret.

"Uh, Yazzy," Seth stammered. "Please tell me you're not using Scrabble to tell me something?"

"What?" Yasmine replied innocently. "Oh, *pregnant*! Lord no, Seth! I am not pregnant. It's just a game word."

"Thank goodness!" Seth sighed.

"Well, what if I was?!" Yasmine snapped. "Nice reaction."

Seth wrapped his arm around his wife and smiled, "Oh, baby, I didn't mean it like that."

Yasmine ducked away from his arm. "You smell, Seth Blanchard. Did you even shower after you left the gym?"

Seth pulled her back into him again, "Aw, Yaz, don't be like that. You know I'd love to have a baby with you. I plan to have a bunch. But not yet. We just got married. Lots of time for that. I'm way too young to be a parent."

"We are all too young to be parents," Beryl added. "I know I am not ready, and I'm the oldest."

Fable thought to herself, *I am too young to be a good mother. I know I'm not ready yet. So why can't I make the decision to end this thing? Why is this so hard to terminate?* She wanted so much to confide in her family. Beryl, Seth, and Yasmine were not just family—they were her best friends. She needed them now more than ever. But it wasn't that simple. If she had been carrying the baby of one of her average boyfriends, that would be one thing. How do you tell everyone that you are carrying the child of the werewolf who tried to kill them all?

Seth took his turn next, applying the word *leap* to the board. "Seven points, write it down."

"As if seven points could help your score," Fable noted. Looking at the words already on the board, she tried to see where she could apply the word *step* for the most points. *Ladder* would have been the perfect spot, but another word crossed it too closely to the space she needed. Then, she saw plenty of room above *father*. "*Stepfather*."

Seth laughed. "Subconsciousness looking ahead?"

"Huh?"

"Aunt Demitra's new boyfriend we met Thanksgiving," he clarified.

"Don't even make jokes," Fable said. "I'm not prepared for that.'

"He seemed like a nice enough man," Beryl noted. "Mother has been alone a long time. She deserves some happiness. I don't like the idea of her with anyone else either, but she's still young. She's mourned Dad for ten years."

Beryl began her next turn. As she laid out the word *photo,* her cell phone rang on the table beside her. She quickly answered it, changing her word to *phone* as she did.

"Hi!" Beryl said to the caller. "Okay...I'm listening...she did? I see...I understand. I'll meet you there tomorrow night."

Beryl ended the call. She seemed disturbed somehow by whomever she'd been talking to.

"Who was that?" Fable asked.

Beryl didn't answer right away. She looked to be still mulling over the call, but in fact, she was thinking up a plausible answer to the question that was not the truth. "A colleague. She needs a consult tomorrow on a patient."

"At night?" Yasmine remarked.

"Huh?" Beryl said snapping back to focus.

"You told her you'd meet her tomorrow night," Yasmine reminded her. "Do doctors do consultations at night?"

Beryl thought fast, "If they are friends and want to meet for drinks to discuss it, they do."

CHAPTER SIX

Candlelight and Cobblestone

Soft music and candlelight encased the little window table at the Cobblestone. Demitra was radiant in her royal blue dress. She looked half her age, nothing like a woman of fifty-one. The soft lighting made her raven hair glisten as she swept it back from her shoulders. Jerry looked quite dashing as well in his suit and expensive silk tie. The dark, tranquil waters lapping up against the wooden pylons below reflected the round moon hanging in the sky above the Black Warrior River.

"Artemis doesn't like me very much, does she?" Jerry asked.

Artemis had come out from the kitchen to say hello to her sister and her new boyfriend, but her greeting felt a little perfunctory and lacked sincerity. She lingered at the table only a few moments, inquiring if the food was to their liking or if she could get them anything. Then she made a clumsy excuse to depart, and they had not seen her again.

"She's just concerned that I am trying to replace my husband."

"Well, aren't you?" Jerry grinned playfully.

Demitra rolled her eyes and tossed a mini cornbread muffin from the breadbasket at her companion. "I do not intend to suffer your teasing tonight, mister," she smiled.

Jerry picked the muffin off his lap, buttered it, and before popping it into his mouth, winked and said, "Then I will refrain and instead simply bask in the magnificent splendor of your beauty."

"Very nice recovery."

"It's true," he said. "Every man in this room has looked at you more than once. Even the ones with much younger dates."

Demitra looked wounded. "Are you calling me old?" she teased.

"Seasoned."

"Better."

She appreciated the compliment, and she knew it was true. Demitra Blanchard was not a vain woman, but she was a woman—a beautiful woman at that. She noticed when men turned 'round to look at her. She encouraged nothing and never returned their stare, but she knew they looked. And her psychic mind also knew their female dinner companions noticed their men were looking as well.

"You're just as gorgeous as you were years ago, Demitra," Jerry smiled. "I am breath taken every time I see you."

"If you are trying to get lucky tonight, Sir, you are succeeding," she teased.

Jerry's eyes widened as he blocked a devilish grin with a sip from his wine glass. "I could love you forever *and three days*."

The overhead candelabra gave Demitra's eyes a glimmery reflection, or perhaps that was just her own doing. "I plan on holding you to that."

Jerry switched gears for a moment, using the opportunity to steer into territory he was curious about. "Have you told the family—most importantly, the girls—that we are going to be married?"

"No," Demitra said. "I haven't. I think Thanksgiving was a good introduction. They met you and liked you. I'm glad they liked you. It would have been too odd if they hadn't. But I am not ready yet to tell them about our engagement. It's a little fast, and I don't want them to become defensive and start to reject you."

"Don't you think you should, Demitra?" Jerry pushed. "Or is it Artemis you are most afraid of? I know how close you two are—I think she'd be shocked at first, but then give us her blessing."

"You give my sister more credit than I think she deserves."

"Do you think the girls will give us much pushback?" he asked.

Demitra reached her hand across the table and held Jerry's. "They really loved their father. They still mourn his loss."

Jerry grinned again. "He was a good man. Larry Mariner is a hard act to follow. Even for me."

Demitra blushed into her smile. "They will learn to love Jerry Miller."

Jerry's face became suddenly grave. He sipped his drink, let out a breath, and leaned closer. "It seems Beryl and Fable are not our only obstacles. My parents are growing concerned."

"What have you told them?"

"Nothing," admitted Jerry. "I have no clue as to what to say or how to handle the situation. I will figure it out though. Don't worry your gorgeous head about it. I have a plan."

CHAPTER SEVEN

Riverside Confessions

It was growing late in the evening when Fable reached the boat landing. It was desolate at this time of night, no one around. In her teenage years, she and her high school friends would come out here at this time to smoke pot. She thought it very strange for her mother's new boyfriend to call and ask her to meet him, especially here of all places. Creepy, in fact. Had she been a typical young woman she would never have agreed to meet him in so isolated a place. However, curiosity—mixed with her ability to summon woodland creatures to aid her in a pinch—helped her decide in favor of meeting him at 10:30 that night.

She had a fairly good idea what this meeting was going to be about. *He cared for her mother. He wanted Fable's blessing to continue their relationship. He had sensed she wasn't on board so far and hoped to win her over. Blah, blah, blah.* Fable thought it absurd to go through this. She wasn't a fourteen-year-old girl, and it wasn't necessary for her to get along with the new stepfather—if, Heaven forbid, that was actually what he wanted to discuss.

She was sitting on a picnic table at the water's edge watching the moonlight glisten off the tiny ripples of the river when she saw him approach. The headlights of Jerry's car swept around the turn of the lonely road, casting shadows of bare spiny tree branches on the ground. He parked just beyond the table and joined her.

"I'm glad you came, Fable."

"I feel weird about this," she admitted. "We hardly know each other. You are just barely dating my mom—what has it been? A month?'"

"Roughly," he replied as she shivered slightly in the breeze. He pulled the collar up on his jacket and put his hands into his pockets.

"It seems a little crazy to need to meet with me privately and here of all places. But let me tell you something right off, if you even think of trying to rape me, I will kill you on this very spot."

Jerry laughed and shook his head. "I assure you nothing like that is in my mind. You are very safe with me."

"That's good," Fable said, though not utterly convinced he was benign. "I also should say right away that if you're here to try and get me on board with your relationship with my mother, there's no need. She is an adult and free to do what she wants. Neither myself, nor my sister plan on trying to talk her out of anything. However, if I am being quite honest, my mother isn't over my father. She's still very much in love with him."

"Is that so?" Jerry smiled.

"You say you were a friend of his, so you know how special he was," Fable continued. "So be patient. Be understanding with her. Take it slowly. If you respect her heart, you and I will get along just fine."

"Thank you," Jerry replied. "I appreciate the advice. I have nothing but the utmost respect for your mother and father's relationship. The fact that she still loves him after all this time makes me appreciate your mother all the more."

"Good," Fable replied, rising from the bench. "So, is that all there is? Are we finished?"

"Not exactly," Jerry answered. "Your blessing isn't really what I wanted to chat with you about."

Fable couldn't possibly fathom what else there was to discuss with this man whom she had met only once before. Politeness dictated she do her utmost to hide her irritability, but Fable was never very good at being polite, particularly with people she had no vested interest in. She plopped back down on the picnic table bench and stared up to him.

"What then?"

"I need a favor from you."

Fable was startled by Jerry's presumptuousness. Was her mother's new boyfriend really about to ask her to do something for him? They barely knew one another. And why the secrecy? Fable began to feel apprehensive. Something was very off here.

"I don't even know you!" Fable exclaimed. "What favor could I possibly do for you?"

Jerry tried to express himself better. This was not going the way he assumed it would. "I need your help with my *parents.*"

It was the disconnected way he said *parents* that struck Fable as the most unnerving. And what sort of help could she offer regarding his parents? She didn't even know them. Or him for that matter. It was all much too strange for her taste.

Fable stood up to leave. "I think I am just going to go. You are nothing but a man my mother just started dating. That does not establish a social bond between us nor an exchange of favors. You don't even know me."

"I know more than you think I do," Jerry said, grabbing her arm as she attempted to pass.

It was not a threatening grab; it was more like one of concern and urgency. She did not like his touching her, but nothing about the gesture caused her to feel alarm. Still, she readied herself to send out a telepathic call to the wild just in case she was underestimating his intentions.

"I know you are a witch," Jerry revealed. "I know you communicate with animals. I know Beryl is a healer." He wringed his hands and smacked himself on the head as if frustrated with himself. "I am sorry that I am going about this so very clumsily. I only wanted to talk. You see, I need you to go to Birmingham and see the Millers... my parents. I need you to do something for me when you are there."

"I am leaving," Fable said, wrenching her arm free. "I don't know what your purpose was here tonight, but I'm not doing anything for you."

As Fable started walking to her car, Jerry shouted across the empty parking strip to her, "Do you know why I asked you to meet me here? Here of all the places in Daihmler?"

Fable turned back to look at him. He was sitting on the picnic table staring off over the murky dark waters of the Black Warrior River. He seemed so familiar somehow sitting that way. Without being aware she was doing so she began walking back towards him.

"Why *did* you ask me to meet you here?" she asked.

"Because I had a little girl once," Jerry said, still staring at the water. "A beautiful, precocious little girl. We used to come here together, she and I. We would talk out all our problems here. We'd skip rocks; we'd watch the barges go by; we'd share secrets. She'd tell me everything happening in her life."

Fable was beside him now, standing by the table, unable to understand why she felt the pull she now felt inside. Almost as if her soul knew something her mind had not yet learned.

"She saved my life once here," Jerry added.

"What?" Fable asked, her voice breaking. "How?"

Jerry faced her with a sly, playful grin she had not seen in years, as he explained,

"There was a rattlesnake on the trail just behind this picnic area. It was just about to bite me when my little girl spoke to it and asked it to leave. It slithered away."

Fable stood motionless. Silent.

"I had a little girl named Fable. Of course, that was before I died. She's all grown up now."

CHAPTER EIGHT

Daddy's Back

Boats passed by sending currents of water washing up onto the riverbank. Fable sat down on the picnic table bench beside Jerry Miller. Dumbfounded and speechless, yet with so many questions swarming her brain, she said nothing. She could only sit there.

"It's me, Fable," he told her. "It's Daddy."

"No," Fable stuttered. "It isn't possible."

"Honey, you know everything is possible."

Fable stood up again; this time anger replaced her confusion. This man was crazy. There was no other explanation.

"How dare you say you are my father! My father is dead. He died a long time ago. You are cruel and unbalanced."

"Ask your mother," Jerry replied. "She brought me back. You know it can be done."

Fable was as confused as before. "You don't even look like him. I mean, yes you have a similar look as my Dad, but you are not him. This is not my father's face."

"She chose a man who resembled me," Jerry explained. "Jerry Miller looked the most like me, so Mama chose him."

"It's not possible."

He was growing weary of finding ways to make her believe. He thought he would try once more, this time using some history to make his case. "Your name is Fable Marie Blanchard. When you were born you weighed 6 lbs., 3 oz. You were born in February, a week early, because your Aunt Artemis could not control her powers very well. It was freezing cold, and she began to worry that the water pipes under the house might burst. But her thought about the pipes ricocheted, and your mother's water broke."

"Mother could have told you that."

"You once had a cat named Mr. Ice Cream. Mr. Ice Cream killed Beryl's pet rat Ricco. Your Aunt Nacaria is a shadow on the wall. Olympia has been married three times. You lost your first tooth when Seth tied one end of string to it and the other to his bow and arrow set. He shot the arrow into the air and yanked your tooth out..."

Fable was shaking now. This man knew too much.

"You cried for two hours," Jerry continued. "I spanked Seth and I bought you a new toy so that you wouldn't tell how you lost the tooth. Demitra had told me not to buy Seth the bow and arrow set, but I did anyway because I'd had one at his age. The toy I bought you was one of those Barbie heads where you could fix the hair in different styles. You styled that Barbie's hair every day over and over for weeks until it broke off."

Fable's face said all he needed to know. She believed him. She had never told the truth about how that tooth had come out, and neither had Seth. It wasn't just the tooth though; she could feel this was real. She could feel her father inside Jerry Miller.

"I don't know what to say."

"I'm just glad I didn't have to break out my ace in the hole," he laughed. "The memory that'd really have cinched it."

"What memory?"

"You know what I'm talking about," her father grinned.

"I think I do," she said, still skeptical. "But just for extra evidence..."

"When you got your first period on that fishing trip with me..."

"Okay, stop!" Fable cringed.

"Nope, you wanted more proof I am your Dad. I stopped at that backwoods store and got all I could find that might help. Ace bandages and gauze tape."

"I thought I'd die of embarrassment," Fable laughed. "I never told anyone about that."

"Neither did I."

She looked into Jerry Miller's eyes and saw her father looking back at her through them. "It *is* you, isn't it?"

"Yes, baby. Daddy's back."

Fable fell into his arms, weeping as hard as she had the day he died. He gripped her tightly and let her cry. "Daddy, I've missed you so much. My heart has never been the same. Please never leave me again," she sobbed. "Please don't go back. I have been so empty without you. Please never leave me again."

Larry Mariner held his daughter. To finally be able to hold his baby again was sublime. His eyes began to stream as his big hands clutched her more tightly to his chest. His baby girl. Oh, how he'd wanted to hold her, and her sister, on Thanksgiving. Now he got to hold Fable, at least, in his arms.

"I'm not going anywhere," he replied, kissing the top of her head as he wiped the tears from her face and his own. "But I am going to need your help. That is why I had to see you today. I had to tell you who I really am, because I need you to help me stay."

She squeezed his hand tightly in her own and smiled at her father, "What can I do?"

He took a deep breath and tried to explain his dilemma, "Your mother and I want to get married. The problem is this body belongs to someone else. Jerry Miller has a family. He has two parents and an ex-wife."

"Any children?"

"Thankfully, no children," he continued. "But enough real relatives to stand in our way. Besides that, no one but you, me, and Demitra know who I really am. We have to keep it that way. We can't even tell Beryl—not right now at least. Your mother could get into real trouble for what she has done. If the Consort found out, she could end up like Nacaria."

A terrible thought came into Fable's mind. She didn't want to ask because deep down she wasn't sure if she was prepared for the answer. But she had to know. She had to know what price had been paid for her father to be returned to her.

"Did she kill Jerry Miller?"

"No," Larry said. "Not technically."

Fable grimaced as butterflies swarmed into her insides. That did not sound like a very good argument. She braced herself for the rest of the story. Sitting quietly, listening, as she looked out over the water again, she heard her father explain the circumstances of his return. Demitra had been doing this for years on their anniversaries—finding some random stand-in, or even hiring one if necessary. She would temporarily infuse her husband Larry's soul into the unsuspecting man's body and have a short-lived reunion with the man she never stopped loving. Fable understood it was far more complicated than that. Her father's soul had long split into fragments, finding new life in other beings, or plants, or animals. To reconstruct that energy field meant stealing pieces of someone else to rebuild someone long dissolved. That alone carried massive repercussions. Yet Fable did not care. It was her father. Whatever it took to bring him back was worth it.

"What do you want me to do, Daddy? Just tell me and I'll do it."

"You could get in a lot of trouble too, Fable. That's why your mother hasn't wanted us to tell you about me returning. She wants us to figure a way on our own."

"I'll do anything it takes to keep you in my life," Fable declared. "Just tell me what I have to do."

"This time, your mother chose this body because she wanted to make it permanent. Last time we did this we decided we simply could not go on with sporadic visits. We want to have our life back. Be together every day again. Jerry was a perfect man to take over. He has no real encumberments except for his parents...and his work. He has no deep relationships. No one gets hurt if he fades away. We naively thought we could do this without arousing suspicion, but it is not working."

"What is going wrong?"

Jerry Miller's nose pulled to the side in that signature Larry Mariner way, as he explained. "Jerry's job wasn't too difficult to take care of. Suspicious as it was, when I called in and quit, it was accepted. However, his parents are proving more difficult to handle. They have heard about the job loss and are growing concerned. They keep calling and texting. I return the texts, replying that everything is fine, but they insist upon seeing me."

"Well, you are in his body," Fable pointed out. "No matter what they think of Jerry's decisions, they certainly aren't going to suspect you're not him."

"But what if seeing them wakes Jerry up and he tries to come back?"

Fable gave him a concerned look. "Wait a minute," she said. "He could come back?"

"We aren't sure," Larry admitted. "He's in here with me, I can feel him. I don't understand all this stuff; you know that. I don't think even Demitra knows exactly what she's done. All I know is I am attached to Jerry's body now and fighting to keep it. I can't go back to death. I know you all believe energy disperses and joins new energy and life keeps going on—and maybe it does—but to me death was death. Nothingness. I want to be with my wife and children again!"

"Tell me what to do."

"Go to Birmingham to see his parents. Find out everything you can about Jerry Miller, so that I can play him convincingly."

"Done."

"See if you can figure out a way to meet them casually."

"No need to say anymore," Fable nodded, finally seeing the whole picture. "You need enough information to really sell that you're really their son and haven't gone insane. Leave the Millers to me. I'll figure something out."

Larry hugged his daughter close. "I knew I could count on you. I love you so much, baby girl."

"And I love you, Daddy. Don't worry about a thing. There is no way on earth I'm losing you again."

CHAPTER NINE

What Are You Doing to Me?

Nacaria had been waiting hours for Nurse Cassie to come in. She waited through the night in a rancid heap of her own waste. The smell, the feel, and the humiliation had all finally twisted together to make her vomit. Nacaria laid in that, too. It was all so disgustingly miserable to endure. She began to realize that Cassie was her only caregiver and if she were not around, Nacaria was on her own.

Why am I still here? Nacaria wondered. *Why hasn't someone come for me? Or released me?* She wished she knew how this all worked. She wished she could remember what was said all those years ago about her punishment. Was this all a part of it? Did no one at home notice her shadow was missing? That she was no longer confined to the walls of Blanchard House? How long had she been in this room awake? When would the person who decides her punishment is over let her go home?

At last, Nacaria heard the metal key scraping inside the lock of her door. The heavy door pushed open, and Nurse Cassie walked in. The odor in the room must have been putrid to the nurse's senses, assailing her upon entry. Nurse Cassie walked to the bed and found Nacaria in her current state.

Angrily she slapped her patient's face and shrieked, "You are revolting!" She scurried to clean her up complaining the entire time. "It's bad enough I have to change your shitty diapers, but now I have to wash vomit off you, too!"

Nacaria could not move or fling her hands to shield her face from the angry nurse's blows. It was simply too tiring to try. She had no strength to her limbs. She could only lay there taking every blow as it came. On the last slap Nacaria took, Nurse Cassie raised her blood-covered hand. She had busted Nacaria's nose. Cassie withdrew another syringe and stabbed into Nacaria's arm this time, rather than injecting the IV tube. Within seconds, Nacaria was unable to think again, unable to do anything but simply *be*. She was like a doll that only came to life long enough to contemplate why it lived and when it would return to the limbo that was before it had developed consciousness.

After locking her patient's door, Cassie walked down the long corridor of the asylum. How she hated being there. Those screams from the other witches locked away in the other rooms had almost driven her to madness. But this was her job, this was what she had to do for the moment, and there was a very good reason behind it. Finally, she made her way through the winding hallways and warped channels of this great catacomb. The front door stood before her, leading outside to where the sun shone—where the air was crisp and new and lifegiving.

The doorman who stood guard tried to speak to her as he always did, and as she always did, she ignored him. The other nurses congregated outside, each one discussing with the others their experience with their patients that particular day. Cassie did not speak to them either. She never did. They were beneath her.

Cassie reached her car in the parking lot and got inside. Withdrawing her phone from her purse, she dialed the number to give her daily report.

"It's me."

"Yes, nothing's changed."

"Yes, I am increasing the dosage."

"Don't worry, no one will ever know her curse has been lifted."

"Of course, I'm sure. The administrator of the sanitarium comes by her cell only once a week. She is always completely unconscious by then."

"I assure you no one is ever going to discover that Nacaria Blanchard is free. From all appearance's sake, she is still in the very same coma she has been in for twenty years."

CHAPTER TEN

The Witch in the City

Blackie D'Angelo lived in the heart of Birmingham. Quinlan Castle once was a large complex of condominiums set on the mountain's rise overlooking the city. The façade of the structure reflected its name. Made of red stone blocks rising five stories tall, the roofline gave the appearance of an ancient castle with its merlon battlements. Each of the four corners of the castle had a parapet connected by a walkway, making all four parapets connected by one path. Sometimes Blackie D'Angelo could be seen at night walking the roofline of her castle, watching over the Magic City, as Birmingham is often called. For many years, Quinlan Castle sat derelict until Blackie purchased the landmark building. Completely gutting the interior, she spent millions turning it into a medieval palace of sorts. She added turrets to every side of Quinlan along with stone balconies so that the lights of the city could be seen from the four master bedrooms. To be invited to Quinlan Castle was a rare honor to which very few Alabamians were bestowed.

Beryl waited outside the building until she saw Arielle pull up beside her. Both women got out and gave each other a brief and perfunctory hug. This was not a social situation or two girls meeting for drinks. There was an agenda.

"I am so confused, Arielle," Beryl began. "Ever since I got your call last night, I have been rolling over what you said."

"You didn't tell anyone did you?" Arielle asked.

"No," Beryl answered. "I made up a story about meeting a doctor friend. Why are we here? And more to the point, why did you reach out to me and not Seth or Salem?"

Arielle took a deep breath of the chilly night air, all the chillier being that they were on top of a small mountain overlooking the city. "My Aunt Blackie called me and told me I needed to come to see her, with a Blanchard—but not one of Nacaria's children or sisters. She said Nacaria's family are not her biggest fans, but she needed a Blanchard since I wasn't able to answer her question."

Beryl was puzzled. "What question was that?"

Arielle looked Beryl square in the eyes and replied, "If I have seen Nacaria's shadow lately."

Beryl and Arielle stood outside the thick, oak, monastery-style arched door waiting to be shown inside after ringing the bell. When the doors were opened, Beryl stepped into an entrance hall with twenty-foot ceilings capped by heavy beams. The walls were the same reddish stone of the exterior. Arched doorways all around seemed to open to what could only be described as *multiple chambers.* An elaborately carved wooden staircase rose to a landing high above where two other staircases rose on either side to reach the upper floors. Rich, intricate tapestries hung on several of the stone walls, and a lush garnet-colored carpet stretched up the stairs reminding Beryl of Scarlet and Rhett's mansion in Gone with the Wind.

The housekeeper who answered the door was a squat little woman with gray hair tied in a bun. Beryl mused that she could have easily been mistaken for Aunt Bee, from The Andy Griffith Show. *I've got to date more and watch less tv*, Beryl thought to herself.

"She does look like Aunt Bee," Blackie said from the window of the chamber nearest the entry.

Her presence startled Beryl. She had no idea her hostess was standing so close. Beryl could see her now, standing before a great window lined with heavy drapes of dark red velvet. Blackie D'Angelo was beautiful. Cascading black hair that stretched to her waist and when she moved it moved with her almost as if it had a life of its own. She was clearly of a generation older than Beryl but, like Demitra and Artemis, she looked young for her age. Blackie wore a slender black dress which showcased her trim figure.

Arielle ran forward and embraced her aunt like a little girl. Blackie's austere facade broke the moment her arms enveloped her niece. Beryl could tell right away that Aunt Blackie was perhaps the only one of Arielle's relations—besides her father—who loved her.

"You read thoughts," Beryl said, joining them in the chamber. It was clear by the décor that Ms. D'Angelo liked a Knights of the Round Table/King Arthur motif.

"I can," Blackie laughed, coming forward to take a seat on the antique sofa. She gestured for Beryl to join her as Aunt Bee poured them each a glass of wine. "It is so good to see you, Arielle. It has been a couple of years since we last had the opportunity."

"I've missed you Blackie," Arielle beamed as she sat next to her aunt, still clutching her hand.

"And I have sorely missed you, my sweet girl."

The next quarter hour was spent going through niceties and small talk. All three being southern women, they all recognized the rules of graciousness before moving onto the real purpose for the meeting. Blackie asked Arielle all about how her life in Atlanta was proceeding as well as tossing a few polite questions to Beryl concerning her career. Likewise, Beryl returned the favor with a few dull but polite questions for Blackie. The final one, sparking the start of the real reason they were there.

"Do you belong to a Birmingham coven?" Beryl asked.

"No," Blackie answered. "I am no longer a member of the Consort. I find it tedious, their politics. My father always said witches are the next level of evolution. I have found the Consort and its Council are more inclined to keep us at mortal levels than I am comfortable with."

Beryl was surprised by this statement. All her life she'd heard Olympia espouse the importance of the Consort and the unity of witches everywhere. The protections and guidance from having a formed government of their kind had been indispensable in helping protect the Natural Order.

Beryl realized Blackie was again reading her thoughts when she added, "I have great respect for Olympia Blanchard and her wisdom. I just do not believe the majority of Council members possess the same depth. You'll recall that my sister sits on the Council."

Beryl sipped her wine and smiled politely at her hostess. "So, you knew my Aunt Nacaria?"

"Oh, my yes," Blackie began. "She was my dearest friend in the world. I met her when we were children—at the Consort in fact. We remained friends well into our adulthood."

Beryl said, "Arielle told us it was you who introduced her to Xander Obreiggon."

"Very true. Of course, it was all quite innocent. Xander and I were close friends, and I introduced them at a meeting. I had no idea his marriage with my sister was as precarious as it ended up being. Of course, I do not fault Xander for that. My sister is a... *challenging* woman at her best."

"Isn't that why you left the Consort?" Arielle chimed in. "Because of Nacaria's trial?"

"Partly," Blackie explained. "After the trial, I began having my own difficulties with my sister. It only fueled the resentment I still harbored for Nacaria's punishment."

Beryl was slightly puzzled by this statement. "It was my understanding that you were the one who testified against Nacaria at her trial," Beryl pressed on. "Not to be rude, but why would her punishment be so offensive to you?"

Blackie did not answer right away. Though Beryl did not possess the same power to read *her* mind, it was obvious Blackie was calculating exactly how to word her reply—perhaps to protect herself.

"I had to tell the truth of what I knew. The Consort required *vows*," Blackie began. Beryl knew the seriousness of vows. Powers are waged when taking a vow. No witch would dare lie and lose their abilities. Blackie went on, "To cover for my friend would have only taken me down as well. Nacaria was wrong for what she did, but you also must know my sister to truly appreciate why Nacaria felt compelled to do what she did. Atheidrelle was always wicked—just short of evil, in my opinion. And maybe not short of it at all. I've no doubt she is still quite reprehensible."

Beryl bristled at this. True as it may be—and she had always heard this same rhetoric about Atheidrelle from her family—Atheidrelle was Arielle's mother. And Arielle was sitting right there. But it didn't appear to be upsetting Arielle to hear her mother so berated.

"It all sounds terribly complex," Beryl sighed. "I've never been able to completely understand what all happened back then."

"Very few people can. There are layers to everything. Some layers come to light, others never do."

A low chime rang out from a cock somewhere which Beryl could not see as she scanned the darkly decorated room. Quinlan Castle felt heavy. Or perhaps it was the energy coming from Blackie. Whichever it was, Beryl wanted to speed things along.

"May I ask why you wanted to see me tonight?" Beryl asked. "I would have thought you'd want to talk with my mother or my aunt or my grandmother or—even more importantly—Salem or Seth. Why me?"

Blackie stood up and strolled back to the window where Beryl had first seen her. It was clear Blackie had something to tell but was unsure how to do so. Perhaps whatever it was involved some of those layers she had just been speaking about. Perhaps she was trying to bring some of them to light yet needed to conceal others.

"I would never upset your grandmother needlessly. Neither would I want to bring Nacaria's children into this matter until I can corroborate my suspicions. Those two have suffered enough already."

"And I said nothing to Salem," Arielle offered. "She believes I am at night classes and then going to a late movie with friends."

Beryl was becoming more intrigued by the second. She rose and joined Blackie at the window where the woman was standing, pensive, staring into the night. "Tell me what is going on, please."

"What do you know about your aunt's condition?" Blackie asked.

Beryl shrugged, "What any of us do, I suppose. She's cursed to be a shadow on the wall at home while her body lies somewhere in a coma, administered by the Council as her penance."

"But she isn't in a coma," Blackie countered with a mysterious air about her. "Not now. At least she shouldn't be."

"I don't understand."

Blackie walked back to the sofa where Arielle was seated. Beryl followed her. Blackie's violet eyes fixed into Beryl's blue. Beryl could tell the woman was genuinely worried about something. Then Blackie asked, "When was the last time you saw Nacaria's shadow?"

"I don't know," Beryl admitted, feeling a little guilty for the answer. They'd all just sort of fallen into the normalcy of it at home. They really didn't pay the shadow attention anymore. "She is always around somewhere. Sometimes we see her; sometimes we don't. We've all just grown accustomed to it."

"But when *exactly* was the last time you saw her shadow yourself? Arielle remembers it at Halloween, but she didn't recall seeing it Thanksgiving when she was last there."

Beryl thought about it. She was not actually sure. She knew Halloween was definite, it was Seth's wedding day, and even after he and Yasmine returned from the honeymoon. Nacaria flashed by while they had been recounting their adventures in Jamaica. After that, Beryl could not be sure. The shadow on the wall had become too much a part of life at Blanchard House; Beryl was so accustomed to it that she paid it little attention anymore.

"I know for a fact that Nacaria's curse has been lifted," Blackie interrupted her new friend's thoughts. "She's served her time."

"How could you know that?" Beryl was astonished. "No one knows that date. Not even my grandmother. That is part of the punishment. The term of the curse was never disclosed."

"Trust me, Beryl. I know."

"Does that mean she's been released and didn't want to come home?" Arielle asked.

"It could," Blackie said. "Or it could mean any number of things. Beryl, your family should have been alerted by Dredmore Asylum the moment Nacaria woke up from the curse. She would have been in no condition to make decisions for herself after having been immobile and detached from her body for so many years. I don't understand why your family wasn't contacted."

"We aren't positive she's been freed," Beryl noted. "I don't mean to sound distrusting, but I'm not actually sure when the last time anyone in my family has seen my aunt's shadow, and I am taking a lot here based on just your word—the word of a stranger."

"Who also happens to be Atheidrelle's sister," Blackie nodded understandingly.

"I'm sorry, but yes," Beryl confessed. Arielle jumped in excitedly, "Oh Beryl, you can trust Blackie! She's not like Mother at all. She would not lie to you about this."

Beryl thought a moment before replying. "I think I need to call home and ask my mother about the shadow."

"Please do," Blackie requested. "If I'm right, then hopefully you will know you can trust me, and we can get to the bottom of this."

Beryl made the call. Demitra did not understand at first until Beryl explained what she'd been told by Blackie D'Angelo. Beryl asked her mother when the last time she had seen her sister's spirit roaming the house. Like Beryl, Demitra could not pinpoint the most recent time. Beryl was quick to warn Demitra not to say a word to Olympia. Beryl feared that at her age, the old woman might become upset and suffer a stroke or heart attack. With Beryl in Birmingham, she would not be there to heal her.

Ending the call with her mother, Beryl turned to Blackie, "Okay, I believe you. What do we do now? Do we contact the Council?"

"No," Blackie cautioned. "We must have complete secrecy. I suspect someone is holding Nacaria against her will. Maybe they took her from Dredmore Asylum forcibly. Maybe they are still holding her there. It is also possible...she may be dead."

"Dead?" Arielle gasped. "That would devastate my father."

"It is a possibility," Blackie continued. "That too would explain the absence of her shadow." Blackie was running through possibilities now, her train of thought exhausting all avenues. "Although if that were the case, the asylum administrators would have contacted the family...unless foul play is involved, and the administrators are part of the plot...but that would be nearly impossible to pull off."

"What do we do, Blackie?" Arielle pressed.

"I must get to Dredmore as soon as possible," Blackie said.

"What if you're right about the administration?" Beryl interjected. "If you go to the asylum, you wouldn't be allowed inside."

"Oh, don't worry about that part of it," Arielle grinned to Beryl. "No one will have any idea she's even there. Show her, Blackie."

Blackie walked to a nearby carved wooden throne and sat down. She stared straight into Beryl's eyes and disappeared. Beryl gasped. She had vanished completely. Then as quickly as she had disappeared, Blackie was back seated in the chair once more.

"What just happened?" Beryl asked. "Did you freeze me and run out of the room?"

"I do not possess time-stopping abilities," Blackie smiled.

"Wait!" Beryl exclaimed. "Salem told me her father has the ability to jump space and time and appear in other locations."

"It's called *leaping,*" Arielle informed. "But she didn't do that either. What she did was hypnotize you into not being able to see her. She basically told your brain it doesn't see her anymore."

"Amazing power," Beryl marveled. "So, you're suggesting you use your ability to enter Dredmore and remain unseen by anyone inside? Then you can see if Aunt Nacaria is still there?"

"Yes, with some assistance. I cannot do it alone. It is impossible for me to actually get inside without being seen. I have to look into their eyes to use my power," Blackie explained.

"But if her sentence has been lifted, why all the secrecy? This sounds like a rescue mission. Don't we have the right to simply go in and get her?"

Blackie tried to explain, "Dredmore is a Consort institution. To just burst in is a punishable crime."

"But if they have done something to Nacaria..."

"It is highly doubtful the institution itself has done anything. It's very reputable," Blackie explained. "Witches locked up in Dredmore are assigned one caretaker. Most of the prisoners are in comas like Nacaria or trapped in cells living out whatever punishments they are forced to endure. Prison officials make routine inspections of the inmates, but the caretaker is their chief warden."

Beryl thought about what Blackie said. "That means Nacaria's caretaker is the one who would most likely know what's happened. Perhaps Nacaria convinced the caretaker not to report her recovery to our family? Perhaps the caretaker was overpowered and Nacaria was abducted?"

Blackie nodded, "We can't know what happened until I can get inside the asylum. But even then, it's not simple. There are hundreds of prisoners, each in a fortified private cell. We don't even know which cell is Nacaria's. Therefore, I need to be able to walk unseen among everyone; I have to locate her cell without anyone seeing me. But first, we have to find a way in."

"So how do we get you inside?"

"Dredmore is heavily guarded and fortified. We can go there, and we can ring the bell, but no one is going to let us in. We will be turned away."

"But you can hypnotize them and get inside?" Arielle noted.

"Not exactly," Blackie replied. "We can't risk the staff seeing us until we can be sure Dredmore's security hasn't been compromised."

"We need Salem's freezing power," Arielle suggested.

"It sounds like we need to assemble a team," Beryl said. "I need to go home to Blanchard House. The family deserves to know what is going on, and we are going to need some help to get you inside Dredmore."

CHAPTER ELEVEN

The Daughter of the Spirit that has Possessed Your Son

Fable parked her Jeep in a vacant driveway three houses down from the one occupied by the Millers. The Crestwood neighborhood was an ordinary one, just on the outskirts of Birmingham. The houses were a mix of styles, all mid-sized, middle-class homes—ranch-style mostly—but updated over the years making for a rather cute little neighborhood. The street was quiet with everyone already home from work or school and settling into another night of dinner table conversations, homework, or family television sessions.

Fable walked toward the Miller house and immediately saw what she was hoping for. Her father had been correct—the Millers did have a dog, and he was lounging quite comfortably under a tree in the fenced back yard. She was just about to approach the fence when she suddenly thought of something she hadn't previously considered. Something that could throw a wrench into her whole plan...her face. If the body of Jerry Miller was going to eventually marry her mother, these people were going to meet Fable Blanchard one day. She had to disguise herself. Quickly remembering a spell she and Seth had played with as children, Fable moved her hands over her face and through her hair as she recited;

"Face to face
Eye to eye
They will see
A face not mine"

As her fingers moved across her features, a new face projected forth to anyone looking upon her. Nothing about her appearance had actually changed, it would merely be perceived as different.

She hurried to the wire fence, speaking to the Millers' Labrador as she went, cautioning him not to bark. She crouched down beside the gate. The dog looked into her deep eyes as she told him, *I am a friend. I need you to help me. I need for you to whimper and limp and act as if your leg hurts. You must stay like that until you hear me tell you to stop.* Fable opened the gate.

She rang the doorbell of the Miller home and waited for someone to answer. It didn't take long before a small older woman in a blue-checked apron came to the door. She saw Fable holding her dog in her arms and gasped.

"Tipton! Is he all right?"

"I was driving down the street and saw him limping in the road. I think someone may have hit him," Fable lied. "I asked a neighbor, and they said he belonged to you."

"Oh yes!" Mrs. Miller cried. "Please bring him inside." She directed Fable to a nearby couch where Fable gently laid Tipton down. Tipton gave a convincing whine for Fable.

"It just so happens I am a vet," Fable told Mrs. Miller. "I can help him. I think he will be alright."

"Oh, thank you so much!" the little woman said, beginning to cry. "I just don't know what Vestus would do without him. Tipton is like a baby to us."

Fable played doctor for half an hour, examining the dog and showing him tender care while Mrs. Miller looked on. She bandaged his leg and made a makeshift splint for him out of two wooden spoons Mrs. Miller supplied her with.

"I cannot begin to thank you enough," the old woman said gratefully when Fable was finished. "I'm afraid I don't even know your name."

"I'm Fa...Felicia," Fable replied, tripping over her real name.

"Oh, Felicia, can I pay you something for your time and help?"

"Oh, no—that isn't necessary. I'm glad I was here to help. If you like, I can stay a little longer to make sure he's all right."

"Please!" Mrs. Miller exclaimed. "And you'll stay for dinner. My husband Vestus will be home any minute."

Fable smiled. "Thank you. Dinner sounds lovely. And we can get acquainted. I can tell you all about myself, and you can tell me all about you and Vestus."

...

Mr. Miller was just as friendly and grateful as his wife. Dinner was scrumptious. Mrs. Miller cooked fried pork chops with string beans and mashed potatoes. Fable hated to admit it, but Mrs. Miller's potatoes were even more delicious than Artemis'. Fable, under the guise of Felicia, concocted a false story of her life then sat glued to every word as Mr. and Mrs. Miller talked about themselves. Fable learned all about Mrs. Miller's church club affiliations, her gallbladder surgery, her two recent gout flare ups. Fable found out her favorite movie was *Driving Miss Daisy* and that she never missed an episode of *Wheel of Fortune*. Mr. Miller was an Elks Lodge member, a retiree from the City Housing and Planning Board, and currently enjoyed his new woodworking hobby. He even gave *Felicia* a tour of his workshop in the garage. She eventually "learned" the Millers have a son.

"Is this his picture here?" Fable asked, lifting the 8 x 10 frame from the living room end table.

"Yes, that's our Jerry," Mrs. Miller smiled proudly. "We're worried about him though."

"Really?" Fable asked. "May I ask why?"

"He was an accountant in Tuscaloosa," Mrs. Miller explained. "But we've heard he quit his job, and we don't hear from him often anymore."

"Hasn't visited us or called us in two months," Mr. Miller added. "When we call him, he hangs up real quick. Something is going on with that boy."

"That's awful," Fable responded, trying her best to sound authentic.

"I'm heading down there next week," Mr. Miller revealed. "I'm gonna see him face to face whether he likes it or not. He's got some explaining to do. Got us worried sick."

"Well, I hope everything is okay," Fable offered. "I really do have to go now. Do you mind if I stop back by in a day or so and check on Tipton?"

"We would love it!" Mrs. Miller exclaimed. "You have been so kind. Let me know when you're coming, and I'll fix you lunch or dinner again."

"Yes, we cannot thank you enough, Felicia," Mr. Miller said, shaking her hand. "I hope you won't be a stranger."

"I won't be," Fable said.

She stopped by the sofa on her way out and stroked Tipton's back. He looked up at her with his big brown happy eyes and wagged his tail. She leaned down and whispered to him, *Keep up the act. Tomorrow you can start walking normally again. Just keep pretending tonight. And thanks for your help, my friend. You're a very good boy!*

...

On the drive back to Daihmler, Fable pulled out her phone and noticed a text from Beryl. *Family meeting ASAP, get home.*

Curious about what was so important, suddenly she panicked. Did Beryl find out about their father? Did Beryl find out Fable was pregnant? Suddenly Fable's anxiety levels hit the roof. She simply had too many secrets going on right now and any one of them was enough to explode in her face. Quickly, she looked up Jerry Miller's cell phone number in her contacts list and dialed him.

"Fable?"

"Hi, Daddy!"

"Your mother just left. Your timing is perfect."

"What's going on with Beryl?" Fable asked. "She's called a meeting. She doesn't know—"

"No, no, honey; it's another matter entirely. Your mother told me it had something to do with Nacaria."

"Nacaria?"

"I don't know anything other than that," Larry told his daughter. "So, tell me, how did tonight go?"

Fable smiled to herself—and the guy in the pickup truck beside her who assumed she was smiling at him. "I just spent the evening with Jerry's parents."

"How did it go?"

"They are wonderful people, Daddy. I learned so much. I'm going back tomorrow."

Larry thanked her for all she'd done, then he added, "Do you think we can really pull this off? Do you think I'll be able to stay in this body without attracting suspicion?"

"At first I wasn't sure," Fable admitted. "But now I really think it's possible. You can pull this off, Daddy. You can remarry Mother, and no one will be the wiser."

"That's wonderful," Larry replied.

"I know," she said. "But Daddy, you have to contact the Millers soon. They are growing more and more concerned with their son's erratic behavior. I've learned enough for you to bluff through a conversation, and I'll get more tomorrow. But what better excuse for acting odd than having met a woman and falling in love? I think telling them that will help a lot."

"You think I should tell them about your mother?"

"I think you and Mother should drive up here and see them. Introduce Mother to them. That alone would drive the conversation away from past things and more toward the present. They are the nicest people. They will be so sweet to her. And do it soon. Mr. Miller is planning to drive down to find you next week. You need to take action now. Trust me."

CHAPTER TWELVE

Oh, Christmas Tree

Christmastime at Blanchard House always came with its own set of rituals and traditions. Every year on December 9, the Christmas tree went up. The date was sacred to Olympia because this was the date many years ago when she and her sister, Pastoria, had successfully convinced their father (after many, many years of trying) to allow them to put up a tree. Normally, everyone in the family would be home for this special occasion, but Fable claimed to have a date and Beryl was meeting a colleague in Birmingham for a consult. Their absences did not deter Olympia from her tradition.

Artemis and Demitra hauled the family tree down from the attic along with several boxes of cherished ornaments from over the years. It was tradition that the family gather together in the living room to trim the tree. Olympia was not helping with the decorating this year, handing that task over to the grandchildren. She felt tired. Being 85 years old did come with a few disadvantages, her energy levels as of late being one of them. She'd overexerted herself on Halloween when the family had taken down the werewolf killer Patric. She hadn't yet managed to bounce back to her full self, but she was still enjoying watching the tree come to life from the comfort of her favorite chair by the fireplace. Seth was sitting on the couch yelling obscenities at the tangle of last year's lights which had not been wrapped properly before being stored. They were never wrapped properly. Every year it was the plan, but by the time the tree came down, no one cared very much for taking time to put anything away tidily.

"Why don't we ever wrap these fucking things in nice, neat bundles?!" Seth raged.

"As I remember," Artemis told him, "You were the one in charge of taking down the lights—just as you are every year. And since you are also the one in charge of putting them up, I guess the fault begins and ends with you."

"Bite me."

Artemis gave a hearty chuckle and continued helping Demitra place the tree in the corner of the room next to the fireplace. Yasmine opened a pack of tinsel and began tossing globs into the branches, spilling more on the floor than she was placing on the tree.

"Yaz, what the hell are you doing?" her husband snapped.

"I like the icicles. It's my favorite part."

"First of all, it's called tinsel," Seth corrected, "and secondly, would you wait until I've got the damn lights on!"

Yasmine Blanchard stomped to the couch and tossed her handful of tinsel onto her husband's head. "Seth Blanchard, you can get the corn cob out of your butt and speak to me a little nicer!"

About that time, Zelda came barreling through the door, stopping once she saw the tree. With a look of disgust on her face, she shook her head and her finger at Olympia as she walked into the room.

"That is still the ugliest tree I've ever seen in my life," she said. "Lympy you've had that same tree since Artemis was little. I tell you ever' year to get a new one."

"I don't want a new one," Olympia declared. "I like the one I have."

"You ortta get a real one. I hate fake trees." Zelda gave the tree one more disdainful glance and let out an exaggerated huff before plopping down in the chair beside Olympia. "You got plenty a trees on this property. Just cut one down."

"I do not believe in the cutting down of trees," Olympia scoffed.

"What'd you think this house is built of…throw pillows?" Zelda chuckled. "Just remember when you get around to buying Christmas presents, I need a new refrigerator."

"Did yours conk out?" Seth asked. "I could try and fix it."

"You don't know how to fix a refrigerator," Yasmine quipped.

"I fixed your electric fan."

"No, you didn't," she said. "I bought another one at Target. It doesn't even look like the old one."

Zelda bellowed out a deep laugh at the bickering newlyweds. "The two a' you sounds like me and Fred. Boy we sure had some doozies, didn't we Lympy?"

Olympia's face morphed into a nostalgic smile as her mind flashed back on the long-forgotten memories of Zelda and her husband's life together. It had been such a long time since she and her best friend had husbands, she sometimes forgot how different their lives were when men were a part of them. "I always felt so sorry for poor Fred, the way you talked to him. Of course, he gave you your share back."

"Best sign of a happy marriage is if you yell at each other all the time," Zelda snickered. "Means you got passion."

Yasmine pulled the tinsel off Seth's head since it hadn't garnered a response and returned it to the box in her hand. "Then I have the most passionate marriage in the world."

Ignoring his wife's jab, Seth asked Zelda, "What happened to your fridge?"

"Door broke off," she answered. "Sarah can't let it be closed longer than a minute. She keeps opening it up looking for a snack. I swear since she moved back in, I'm bein' eat out of house and home. Now Melinda's over every night too."

Demitra stopped mid-way through stringing the first set of lights Seth had untangled and asked, "I thought Melinda and Sarah couldn't get along? I'm surprised she even comes over with Sarah moved back in."

"Oh, they made up and now they're inseparable," Zelda sighed. "Hell, the best part of getting old is finally having a house all to yourself. Thought I'd get some peace when Fred died, but those blame girls of mine..."

"Now, I know for a fact you loved Fred and miss him," Olympia said, giving her friend a side-eye.

"Oh, I ain't sayin' I didn't love him. I'm just sayin' I thought he never would hurry up and die."

"Yaz!" Seth shouted, looking up from his knot of Christmas lights to spy his wife continuing to place tinsel on a completely undecorated tree. "I'm not kidding. Stop it with the damn tinsel."

"Grandmother, make Seth stop picking on me."

"Yasmine," Olympia scolded. "You are no longer twelve, and he is your husband. Handle him yourself."

Demitra was seated on the floor now with a brown cardboard box before her. Inside were the family's Christmas stockings. She pulled the box closer to the fireplace and began to hang them on the mantle with thumbtacks. Every family member had their name stitched on their individual stocking. When finished, she went to a plastic bag on the coffee table and withdrew the new additions she'd purchased that morning in town. Olympia twisted around in her chair to look at the mantlepiece now very crowded with a row of stockings dangling above the hearth.

"Wow," she said reading the names. "Myself, Artemis, Demitra, Beryl, Salem, Seth, Fable, Yasmine, Howard, Zelda, and now Arielle and Jerry. We may need a larger fireplace."

"Jerry?" Artemis noted, as she gave her sister a concerning look. "Already on the mantle?"

"Don't start with me, Artemis," Demitra warned. "Jerry is important to me."

"Just seems rather fast, little sister."

Zelda gave a hearty chuckle and commented, "Looks like Demmy better be careful 'fore she runs out of fool!"

Demitra shot Zelda a resentful look. "And in the dense vacuum which we charitably call your mind, is that comment supposed to mean something?"

Artemis intervened. "Oh, don't lash out at Zelda for saying what we are all thinking. This little romance is moving extremely fast. But it is your business. I just hope the girls won't be upset by it."

"My girls," Demitra asserted, "are happy for me. In fact, Fable told me just last night how happy she is that I have Jerry in my life."

"That was quite a turnaround for her," Yasmine commented.

"I thought so too," Demitra agreed. "But she says she's on board. Speaking of the girls, Beryl phoned a little while ago. She said we are to all be home tonight. She is coming back late, and she's called a family meeting."

CHAPTER THIRTEEN

Blackie Comes to Blanchard House

The twinkling lights of the Christmas tree gave the illusion of tranquility to the living room of Blanchard House. Yet the illusion was only moments from fading as everyone gathered around the Blanchard living room to hear why Beryl had called a special family meeting—and why Blackie D'Angelo, of all people, was now standing before them after all these years. Beryl and Blackie took turns recounting their conversation in Birmingham, announcing to the family the real possibility that Nacaria's curse might have been lifted. Everyone was shell shocked by the revelation. Olympia began to cry. Demitra moved to stand beside her mother's chair, her reassuring hand resting on the old woman's shoulder. Olympia's heart was fluttering. Discreetly she pressed her hand to her chest, pretending to fiddle with her pendant. She did not want her family to worry.

"Why didn't we notice if she wasn't here anymore?" Seth cried. "Why didn't I notice?"

He took off, charging through all the downstairs rooms from the office den through the dining room, the kitchen, and back to the foyer. Searching every wall for his mother's shadow, he bolted up the stairs to search the upper levels. Yasmine chased behind him.

"She isn't here," Demitra told her mother. "I searched every floor after Beryl called."

After their fruitless inspection of every wall in Blanchard House, Seth and Yasmine rejoined the family. Blackie continued with her story and her concern over what could have happened to Nacaria after the curse had lifted.

"How do you know the curse has been lifted?" Artemis asked.

"Because I know the date it was set to end," Blackie revealed.

"No one knows that date," Demitra shot back with a suspicious tone.

"I do. I always have."

"How could you know?" Seth asked.

"Is that important now?" Blackie asked. "We know she isn't here. That means she is free of the curse. Now we have to discover why she hasn't come home."

"Couldn't it just take a while for her to be able to come home?" Demitra asked. "From what I understand her body has been in a coma all this time. It would take quite a while for her body to acclimate. Perhaps she's just in a recovery period and they will call us once she has regained her faculties."

"Normally, perhaps," Blackie admitted. "However, considering Nacaria has a niece with healing powers, I doubt they'd wait for Nacaria to recover on her own. It'd make even more sense for them to have called the family."

The front door flew open as Salem rushed inside, Arielle trailing behind her. Blackie turned to see them. Arielle announced she had caught Salem up to speed on the drive in from Atlanta. Seth looked at his big sister and saw it all—everything he was feeling—shock, joy, trepidation. He jumped up from his chair and grabbed Salem's hand. "Salem, Mother's free!"

"I know," she replied. "Arielle told me. I just don't know what to make of any of this."

Seth walked over and gave his new little sister a brotherly hug. "Hey, kiddo," he said kissing the top of her head. "I'm glad you're here."

Beryl motioned for everyone to rejoin the group so that the family could hash out what lay before them. "Salem has already heard most of this, but for the rest of you the reason we called this meeting isn't only to tell you Aunt Nacaria is free, but to tell you Blackie and I believe something has happened to her."

"Explain," Seth said.

"No one has contacted us," Beryl went on. "This means she has either left Dredmore Asylum on her own or has been taken from it against her will."

"Or..." Blackie added. "She's still there, captive."

"Who would do that?" Fable asked.

Blackie looked at her niece without saying a word. The room fell silent.

"Oh," Fable said.

"It's possible," Arielle said softly. "My mother is capable of anything."

"Or has Aunt Nacaria run away with Xander?" Fable posed. "Salem said when she met him last summer, he was still very much in love with her. Could he have taken her?"

"I could call him?" Arielle offered.

"No," Olympia said. "It's best no one else gets involved until we know more."

"Olympia is right," Blackie said. "If my sister, or the facility itself is involved in any way, we cannot risk tipping them off that we know Nacaria is free."

Beryl picked back up to explain everything she and Blackie had previously discussed. She told them the details of how Dredmore Asylum is a witches' prison, complete with guards and security measures. Hundreds of rooms housing hundreds of prisoners would make it impossible to rush in and find Nacaria. The team would need to comprise only those with powers needed for the mission.

"Blackie will need to be able to walk around Dredmore unseen," she explained. "She has that power. She can hypnotize people into not seeing her, but even if she were able to hypnotize them into not seeing her any longer, they would have still seen her when she originally looked into their eyes."

"I follow," Seth said. "The staff would already know there was an intruder. They would just think she had *blinked away*. They might still ring the alarm and alert the entire prison."

"What I need," Blackie said, walking toward Salem, "is someone who can freeze people before they see me."

"Done," Salem nodded.

Yasmine raised her hand like a schoolgirl, "I have a silly question. Why can't you guys just blow out each door until you find her? Why the need to sneak around unseen?"

"It is still a prison," Olympia explained. "The witches imprisoned there are guilty of terrible crimes. If just one prisoner got loose accidentally, there's no telling what could happen."

"You have Salem's freezing power to help," Seth said to Blackie. "What should the rest of us do? I can control weather. Fable can control animals. Artemis can make almost anything happen if she sets her concentration to it."

Blackie held up her hand to stop him. "I think it's best if we keep the team small. My power, Salem's freezing ability, Beryl's healing power in case guards attack us or Nacaria is injured, are all we need."

"Arielle should go," Salem suggested.

"Arielle? And not me?" Seth grimaced. "No offense, Ari, but it's my mother in there."

"Yes, but you do not have the power of telekinesis like our little sister does. I can unlock doors if I focus really hard, but I'll also be busy freezing anyone coming around any given corner. Arielle can handle the locks while Blackie and I handle the people."

Seth didn't argue. He understood she was right and that this was not a time for his ego to strut around. The point was saving his mother. It was Arielle who argued in his favor, bringing up an important point no one had thought about.

"Exactly how large is Dredmore, Aunt Blackie?"

Blackie turned to the only other person she knew who'd probably ever seen it, "Olympia? What would you say—300 rooms?"

"It looks like a very large hotel," Olympia began. "Disguised as such so that outsiders never know what it truly is. It is all an illusion. Inside, it is perhaps the most frightening place on earth."

Arielle turned to her sister. "Salem, how far of a freezing range do you have?"

"Pretty good, I'd say."

"An entire 300 room building with cinder block walls?" Arielle asked.

Salem shook her head. "I don't think so."

Arielle clasped Seth's hand. "Remember when we rescued Yasmine? You, me, and Salem—we held hands and amplified our powers. The three Obreiggon witches—full witches—sharing the same blood in our veins."

Seth's face lit up. Grinning he replied, "With Salem drawing power from you and me, she can freeze that whole building."

"Then it is decided," Blackie announced. "Myself, Beryl, Salem, Arielle, and Seth will go."

Olympia stood up. She had not meant it to appear ceremonial, but as she stood everyone else moved back to reverently give her space, as though she were a queen. She walked toward Blackie D'Angelo with her hand outstretched to clasp with Blackie's. "Many years ago, you testified against my daughter. I understood your reasons then, as I do now." Olympia's hand squeezed Blackie's. No one else noticed. It was a private exchange—an indication of an understanding only the two of them shared. "Bring my daughter home to me now and all is washed away."

Blackie turned to Beryl, Seth, Salem, and Arielle, "Then we should be on our way. It is quite a drive to the Louisiana bayou. We can reach Dredmore by morning."

CHAPTER FOURTEEN

Dredmore Asylum

The drive into Louisiana was deafeningly silent for the most part. Everyone in Salem's car seemed lost in their own thoughts about the situation. Salem guided the car along the road past ugly billboard advertisements of accident lawyers, chain gas stations, rusty sheds, dilapidated houses, and farmlands. She didn't look at the landscape very much, too distracted by conflicting emotions which she assumed only her brother probably also carried. There was a natural fear at work in the pit of her stomach at the fact that they were about to break into a prison—a witches' prison. That alone came with countless concerns and dangers. Behind that was a fear of came one even more potent. Finding their mother. *Their mother* whom they hadn't been around since they were little children. Having their mother restored to them had been their life's dream, but now as it loomed before Salem, she was afraid to have that dream realized. What if she wasn't the same? What if they didn't like each other? What if Nacaria wasn't the good person everyone insisted she used to be? Salem lived her life with an image in her head of what her mother had been like. What if that had only been a little girl's fantasy?

Through the swampy wetlands of the backwoods bayou, they found the cutoff road which led to their destination. Nothing else existed on the road other than forest and murky river tributaries flowing under an occasional creaky wooden bridge. In the distance they saw it—a large structure that did indeed look very much like a curiously-placed hotel which had gone out of business.

Dredmore stood like a great manor house from days gone by when land barons paid no property taxes and were free to build their monstrosities without constraints of a yearly penalty. Olympia had been correct, the great structure stood four stories tall with several wings branching off. The windows were all shuttered to conceal the fact that there were no windows at all. It looked serene from afar, like an exclusive hotel.

But the wings of the great building wrapped around and reconnected themselves shielding from view whatever might lurk inside or out. It was an ornate fortress.

A massive wall surrounded the property, shutting out the world and locking in Dredmore itself. There was only one gate, sentried by two guards with guns. Beryl did not approach with the car. She stopped on the east side of the wall, well out of sight of the gate watchmen. She, Blackie, Arielle, and Seth exited the car and hid against the wall out of sight as Salem drove the car around to the front and only entrance to Dredmore Asylum.

Salem did not steer the car into the small driveway running to the guarded gate. She worried hidden cameras might pick her up if she came into view. Instead, she pulled off the road so that only the driver's side of the car faced the guards. She wanted to give the impression she was merely a traveler asking directions. Rolling down her window, she motioned to one of the guards. Neither guard abandoned their post, they simply stared at her, hands ready on their holster.

"Excuse me," Salem called out to them. "I am turned all around. I'm looking for Owens Road."

Before they could reply she threw her hands to the air and sent her magic hurtling toward them. Both guards stood still as stone as her freezing power took effect. Salem whipped the car around in the road and drove back to the east wall. Joining the others under the canopy of a tree, Salem tapped her brother on the back. It was his turn. Seth stepped forward and looked to the skies. Overhead the sporadic cloud cover began changing. Clouds began to drift toward one another from all directions until a much larger, ominous gray cloud rumbled overhead. Seth raised his arm and jerked it down sharply toward the thick stone wall. A bolt of lightning burst from above crashing into the wall. Shards of rock flew out as larger stones crumbled amid a heavy cloud of dust and debris. In their place was a hole in the wall.

"Your door, ladies," Seth said bowing.

Everyone climbed through the hole. Salem kept alert for any additional guards as they ran across the lawn to the front doors of the building. A heavy iron knocker hung centered on the right-side door. The others hid, backs flat against the stucco flanking the doorway. Salem lifted the knocker and let it fall to the pad beneath, sending an echoing sound from behind the door. Within seconds the door pulled slightly ajar.

Salem wasted no time before she froze the person behind the door. Seth pushed his shoulder into the door, shoving it open enough to move the man behind it out of the way. No one else was in sight. He rejoined the others on the front steps and joined hands with his two sisters. Beryl and Blackie stepped behind them, out of Salem's range. Salem drained power from her two siblings, sucking enough energy to magnify her abilities fifty-fold. Thrusting her arms in front of her, power bounded out with such a force she stumbled backward, nearly falling until Beryl caught and righted her.

"That had to do it!" Salem exclaimed. "I have never felt that much surge through me before. Wow! That was a rush!"

Salem felt exhilarated. Then suddenly she didn't. The others watched as she slowly became a little wobbly and closed her eyes. Seth darted into the doorway, his quick reflexes catching her before she slammed herself into the concrete floor.

"She drained herself," observed Blackie.

Seth lightly slapped at Salem's cheeks until she came back around. His sister managed to get herself to her feet but remained unsteady. She insisted she was able to walk and continue the mission. With a little help from Beryl's arm around her waist, she and the others went inside.

Beyond the doors of Dredmore, things were rather bleak as the group looked around. The pristine, although disintegrating, beauty of outside was not reflected indoors. Before them stretched a maze of cinderblock corridors. There was no entry lobby, or front desk. Only a hallway which broke off into other hallways. The lighting was dismal. Dull fluorescents, suspended by chain overhead every ten feet or so, lent a greenish tint to cinderblock walls. Every so often, the group would come across a door of thick oak or steel, otherwise every direction was windowless and deplete of furnishings. Dredmore Asylum was only a collection of indistinguishable passages and holding chambers.

"I guess there's no way to know which one is Mother's," Seth whispered as they twisted along the hallways. "Could we perform a honing spell of some sort? Maybe Salem and I being her closest relatives can locate her using our blood."

"Not here," Blackie informed them. "This place will be protected from spells and charms."

"How do my freezing powers work then?'

"Powers are different," Blackie explained. "There are too many varying kinds of powers to protect from. And people have varying degrees of strength of power. Simple spells are pretty easy to shield for a place like this, but our powers are different.

There isn't a witch alive strong enough to safeguard against another witches physical power, especially multiple forms."

"Makes this place rather susceptible to break-ins, doesn't it?" Seth commented as they walked.

"I don't think this is the kind of place people typically try to break *into*," Arielle whispered. "This place is filled with bad, bad witches."

The group turned a corner and entered a square room with two additional corridors jutting off in other directions. A group of staff members filled the room, each displaying various degrees of frozen movement.

"This is a hub," Beryl observed. "That first stretch of hallway we were on all the way to here needs to be the first place we check. Arielle, you unlock all the doors on the hallway we just came down. Blackie, you hypnotize these people then keep going and do the same thing to everyone you find. The rest of us will search the unlocked rooms one by one till we find her. If anyone finds Nacaria, *mindspeak* to the rest of us, and we'll find you."

Everyone did as Beryl suggested. Arielle walked from door to door, unlocking them each with her telekinesis. The moment one unlocked, Seth, Beryl, or Salem inspected it for Nacaria. Once cleared, Arielle relocked the door. Blackie moved through the building hypnotizing every frozen staff member she found.

Salem went into the first room. It was empty except for a desk, chair, phone, and bookshelf. It appeared to be a kind of receiving office. Beryl and Seth discovered much the same among the first few rooms of the first hallway. Only one prisoner was on that hall. A child. Frozen still in a cell, she looked as if she had been pacing before having been stopped by Salem's magic. *What could she have done to end up here?* Salem wondered.

Seth met Beryl and Salem back in the square hub, waiting for Arielle to finish relocking the doors. He told the others he had found no prisoners in any of the rooms he had checked. They were either empty or being used to store supplies. Beryl had much the same experience. Salem told them her findings, including the disturbing caged child she found. Arielle finished locking the checked rooms and went on ahead down the next corridor, unlocking doors as she walked. Seth, Beryl, and Salem followed behind, darting into now-opened rooms to search them.

Seth found an incredibly old woman laying on a hospital bed. Tubes and wires and pouches of fluids all connected her to machines. She was frozen like all the others by

Salem, but he knew that even had she not been, she would have been unconscious. Coma. Just like his mother had been placed in for most of his life. *I wonder what mother even looks like now. She used to be so beautiful. What does age look like on her after twenty years? Will I even know her when I see her?*

Beryl opened a door to find a very strange sight indeed. Two men were fused together at the wrist as if their hands had been connected permanently. *This is not a Siamese thing. This looks magical.* The men were oddly in different states of captivity. One man was standing inside a thickly barred cage, frozen in place by Salem's powers but from the expression on his face, he had been awake at the time her spell was cast. The other man fused to his arm was lying on a bed, connected to the same equipment as other prisoners who were comatose.

Room by room, the trio found many prisoners. Most were in sedated states of medically induced coma, while others were caged or shackled to walls. The most disturbing sight of any they encountered came when Seth went into one exceedingly small chamber where he discovered a man suspended from the ceiling by chains. The sight was so unnerving that he called his cousin and sisters in to observe. The man was young, not too much older than Seth himself. He was completely naked and utterly surrounded by hovering razor tipped spears enclosing his entire body. On the floor beneath him puddled little pools of blood—some fresh, some long dried up.

"What the hell did he do?" Beryl gasped.

"It looks like anytime he even barely moves, he gets cut," Arielle shuddered.

Seth walked around him. He felt empathy for the guy. Every area of his body had slices and cuts. His thighs, his chest, his face, his buttocks, even his penis.

"We have to help this guy," Seth urged the others.

"No," Beryl said. "Don't forget that everyone here committed a crime. A violent crime. The punishments fit the crime."

"But this is sadistic!" Seth gasped. "What could he have done to warrant this?"

"We are only here to find our mother," Salem reminded him. "And we are only here because her punishment has been lifted. We do not break criminals out of prison."

For half an hour, Salem, Beryl, Seth, and Arielle went through the asylum with no luck finding Nacaria. A new corridor presented itself before them and Arielle led the way. As she took a step into it, she immediately jumped back and thrust herself flat against the cinderblock, reaching her arm out to block the others from going forward.

There are unfrozen people, she mindspoke.

Salem's original spell was wearing off. She outstretched her hands to refreeze the place. Again, the act drained her, but the recovery time was shorter than before. They continued their search, still turning up nothing. Blackie ran back into the others somewhere near the center of the building.

"I have hypnotized everyone I've seen," she said. "We can't keep these people frozen too much longer. It is risky enough that this much time has passed. You guys get out of here and leave me inside. I'll move around unseen until I find her."

"But you can't unlock any doors without me," Arielle said.

"I know," Blackie replied. "But you four have already eliminated half of Dredmore while I was hypnotizing people. I only have half to search. I'll just follow caregivers around on this side of the asylum and go in to see their patients with them, until I find Nacaria."

"I don't think it's going to take that long," Salem announced staring at something down a long corridor they had not searched yet. "Arielle, come here. You'll know better than me."

Arielle walked to the start of the hallway and gasped. "Cassandra!"

"I thought that was her," Salem replied.

"Who is Cassandra?" Seth asked.

"Your other sister," Salem said sarcastically.

"Cassandra Obreiggon is here?" Beryl asked. "Why?"

"I didn't see Cassandra," Blackie gasped staring down the hallway. "I went down this hall earlier and she wasn't there."

"It looks like she's coming out of that room," Salem pointed out. "It's possible she was frozen inside there while you searched this hall and stepped out during one of the times I was refreezing everyone."

"Cassandra is dressed as a nurse," Beryl gasped. "*She's* been Nacaria's caretaker."

The group collectively gasped and looked at one another as they let soak in the full despicableness of this development. Atheidrelle Obreiggon's daughter was the caregiver assigned to look after the woman Atheidrelle hated more than any other in life.

"Quite a brilliant plan," Blackie acknowledged. "Put your daughter in place to look after your enemy, so that when your enemy wakes up, you can keep her prisoner. I suspected Atheidrelle was behind this, but I wasn't completely sure."

Arielle suddenly felt so embarrassed. Ashamed. She felt as if somehow the sin was sitting upon her as well. "My mother has been holding your mother captive," she teared up. "I am so sorry."

Salem saw the despair in her young sister's face. She pulled Arielle into an embrace and pressed her cheek to her own. "Hey, none of this is your fault."

Seth, tired of waiting to act upon their discovery, charged forward, "Let's go get our mother out."

"Wait!" Blackie ordered. "It is a mistake to pull her out now. We don't even know for sure if she's even in that room. To rescue her now would let Atheidrelle off scot free."

"Are you suggesting we leave my mother here?" Salem asked.

"No, of course not. Nacaria is leaving here with us," Blackie said. "But I need to witness what Cassandra is doing inside that room. A lot is at stake. What Atheidrelle is doing is a crime—if indeed she has put Cassandra up to this."

"What do you mean *if*?" Salem asked.

"It's rather simple, my dear," Blackie explained. "So far we have no evidence of a crime. Cassandra clearly has a job here. That is not illegal. Even if she has been assigned to your mother, that is inappropriate, but not illegal. Holding your mother hostage is illegal. But who is doing it? Cassandra? Atheidrelle? I need to catch Cassandra *with* Nacaria. If Atheidrelle is behind it, we need evidence to take to the Council. I will hypnotize Cassandra and follow her around. If Nacaria is in that room, I'll find her. And hopefully I will find out what is going on. Then I can go to the Council, take *vows* and report the crimes I have witnessed. If I can incriminate Cassandra, they can force *vows* on her as well."

The others decided to hide nearby in the chamber next to the one where Cassandra stood frozen. That chamber housed no prisoner they could see, however in the center of the room was a coffin, bound with heavy chains. This was an odd enough sight to behold, but the room itself was much different than any of the other rooms the witches had explored during their time in the asylum. Every other room they had seen was dimly lit, dark and gloomy. This room was filled with light. Sunshine streamed down from glass windows in the ceiling completely illuminating the entire space.

"This is new," Arielle observed, sarcastically.

Salem and Seth looked to each other and immediately uttered the same word, "Vampire."

Beryl, being a doctor, naturally took notice of a metal chart case hanging on a wall peg. As she did every day of her work life, she flipped through it, curious as to what she might find regarding the inmate of this room. Near the very front of the file, her eyes stopped moving further, unable to move past the background information of this particular prisoner. She let out an audible gasp.

"Guys, this is a vampire!" she said. "And right here it says he was captured by Olympia Blanchard, Pastoria Blanchard, and Zelda Markenson more than 60 years ago!"

"What?!" Seth exclaimed rushing over to view the file.

Beryl's astonished face released a smile of pride. "Hecate really was some kind of superhero back in her day!"

Out in the hall, once Salem unfroze the inhabitants of Dredmore, Blackie followed Cassandra to a storage closet where she gathered an IV bag and new catheter before returning to the room where they had first discovered her. As Cassandra unlocked the chamber door, Blackie hurried to slip inside before her niece closed and locked it behind her.

Blackie stood dumbstruck at the sight before her eyes. Nacaria. Beautiful Nacaria Blanchard lay like Sleeping Beauty on the bed. But Nacaria was not sleeping. Nacaria was awake, turning her head to see her nurse coming into the room...and Blackie.

"Friend..." Nacaria muttered indistinctly. "Save me."

Don't say anything. Blackie told her with her mind, hoping Nacaria's groggy state would not inhibit her reception of the warning. *She can't see me. But you can Nacaria. I am here to help you.*

Nacaria said nothing to alert Nurse Cassie to her old friend's presence. Blackie watched, overcome with emotion, seeing the poor wretch laying in the bed before her. Nacaria was just as beautiful as she had always been. Being locked away from sun and air had preserved her youth in many ways, yet fear had warped her face leaving a tortured soul strapped to the bed. Blackie watched as Cassandra injected Nacaria with a serum, knocking Nacaria back into a state of unconsciousness. Tears fell from Blackie's eyes seeing her friend drift back into that lonely, desolate waiting.

"I'm not your friend," Cassandra told the frail creature as she faded into nothingness again. "No one is coming to save you. Ever. No one even knows you are free. You are never waking up, Nacaria. You are never getting out of here."

Now! Blackie said with her mind.

A sudden explosion rang out, causing Cassandra to stagger backward and land with a sharp thud on the floor as brick and dust flew out in all directions from the side wall. She sat bewildered at the sight of her sister stepping through the hole amid clouds of brick dust.

"Arielle."

Cassandra nearly fainted as she saw the identities of the others coming through the swirls of dust behind her sister. Salem Blanchard. Two other people, most likely also Blanchards. And her Aunt Blackie.

"What are you doing here?" Cassandra demanded. "And with them?"

"Freeze her, Salem," Arielle said smiling down to her sister on the debris covered floor.

Salem froze Cassandra still as a statue before rushing to her mother's bedside. For the first time since she was a little girl, Salem looked upon her mother's face. Beryl motioned for everyone to stand back, to give her cousin the moment she had waited all of her life for. Gently, Beryl pushed Seth forward to join his sister. Salem lifted her fingertips to Nacaria's motionless face and traced the gentle bone structure she barely remembered. Seth was breathing heavily, unable to make sense of the feelings bubbling up inside him. Salem linked her arm with his and looked at him.

"Seth, she is alive. She is here. She's flesh and bone. Our mother, Seth! Can you believe it!"

"She's so beautiful," Seth whispered. "I forgot."

"She's not a shadow on the wall. She is real." Salem sobbed as tears broke through.

"How long will the drug last?" Arielle asked Blackie.

"Only seconds," Beryl smiled stepping forward. She placed her hands on her aunt's body and began doing her magic.

Nacaria's eyes began to twitch. She slowly moved her head to the side. Beryl moved her hands down Nacaria's body. There was so much to heal. Nacaria's body had not moved in years. Beryl began with her legs. As she worked, Salem continued pleading with her mother to awaken.

"Momma, Momma, it's me, Salem. Open your eyes Momma. It is your daughter Salem. We've come to rescue you. Seth's here Momma. Seth is here."

Nacaria opened her eyes halfway, still very groggy. But the light that twinkled from behind her half-closed lids let Salem know her mother understood what she was saying. Nacaria tried to speak, but it came out garbled. Beryl quickly moved her hands to her aunt's throat.

"Speak, Aunt Nacaria," Beryl ordered. "You can speak again."

"Salem," Nacaria said, eyes fully opening now. "Salem. Salem. Salem!"

With every repetition of her daughter's name Nacaria came to life again. Beryl finished with her arms and Nacaria lifted her hand, amazing herself by the action and displaying a look of awe in her expression as she lifted it to her daughter's face. Salem pressed her mother's soft hand to her cheek and wept.

Nacaria looked to Seth next. "My boy."

"Hi, Mom," he said breaking down into sobs. "Momma, Momma, you're back." He fell over her, hugging her body to his. "Oh, Momma we missed you."

The rescue party helped Nacaria to her feet. Despite her newly healed body, the act of walking was unfamiliar. Though capable of movement again, bodily motion was too foreign for Nacaria to achieve without assistance. Seth saw no point in her trying to reacquaint herself with the act of walking while time was of the essence. He picked her up and carried her out of Dredmore. Salem stayed behind with Blackie, Arielle, and Beryl. Salem and Arielle placed Cassandra onto Nacaria's bed. Beryl hooked Cassandra to all the tubes, wires, and bags which had been connected to Nacaria. She injected Cassandra with the very serum which the nurse had dosed Nacaria with for months.

"Hopefully, that will keep her knocked out for a while," Blackie said. "We need her to stay here until the Witches Council can send someone to get her. That could take a few hours. There is a Consort office not far from here."

"In the meantime, if anyone comes in here, they will just think she's a prisoner," Salem noted.

"What about the wall?" Arielle pointed out.

Blackie looked back at the massive hole blown out in the wall of the adjoining cell. "We will have to hope no one comes in here until Council authorities arrive. I will remain here until they do. It should not be more than an hour or two. Salem, you phone Queen Ursula and let her know what we have discovered and that I am here at Dredmore waiting. No one who is here presently will be able to see me. I will be quite safe until the Queen gets involved. The Consort meeting is in a few days. We will bring charges against Cassandra and Atheidrelle then. Salem, make sure Ursula keeps this quiet. We want to take Atheidrelle by surprise at that Consort meeting."

Salem looked down to her evil half-sister, now unconscious. She felt such a rage toward her. She wanted to hit her. Hit her hard. The thought of Nacaria laying in that bed every day, sick, afraid, thinking no one cared enough to come rescue her. She wanted Cassandra and Atheidrelle to pay for this.

"Let's get out of this place," Salem finally said. "I want to unfreeze this building and get my mother home."

CHAPTER FIFTEEN

Meet the Family

Fable spent the better part of the day with the Millers. Tipton the dog was feeling much better after his pretend injury. The Millers were as grateful to "Felicia" for her assistance as they had been two nights ago. Felicia was having lunch with the dear elderly couple when a knock came at the front door. Mrs. Miller's squeal of delight alerted Fable that everything was going as planned. The old woman rushed back to the kitchen dragging Jerry Miller's arm along with her.

"Vestus! Vestus! Jerry is home!"

Mr. Miller hopped from his chair to give his son a welcoming hug. "Boy, we've missed you! We've been so worried about you."

Tipton was the only person who did not seem at all pleased with the prodigal son's return home. The dog began growling and barking, snarling his teeth viciously at the man he knew to be an imposter. Fable, thankful to be present for this unforeseen wrinkle, rushed to Tipton's side and began stroking his fur. She whispered in his ear, *This man is a friend. Do not be afraid of him.* Tipton did not seem convinced, but he ceased his theatrics. He did, however, continue to regard Jerry Miller with distrust and gave him a wide berth. Tipton took a seat beside his owner's leg. He protected Mr. Miller by keeping himself between he and Jerry at all times.

"Jerry," Mrs. Miller said, remembering she had a guest. "This is Felicia. This dear girl saved our Tipton's life the other night. She dropped by to check on him. Isn't that so thoughtful? We have become such good friends. Felicia, this is our son, Jerry, we've told you so much about."

"It's nice to meet you, Jerry," Fable smiled at her father.

"Likewise," Larry said with a grin, trying to not show his bewilderment at how different Fable was able to make her face look with magic.

Fable offered to leave to give the elderly couple time with their son, knowing that manners would force Mrs. Miller to insist she stay, even if in truth she would actually have preferred the privacy. When Larry, in Jerry's body, also insisted Felicia not leave on his account, Fable remained a little while longer.

Having a stranger among them forced the conversation between parents and son to remain light and frivolous—exactly how Larry and Fable planned. Jerry explained away his quitting his job citing that he had larger plans in the works that he could not talk about yet due to confidentiality agreements. This story appeared to satisfy his father's concern. Moving the conversation away from work and into more private areas, Jerry informed his parents that he had met a woman and their relationship had become quite serious.

"What's this lady's name?" Mrs. Miller asked.

"Demitra," Jerry replied. "Demitra Blanchard. She is remarkable, Mom. You will love her as much as I do."

"How old is she?"

"She's in her early fifties, like me."

"Good," Mrs. Miller replied. "If there is one thing I don't hold with, it's men marrying women young enough to be their daughters. Glad you found a woman your own age."

"Has she ever been married before?" Mr. Miller wanted to know. "Is she divorced, like you?"

Jerry shook his head. Fable had already informed her father that Vestus Miller didn't believe in divorce and hadn't approved of Jerry's divorce when it happened.

"No, Dad, Demitra lost her husband many years ago. She's never even dated since then, until me."

"Did you say Demitra Blanchard?" Fable asked.

"Yes, I did."

"Does she happen to live in the little town of Daihmler, near Tuscaloosa?" Fable continued.

"Yes, she does!" Jerry answered.

"Oh, I know her!"

"You know Jerry's girlfriend, Felicia?" Mr. Miller cried. "Now that is a small world. How on earth do you know Jerry's girlfriend?"

Fable winked at her father and answered. "I don't exactly know Demitra Blanchard. I've met her a few times, though. She is a very nice lady. Always sweet to me. I'm friends with her daughters Fable and Beryl."

"Is that so?!" Mrs. Miller exclaimed.

"Yes," she replied. "I went to veterinary school with Fable. She was the smartest one in our class. And beautiful, too! I mean gorgeous!"

"I've met the daughter," Jerry said. "I'd say she's average."

"Would you?" Fable scoffed, sneering at him.

"Well, if Felicia here thinks your girlfriend is nice, then I am sure we will like her very much," Mrs. Miller declared. "I have an idea! Call your lady friend and invite her tonight for dinner. I'll prepare something real nice. You have time to drive down and get her. Felicia, you are invited too! Maybe she can bring your friend from school as well! We'll have a wonderful time."

Fable and Larry exchanged concerning glances. "I don't know if I can make it," Fable replied.

"And I'm not sure if Demitra can either on such short notice," Jerry offered.

"Nonsense," Mr. Miller declared. "Our boy comes home after two months of almost no contact, and he tells us he's got a girl. I think your new lady will respect the fact that your parents are eager to meet her. And Felicia, you can surely arrange things, can't you? I'm sure Jerry's lady would love to see you again."

There was no way out of it without appearing rude. And for some strange reason, Fable could not bring herself to be rude to Mr. and Mrs. Miller. They were such gracious people; she would not want to hurt them for the world. She also felt very guilty since she and her father were basically hijacking their son's life forever; she owed them whatever little happiness they requested.

Fable assisted Mrs. Miller in the kitchen all afternoon preparing dinner. By the time Jerry walked through the front door with Demitra, the aroma of pot roast, potatoes, carrots, and steamed vegetables filled the house. Mrs. Miller had even found time to bake a pound cake. Fable helped glaze it.

As Fable came into the living room, introductions were being made all around. Demitra shook Mr. Miller's hand, but Mrs. Miller was not satisfied with such formalities and swooped an unsuspecting Demitra into a hug. It was clear to see that Demitra was just as uncomfortable in this situation as Larry, but she had the cover of *meeting the parents* to excuse her nervousness.

"And who is this?" Demitra asked suspiciously as she caught sight of Felicia in the doorway.

"Hi," Fable said coming forward to shake Demitra's hand. "I am Felicia Cooper.

I'm a new friend of the family."

"I'm sorry—Jerry didn't tell me anything about you."

"We just met today," Jerry said.

Mrs. Miller patted Felicia's hand and told Demitra, "Felicia is a vet. She saved our dog's life a few nights ago. She's become very dear to us. I asked her to join us tonight because she is a friend of your daughter."

"I thought you two knew each other," Mr. Miller said questioningly.

"We do," Felicia replied. "It's been a long time, Ms. Blanchard. I went to school with Fable. We met a few times years ago."

"Did we?" Demitra said, raising a brow.

"Yes," Felicia nodded. "I was amazed at her skill with animals. She was the best in our class."

Mrs. Miller directed everyone to come to the dining room where she began serving dinner. Felicia helped her lay everything out and the five of them enjoyed a delicious meal. The Millers had many questions for Demitra, all of which she answered.

"Yes, I have two daughters from my previous marriage," Demitra said. "They are all grown up now. One is a vet, as you know, and the other is a doctor."

"How proud you must be of them!" Mrs. Miller cried.

"Most of the time," Demitra said, eyeing Felicia. "Children can be a handful."

"Oh, this one surely was," Mr. Miller chuckled as he patted Jerry's arm. "Broken arm when he was ten. Broken collar bone when he was 14. And I was getting awful worried these past few weeks when he all but disappeared. Come to find out, he just got captivated by you. Can't say I blame him."

The evening was a roaring success. The Millers liked Demitra Blanchard and approved greatly of their son's relationship. Larry would not have to worry so much about dodging Jerry's past now that he had provided Jerry's parents with a sunny new future to focus upon. Felicia decided to take her leave early, to allow Jerry and Demitra some private time with the Millers. As she said her goodbyes and made her way for the door, Demitra stood in her way.

"It's rather dark out there. Jerry, why don't we walk Felicia safely to her car?" Demitra turned to Mrs. Miller. "And perhaps when we come back inside, I might have another piece of your delicious cake."

"Why certainly!" beamed Mrs. Miller, happily leaping up to cut a slice for her son's new love.

Jerry opened the front door for Demitra and Felicia and they stepped outside. Halfway to the rental car Fable had used for this visit, Demitra clutched her arm. Felicia stopped abruptly and turned around with a startled expression.

"Do you really think I am that stupid?" Demitra said. "An appearance altering spell is not going to keep me from knowing my own daughter."

"Oh my god!" Fable exclaimed. "You knew the whole time?"

"The whole time," Demitra scowled. "Which means one thing." She turned to Jerry. "Obviously Fable knows you are her father."

"Yes, angel, I told her."

"Don't angel me, Larry!" Demitra cried.

Larry tried to soothe her fury. He placed his hand to her soft cheek and said the phrase he'd been saying all of their lives since they were very young. "I love you, Demitra. I will *forever and three days*."

It didn't work. She was still angry. "Why? Why did you tell her?"

"We needed her help with Jerry's parents! And it worked. They love you, and they are no longer suspicious of me. Fable did all that."

"It's going to work, Mother," Fable beamed. "Daddy is home again, and this is going to work!"

Demitra did not look pleased.

"Why are you so angry that I know?" Fable demanded. "He is my father. I deserve to know he's alive again."

"Yes," Demitra explained. "And so does your sister! Having just one of you know is not fair to the other. But telling her runs too much of a risk of the secret coming out. You know as well as I do there is no way my mother or your Aunt Artemis is going to allow Larry to stay here. It flies in the face of everything we have always lived by. I have defied the Natural Order of things. If they find out, they will send him back."

"They aren't going to find out," Fable said. "No one else is going to find out."

CHAPTER SIXTEEN

Another Witch?

Olympia Blanchard did not generally leave her home very often. In her old age, she had found the peace of home far more appealing than anything else going on in the outside world. In her youth, she had been a rather active witch who'd had more than a fair share of adventures. In her womanhood she had been a dedicated wife, mother, and teacher of the arts of witchcraft to her children. She spent her autumn years as an activist doing what she could to help save and protect the environment. She more than earned a rest for her winter years. However, since her eldest daughter opened The Cobblestone restaurant, Olympia made a point of leaving the house once a week to take lunch there with some of her friends.

She was not in the mood to go this week—too concerned over what might be happening in Louisiana with the mission to find her youngest daughter. Yasmine insisted she get out for a few hours to clear her mind and enjoy the company of friends. Yasmine drove Olympia to the restaurant and said she would return to collect her in two hours. Zelda had already arrived. She was waiting on the long wooden stairs leading to the front door when Yasmine pulled up with Olympia. The friends they were meeting had already arrived as well and were holding the table inside. Mae Hemsley (the mayor's wife) and Constance Daihmler (descendant of the town's founding family) were lifelong friends of Olympia and Zelda's.

Yasmine let Olympia out and waved goodbye. She was late to work by a couple of hours, but Howard never minded. Yasmine long ago proved herself as a person who could accomplish an entire day's work in half a day's time—which made her indispensable to Howard. Even if it had been a problem for her to come in late, Howard would have never said anything about it. He genuinely held Yasmine Blanchard in high regard. She was not only the granddaughter of his best client and the niece of the woman he still harbored romantic feelings for; she was also the most dedicated and capable assistant he'd ever employed. Knowing Yasmine was wealthier in her own right than he would ever be meant she didn't need the work, she enjoyed it. He did not ever want to do anything to cause her to quit.

"Sorry I'm late," she said, rushing into the small office. "I took Grandmother to meet her friends for lunch."

"Anyone I know?'

"Everyone you know. Zelda, Constance Daihmler, and the mayor's wife."

"Oh—that reminds me—I need to messenger some documents to Mayor Hemsley," Howard remembered.

"Give them to me," Yasmine said. "I have to pick Grandmother up after, so I'll just give them to his wife."

Howard dug through his desk and found the manilla envelope with the word *mayor* jotted down in Sharpie on it. He rose to hand it to Yasmine and hit his knee on the edge of his desk. The envelope flew out of his hand. It would not have been a catastrophe for the envelope to fall on the floor. It was only an envelope. Yasmine could have easily bent over to pick it up. But the envelope did not fall. It simply hovered in the air as both Howard and Yasmine stared at it.

"Uh...do you see what I see?" Howard stammered.

"Yes, I do," she replied in astonishment.

"If we were at your house this would not be so disturbing. But it's just you and me."

"I know," Yasmine said. "So, are you doing it, or am I?"

Howard rubbed his chin as the envelope broke loose of its hold in the air and continued its fall to the ground. Yasmine picked it up and turned it over in her hands as if to check it for strings. She looked at her employer and shrugged.

"You've been around the Blanchards as long as I have," she smiled. "Maybe they're rubbing off on us."

"They always said that everyone is capable of magic, if they can focus their mind to summon it," Howard stated. "But I wasn't focusing my mind on anything."

Business went on as usual until it was time for Yasmine to collect her grandmother. She grabbed the mysterious envelope and drove out to the river to where The Cobblestone restaurant loomed over the water. She'd sent her grandmother a text letting her know she was on the way. She sent one to Zelda as well knowing that Zelda was far more likely to check her cell phone than her grandmother would be. Olympia Blanchard was not a fan of technology, nor being obligated to check a device for contact with people. After weeks of arguing with her daughters to carry a cell, Olympia relented and did as they asked—but everyone knew she rarely even touched the thing. But Zelda had checked her messages and alerted her friend to Yasmine's impending arrival.

"Yasmine is on her way to pick me up," Olympia told her friends. "I guess I need to go outside in a few minutes."

"Speaking of Yasmine," Mae Hemsley said, "how is she enjoying married life?"

Olympia laughed a little and replied, "Some days they are the picture of romance, and some days she and Seth revert back to bickering cousins. It's actually a very interesting situation. But they are so in love with one another, it is unbelievably cute to observe."

"I'd drive you home, but I got a readin' with Moosey Foster at 2 o'clock," Zelda told Olympia.

"Oh, and I have a nail appointment, or I'd drive you," Mae frowned.

"I can drive you home if you like, Olympia," Constance Daihmler said. "I have no appointments or plans for the afternoon."

"No, it is all right," Olympia replied. "I appreciate the offer. Yasmine is on the way. Besides, I am rather anxious. I know I have not been very good company for this week's luncheon. I won't subject you ladies to anymore of me today."

"It's perfectly understandable," Constance smiled. "You are worried about your child. I hope all goes well. I know Mae and I don't completely understand how things work in your world, but I pray that Nacaria is safe and that she finds her way out of that dreadful place soon."

"You will call us and let us know how she is, won't you?" Mae asked.

"Of course, I will," Olympia smiled. "Thank you for being such good and supportive friends. There aren't many people outside the witching world I can talk to about such things."

"Well, you can always talk to us," Constance said. "I still haven't forgotten how you saved me from that poltergeist in my house when I was first married."

Mae grinned and lowered her voice as she clasped hands with her friends, "Having two witches as two of your best friends has come in handy many times in our lives. We are always here for you. Keep us posted on Nacaria."

Olympia said her goodbyes to her friends and dropped a twenty on the table for the server since Artemis refused to ever charge her mother or her friends. Zelda walked to the exit with her after also adding a tip to the pile.

"You know Mae is gonna lift up one of those bills to tip her nail tech," Zelda snickered as they opened the door to The Cobblestone's porch.

"She's married to an honest mayor," Olympia grinned. "He doesn't have much money."

Yasmine could see her grandmother standing with Zelda when she pulled up. Mae and Constance were coming outside as well which reminded her that she had papers for the mayor on the seat beside her. Yasmine parked in front of the long wooden steps leading up to them and waved to her grandmother. She took the envelope and got out of the car to take to Mae. Olympia said goodbye again to her friends and started down. Through a construction miscalculation, the top step of the Cobblestone stairs was three inches higher than the other treads. As Olympia stepped down, the jolt she felt on her body as it reached the lower step sent a fluttery sensation through her body—as if she'd been inverted on a roller coaster. But the flutter didn't go away. She felt disoriented. *It's my heart again.*

The group all watched in horror as Olympia's foot slipped from the upper stair tread. The old woman began to topple forward, heading face-first toward the ragged edges of hard steps beneath her. Instinctively, without any thought about it whatsoever, Yasmine raised her hands into the air as if to catch her despite the fact she was much too far away to be able to do so. Then the strangest thing occurred. Zelda, Mae, and Constance looked on in utter disbelief as Olympia did not fall. She raised. She raised into the air as if floating. Olympia was floating above the stairs.

"Lympy!" Zelda shrieked. "How are you doing that? You can't levitate!"

"I-I-I'm not doing this," Olympia cried.

"Zel-Zelda," Yasmine stuttered with her shaking arms still raised mid-air. "I'm not sure. But I think I am."

Yasmine's brow was furrowed in utter astonishment. She could feel a tiny tingle surging within her. It felt a little like getting shocked by static electricity. Only the shock didn't begin at her fingertips; it started somewhere near her core and flowed outward through her hands.

Zelda snapped to, rushing forward to Olympia with Mae and Constance at her side. They clasped their hands onto Olympia's waist. "Try to set her down," Zelda called to Yasmine.

"I don't know how," Yasmine declared, terrified she would lose the ability and drop her elderly grandmother painfully to the ground.

"We got her waist," Zelda shouted. "She ain't gone fall."

"Just lower her while we right her legs so that she lands on her feet," Constance called out.

"I don't know what I'm doing!" Yasmine shouted. "Zelda, what do I do?" Yasmine was beginning to shake now, as was Olympia. Whatever Yasmine's hands did, her grandmother's suspended form reflected.

Zelda shouted down the stairs to Yasmine, "Just slowly—SLOWLY—lower your hands."

Yasmine did as she was told as inch by inch her grandmother came down. Olympia's friends directed her hips so that Olympia landed carefully on both feet to the stair tread. Olympia was bewildered by the experience. Her heart was racing, but the weak, fluttery feeling had passed.

"This is why old buzzards like us should use the wheelchair ramp," Zelda commented. "You're way too old to be climbing these steps, Lympy."

Once Olympia reached the bottom of the stairs, she approached her non-witch granddaughter. "All that work in the magic room is paying off, Yasmine!" Olympia delighted, referring to the family's weekly practice of expanding their powers in the upmost tower room of Blanchard House which had long been dubbed *the magic room*. "Years and years of your trying to move objects has started paying off. You are developing powers!"

Yasmine was thrilled. All her life she watched her cousins working their powers around that special room. She had always been there with them, trying with all her might to make anything from feathers to lint on the table flutter or jolt or do something to prove she could move it. And now when she'd feared her grandmother's life was in danger, she had manifested powers! Yasmine truly felt like a Blanchard now. And the news of what Yasmine had achieved certainly distracted Olympia's mind from whatever was going on in Louisiana.

CHAPTER SEVENTEEN

Nacaria Comes Home

Olympia meant to come home to rest for a while. She then wanted to run Yasmine through a battery of tests in the magic room on the top floor of the Blanchard House tower. However, her granddaughter's potential new powers slipped her mind, replaced with the phone call that the rescue mission to Dredmore had been a success, and Nacaria was on her way home.

It had been twenty years. Twenty years since her youngest daughter's feet crossed the threshold of Blanchard House. Olympia had not heard her daughter's footsteps or heard her laughter or seen her smile in all that time. Olympia stood in the upstairs hallway, captivated by the photographs of all her children, but most especially Nacaria, and most especially now. At any moment, Olympia would hear Salem's car pull into the driveway. She would hear the car doors shut and would know her prodigal daughter had returned.

Standing before the last picture taken of Nacaria, Olympia wondered what she would look like now. Artemis and Demitra had not aged very much over the years. Would her youngest be the same? Or had the ordeals she had been through taken a toll on that celestial beauty she had once been? Olympia was remembering that awful day now—the day when they came and took her away. She could still recall the screams from young Salem and little Seth as their mother was dragged out by Consort officials. Nacaria was mad then, her eyes showed her madness. Olympia still blamed herself for those days. She should have seen the warning signs. Just a week before they came for Nacaria, Olympia had found traces of bone dust that Nacaria used in her spell. She had also discovered one of the forbidden books missing from the vault. Olympia should have suspected something, but—like most mothers—she had not been able to realize her own child could be capable of such a crime.

"Mother," Artemis called from the foyer below. "They're here."

Olympia's heart raced. She wanted to run down the stairs. She wanted to slide down the banister or leap the railing of the landing—anything to get there faster—but she couldn't. Anticipation paralyzed her. The moment she had been waiting two decades for, a moment she doubted she might even ever see in her lifetime, was happening just a few stair steps below. And Olympia could not move. Struggling to unstick her feet from their place and get them down the stairs, Olympia saw Salem and Beryl coming through the doorway. Just behind them, Nacaria.

Trembling, nervous, like a poor wretch freed from a POW camp, Nacaria Blanchard crept slowly over the threshold of Blanchard House. Olympia still could not move. Standing still on the stairs, all she could do was watch with tunnel vision as her daughter returned home.

She was still so beautiful. Her long, blonde hair cascaded to her shoulders. Those piercing green eyes still shone as brightly as they used to. Time had not changed her face. She was definitely older, but not aged. Not aged one bit. She was still the most beautiful Blanchard there had ever been.

Seth came in behind his mother, followed by Blackie and Arielle. Demitra stood with Artemis in the foyer staring at the sister they had been separated from for so many years. The trio of sisters who were once so inseparable, who had to live as merely two for twenty years, now had their missing third before them. Each of them now secretly worrying that they may have forgotten how to be three again after all this time.

Artemis came forward first. "Sister."

She took Nacaria gently into her arms. Nacaria melted into the embrace. They opened for Demitra and for a time it seemed to the others in the room that the three entities had merged into one. It suddenly occurred to Olympia how everyone's focus, even her own, had always been centered upon Salem and Seth and the loss they had suffered having their mother removed from their lives. But, standing on the stairs watching her three daughters reunited, Olympia realized the true devastation had been felt among the sisters. Those three beautiful girls who had shared their entire lives together. Their children would never understand that the strongest bonds in the family had always been the three Blanchard daughters. All close in age, growing up together as each other's best friend. They went through everything together—love, heartbreak, life, death, and always magic. No matter what happened in their lives, the Blanchard sisters were their own circle of support. Then that circle was broken.

Olympia was now watching it mend, and she felt guilty that its beauty was something she had forgotten.

She could now break her feet loose from the place they were stuck and descend the stairs to her daughter. Nacaria pulled away from her sisters' hold and looked into her mother's wizened eyes. Quietly, Olympia embraced her child and wept. Nacaria wept. The entire family wept together as the last limb of the family tree was resewn to the trunk.

Olympia took her daughter into the family living room where everyone else was gathering. Fable and Yasmine came forward for their turn to greet her. Fable, for a reason she didn't even understand, gave a slight bow.

"I have no idea why I just did that," she laughed, breaking the tension. "I'm your niece, Fable."

Nacaria smiled. "I know." She stroked Fable's face and then turned to Yasmine. "And you. My daughter-in-law. I have watched you all grow up, and I have been so proud of you all. But I have never been prouder than when my son married you, Yasmine. My newest daughter." Nacaria gave Yasmine a warm hug and kissed her cheek.

"I guess we forget," Yasmine said, wiping a tear away, "you've been here all along. You know everything about us."

Nacaria walked to the center of the room and whirled around, outstretching her arms. "Do you all know how long I've waited to stand in *the middle* of this room! No more clinging to walls! And to sit!" she plopped down in one of the winged-back chairs by the fireplace. "I can finally sit down."

Salem took a seat at her side on the floor; Seth joined her on the other side. Nacaria went on talking, telling them how much she had seen from the walls during her incarceration there. The secret stories. The teenage years when the kids would sneak in and out despite curfew. The times Seth came in drunk from a night out with friends, or how Fable was the one who really broke the expensive vase on the mantle. Nacaria shared her experiences. Some brought sadness, some brought laughter.

"My deepest regret," she said, "was never being able to hold my grandson." She stroked Salem's hair as she reflected. "Michael was such a beautiful boy. I ache from the time I lost."

Blackie interrupted the momentum of the night with pressing and serious business. "I hate to be the one to put a halt to such an emotional time, but we have some pretty consequential things to decide. Tomorrow night is the Winter Consort.

We have to discuss what we plan to do to bring Atheidrelle to justice for what she's done to Nacaria these last weeks."

"Can't we wait?" Nacaria asked. "I just want to be with my family tonight. I want to walk outside through the meadows and trees. I don't care how cold it is. I don't care if I get frostbite. I have not walked the acres of this place in twenty years. I promise tomorrow I will tell you all you need to know, and we can plan anything we need to plan. But for tonight, I want to walk with my children."

...

The family sat quietly early the next morning to listen to Nacaria relive her experiences at Dredmore Asylum. What they did not expect was for her to rewrite the history they'd long accustomed themselves to believing. There was more to her story than what the others knew, and she had waited two decades to clear herself and explain her version of events which the Council had not allowed her to tell.

"Xander and I were in love," Nacaria began her story. "It's important for you all to understand that, especially Salem and Seth."

"We already know, Mother," Salem interrupted. "I've met Xander. He told me."

"That's right, Nacaria," Arielle added with a smile of understanding. "My father has never stopped loving you. Even I know that."

Nacaria felt awkward for a moment. She had half forgotten that Arielle was there and who she was. "I'm sorry, Arielle. The things I have to say might be painful for you to hear. You were so kind to help rescue me. I wouldn't want to hurt you."

"It's all right, Mother," Salem informed. "Arielle's more of a Blanchard now than she is an Obreiggon. You can speak freely with her."

"That's right," Arielle smiled. "Though I will say I don't like that you once tried to kill my mother, I'm not on very good terms with her and never have been. I can see how she could push someone to the edge. And I think my father is wonderful, so I can also understand your desire to be with him."

Nacaria sighed and looked away at the wall. The wall which had been her prison for so long. The place where she had been trapped, unable to tell the truth of what happened all those years ago. She found herself almost fading away into her thoughts, into her isolation. The grain of the wood in the paneled wall seemed to beckon to her. It had been her world too long. She was not accustomed to interacting with people now. She had to snap herself back into the present.

"That is what is most troubling for me," Nacaria said, looking over to Arielle, and her own children. "I did love your father. I did want to be with him, and he with me, but I didn't try to erase your mother's existence because I longed to have a life with him."

Olympia was puzzled by this statement. It was common knowledge that Nacaria's crime of trying to undo the birth of Atheidrelle D'Angelo was so that she could have been the one to marry Xander Obreiggon. "What are you saying, dear? You did go back in time to try and undo Atheidrelle's birth. That was attempted murder, Nacaria. That was why you were cursed."

Nacaria took a breath and tried to clarify the misconstrued ideas her family had held for so long. "I did try to undo her life, but not because I wanted her husband. I did it to save my own children a lifetime of unhappiness."

"Explain," said Artemis.

"Atheidrelle knew Xander loved me. He never loved her. Hugh D'Angelo and Lotek Obreiggon wanted their families merged. That pressure is the only reason he married her. Had he met me first, he never would have even considered her. But Atheidrelle genuinely loves Xander. I believe that to be so. Xander never loved her back. She is cold. She is ruthless. She is evil."

Salem gripped her sister's hand. Arielle felt pangs from the description of her mother, but she knew in her heart they were not untrue words, so she said nothing to defend her. Nacaria continued her statement.

"Xander and I met, and we fell in love. It was clandestine at first, until Salem was born, and it became all too public. We tried to stay away from each other. We failed. He was so miserable. Cassandra was born first so Hugh and Lotek had their heir. Xander couldn't take another day with his wife, and he came to me. He and I were going to build a life together with our little girl."

"I remember all too well," Olympia reflected. "You went away for a while, then you came back again, pregnant, with Seth."

"Hugh and Lotek found us and demanded Xander return," Nacaria said, turning to Arielle. "Your father is an honorable man. A dutiful man. Unfortunately, he never was very strong. It was not easy to be an Obreiggon, particularly when Lotek Obreiggon is your father and Hugh D'Angelo is your father-in-law. Xander had lived his entire life under his father's thumb. I wish he'd been stronger back then, but he wasn't."

"He still isn't," Arielle frowned. "Within the Obreiggon and D'Angelo family, he and I are mostly dictated to. We endure our family as best we can."

"He found the courage to finally leave when Seth was four years old," Nacaria continued. "We were doing it, asserting our independence and were going to be married. Atheidrelle refused to give him his freedom. She came to me one day. I will never forget it. She was so smug. So vicious. She told me she had cursed my children."

"What?" Salem gasped—horrified by this new information. "How?"

Nacaria looked into her daughter's eyes. She ached from Salem's recent losses. "Don't you know, my sweet girl? I stole Atheidrelle's love from her. The only man she ever wanted, and he wanted me. She cursed our children to a life of lovelessness. Anyone who dared to love a child produced by Xander and myself would die."

The Blanchards were silent. No one quite knew what to say or how to process what they had heard. It seemed so silly a curse. A childish one, in fact. More a threat than an actual danger. Until their minds, one by one, looked back and saw the path of damage the silly curse had wrought.

"David," Salem said softly. "And my baby."

"And Seth lost Susan the summer after high school graduation," Fable recalled. "They were planning to get married that fall."

"Jet ski accident," Seth replied.

"Car crash," Salem muttered.

"And what happened only two months ago?" Nacaria said, looking at Yasmine. "A werewolf tried to take you away."

"This is ridiculous!" Seth cried. "Are you saying that Susan and David and Michael died because twenty years ago Atheidrelle—out of jealousy—put a curse on me and Salem?"

"Yes."

"But Patric was Yazzy's brother," Fable noted. "I don't see how her situation is related."

"If the family hadn't intervened, she'd be gone," Beryl pointed out.

"If this is true, and it's kind of hard to believe," Fable said. "Then Yasmine is still in danger."

"Yasmine will fall under the power of the curse," Nacaria said. "I have no doubt. I cannot tell you when or where, but Atheidrelle is a horrifically powerful witch. I don't even understand how one witch gets so powerful. Her curse is unbreakable."

"But Yasmine has been around for years and years," Fable said. "Nothing has happened to her so far."

"Yes," Salem began. "But how long have she and Seth been together? It was just a few months ago when they realized they were in love."

"Meaning the curse on Yasmine has really just begun," Beryl pointed out.

Demitra turned to Blackie. "Did you know anything about any of this?'

"I had no idea. But it sounds very reasonable, considering my sister."

Nacaria took the conversation back. "You have all spent years thinking me an unstable love-sick witch who tried to kill the wife of her lover. I did not want to kill anyone. I just wanted to undo the existence of a very evil woman who had damned my children to a life of pain and disappointment. Yes, I loved Xander and her removal from his life might clear the way for me. But my reason was my children."

"Nacaria, why didn't you come to us?" Olympia asked her daughter. "You, me, your sisters, Zelda, we would have figured something out. The Council could have been notified. We could have stopped Atheidrelle, punished her for such a crime."

"A witch cannot break another witch's spell," Blackie reminded the old woman. "The Blanchards might have brought Atheidrelle's curse to light, but it wouldn't end the curse. And I think we all know that my sister would never have been compelled to lift it. Not even the Council of Witches could persuade her."

"Couldn't the Council all pool their powers to lift the curse?" Yasmine asked.

"It isn't possible to undo another's magic," Blackie answered. "This is the whole reason places like Dredmore exist. To punish and to stand as a deterrent. Besides, what Nacaria said is true. My sister is filled with more power than any witch I have ever encountered. If Atheidrelle casts a spell, even one so elementary, I assure you it is serious, and it is forever."

"Am I going to die?" Yasmine asked her grandmother.

Olympia patted her hand and shook her head, "Of course you aren't my dear. You have all of us to protect you. We will place protections on you to shield you now that we know."

"What do we do?" Seth asked.

Olympia took charge and formulated their plan. "Tonight is the Consort. We will all be in attendance. The most urgent matter at hand is the punishment of Cassandra and Atheidrelle for holding Nacaria captive after her time served at Dredmore was lifted. Queen Ursula has already taken Cassandra out of Dredmore and is holding her in custody until the meeting tonight."

"What about everything Nacaria just told us?" Demitra asked. "Atheidrelle's curse on Salem and Seth? David and Michael died! Yaz is in danger! We need to address this."

"It can't be proven," Olympia sighed. "We only have Nacaria's word. I am afraid her word carries little weight to the Council. Atheidrelle will deny the allegation."

"Hecate, what if Nacaria took *vows*?" Beryl suggested.

"Unfortunately, this situation is complicated," Artemis pointed out. "So many years have taken place, and Nacaria has been comatose for two decades. It can be argued that the medications administered may have damaging effects to memory."

"I don't understand," Seth said.

"I do," said Beryl in her professional medical voice. "Medication, especially ones of that caliber and duration of time, can alter the brain. It's easily arguable that Aunt Nacaria could be suffering from false memories now. Vows would have no effect. Not if she really believed what she was saying was the truth. Her testimony would be inadmissible on the sheer fact that she's been so heavily medicated all these years."

Nacaria was flattened by this possibility. "I am telling the truth."

Artemis placed her hand on the back of her baby sister's head and pulled it toward a kiss of support to the forehead. "We know you are. We just probably can't prove the curse part."

"Artemis is correct," Demitra said. "We have an open and shut case against Cassandra for holding Nacaria hostage. Hopefully, Cassandra will be able to take vows and incriminate her mother. I'm afraid that is about the best we can hope for."

Olympia gave her family and friends a warning, "Tonight's meeting is going to be critical. At the Autumn Consort, Ursula declined another term as queen. Tonight, a new king or queen will be chosen to rule the Consort. And Atheidrelle is running. If we can get Cassandra to incriminate her mother, Atheidrelle will not only be denied the chance of being elected, but she might also be stripped of her powers..."

"And that could actually lift the curse on Seth and Salem," Beryl observed. "That might keep Yazzy safe."

"If Cassandra takes vows and incriminates her mother, could the council force Atheidrelle to take vows too?" Yasmine asked. "Then maybe Nacaria could ask her about the curse and she would have to answer truthfully."

"Frankly, I doubt Atheidrelle could be compelled, even by the Council, to take vows for that line of questioning, and you can't force a person to take vows. Atheidrelle might be more willing to take her chances and keep her powers," Olympia admitted.

"Wouldn't the very refusal to take vows be a sign of guilt to the Council?" Fable asked her grandmother.

"Not at all," Blackie answered for Olympia. "Many witches have refused to take vows in past trials. Much like pleading the 5th Amendment in the U.S courts."

Artemis added to Blackie's thoughts, "Taking vows is risky, even when you are giving honest testimony. Everyone lies, even about tiny insignificant things."

Blackie elaborated to make sure the others fully understood. "We lie sometimes without realizing it. *How are you doing this afternoon?...I'm great!* But you're not actually great. You might be having a rough day. And if so, you just lost your powers. It's not something witches take lightly. Besides, my sister would fear losing her power far more than being found guilty of a crime."

"We really have nothing on her for the curse she placed on Nacaria's children," Olympia decided. "Our only provable crime is Nacaria's being held captive these last two months."

CHAPTER EIGHTEEN

The Winter Consort

United as a family force, the Blanchards, plus Madame Zelda, drove in four cars to the Consort Meeting of the Witches Association. This season, it was conveniently being held at the University Club only a few miles away in neighboring Tuscaloosa. Built in the classic Greek revival style in the 1834 the magnificent mansion did not suit the original owners primarily due to its proximity to The University of Alabama. Historical lore was that students often trapsed through the gardens, uprooting the flower beds—and sometimes stealing hens from the chicken houses in back. The biggest controversy occurred when a group of students, captivated with a servant of the house, spirited the young woman away to their quarters on campus. When her master stormed the dorm searching for her a riot erupted. Several students were injured. The owner sold the house two years later and moved his family and staff away. The antebellum mansion changed hands many times through the years, even becoming a venue to entertain soldiers during World War II. It eventually was purchased by the University in 1944 to be used for social activities and parties.

It was a fitting choice for the Winter Consort, although undoubtedly the University had no idea the event being held there was for a convention of witches. Eleanor Branson rented the club out for the evening. Eleanor was not only a leading citizen of Tuscaloosa, and a hefty donor to The University of Alabama, she was also surreptitiously a member of the Witches Association. Anytime she was chosen as hostess for the season's Consort meeting, she rented out the University Club. Consort members liked the venue very much. Eleanor always thought of everything from parking valets to the best caterers. The last time she hosted a Consort, she even had gift bags of scented candles and small potions for every member as they departed. Olympia often marveled at Eleanor's attention to detail.

Olympia thought several times over the years of placing Blanchard House on the roster as possible meeting locales. She hosted a meeting once, when the grandchildren were teenagers. She found most people were too preoccupied with trying to find Nacaria's shadow somewhere in the house than they were in actually using the meeting to mingle with fellow witches. It was a shame, too, because hosting the meeting at Blanchard House was the only way Olympia had ever been able to get the younger generation involved in a Consort meeting. Of course, tonight's would be different, as every Blanchard in the family descended upon the University Club.

As if they were soldiers marching on the front lines, the Blanchard crew came through the wide-open doors of the mansion as a force to be reckoned with. Olympia led the pack, followed by Artemis, Demitra, Zelda, Salem, Beryl, Fable, Seth, and Yasmine. They were on a mission, confident, and ready to bring Atheidrelle down—or at the very least expose her. Nacaria and Blackie were waiting at home until the meeting commenced. No one wanted to give Atheidrelle Obreiggon any indication that her devious plan had been uncovered. Olympia instructed Nacaria not to show her face at the Consort until 8:30 p.m.

The Blanchards lingered inside the entrance hall of the mansion, searching the faces of people they knew, hoping there would be more friends of the family than allies of Atheidrelle. Olympia knew the deck was stacked against her when it came to the subject of Nacaria and public opinion. Olympia was one of the most respected and admired members of the Consort. In matters concerning all other things, people generally considered Olympia Blanchard's opinion the right side of an issue. The only time in Consort history when someone felt inclined to side differently than she was at Nacaria's trial. Nacaria's crime against Atheidrelle could not be excused no matter how many people disliked Atheidrelle Obreiggon. Tonight's meeting could set the record straight about what really happened all those years ago, and Atheidrelle might find herself on the hotseat.

Olympia liked that idea. Never one to wish ill upon others, even Olympia Blanchard was not above taking pleasure at the thought of having Atheidrelle be taken down a peg or two. Olympia never liked the D'Angelo family. Her father, Constantinople Blanchard, always said Emmerick D'Angelo and his family operated in the darker spectrum of the world. Their magics and powers were not of the light. Olympia never quite understood what that meant exactly but whatever it meant, she had always strongly suspected Emmerick's son, Hugh D'Angelo, and his children were not far removed from that darkness. Blackie had seemingly proved her wrong, but even Blackie was cloaked in a mysteriousness which sometimes worried her. However, Blackie had never been anything but kind to the Blanchard family, and especially Nacaria. Even in the days after the trial—after Blackie was pushed to testify against Nacaria—Blackie had come to Olympia heartbroken at the role she had been forced to play in her friend's downfall.

Olympia was mid-thought, remembering the past, when she heard a voice call out to her. She looked up to see a regal older woman, slightly younger than herself—but not much—descending the stairs in the University Club foyer. The woman's hair was the same cotton white of Olympia's, only it hung straight in an angular cut with two longer tips meeting just under the chin. She wore a pale blue dress, with two long strings of pearls. Olympia smiled. She had given her those pearls on the woman's 50th birthday, almost 30 years ago.

"You certainly are a sight for sore old eyes, Sister," Olympia said, moving forward for a hug.

The woman pulled Olympia close and kissed her cheek. As they embraced, the thought was not lost on Olympia how this woman completed her in the same way Artemis, Demitra, and Nacaria completed each other. Long before having children of their own, Olympia and her sister, along with Zelda, had been their own circle of family. That was a long time ago, but the power of that bond never faded.

Over Olympia's shoulder, the woman caught sight of Salem. Pulling away from Olympia, she approached her grandniece. "Salem, Salem my sweet love. I was so sorry I was unable to attend the Autumn Consort. I had no idea you had lost David and Michael. I have no excuses. My family was having some struggles which kept me from the meeting. Had I known about Michael's cremation I would never have missed it."

"Aunt Pastoria," Salem said hugging her grandmother's sister. "It's all right. Everything happened very fast, and we just didn't have time to tell you. I'm sorry for that."

"Well, Olympia has informed me about what's happening tonight," Pastoria Blanchard said. "I want you to know I have my brood here with me, all of them. Tonight, every living Blanchard stands behind you and Seth." She raised her head slightly and called to the air, "Boys!"

Two handsome men in their early fifties appeared next to her. With them came four others, three men and one woman, much younger—late teens and early twenties.

The older men gave Artemis and Demitra boisterous hugs as if long lost brothers reunited with their sisters for the evening.

"Seneca Blanchard!" Artemis cried. "It's been too long. Ten years maybe?" She turned to his brother. "And Drake! You boys look the same!"

"I think my crow's feet and gray hair say otherwise," Seneca laughed. "You girls, you're the ones that don't age."

"Is he really calling them *girls*?" Fable snickered behind them to Yasmine. "*Golden Girls*, maybe."

"Hey, you should hope you inherit your mother's graceful aging," Seneca Blanchard teased. "Fable, I remember you. You always were the mouthy one of the kids. Do you remember my boys, Ocean and Forest?"

"I do!" Seth exclaimed. "Your visits were the only time I had fellas to play with. Hey guys! Good to see you again."

"And these are my kids, Sage and Sydney," Drake Blanchard said pulling his son and daughter forward, they were clearly twins.

"It's been a while since we've all been together," Beryl smiled. "But I see the children's faces I played with in all these adult people."

Olympia and Pastoria watched, arm in arm as their offspring reacquainted themselves. A hoard of cousins, all catching up on the ins and outs of their lives. To casual observers passing by, it looked like an innocent family reunion. And it was. But it was also the unification of an army. A Blanchard was in need tonight, and so all Blanchards had come for backup.

Pastoria pulled Arielle aside for a moment and smiled gently to the girl, "I hear from my sister that you are on our team?"

"Yes."

"If that bitch mother of yours tries to punish you for this, you just let your new adoptive Aunt Pastoria know. My brood will run to your rescue anytime you need us."

Pastoria was not the only member of the Mobile branch of the Blanchard family interested in Arielle Obreiggon. Forest Blanchard stepped forth to ask, "Do you happen to know where the bar is? I really could use a drink. I've never been here before."

"I do know where it is," Arielle smiled. She then looked to Olympia as if asking permission to accept the flirtation with her grandnephew. Olympia found the gesture charming and admired her respect. Olympia gave her a wink, and off Arielle and Forest moved in search of liquid refreshment.

The family reunion was broken up when one of the waiters ushering through with drinks on trays handed Olympia a note. She read it and motioned for Salem and Seth. The note was from the queen, requesting a private and secretive meeting with the two of them in one of the upstairs sitting rooms. The two of them made their way up to meet her, doing their best to appear casual and not draw attention.

Salem and Seth found Queen Ursula seated on a chair of English floral chintz of light green with pink roses. She motioned for them to close the door and take a seat on the settee across from her in the same design. The room was done in pinks and greens with yellow accents. It felt a little precious to Seth.

"I feel we should discuss matters prior to entering tonight's meeting," Ursula began. "My men have Cassandra in holding nearby. She will be brought in once you make your allegations. But I want you to go over once again, in person with me, what happened and what your exact charge against her is to be."

"Not just her," Seth offered up, "Atheidrelle Obreiggon, too! After all she's the one behind this."

"Tell me exactly what you think the Obreiggons have done."

Salem took charge. "Our mother's curse has been lifted, but we were never contacted."

"The authorities at Dredmore are Council-bound to alert relatives as inmates are reanimated," the queen explained. "If you were not contacted, how can you be certain the Obreiggons had anything to do with it?"

"Your men must have seen for themselves," Salem replied, "when they found Cassandra?"

"My men found Cassandra precisely the way you said they would, unconscious and hooked up to tubes and wires in the room assigned to Nacaria."

"Yes!" Salem cried. "Just like I told you when we spoke that night. Cassandra Obreiggon has been posing as my mother's caretaker, but in reality, she has been holding her hostage."

"Asylum administrators perform weekly checks on all inmates. If your mother had awakened from the curse..."

"Not if Cassandra was keeping her unconscious," Seth interrupted.

"It's a serious charge," Queen Ursula stated. "I felt the need to warn you before you make it. If you accuse a witch of a crime and that witch is found innocent, you can be held accountable for false allegations. You could serve time in Dredmore yourselves. I need for you to both understand this fully. Be very certain you can back up these charges before you wage them."

"We have a witness. And we have our mother," Salem said. "I think we can prove these charges."

"You mentioned Atheidrelle's involvement," Ursula reminded them.

"Yeah," Seth said. "Obviously, she's involved. Who else would have sent Cassandra?"

"Dredmore is not a place easily compromised. If Cassandra was there, it is highly likely she is employed by the asylum," Ursula noted.

"We broke in rather easily," Seth remarked. Salem gave him a dirty look.

"Your majesty, we do not intend to sound disrespectful," Salem smiled. "Please excuse my brother. I do not know whether Cassandra Obreiggon is an authorized staff member of Dredmore Asylum or not. I am confident that we can prove she willfully kept my mother sedated as to give the appearance that the curse was still in effect. I am willing to make the charge."

"And Atheidrelle?" Ursula asked.

"Why else would Cassandra do what she did?" Seth sighed. "Obviously, her mother put her up to it!"

"The Witches Court does not operate under obviouslys," Ursula declared. "There was a time in this country when too many innocent people were killed due to suggestion, happenstance, and willful innuendo. This Council takes crimes and guilty verdicts very seriously. My advice, children, is that you leave your charges solely to Cassandra Obreiggon. Nothing I have been told about this matter proves any guilt lay at Atheidrelle's feet. Oh, it suggests a great deal. It proves nothing."

"Why else would Cassandra do it then?" Seth exclaimed. "Unless her mother told her to."

"I can think of a very clear reason," Ursula answered. "Nacaria had an affair with her father, and she did not want Nacaria to wake up and try to split up her parents. That alone explains Cassandra's motives."

Seth and Salem remained silent. Although they knew Atheidrelle was involved, the queen made an excellent point. On the surface, the argument that Cassandra was acting alone was not unreasonable. It was plausible Cassandra could have done what she did for her own reasons.

Queen Ursula looked Salem directly in the eye and continued. "Salem, you are well respected here. You won over a great many hearts this summer when you came to cremate your child. Listen to the advice I offer. You can win against Cassandra. You have no evidence to support a charge against Atheidrelle. Atheidrelle has many friends. She and her husband share a Council seat. She has campaigned rather deftly in her quest to be elected the new queen tonight. Becoming queen is of the utmost importance to her. When we get in there, keep these things in mind. Do not charge Atheidrelle with anything you cannot emphatically prove. You will not bring her down merely with what you have."

...

Downstairs, Olympia waited with her granddaughters for Salem and Seth to return from their discussion with Ursula. Olympia was interested to hear what the queen might be telling them about the charges they planned to wage. Ursula and her family were age-old friends to the Blanchard family, and Olympia knew she had Salem and Seth's best interests at heart.

The waiter came by two or three more times with trays of drinks. The University Club was a massive house, but as massive as it may have been, packing hundreds of people inside on a cold winter's night did not make moving around very fluid. When the waiter accidentally tripped over a passersby foot, his tray of champagne went airborne, spilling all over one of the delicately wallpapered walls. As the drinks went one way, the waiter went the other, stumbling forward and falling into Yasmine, bumping her into a tall roman pedestal which housed the bust of James Dearing, the steamboat captain who originally built the house.

Yasmine reached forward in an attempt to grab the falling art piece before it smashed to the floor. She missed. But the bust did not smash. It did not fall. It hovered three feet above the floor before everyone's eyes. Yasmine knew she was the one doing it. She could feel it inside. Everyone else knew she was doing it as well. The position of her hands was in direct line to the floating bust of old John. Slowly, she began directing her hands back toward the pedestal. As she did, the bust moved in sync with her motion until it rested itself back in place.

"Oh my God!" Fable cried. "Yaz, you really have learned some magic after all these years! When Hecate said you'd developed abilities, I really didn't know what to think, but now I see it!"

"I guess so," Yasmine stammered. "Crazy huh? I can now just suddenly do stuff.

Mostly float things, I guess. I haven't had anything else happen. But yeah, I think I've developed powers."

Beryl let out a laugh. She hadn't meant to. It was an involuntary reaction to her family's gross misinterpretation. She didn't know why everyone was missing the most reasonable conclusion. Olympia shot her a disapproving look, as Yasmine and Fable turned to her with confusion.

"What's so funny about this?" Fable scoffed.

"It's funny because you two idiots are missing the obvious," Beryl said. "I think it is highly unlikely Yasmine just suddenly developed powers."

"Then explain what you just witnessed?" Fable demanded.

"It is always the doctor who has to figure it out isn't it," Beryl smiled, nudging her grandmother, who had only now worked it out herself as well. "Yaz, you're pregnant. That is why you have spontaneously manifested powers. Seth's baby is a witch—apparently with some sort of levitation ability."

"Pregnant!" Yasmine gasped. "But I'm on the pill!"

Beryl gave her a suspicious side-eye. "I know you, Yaz. Are you sure you remember to take it every day?"

"Well, practically."

"You're pregnant," Beryl nodded.

Yasmine's eyes bulged in complete surprise before being replaced by the happiest smile anyone had ever seen upon her face. She placed her hands on her stomach and looked to be almost hugging herself. She snapped back to awareness and faced the others.

"Don't say a word to Seth! Not anyone. I'll tell him later," Yasmine ordered. "Once I take an actual test to make sure."

Leaving Yasmine with their grandmother to giggle and daydream about motherhood, Beryl edged Fable away from the crowd for a private conversation. Tucking themselves away down an empty hall, Beryl confronted her sister.

"Speaking of pregnancies..."

Fable's mouth dropped. Beryl knew. Wordless understanding passed between them for a moment before Fable gave a gentle nod of confession. "I'm not discussing this tonight," she said.

"You better start getting ready to discuss this soon," Beryl warned. "It is Patric's, isn't it?"

Fable frowned but gave a second nod.

"You are having Patric's baby!" Beryl howled. Fable shushed her and pushed her into a coat closet nearby.

"Lower your voice!"

Beryl was not terribly concerned with the decibel amount of her words. She was more concerned with her sister's lack of common sense. "You are planning on bringing another monster into our lives!"

Fable grabbed her sister's hands and squeezed them to her chest in plea, "Look, I don't know what I'm going to do yet," she said. "There's still time to abort. I just need to think. I'm not ready yet. But there is time."

"Fable that baby's father tried to kill all of us!!!"

Fable gave her sister's hands another squeeze, beseeching her compassion. "It's a baby, Beryl! It's not Patric. We aren't even sure Patric's curse is inheritable. This could be a perfectly normal child. My child. My baby, Beryl. What if there's nothing wrong with it? Are you—a doctor, sworn to protect lives every day—really asking me to kill my child?"

Beryl did not know how to respond.

"Just give me some time. You and I will talk it all out later. But right now... right now I need time to think. I always make the wrong choices. This is too big a decision to get wrong. Please, trust me. And keep my secret."

"I don't know, Fable. This is too big."

"We are sisters, Beryl. Sisters! You and me, forever. As your sister, I am begging you."

Beryl shook her head and paced around the closet floor a few seconds, considering the options. Inhaling a deep breath, she acquiesced, "Okay look, for the time being I will keep this quiet. We do actually have some more pressing things to deal with right now. But this is not over. You and I are going to sit down and figure this out and figure it soon, while there's time to end this pregnancy."

"We will figure it out, together," Fable said, buying time. Then she asked, "How did you know I was pregnant?"

Beryl rolled her eyes at her little sister, "I was looking for my green sweater you always steal, and I found prenatal vitamins in your drawer. But even if I hadn't found those, haven't you noticed the tiniest formation of that baby bump you have going on under that dress?"

Fable clutched her stomach in vanity. She had no idea she was showing. "I'm not far along enough to be showing."

Beryl gave her sister a not-so-gentle forehead slap, "You are not pregnant with a human baby Fable!"

...

Back at the bust of John Dearing, Yasmine was beginning to panic a little. The thought of becoming a mother was enough on its own to frazzle her, but Seth had already made it quite clear he was not ready to be a father yet.

"What is he going to say?" Yasmine frowned at her grandmother. "We were playing Scrabble not too long ago, and I made the word *pregnant,* and he almost fainted. He doesn't want kids right now."

Olympia laughed, mostly to herself. She wasn't intending to be dismissive of Yasmine's fears, but a long life had taught her much—much more than her youthful offspring would understand until they too were old. She placed her reassuring arm around her youngest grandchild and smiled. "I have never known a man who was ready to be a father. Becoming a parent is never something you are ready for, but it is something you would not trade for the world. Seth will be delighted."

"How can you be sure?"

"Because, my sweet girl, I know all of my children better than they know themselves. You and Seth included. Deep inside that boy he longs to be the father he never had. I can guarantee you that Seth Blanchard will be the most devoted dad any of us have ever seen. Once he's past the shock of it happening now, and he gets all the cuss words out."

CHAPTER NINETEEN

I Hate You Because You Smile

Xander Obreiggon stood in the main lounge of the University Club, his wife entwined around his arm, flashing her smile to anyone they encountered as if she were a movie star at a premiere. She waved across the room to far off faces of Consort members whose names he knew she did not know. He grimaced every time someone approached and told her she had their vote that evening. He did not understand why the idea bothered him so. She was his wife after all. Regardless of whether he felt affection for her or not, it behooved him just as much if his wife became queen. The problem plaguing Xander's heart was that he hated to see her succeed at anything. Perhaps because she succeeded at everything. Atheidrelle was always getting her way in everything since the day they met. Xander Obreiggon had spent the better part of his life waiting patiently for the day to come when—just once—she didn't.

"She has nerve, I must say," Olympia scowled quietly to Zelda from the other side of the room. "And look at that ridiculous fur coat."

"Yeah, that thing musta cost a fortune," Zelda said. "She could'a checked that thing at the door, but you know she's gotta be seen in it by everybody first."

Behind Zelda and Olympia, two of the new Wiccan members were overheard admiring Atheidrelle. Each girl felt it their mission to make her acquaintance that night because as they phrased it, "She's probably going to be the queen after tonight. We should buddy up to her."

"Don't pay any attention to them young'ens, Lympy. They're just Wiccans. Ain't never seen no real anything before."

"But they are correct, Zelda. Atheidrelle wields a lot of influence. Imagine if she becomes the queen tonight."

"That bitch don't hold half the friends you got, Lympy!" Zelda cried. "She may not go down for what she did to Nacaria, but she ain't gone look too good after the

Council gets through with Cassandra."

"It may not have any effect on her popularity," Olympia worried.

"Popularity," scoffed Zelda. "Who the hell is she anyway? Her granddaddy Emmerick D'Angelo was nothin but a black magic crime lord windbag. Your Daddy on the other hand, now he was a real witch. People don't forget men like Constantinople Blanchard!"

"Zelda," Olympia smiled. "We are nearing our nineties. I don't think there's anyone left who even remembers my father."

"Well, they know you! I'll lay my odds on Olympia Blanchard any day of the week! There ain't a soul in this place you ain't helped in some way at some place in time. Hell, you should be queen!"

"I'm afraid that's a job for younger witches. Let us face it, Zelda, our days have passed. It's now our children's world." Olympia smiled. "Speaking of children, where are Melinda and Sarah? We could use them tonight."

"You know well as me you can't count on my sorry girls for nothin'," Zelda moaned. "Sarah won't miss her Weight Watcher class, and Melinda is judging the Miss Christmas Spirit Pageant."

"I don't believe I've ever heard of that," Olympia said.

"Cause it ain't a real pageant! It's a drag contest."

"A what?"

"Oh hell, Lympy, don't you know what a drag contest is? You ain't that damn old. Men dressing as women. Drag Queens! Lord, you gotta get your grandkids to take you out more."

A ballroom lay in the back of the University Club. A light-tone parquet floor covered the room. The ten high windows covering the three sides of the room were flanked with plush green velvet. Had Scarlet O'Hara been there, she could have made ten gowns to parade through the streets of Atlanta in. The walls were painted with a summery scene to give the appearance of outdoors and a verandah. The murals were as old as the house itself, so the illusion of outdoors was a flimsy one.

Eleanor Branson outdid herself with the decorators she hired to swath the ballroom rafters in cedar bunting with holly and lights. The band she hired was the best in the state, and all around the room happy couples danced joyously along the floor in celebration for the upcoming holidays as well as the last Consort meeting of the year.

Seth Blanchard moved through the crowded drawing room pulling his sister's arm, dragging her to the ballroom. Salem had an incredulous look on her face at her brother's uncharacteristic gesture. As the music reverberated in the room, she stared at him as if he had lost his mind.

"Dance with me," he said.

"I don't feel like dancing," she replied.

"Shut up and dance with me, Salem."

"Where is your wife?"

"Off somewhere with Beryl and Fable. Are you going to dance with me or not?"

Salem gave in and moved into his arms. Seth placed one hand on her waist and clasped her hand with the other and began twirling his sister across the dancefloor as if in celebration. At first, she couldn't understand what had gotten into him. Was he posturing for the crowd? Was he trying to temporarily forget the seriousness of why they were there tonight? But it then occurred to her, he was happy. It was Christmastime. He was married to his best friend. His mother was back. Justice was going to be handed down later that night to their sworn enemy. He had many reasons to celebrate, but mostly, he just wanted to dance with his big sister.

After the dance ended, both Seth and Salem were winded. With a mutual nod they both agreed one dance was enough and so, hand in hand, they departed the ballroom and reentered the drawing room. Salem noticed her father right away. Xander was standing with Atheidrelle as she surveyed the room, still occasionally taking a few moments of her precious time to acknowledge the presence of someone else. Salem watched from afar. Her father looked miserable. She hurt for him. Then, Atheidrelle saw her. Salem did not overt her eyes, she stared directly back at her in defiance. The sight of Salem shook Atheidrelle. She betrayed her discomfort for a few seconds before returning to her icy reserve, but Salem saw it.

"Is that him?" Seth asked when he saw where Salem was looking.

"Yes," Salem whispered. "That's our father."

"I *do* look like him," Seth observed.

"Yes, you do."

"His wife keeps looking over here, but I don't think he sees us," Seth noticed. "She is clearly worried he might."

"She has no idea Xander and I have met," Salem smiled. "You can tell she's already figured out who you are. You can bet she isn't going to share that information with him. She's remaining cool as a cucumber. She's going to pretend we don't exist."

Seth grinned wickedly at Salem, "But we do exist."

Tugging his sister along with him, Seth crossed the room, dodging and swaying through dozens of people—all of whom were now watching the scene play out because they knew exactly who Salem and Seth were, and they could not wait to watch the Obreiggons' reaction to their presence. Atheidrelle felt her own eyes begin to widen as the shock of seeing Seth Blanchard marching straight toward them set in. She steeled herself quickly, hardening the muscles of her face as to not show any emotion whatsoever.

"Hello," Seth said to Xander as he stepped next to him.

Behind them, Salem could hear the whispers faintly growing from around the room. *They are talking to him. Nacaria's children are here. Look at Xander with his other children, his children by Nacaria.*

Xander, who had not seen them approaching, turned to greet whomever just spoke to him. He couldn't conceal his surprise well once he recognized the young man at his side. "Seth? Seth is it you?" All the misery which had been in Xander's eyes drained out, replaced with a bright shiny joy at the sight of Seth and Salem.

"Yes," Seth smiled. "It's Seth."

"How are you?" Xander cried with a huge smile as he began to rigorously shake Seth's hand without stopping. "Oh, my boy, how are you?"

"I'm having a great night so far," Seth beamed, his peripheral vision catching Atheidrelle's menacing glare.

Xander looked as if he were about to burst with happiness. His children were here. He was actually talking to his children, and he was thrilled. He looked at Salem, his beautiful Salem. "Salem, hello my dear."

"Hello," she said.

An audible, collective gasp rang out from around the room as she stepped forward to offer him a brief cordial hug. He embraced her lovingly, lingering a moment longer than his wife appreciated.

"I wasn't aware the two of you had met before," Atheidrelle said, continuing to hold her gracious façade as she seethed inwardly.

"Yes," Salem said flatly, "Xander and I know one another."

Atheidrelle fortified herself so that her reactions would not cause her more embarrassment than this scene was already doing. She needed to give all appearances that she had previously known the Blanchard bastards would be there and that she approved this exchange with her husband. Salem drank in every awkward second of Atheidrelle's misery. And, as if scripted for perfection, a voice rang out over her shoulder making it all the more splendid.

"Well, isn't this cozy," Arielle cried, walking up and giving her father a kiss on the cheek. "Hi, Daddy."

"Arielle," Atheidrelle said in surprise without loosening the smile on her face as the onlookers watched without blinking. "What are you doing here, darling?"

"I'm a witch. This is a Witches Association meeting. I have every right to be here."

"Of course, you do my dear," Atheidrelle said calmly, even placing her hand gently on her daughter's shoulder. Her nails just barely digging into Arielle's flesh. This was a dead giveaway to Arielle that her mother was truly reeling from this loss of control of the events around her. Atheidrelle never touched Arielle. Arielle couldn't even remember the last time her mother had hugged her. Possibly never. "I wish you'd have let me know you were coming tonight. Your father and I have missed you, and we could have all arrived together as a family."

"I came with *them*," Arielle announced, a little louder than necessary. "I came with family."

Atheidrelle could barely contain her rage under that concocted smile. "You came with them? You don't even know them."

"Of course, I do, Mother," Arielle said, even louder. "Don't you know who they are? This is Seth and Salem. My brother and sister."

"Your *brother* and *sister*," Atheidrelle repeated, the smile slowly evacuating her icy porcelain face. "I was not aware you knew one another. When did this happen? You've been away at school."

"Yes," Arielle grinned triumphantly, relishing the opportunity to finally have the upper hand with her mother after a lifetime of it being the other way around. "I have been at school. The University of Georgia."

"Georgia," Atheidrelle sneered as if the very name of the state filled her with repulsion. "It was my understanding you were enrolled at—"

"But I'm not," Arielle replied. "I go to Georgia."

"And that is where you met..."

"My *sister*?" Arielle injected. "No. I met my sister last year at the Consort. Then we reconnected in Atlanta when I went to visit her. I live with her now."

"You what?" Atheidrelle dropped the faux smile. Her fury was bigger than her ability to hide it. "You live with Salem Blanchard?"

"Yes. She does," Salem said, now possessing the smile, only hers was genuine. "We've become very close. Of course, sisters should be—don't you agree?"

Atheidrelle regained her public face and leaned into her husband, placing a playful hand on his chest as she laughingly, yet venomously asked, "Have you known about this, my love? You should have told me."

"I've known from the beginning," Xander replied. His face was white with uneasiness yet there was something about him that was changing in front of their eyes. His instinctual fear of his wife was losing its grip on him, empowered by the presence of his children. He was proud of his children and proud to be seen standing among them, talking with them. Xander Obreiggon was slowly becoming a man again after a lifetime of having been reduced to something else.

"You met Salem at the last Consort, didn't you?" Atheidrelle asked. "I should have known you'd return early to see her. But Seth?"

"I am officially meeting my son for the first time," Xander said beaming again at the sight of his boy. "Although I did watch him from afar on his wedding day." Seth grinned at his father. "I would not have missed that moment for anything," Xander added.

Atheidrelle took inventory of the room around her and realized every witch in sight was watching this entire scene play out. She could not afford to unleash the emotions she wanted to unleash. Not tonight. Not before elections. She sculpted her face into perfect graciousness as she outstretched her arms to place both hands on her husband and daughter's shoulders.

Giving onlookers the impression that she was saying something kind, she looked directly at Salem when she said, "I'm sure you meant to make me look foolish tonight. But you will not cause me to stumble. I'm still smiling."

Salem returned the gesture, placing her hands on Atheidrelle's shoulders, staring her directly in the eye and replying, "You always seem to be smiling. You smiled at my mother's trial. You smiled at my son's cremation. I hate you because you smile. I can't wait to watch you fear."

Salem Blanchard linked arms with her brother and her sister and victoriously guided them away. Everything was going to be at stake now in this Consort meeting. Queen Ursula warned her not to make charges she could not prove against Atheidrelle. Now Salem didn't know what she was going to do. It just might be much too difficult to leave Atheidrelle the chance of still standing.

CHAPTER TWENTY

The Meeting

Five long rows of chairs were arranged in circular patterns throughout the convention room of the University Club. At the center of the first ring stood a large round table. The members of the Consort began entering the convention room taking seats among the circular rows. The Council of the Consort filled the center roundtable. There was no front or back, everyone faced fellow members in five round circles symbolizing infinity and how everything and everyone in nature is connected with no beginning or end.

Olympia, her sister Pastoria, and their individual families sat together in a cluster, some in every row. It did not take long for the Consort members to find seats, as everyone knew not to dawdle once a meeting commenced. Queen Ursula stood at the center round table where the rest of the Council members were seated, and she began her opening speech. As she talked, welcoming everyone to the Winter Consort, Seth and Salem watched their father in the center ring in his Council seat. Across the room, Atheidrelle stared daggers at Arielle who was seated with Salem and Seth.

"Welcome to the Winter Consort of the Witches Association," Queen Ursula began. "Before we begin tonight's meeting, I would like to take a few moments to speak to you for the last time as your queen. As you know, my reign ends tonight, and I have chosen not to run again. During the Autumn Consort, those of you who wished to be considered as my replacement were given the opportunity to place your names on the ballot. We will be voting shortly, but before we commence, I wanted to thank you all for the support you have shown me over these last nine years as your queen. We have accomplished many wondrous things together in that time, and I have every confidence our new leader will achieve even more. It has been my sincere pleasure and honor to serve you as well as lead you. I leave my post all the wiser for having been blessed by your encouragement and affection."

The crowd rose to their feet to applaud Ursula for her years of dedication and service. The room was an uproar for three solid minutes. Ursula's tears evidenced her thanks to them. The applause was justified. She had been a wonderful leader. Under her watch the Consort thrived, and the rest of the world would never have any idea just how many times Queen Ursula's decisions and interventions saved mankind from untold trouble.

Ursula continued her speech once the cheers died away. "Five of you have tossed your hats into the ring for king or queen, and tonight we will begin the meeting with the vote. For those of you new to the Consort, I will explain our election procedure."

Ursula knew everyone had already been informed via email and the older members had been through the election process before, but Ursula was stalling for time. Stalling long enough for her guards to arrive with Cassandra and for Nacaria to get there. Though propriety dictated she remain neutral, Queen Ursula secretly hoped to see justice for her old friend Nacaria.

"Beneath your chairs, you will discover a small box containing five colored medallions. On each medallion is the name of one of the five candidates. You will choose one coin and drop it into one of the three chests guarded by our officials as you exit this meeting. Votes will be tallied by our electoral staff and the results returned to us within two hours' time after this meeting is adjourned. You may mingle, dance, eat, drink, do whatever you wish while the results are tallied. Do not fear the integrity of our electoral staff, as each of the three officials have staked their powers on the honesty of their count.

"The five candidates up for the role of King or Queen of the Consort are as follows: Desmond Tanner, Lois Cavanaugh, Desiree Talbot, Geoffrey London, and Atheidrelle Obreiggon. Now, let us get on with our meeting so we can vote and enjoy the evening. I introduce to you all, Councilman Jason'te Barstow."

Councilman Barstow stood and bowed to the congregation. For a second, he caught sight of Yasmine Blanchard seated in the audience and gave her a wink. It was rather uncommon for non-witch spouses to attend Consort meetings. Her presence was an anomaly so there was really no reason he should have even known who she was except for the simple fact he'd performed her wedding ceremony on Halloween.

"We will begin tonight by completing old business," Jason'te began. "At our last meeting, there was a request by Norma Connelly to install her sister Clara as the new coven leader for their family. The request was due to the fact that their prior leader,

Jewel Connelly, now suffers from Alzheimer's. The family did not request a healing, therefore the Council investigated and determined Jewel's diagnosis to be correct, and we have bound her powers and granted the new coven leader request. I ask now if there are any Consort members who have new business to bring to the Council?"

She had said nothing to anyone prior to the meeting, so when Arielle rose to her feet before the entire Consort, Salem was caught off guard. Olympia, Seth, and the others all appeared to be equally surprised. "I have a request to put before the Council."

All eyes fixed upon Arielle as she stood facing the Witches Council. She could see her mother on the other side of the room. Atheidrelle's virulent face was clouded with a mixture of confusion and apprehension. Xander looked on from the Council table just as perplexed as his wife seated several rows behind him.

"Go ahead, Miss Obreiggon," Jason'te permitted.

She spoke matter-of-factly, never allowing her gaze to stray from her mother's icy glare. She wanted this act of defiance to send the clear message that she was grown up now and not afraid anymore. "I would like to withdraw from the coven of D'Angelo/Obreiggon and join the Blanchard coven."

A tidal wave of gasps and rumbling voices erupted through the room. Never in life had Atheidrelle been more furious nor more humiliated than this exact moment with the eyes of the witching world looking on. She did her best to hold her composure knowing all eyes were darting back and forth between herself and her youngest daughter.

"Have you given this matter due consideration Miss Obreiggon?" Jason'te queried. "It is not a move to be made lightly, after all the D'Angelo/Obreiggon coven is your family."

"So are the Blanchards," Seth chimed in standing up beside his little sister. Arielle looked at him and smiled. He clutched her hand and winked. Salem stood up on the other side of her as well.

"I see," Jason'te muttered in bemused amazement.

All around whispers were raging. *She knows them. She knows who they are.* Other voices could be heard muttering *I hear she lives with them*. Still others even murmured, *I hear she sometimes stays at Olympia Blanchard's own house. Atheidrelle's daughter, at Olympia's own house!*

Jason'te Barstow's astonished face addressed Olympia, "Is her move acceptable to you Olympia, as head of your family's coven?"

Olympia rose and switched places with Salem to stand beside Arielle. Olympia placed her authoritative hand on Arielle's shoulder and declared, "Quite acceptable. The Blanchard coven happily accepts Arielle as a member."

Jason'te addressed Xander seated beside him, "Any objections from the Obreiggons?"

"Yes!" Atheidrelle objected. "I strenuously object to my daughter's motion. She is young and cripplingly naive. She has been the unfortunate victim of a targeted manipulation to alienate her affections from her own family loyalties."

"That is not true," Arielle shot back.

Unexpectedly, Xander Obreiggon rose to his feet to address the Consort at large. "There is no objection to my daughter's request."

"Xander!" Atheidrelle cried out before remembering herself and what it might look like to the others.

"I said there are no objections," Xander repeated. "As her father I release my daughter with love, pride, and my blessing." He winked at Arielle and returned to his seat.

"In that case," Jason'te moved on, "Arielle Obreiggon you are hereafter a member of the Blanchard coven of Daihmler. You are now answerable to their leader, Olympia Blanchard." Arielle smiled and hugged Salem before they all returned to their seats.

Atheidrelle was seething now. Not only was this an utmost public humiliation, but it was not like Xander to be so defiant. She had spent too many years caging him into submission. To now see him so emboldened by the sight of his three children united was more than she could withstand. Atheidrelle Obreiggon hated the Blanchard family. They'd caused her enough torment in her life. She stared at them and their victorious faces, and she wanted to unleash her great power upon them. Those stupid fools. They had no idea what she was capable of doing. Neither did Xander. It took everything in her to hold herself together. There would be time enough later for revenge.

Jason'te Barstow continued with new business. "Any other Council requests?"

A woman rose. "I am Gina Meadows. I belong to the Sallinger coven. I have a request for one of my coven members, Irma Sallinger. I'd like a healing witch to visit Irma's husband Robert in Sarasota, Florida. He has suffered a debilitating stroke."

Jason'te addressed the Consort at large, "Are there any healing witches willing to travel to Sarasota?"

Beryl and four other people stood up.

"Beryl Blanchard lives in Alabama. Any of the rest of you nearer than Daihmler?" Jason'te asked.

A woman raised her hand. "I live in Bradenton. That's just a few miles from Sarasota."

"Thank you," Jason'te replied. "See Miss Meadows after the Consort and make arrangements for the healing."

Jason'te moved on to inquire if there was any additional new business before the meeting moved into other areas. Olympia noted the time on her watch and gave a slight nod to Salem and Seth. Salem stood to her feet and addressed the Council.

"I apologize if it seems my family is monopolizing this entire meeting," she said with a slight nervous grin, "however, my brother and I wish to place a charge on a fellow Consort member."

The night of whispers and astonished gasps continued as everyone around waited breathlessly to hear what Salem was about to allege.

"First, let me warn you Salem," Jason'te instructed, "a false charge is a crime in this association. You should be definite in your proof before you irrevocably assert an accusation."

"We are fully aware of the seriousness of a charge and the repercussions should that charge be inaccurate," Salem concurred.

"State your charge."

Every member of the Witches Consort sat with bated breath wondering what words might spill forth from the young witch's mouth. Salem too was unsure. In the fraction of seconds left to her to state her charge, she wasn't sure what she was going to say. Should she implicate Atheidrelle as well or take the advice of those wiser than herself and only address Cassandra's participation? Seconds were passing without her utterance of anything whatsoever. Seth was now staring at her, wondering why she wasn't saying anything. Finally, he took command.

"My sister and I would like to place a charge on behalf of our mother against Cassandra Obreiggon for illegally confining our mother to Dredmore Asylum even after her curse was lifted."

The audience erupted. Simply the news that Nacaria Blanchard's curse had been lifted was enough to send everyone into a frenzy, but to also add the accusation that Cassandra Obreiggon held her against her will after—the commotion forced Ursula to command silence from all witnessing.

Atheidrelle grimaced as she listened. Salem watched every flick of her facial muscles, every tick of her chin, every glint and shadow in her eye. Atheidrelle was not surprised by the news Nacaria's time was served. She was not surprised by the allegation that Cassandra had kept her locked away. Had Salem ever possessed any doubt of Atheidrelle's compliance—nay, masterminding—of Nacaria's captivity the expressionlessness coming from Atheidrelle quelled the doubts. *I cannot let her get away with this. I cannot allow her to sit back while Cassandra takes the fall.*

"I also charge Atheidrelle Obreiggon as accomplice or possibly even orchestrator of the entire plot to hold my mother captive," Salem announced. She took a deep breath. She thought one final time before she said what came next. She owed it to them to say it, no matter what the personal cost. "I also charge Atheidrelle Obreiggon with murder. The murder of my husband and son!"

Olympia grabbed her arm, "Salem, no! You cannot prove this." Olympia's heart trembled again. She slowly placed her free hand on her chest, as if attempting to stop its fluctuations with her wrist.

Salem wrestled her arm free and reasserted her claim to the Council. Xander was staring at her, his face crestfallen yet something else as well. Was it perhaps hopeful? Hopeful that Nacaria might be free?

"I dare you to prove this libelous blackening of my character," Atheidrelle said defiantly.

"Dare *me*," shouted a voice from behind Salem. Heads turned to see two figures coming through the double doors of the convention room.

No one had seen Nacaria Blanchard's face in twenty years. And there it was, just as beautiful and delicate as ever. Her long blonde hair swishing behind her as she marched forward through the aisle between the circular rows, marching toward the Council table. Behind her walked Blackie D'Angelo, but all eyes were on Nacaria. And no pair more so than Xander Obreiggon.

"This is my mother, Nacaria Blanchard," Salem announced.

Nacaria continued walking toward the Council table but veered to the left to encircle the table so that she passed by her nemesis. "You should see your face," she sneered at Atheidrelle as she walked by.

Never in her life had Atheidrelle felt as much hatred for another person. Looking straight into Nacaria's eyes, she knew the evening was no longer going to go as she planned.

"As you all can see," Salem continued, "my mother's curse has been lifted. Yet we found out quite by accident."

"What do you mean accident?" short, stodgy Councilmember Brimford Uding asked. "When a witch is released from their penance, the family is contacted by Dredmore Asylum administrators."

"No one contacted us," Salem announced. "And why, you may ask? Because Atheidrelle Obreiggon placed her daughter Cassandra on staff to serve as my mother's caregiver. When my mother awakened, Cassandra kept her drugged and unconscious whenever asylum administrators made their inspections. Thus, making it appear the curse was still in effect."

Atheidrelle pounced to her feet. "I demand Salem Blanchard be magically silenced by the Council and punished for these egregious lies."

Nacaria laughed. It was a genuine laugh. She was legitimately amused by Atheidrelle's response. "That is how you prefer to do things isn't it, Atheidrelle?" she said. Nacaria felt light. Free. She had not felt this electric in two decades. "Twenty years ago, you persuaded the Council then to silence me while you delivered all the evidence needed to convict me. I never even got to say a word."

"What was there to say?" Atheidrelle declared. "We gave you vows, and you admitted guilt."

"And I was silenced before I ever got to say anything more," Nacaria said, glaring at her. "But tonight, you are all going to hear everything."

CHAPTER TWENTY ONE

Comeuppance

Nacaria had the full attention of the Council and all the members of the Witches Association Consort. She had waited a long time to tell her tale, and now nothing was going to stop her. As every face looked to her and every voice was quieted, Nacaria Blanchard made up for all those silent years.

"This Council, some of you even members back then, tried and convicted me without hearing my version of events. You did this because of your disapproval of my affair with Xander Obreiggon."

Her eyes looked to Xander. She was seeing him for the first time in two decades. He looked broken, shrunken, a shadow of what he had once been. Still, she loved him. One look to his weary eyes was all she needed to know. What they felt was still alive.

"Miss Blanchard," Councilwoman Millicent Davis chimed, "you were convicted because it was proven beyond doubt that you tried to kill Atheidrelle Obreiggon."

"You are an idiot," Nacaria laughed. "An egocentric idiot who has lived her entire Council career in the D'Angelo family back pocket, and everyone knows it."

The crowd erupted into muffled deliberation and not a small amount of laughter. Many enjoyed hearing the candidly truthful account of Millicent's loyalties.

"Miss Blanchard, you will not disrupt this serious hearing with crude insults and sublimation," Amory Vendell, another member of the Witches Council snapped.

"I learned many things during my time haunting the walls of my house, Mr. Vendell," Nacaria said. "One of which is to speak my mind when I have the opportunity because you never know when you'll be robbed of the chance in the future. You would defend Millicent. If she sits in one of the D'Angelo's back pockets, you are tucked away in the other one."

"Give 'em hell, Nikky!" Zelda cheered from row two.

"Enough of this commentary," Queen Ursula commanded. "Nacaria, I urge you to swiftly make your point."

"I will tell you all everything. The truth of what happened to me at Dredmore. The truth of why I committed my crime years ago. I will tell you why the blood of my daughter's husband and son sits on the hands of Atheidrelle Obreiggon. But before I tell anything, I want to call for vows. I will take a vow. I request all witnesses be bound to vows before questioning, including Atheidrelle Obreiggon."

Emory Vendell jumped to Atheidrelle's defense. "The call for vows is too serious a request for such frivolous and childish allegations. Mrs. Obreiggon is a well-respected member of this organization, and she will not be insulted by such a ridiculous measure."

"Miss Blanchard," Brimford Uding said clearing his throat, "before we could even consider a vote to call upon vows, I'm afraid you need to be a little clearer in what you are alleging and how you can prove it. Particularly regarding this sudden murder allegation."

"Murder is perhaps the wrong terminology," Nacaria answered. "Twenty years ago, Atheidrelle Obreiggon placed a curse on my children. Because her husband loved me and not her, she condemned our children to a life where anyone they ever truly loved would die. Imagine a life in which you could fall deeply in love with the person you have waited your whole life for—then have it ripped away in seconds. Robbed of life's passion, partnership, and any meaningful longevity."

"My husband died," Salem said angrily. "Our infant son died."

"A curse or a coincidence?" Millicent remarked. "Or perhaps just the rantings of a vengeful mistress concocting fanciful curses to explain natural tragedies."

"My wife was almost killed by a werewolf recently," Seth announced. "Many years ago, my fiancée at the time was killed tragically and unexpectedly."

"Again—coincidence," Millicent said rather condescendingly.

"Let's find out," Salem said. "Let's ask Atheidrelle to take *vows*."

"Explain more about this claim of being held against your will at Dredmore," Ursula asked. "I feel the Council might be better persuaded by your claims if the immediate evidence of one was brought forth." *We will bring Cassandra in. That might help your credibility here. State that charge.*

Salem heard the queen's mindspeaking very clearly. She gave Ursula a slight nod, then announced to the Consort at large, "Let's table my mother's claims from the past for a moment. The most immediate crime being charged here tonight is the captivity of my mother by Cassandra Obreiggon."

"Yes, explain this charge," Brimford requested.

"My Mother was released from her curse months ago. We only discovered this days ago."

"How did you discover this?"

Blackie stepped forward giving her sister a sly mischievous smile. "I brought it to the Blanchard family's attention. I knew the date had come and gone for Nacaria Blanchard's release, yet she had not been returned to her family. I suspected my sister might be involved."

"How could you know the date?" Brimford asked. "Only King Perrimont knew that date. He set it himself all those years ago when Nacaria was sentenced. The date was to be concealed as part of the punishment."

Blackie laughed. "I have ways of being in rooms unnoticed."

"Blackie is also a witness to what we found at Dredmore," Salem informed the Council.

"Tell us your version of events," Brimford demanded.

"First thing's first," Blackie bowed. "Queen Ursula, would you be so kind as to have your guards bring in our culprit?"

As Cassandra Obreiggon was brought in, hands bound and mouth covered, the room descended into chaos. Salem watched Atheidrelle's face turn from faux indignation to actual terror. Cassandra had been caught, and now Atheidrelle knew it. But Salem knew there was still no way to tie Atheidrelle to Cassandra's actions unless Cassandra willingly implicated her own mother. And there was no way Salem could know if that would happen.

"Now," Blackie smiled, "before we waste any more time discussing matters that would only have to be discussed again after taking vows, let us just cut right to it. Will someone make the call?"

"I will," said Pastoria Blanchard standing up from the fourth row. "I call upon the Consort of Witches to invoke vows for these proceedings."

"I second my sister's recommendation," Olympia said standing up next.

Ursula addressed the Consort, "We will take an oral vote of yea or nay. There are 389 Consort members present. A majority of 233 is required either way."

Jason'te stood once again. "I will quickly read off the names of members present. Cast your vote as instructed—yea for a call of vows; nay, against. Ernestine, if you will help me keep tally."

He began reading the names of the members of the Consort as one by one everyone in the room voted. "Serene Attaway?"

"Yea"

"Calvert Avery?"

"No."

"Shawna Babcock?"

"Against."

"Dirk Babcock?"

"Nope."

"Denise Babcock?"

"Definitely for the vows."

"Artemis Blanchard?"

"Yea."

"Beryl Blanchard?"

"Yes."

"Demitra Blanchard?"

"For vows."

"Drake Blanchard?"

"Yes."

"Fable Blanchard?"

"Oh yeah."

On and on it went. Every Blanchard in the family voted for the call for vows (which was exactly why every Blanchard in the family was in attendance that night). Every member of every coven cast their vote until the final Consort member had voted. Atheidrelle, naturally voted *against*. To her surprise and dismay, her husband supported the call *for*. When the counts were tallied Jason'te announced a narrow margin... in favor of the call for vows.

Nacaria began, "I vow to speak truth and pledge my powers be stricken if I betray my vow."

"Begin your account now, Miss Blanchard," Ursula instructed.

"Beginning at the beginning," Nacaria said. "Twenty odd years ago I was in love with Xander Obreiggon, and he was in love with me." She looked to the Council table at her beloved again. "It has been long believed I tried to undo Atheidrelle's life simply to be with her husband. But that is not why. I like to believe he and I would have found a way to be together regardless. Our love was strong. I did not have to kill anyone to hold him.

"Atheidrelle Obreiggon had come to me and told me that she had cursed my children. She called it poetic justice. Since I'd stolen the one she'd loved, she'd damn our children to life of continuous loss and heartbreak. I am very skillful with spells and potions. I know how to wrap time back around and step into it. I went back in time to undo the birth of Atheidrelle D'Angelo because undoing her existence would eradicate the curse."

"Why did you take her claim seriously? She might have been simply attempting to frighten you," Ursula asked.

"Because it was Atheidrelle Obreiggon," Nacaria remarked. "Everyone who knows her knows what she's capable of."

"Why didn't you report her curse to the Council?"

"Reporting it doesn't lift it," Nacaria said. "I knew there was no way even the Council could enforce her to lift the curse. I had only one sure-fire way to save my children a lifetime of unhappiness. I took it."

"And that was attempted murder," Millicent Davis projected loudly with a smirk on her face as if she had just settled the entire matter.

"Yes, it was," Nacaria concurred. "And it was a crime I have already paid for."

"You believe this curse to have been real?" Ursula redirected.

"My husband is dead," Salem replied. "My son is dead. My sister-in-law was almost killed by a monster. My brother's first fiancée was killed."

"Again, accidents," Emory declared.

"Perhaps," Nacaria said. "I guess the only real way to know is for us to question Atheidrelle."

Atheidrelle's eyes burned with fury. Nacaria took great pleasure watching her squirm, wondering if the Council might become convinced enough to force vows upon her.

"Let's return to your alleged captivity," Ursula directed. "Tell us about that."

Nacaria began walking toward the Council table. Pacing in a way. "I have so few recollections of that place," Nacaria admitted. "I awoke. I do not know when. All I know is every time my nurse came into my room, I could feel she hated me. And always she injected me with a serum which would drift me back into unconsciousness."

Xander spoke now. It was difficult to tell which emotion of the many streaming through him, was the strongest. His love for Nacaria and the thrill of being able to once more lay eyes upon her? Or his contempt for his wife because he knew in his heart these claims were real? Or was it his disappointment in his eldest child—Cassandra—now standing bound and gagged by the guards of the queen?

His voice betrayed him and broke as he began to speak. "Nacaria..." For several seconds, he could not add more to his sentence. The very utterance of her name paralyzed him. He had not spoken to her in two decades. He tried to regain himself and continue. "Nacaria, is this woman bound here before us—Cassandra Obreiggon—was she the woman presenting herself as your caregiver at Dredmore?"

"Yes, Xander," Nacaria frowned. "I'm sorry to say that she was."

"How did your captivity at Dredmore come to an end?" Brimford Uding asked.

"One day I saw my friend Blackie looking at me behind Cassandra. Cassandra couldn't see her. Blackie told me she was there to save me. The next thing I remember is my children being there as I awoke again. They'd come to rescue me."

"Let us hear now from Blackie D'Angelo. You must take vows."

"Gladly," Blackie stated. She knew that Nacaria's testimony, though true, might not be enough to make an impact. Nacaria's word and mental stability carried a compromised stigma. Blackie knew it was up to her to sway the Council and the general assembly of witches there tonight. "I vow to tell the truth, and I pledge my powers be stricken if I betray this oath."

"Begin your version of events please," Xander requested.

"I approached Beryl Blanchard a week ago because I hadn't heard any news of Nacaria's return. As I stated before, I knew what that return date should have been. Beryl was as confused as I was to where her aunt might be. I had my suspicions that my cunning sister might be involved."

"So far, there is not an ounce of evidence to substantiate any involvement from Atheidrelle Obreiggon," Millicent Davis noted. "I want that made clear to the Consort."

Ignoring the very fact that Millicent even spoke, Blackie continued. "I knew Atheidrelle had done something. I met with the Blanchard family and we formed a group—a rescue team of sorts—to infiltrate Dredmore and find Nacaria."

"Dredmore Asylum is impenetrable," Jason'te Barstow commented.

"Really?" Blackie laughed. "We had very little problem getting in."

"Who is we?" Emory demanded. "Who assisted you as you broke into a Consort institution to free a condemned criminal?"

"The group which entered Dredmore to rescue a free, yet unreleased inmate, consisted of myself, Beryl Blanchard, Salem Blanchard, Seth Blanchard, and Arielle Obreiggon."

Atheidrelle and Xander both looked to their youngest daughter who stood radiating with pride at the defiance she had struck and the adventure she'd had with her new family.

"We were all careful to search every cell while painstakingly ensuring no other prisoners were released or harmed as we looked for Nacaria. We found Nacaria in the care of my niece Cassandra Obreiggon. As I have stated before, I have the power to move unseen. I watched Cassandra inject her patient with medications to knock her out. This helped her to continue the illusion to administrators that the curse on Nacaria was still in effect. We captured Cassandra and left her locked in the room. We rescued Nacaria, and Salem Blanchard immediately alerted Queen Ursula as to what had taken place. The queen sent her men and they restrained Cassandra until bringing her here tonight."

"Does this conclude your testimony?" Brimford asked Blackie.

"It does."

Salem stood up and walked forward to the Council table. "I am ready to take vows now myself."

"Do you have new information to impart which we have not already heard?" Xander asked his daughter.

"No," Salem said. "I guess I don't. Blackie pretty much covered it, although I can corroborate her version of events."

Xander smiled. "That isn't necessary. Her version of events are about to corroborate themselves." He turned to his sister-in-law. "Demonstrate your powers Blackie."

Blackie approached the Council table. She looked Queen Ursula directly in the eyes and said, 'You do not see me.'"

Suddenly, Ursula could be seen looking around as if confused. The crowd gave a slight chuckle. Blackie then asked Ursula if she could hear her, to which the Queen answered yes while still glancing around to locate where Blackie's voice was coming from. Blackie did this to several council members as well as a few random, willing Consort volunteers, until she had proven beyond doubt—she had not lost her powers and no one was covering for her.

"Blackie D'Angelo continues to retain her magic," Xander announced. "Her vow has not been broken. The Council will regard her testimony as truth." He looked back at Salem and smiled. "See my dear, we really don't need your testimony." Returning his focus back toward his fellow councilmembers, Xander added, "I would, of course, like to hear from my eldest daughter, Cassandra."

Cassandra was unbound, ungagged, and presented to the Council table. She looked afraid. She looked humiliated. The pride she carried like armor—pride taught to her by her mother—was a broken shamble now. Looking into her father's deeply disappointed eyes, Cassandra realized she felt shame. It was not an emotion she had often felt, but she truly understood it now as her long-suffering father's eyes looked upon her.

"Cassandra," Xander began. "Take vows."

"No," Atheidrelle roared from the audience. "Our daughter does not have to answer to these people. She will not be lowered to such levels."

Xander faced his wife. "You do not have power here at the present. Tonight, I sit upon this Council. You have no say. Our daughter is guilty, and I want to hear from her."

"She is not guilty!" Atheidrelle shouted. "All we know is Blackie believes her to be guilty. Blackie's vow is unbroken, but that only stands as evidence that Blackie believes her own words. That isn't proof."

Xander knew what his wife was doing. She was leading the witness. Making a case, however flimsy, to argue Cassandra's innocence. Xander returned his focus to his daughter. "I want you to make vows."

"I don't have to make vows, Father."

"Please, Cassandra," Xander pleaded. "Do not follow your mother's directions anymore. Stand on your own and take responsibility. Take the vow."

"You don't understand, Father," Cassandra sighed sadly. "I don't have to take vows. I'll tell you what you want to know without them."

Xander nodded and gave her an encouraging smile. "You posed as a caretaker, and you infiltrated Dredmore Asylum, where you kept Nacaria Blanchard prisoner after her release, didn't you?"

"I didn't pose," Cassandra clarified, "I actually took a job at Dredmore as a caregiver. I am certified legally."

"They assigned you to Nacaria's case?"

"No, I arranged that myself."

"Why?" Xander asked.

"To keep her unconscious when she awoke."

"How did you know when she would awaken?"

Cassandra looked at her mother then back to her father. "My mother told me."

The members of the Consort burst forth into disarray as everyone gasped, or shouted pleas to force Atheidrelle to testify, or defended Atheidrelle's honor. Atheidrelle now looked frightened. Cassandra had not incriminated her; she'd only mentioned she'd known the date of Nacaria's release. However, it was not over, and Atheidrelle could not be sure exactly how much her daughter planned to reveal. Atheidrelle looked toward Salem and saw her glancing her way. She remembered the words Salem had spoken earlier; *I can't wait to watch you fear.*

Xander returned to questioning Cassandra. "Why did you hold Nacaria in that room after her curse was lifted?"

"All my life the name Nacaria Blanchard has hovered over my family. We have never known happiness. I thought her return would destroy what little bonds we have left."

Salem stood up from her seat and shouted, "Did Atheidrelle tell you to hold my mother prisoner?"

Cassandra turned around and saw the fiery face of Salem Blanchard demanding an answer. She looked to her anxious mother whom she loved and feared, then back to her father standing before her, begging her with his eyes to tell the truth. Cassandra Obreiggon had never felt close to him. Now she found herself wanting to. Yet to tell the truth would betray the only person she had ever been aligned with...her mother. As the crowds waited eagerly for her response, Cassandra closed her eyes and tried to center herself into a peace. It began to dawn upon her that she had always sided with her mother, but should families have sides? Why was her own family divided? All her life it seemed to be her and her mother ruling over or manipulating Arielle and her father. They had never been one whole. Opening her eyes and looking to her sister, she saw Arielle standing with Salem and Seth, waiting for her reply. A flicker of light sparked a moment in her little sister's eye and Cassandra noticed it. It was a tear.

"Tell the truth, Cassandra," Arielle pleaded.

"Cassandra?" Xander repeated. "Did your mother ask you to keep Nacaria locked up?'

"No," Cassandra answered. Atheidrelle's face showed momentary relief while Arielle's displayed disappointment. Yet, neither should have reacted quite so soon because Cassandra had not finished her statement. "No, she did ask me to keep Nacaria locked away. She *ordered* me to."

CHAPTER TWENTY TWO

The Verdict

The Blanchard family secluded themselves in an upstairs sitting room while waiting. So much had occurred in the last two hours. No one quite knew what to say to one another as the time ticked quietly off the hands of the clock on the mantlepiece. Cassandra and Atheidrelle had been taken into custody while the Council convened to discuss matters. The Consort members continued their mingling and revelry downstairs in the banquet rooms, sitting rooms, parlors, and ball room of the University Club. Everyone was abuzz with the newly revealed scandals and dramas between the Blanchard and Obreiggon families. Olympia had preferred to isolate her coven away from the gossip mongers and information seekers while awaiting the Council's return.

"What do you think will happen now?" Seth broke the silence and asked.

"Well, the Council's gotta lot to figure out," Zelda replied. "Cassandra never took any vows, and Atheidrelle refused to 'fore they took her out, so it's anybody's guess. I figure they'll still find 'em both guilty."

"Do you think they will bind Atheidrelle's powers?" Fable asked. "If so, that would break the curse and keep Yazzy safe."

"We will have to wait and see," Olympia declared.

Demitra pulled back the curtain from the sitting room window and looked down on the few witches congregating outside. "It's probably a safe bet no one cast a vote for Atheidrelle as queen on their way out of the meeting room."

"I'm in agreement with that," Artemis grinned. "I think she came here tonight believing she would leave queen, but I seriously doubt that will occur now. That at least is something, even if they do not find her guilty."

"They have to find her guilty!" Salem cried. "I've lost too much for her to walk away free."

Beryl sat down beside Arielle and held her hand. "This has to be hard on you. Your mother and your sister both charged with crimes. People talking about your family. Know we are here for you."

Arielle rested her head on Beryl's arm.

"We are your family now," Seth nodded. "You're a Blanchard. You are not alone. You never will be."

Artemis smiled at her nephew's thoughtfulness, remembering a time not too long ago when he had not been so welcoming to his little sister. She felt proud of him. She was about to say so when Nacaria spoke out.

"You're quite a man, Seth Blanchard. And quite a son."

"When this is all over," Forest said, "I think Arielle should come stay with us awhile in Mobile. It would do her good to get away. You, too, Salem?"

Arielle smiled at him and continued laying against the comfort of Beryl's arm. Pastoria winked at her sister and said with her mind, *I believe we know who it would do the most good if Arielle came to Mobile. I think my grandson is smitten.*

A knock came to the door. It was Blackie, announcing the Council was reconvening downstairs. The family marched down and took their seats. Atheidrelle was seated beside her daughter to the left of the Council table where two chairs had been placed. The two Obreiggon women wore arm shackles similar to what Cassandra had been wearing when she'd been presented to the Council. Nacaria instantly recognized the restraints as the same long-standing shackles used in the past by the Council—magically imbued to suppress a witch's powers when worn. She had worn a similar pair twenty years ago.

"We will dispense with formalities, for this Consort has drawn out long enough already," Ursula announced. "We the Council have deliberated and reached a conclusion on the charges brought forth tonight."

Jason'te Barstow carried on from there, "A great many revelations have come forth tonight, some proven, some speculation. Yet there seems to be little doubt that there is merit behind these claims. Many of these events took place many years ago, making it difficult to ascertain—"

"You ain't doin' a real good job of dispensing with formalities and speed'in this up," Zelda shouted from the audience. The Consort members laughed and a few even applauded.

"Right," Jason'te replied. "Will the two prisoners stand."

Atheidrelle, snarling at the crowd now staring at her as if she were a common criminal, rose to her feet as she glared at the Council before her. Cassandra rose herself—meekly, disgracefully—and stood with her head down.

Jason'te read from a notepad as he addressed the room. "Cassandra Obreiggon has been charged with willfully holding a fellow witch captive. She has been found unanimously guilty by this Council. She is hereby sentenced to 10 years in waking captivity strapped to a bed in Dredmore Asylum whereupon she will relive, day by day, the experiences she inflicted upon her victim."

Cassandra never raised her head. The shame befallen her kept her eyes glued to the parquet floor. Around her the gasps, moans, and whispers said it all. The Consort agreed with her verdict.

Jason'te turned toward Atheidrelle next, who glowered at him insolently. "Atheidrelle Obreiggon is charged as coconspirator in holding a fellow witch captive. She is also charged with bestowing a curse which triggered the deaths of three persons."

All voices fell silent through the room as the gravest of crimes was about to be decided. Salem clutched Seth's hand for support as the verdict was read.

"On the first charge of accomplice in the wrongful imprisonment of Nacaria Blanchard, the council finds Atheidrelle Obreiggon, guilty." Jason'te paused for the reactions of the witches in the room to die down. "On the second charge of complicity in the deaths of three others, the council has broken each death into three separate charges. On the first charge regarding the death of Susan Cantrell, the Council finds we have no authority to declare verdict, as this was a human and not under the jurisdiction of this Council."

Seth hung his head. Yasmine stroked his hair and gave him a slight kiss on the back of his hand. Salem gripped his other hand tightly, knowing that if Susan had been out of their jurisdiction, David probably was as well. She was correct. Jason'te went on to say that David's demise bore no repercussions from the witches' court, being he was not a witch. She did not give herself time to process this setback, as Jason'te moved on to baby Michael.

"On the third charge regarding the death of Michael Lane Blanchard, a witch, the Council finds Atheidrelle Obreiggon guilty."

Atheidrelle's stony face betrayed her as she was now reduced to panic. The slightest hint of teary eyes could be seen as she realized her hopes of being queen, as well as the life she was accustomed to living, was all over now.

Brimford Uding had to silence the room as the assembled witches cried out in support or contempt for the verdicts. Salem's heart lifted. Somehow it lifted a little. She had spent so many months with an indescribable weight suffocating her heart, and it was lifting. Her baby's death was avenged. Atheidrelle had not gotten away with it.

"Atheidrelle Obreiggon," Jason'te directed, "for the death of Michael Lane Blanchard and the imprisonment of Nacaria Blanchard, I sentence you to the same fate as the one you banished your enemy to twenty years ago. You will be taken from here and confined to Dredmore Asylum, where you will be stripped of your soul and rendered lifeless until some unknown future date when your spirit and your body may be reunited. I direct your soul be imprisoned in the walls of Oleander where you watch the world you presided over continue forth without your influence."

Atheidrelle made no effort to protest. She simply stared at her husband, perhaps hoping for a modicum of sympathy in his eyes. She never discovered any because his eyes were solely focused upon Nacaria Blanchard and her children.

The queen's guards rose to remove Cassandra and Atheidrelle from the room and take them into custody, however before they could, a request rang out from the audience. Nacaria was standing with her hand raised for permission to address the Council again.

"Yes, Miss Blanchard," Queen Ursula granted.

"Before you take the prisoners away, I would like to ask the Council to forgive the crime perpetrated upon me by Cassandra Obreiggon."

"Whatever for?" Brimford gasped. "Do you not feel she should pay for what she has done?"

"I think she already has," Nacaria replied. "The real blame here lies with a vindictive and manipulative mother. Atheidrelle raised her daughter to hate—to hate me and my family. And Cassandra was raised in fear—fear of her mother's wrath. To live so dominated could not have been easy. I truly feel her honesty tonight reflects a sorrowful heart. I forgive Cassandra. I ask the Council's leniency for her sentence."

Xander bowed his head to the woman he still loved. That gracious beautiful creature who still had the same warm, generous heart he had remembered. Jason'te Barstow looked to Ursula in confusion. Unsure what to do exactly.

Ursula spoke out. "As my final duty as queen, I absolve Cassandra Obreiggon of her punishment. If her victim can be so forgiving, this Council shall be as well. Oh, I also need to announce that the results are in and our new Consort leader is—"

"Wait!" Xander shouted. "Queen Ursula, before you hand over your throne to whomever's name you are about to announce, I would like to make a request of you as well."

"Go ahead, Xander," she replied.

"I would like to resign my post on the Witches Council."

More gasps and whispers ensued.

"Xander, do you know what you're saying?" Ursula cried. "You've served on this Council since your father died. My own father appointed you himself to take your father's place. Are you certain you wish to resign your seat?"

"Absolutely," Xander said. "I do not deserve to oversee this association of witches. Because of my actions twenty-eight years ago, all of this has come to pass. I married the girl my father told me to marry. Then, when I met the girl I loved, I made a mess of things. I would like my seat to be awarded to my daughter, Salem Blanchard. As in accordance with our rules of governance, a retiring Council member has the right to propose his or her replacement for consideration by the ruling king or queen. I ask for that consideration now, Queen Ursula. I would like my daughter to sit in this chair which has housed an Obreiggon Council member for more than 200 years."

No one said a word. Pure silence filled the air. Salem could not believe what she was hearing. She watched her father move away from his chair and take a seat in the front row with the rest of the general Consort. Atheidrelle, still standing bound and shackled, watched her husband vacate the seat of power she herself had wielded for years. She had lost every vestige of dignity tonight.

Ursula—still shaken by the shocking development—took a breath, regained her composure, and addressed the room. "I, Queen Ursula, grant your request. The seat of Xander Obreiggon now belongs to Miss Salem Blanchard. All welcome our newest Council member!"

The room was cheering for the most part, but none of the Blanchards could tell who was on the side of the ruling because the entirety of the family was howling and clapping in celebration. One of their own now had a seat on the Council of Witches. There had not been a Blanchard on the Council since Olympia's father.

"Oh!" Ursula laughed, calling the meeting back to attention. "Let's wrap this thing up and go home. Your new king is Geoffrey London! King Geoffrey will begin his reign at midnight tonight and will head this Council at the Spring Consort meeting in March. I ask you all to go home now as we adjourn this meeting of the Winter Consort."

Salem stood flabbergasted at what all had transpired over the course of the evening. It was all too much to comprehend. She watched as the guards dragged Atheidrelle away. She watched as Cassandra was unshackled and set free only to disappear as quickly as she could away from the crowds who had seen her downfall. Salem stared at the vacant seat which her father just awarded her. The prestige of a Council seat—the respect and responsibility that accompanied it—it was hers now. But most of all, she thought of her son. Baby Michael. His killer was now going to pay. This chapter in her life could close.

CHAPTER TWENTY THREE

After the Storm

The days following the Consort meeting found the Blanchard family adjusting to the aftermath. There were some members of the Witches Association who did not support Salem being awarded her father's seat at the Council table, and those people were very vocal to everyone but the Blanchard family. Zelda kept Olympia informed who they were and what they had been saying. Olympia paid it little heed. They were typically the same people who squawked every time a Council seat came up for appointment and did not believe Council seats should pass through generations of the same family. Olympia shared this belief, which was why she never asked for her father's seat on the Council after his death. However, in Xander's case, the Obreiggon chair had always been the Obreiggon chair, and it warmed Olympia's heart that Salem was being recognized as the next Obreiggon in line.

Yasmine spent the last days after the meeting trying to find a way to tell Seth she was pregnant—once she had confirmed it at the hospital with one of Beryl's OBGYN friends. There never seemed to be the proper time. Too many people were always around. Finally, at breakfast three days later, she blurted out, "Pass me the pancakes please, Fable. And by the way, Seth... I'm pregnant." Seth was overjoyed and scared to death at the same time. After he stopped choking on the bite of pancake he'd just swallowed, he swept his wife up in his arms and professed his joy.

Fable's pregnancy was proving to be a bit more worrisome for Beryl. Beryl could not risk bringing Fable in for an appointment for fear of what an ultrasound might show. Everyday Fable's baby bump grew making it very difficult to hide from the family. Thankfully the cool weather provided a shield with heavy sweaters and oversized coats. Fable no longer feared Beryl pushing her into an abortion. She looked too far along now for any clinic to agree to such a procedure. For the time being, it was a secret only Fable and her sister shared.

Nacaria was adjusting to homelife again after so long an absence. Christmas was only days away, and she desperately wanted to buy presents for her family. Salem took time off from work for the holidays so she could be in Daihmler with the family and decided she would take her mother shopping.

"Please, Salem, let me drive," Nacaria urged.

"No Momma," Salem repeated as they climbed into her SUV.

"But it has been so long since I've driven," Nacaria persisted.

"That is exactly my point," Salem said. "A lot has changed. You're going to have to relearn all kinds of things."

Nacaria was baffled. "What could possibly have changed that much? Have they stopped using gas? And Salem this car is enormous! What is this?"

"See?!" Salem exclaimed. "This is an SUV. And yes, cars still run on gas, but some now run on battery. In fact, Hecate is constantly on my case for driving this thing. She said she'll buy us all new cars if we switch to Teslas."

"What's a Tesla?"

"A kind of car that runs on battery power."

"Besides that, what else could be different?"

"Lots of things since your time, Momma," Salem said starting down the winding drive leaving Blanchard House. "Air bags, mandatory seatbelt laws, GPS..."

"Air bags!" Nacaria gasped. "What's wrong with regular air? Oh, is it because the exhaust fumes are so bad now we have to breathe air from bags?"

Salem shook her head. "No. Air bags pop out if you are in an accident."

"Like if an airplane crashes?"

"Sort of, but you don't breathe the air. It is an inflated bag that pops out to keep you safe in a crash," Salem explained.

Nacaria reached down and turned on the radio. Music began playing through the speakers, but she did not care for it. She reached down to change the channel.

"No Momma; it's on my Bluetooth."

Nacaria stared at her, "I didn't say anything about your teeth. And your teeth aren't discolored."

Salem rolled her eyes and gave an exasperated laugh. She then gave her mother a tutorial on how the music industry, like the automotive industry, has made many changes since her day. Nacaria had a great deal to learn if she was going to exist in the new world.

As they drove through town, Nacaria noticed the many changes in Daihmler since her incarceration on the wall. Stores she had never heard of had sprouted up everywhere. Shopping centers seemed to be prolific now. It was hard to fathom. Her memory of old Daihmler was nothing like new Daihmler was. Her hometown was almost unrecognizable.

"I can't believe the number of shops and restaurants," Nacaria said admiringly. "When I was young, none of this was here. Daihmler did not have much commerce. If we wanted anything, we had to drive into Tuscaloosa."

"As I said, a lot has changed," Salem nodded. "Daihmler is a pretty good town. Still not as large as Tuscaloosa, but we don't have the university to grow our community."

"Are we going to a mall?"

"Malls aren't really much of a thing anymore," Salem explained. "There are still a few, but typically none of them have any stores anyone ever wants to shop in. Most popular stores are free standing."

"That's how it was when I was little," Nacaria reflected. "Malls were made to make shopping easier. Put it all in one place. Seems like everything just went back to the hard way."

"I guess you have a point," Salem smiled. "I haven't thought about that before. In Atlanta we have a couple of great malls. Larger cities still have strong mall business, but in regular communities we just go to the store we need."

"Well, can we go to Google? I heard Beryl saying she can find anything there."

"Where?"

"Google," Nacaria repeated. "Strange name for a store but in my day, we had Pier One and Chess King, so I guess it's not that odd."

"No Momma," Salem giggled. "Google is not a store or a place, it's—well, I don't really know how to explain. I'll just have to show you." Salem withdrew her phone from her purse and started the search engine. She looked up everything from high heel shoes to last year's Oscar winners.

"It like a pocket library!" Nacaria exclaimed.

"Exactly," Salem said. "Now for shopping I usually go to Amazon."

"Is that a store for large women?" Nacaria asked. "You're very petite."

Salem laughed. "No, Mama, look." She flipped to her Amazon app.

"Salem, what is all this? A TV screen! Look at that! Things for sale with prices and everything. Is this so you know what it costs before you pull up to the store?"

"Momma, we have a lot to teach you today."

Salem spent a pleasurable day with her mother. They shopped, they talked; Salem taught and Nacaria learned. But mostly they just enjoyed each other, mother and daughter—something they had not had the privilege of doing since Salem was a small child.

Shopping was cut a little short when Salem received a text from Beryl saying the family needed to have a meeting. The message filled Salem with dread as they'd all just put an ugly part of the past behind them and were in high hopes of having a stress-free Christmas.

"Did she say what it was about on that text...app, is it?" Nacaria asked as they were leaving the shopping center.

"Close," Salem said. "Apps are on phones, but text messaging isn't considered an app. It is just like having a call, but you're typing it. And no, she didn't say."

"Do you think Atheidrelle has escaped?"

"I think she'd have just called us if that were the case," Salem replied. "Speaking of Atheidrelle, I know none of us have wanted to talk about the Obreiggons or anything reminding us of the Consort night. But you know, now that I am a Council member, I am in the loop with the goings on of things. I checked my email this morning—"

"Those are the letters that come over the internet?" Nacaria clarified.

"Right," Salem said. "I was sent an email two days ago telling me that Atheidrelle's punishment had been carried out. Her body is now in a coma at Dredmore, the way you were. Her spirit, I presume, is confined to the walls of Oleander now."

Nacaria's eyes drifted toward the window, but she didn't seem to be looking at anything in particular. She took a big breath in as those same eyes got heavier and unfocused. Salem finally broke the silence and asked, "Are you all right?"

Her mother gave an almost imperceptible nod. "Just remembering," Nacaria said softly. "It hurts when they do it. It feels like a hand has grabbed a piece of you inside your chest and snatched it out. You feel the burn from your fingertips and toes at first. And your head. Then it moves through the limbs and comes tearing out of your belly. For a moment you see your body laying there, then you're sort of flung out into the universe at a dizzying speed—like the fastest, most nauseating roller coaster ride. Over land, water, trees...moving in seconds over such space until suddenly you just stop. Then I was there. On the wall..."

Salem had never even thought about how it happened or what that must have felt like.

"I could hear all of you," Nacaria continued as her eyes filled with tears. Her voice began to break in sections as she continued. "I could see all of you. And in those first weeks when you would look at me with fear and confusion...that alone could have killed me. Seeing my mother unable to turn a corner without bursting into tears because my shadow was there, seeing my children hide from me. Seeing my sisters avoid whatever room I may be in, because it was too painful for them—all the while my pain was excruciating. You all had each other. I had no one."

"I'm sorry, Mother."

"It is a miserable condition," Nacaria remembered. "I would say I wouldn't wish it on my worst enemy, but I am very glad my worst enemy is currently experiencing it."

They didn't say anything for a few moments as Nacaria wiped her eyes and used the visor mirror to remove the mascara smudges. Salem had more questions but decided to change the subject.

"Have you spoken to Xander?" Salem asked.

"I have been wanting to ask you the same question."

"No, I haven't," Salem admitted. "Arielle is at Oleander now with him. I don't know whether she'll be here for Christmas or not. She might stay with him considering all that has happened. Do you think you will try to see him at some point?"

"I would like to," Nacaria admitted. "Even speaking of him makes me feel so many things."

"Good things?"

"Yes... and bad things. Regret, loss, hope, but mostly the feeling of being completely unsure."

"Unsure about?"

"Everything," Nacaria explained. Her face grew solemn as she turned her head to look out the car window. "Is our love still real? Is there a chance for us? If so, then why hasn't he come to me? Why haven't I gone to him? Is it too soon? Is it too late? So, I sit and wait for something to happen. Or not to happen. It isn't my place to try and forge a future, and yet everything about his life involves my every thought."

Salem patted Nacaria's hand and asked no more questions. It was hard for her to fully comprehend what must be going through her mother's mind. It was all so complicated. She felt pity for her. As they pulled into the driveway at Blanchard House, the two women left their shopping bags in the trunk as they saw Demitra standing on the porch waiting for their arrival.

"I sensed you two were near, so I thought I'd wait out here for you," Demitra said as they were getting out of the SUV. "Beryl won't tell us anything until everyone is here. We've been waiting for you."

Demitra, Nacaria, and Salem took a seat at the dining room table where Olympia, Artemis, Beryl, Fable, Seth, and Yasmine were already gathered. Everyone looked confused and a little unsettled. Nacaria and Salem hadn't even stopped to take off their coats, but neither had Yasmine or Fable.

"I see we aren't the only ones who rushed back home," Salem said, removing her jacket.

Beryl began to address the family. "We've been through a lot the last few days—hell the last year. But we still have a little more to go through. Fable needs to tell you something. I need for you to hear her without attacking her. Then we will discuss this as a family."

Fable stood from the table and removed her coat. It required no words to explain why the Blanchards had been assembled for the family meeting. Her small, round stomach said it all. A collective gasp circled the dining table. Suddenly Yasmine's surprised face turned into a huge smile.

"Oh my God! You're pregnant, too! We are going to have babies together!"

Demitra shook her head. "I don't believe this. Look at you, Fable. How long have you been hiding this?"

"Just a couple months."

"Two months!" Artemis exclaimed. "Surely you suspected something, Fable. Look at you! You're at least five months along."

Beryl and Fable exchanged glances. "That's the thing," Beryl said. "She isn't. She is roughly two months along."

Seth guffawed and elbowed his cousin, "Dang, girl, you've had serious cravings then, haven't you?"

Fable did not laugh. In fact, she was beginning to tire of this banter back and forth. She wanted to cut to the chase and have it out so the conversation could end. "I am pregnant by Patric."

All mouths fell silent and hung open. Artemis and Demitra exchanged alarmed glances. Olympia took a few deep breaths without drawing attention to herself. She needed to remain calm. Yasmine's eyes enlarged as she realized the gravity of what Fable revealed. But also, its silver lining—her brother's child.

"Patric?" Demitra asked slowly, quietly, as if disbelieving the words. "Patric who tried to kill all of us? Patric, werewolf Patric?"

"Yes."

Artemis turned to Beryl, "Can we abort?"

"I am not having an abortion!" Fable cried.

"Yes, you are," Demitra demanded. "This child is a monster."

Beryl intervened on her sister's behalf. She understood everyone's concern, in fact she shared it. But with her sister on the hot seat, the recipient of everyone's scorn and judgment, her loyalty kicked in and she had to defend her sister. "It's too late for a legal abortion. She is only two months along, but as you can see the baby is growing rapidly. No clinic would do it. And before anyone asks me, I will not do it. I save lives, I do not abort them."

"This thing's father tried to kill Yasmine!" Seth shouted.

"Patric did not try to kill me," Yasmine corrected. "Patric wasn't even his name. His name was Ollie, and he was my brother. He did not try to kill me; he just wanted me to go away with him."

"Whatever," Seth scoffed. "This freakazoid baby has to be killed."

Fable turned on Seth, "Nobody is hurting this baby! You try, I'll kill you. This child is my child. I don't care who the father is."

"It's a werewolf, Fable!" Demitra shouted.

"Hold on everybody," Salem said calmly. "Yelling at Fable isn't going to solve anything. And I agree we are not going to abort this baby. Having lost a baby myself, I cannot support ripping Fable's child from her."

"This isn't a child," Seth countered. "It is a werewolf."

"It is my nephew or niece!" Yasmine shouted at her husband. "No matter what else it might be, it's my family."

Olympia listened to enough squabbling among her children and decided it was time to give her word on the matter—the last word. "Fable will not terminate the pregnancy. I confess I do not know if having this baby is a mistake or not. I have never heard of werewolfism by heredity. Then again, I have never known of a werewolf procreating. This is a first, even for me. What I do know is that this child is also a Blanchard."

"Mother, what if this child is a werewolf like his father?" Artemis asked.

"Then we will destroy it as we did his father," Olympia declared. "But we will wait and evaluate once it is here."

"Hecate," Fable said. "Even if it is like Patric was, I don't think I can kill it."

"You won't have to, dear," Olympia informed. "I will." Her heart fluttered once more. "This family will not introduce a monster into the world. If it turns out to be one, we *will* destroy it. But there is every bit of chance it will be a perfectly harmless infant."

"Growing at that rate?" Demitra noted.

"Lest we not forget, daughter," Olympia smiled, "Fable's child is also a witch. Perhaps this rapid growth stems from its powers and not its paternity. We will have to simply wait and see."

CHAPTER TWENTY FOUR

It's Beginning to Look a Lot Like Witchmas

Demitra was wearing the floors thin traipsing back and forth from the dining table to the living room, placing all the presents she had finished wrapping under the tree. Her yearly efforts to balance the bottom of the tree with just the exact amount of height and depth while also spreading the different wrapping paper selections evenly were a thing of legend among the family. It was the family's running joke at how obsessed she was with planning the perfect present presentation. And you could always tell when a gift was from Demitra by the way she never broke the paper's pattern when she taped the two ends. No one ever needed a gift tag to spot a Demitra Blanchard present.

"Whenever you are finished with this exercise in anal retentiveness, Clara Cummings is coming by to pick up a potion I made her. I left it on the counter if she comes," Artemis told her sister as she grabbed her purse to rush out to work. "Ya'll have a good day!"

"Clara Cummings is a freak," Fable laughed from the couch where she was sipping hot chocolate while watching her mother's frenzy. "She is the only woman in town with three separate nativity scenes in her yard, and one of them is made up of *Peanuts* characters."

"She added a *Simpson's* one this year," Demitra remarked.

Fable laughed. "I remember when she had to replace the Linus Joseph last year because she put in too strong a bulb and half his head melted off." Fable began to giggle at the ridiculous thought until suddenly she did not feel very well. She doubled over clutching her stomach. Demitra rushed to her side, but Fable was already straightening up, the pain subsiding.

"I'm fine," she said. "Just a bad cramp."

"You are not fine, Fable. Your face is dead white."

"I'm fine, really Mother. The baby kicked, that's all."

"Babies do not kick like that! And they really don't kick like that at two months."

"Drop it. I'm fine," Fable asserted. "Besides, I'd rather talk about when you and Daddy are getting married."

"Hush!" Demitra scolded, looking around. "This house is never empty."

"Relax," Fable replied. "Seth and Yasmine are at a doctor's appointment. Salem took Nacaria practice driving on Butterfly Road because nothing is out there anymore; then they had an appointment with Howard. Hecate is off with Zelda visiting a sick friend, and Beryl is at work. It's only us."

Demitra softened. She excitedly grabbed her daughter's hand and snuggled in beside her on the couch. "Tomorrow, at the family Christmas dinner, we are announcing it. We are going to get married on New Year's Eve!"

Fable gave her mother a big hug and exclaimed, "I am so happy! Oh, Mother, it's fantastic! I can hardly believe we are going to start the brand-new year with Daddy back!"

...

Across town at Howard Caldwell's office, Salem and Nacaria were right on time for their appointment with the family solicitor. Nacaria had not laid eyes on Howard since her return even though they'd once been good friends. She excitedly rushed into his arms the moment he met her at the door.

"Nacaria Blanchard—I just don't believe it!" he bellowed. "You look exactly the same."

"Well, not exactly," she smiled. "But I'll take the compliment."

He showed them inside to his office and made them comfortable. He had many papers for Nacaria to sign—many legalities to get out of the way. She did not understand why it was so important or as urgent as he had made it sound to Salem, but she signed where he told her to and trusted he knew better than she.

"Sorry to make you come in here two days before Christmas," he apologized. "But you've been away a long time, and for Nacaria Blanchard to suddenly reappear after all these years requires a paper trail of explanations."

"I suppose so," Salem observed. "I hadn't really thought about it."

"You don't have to," Howard grinned. "That's what your grandmother pays me the big bucks for." Howard reached into his desk and withdrew a bank book and a few more papers for Nacaria to sign. "Sign these where I have marked. This is your new bank account."

"Bank account?" Nacaria asked.

"Yes," Howard explained. "You inherited monies when you reached adulthood that your father left you when he died."

"Yes, I know," Nacaria said. "I lived on that before my curse."

"Coma," Howard corrected. "Please try to use the word *coma*, not *curse*. You spent a few years in a coma in a hospital out of state. When you came out of the coma, you were sent to a facility in Europe where you underwent extensive physical rehabilitation. Once you recovered you chose to remain in Europe until just recently. That is the cover story for outsiders. I have papers to back it all up. Learn your new history. We cannot tell people you were cursed to a witches' prison for two decades."

"I'll make sure she has the story straight," Salem said. "Now go back to her money. What were you saying?"

"Yes, this new account. When Nacaria went away, I closed her bank accounts and took over her finances. I made some investments here and there, and her money has grown exponentially over the years. I still have the vast majority in funds which she is free to draw from when needed. But for general living expenses I opened this checking account for her. There is $10,000 in there now and I will deposit another $5000 every month. If you need more, just let Yasmine or myself know and I'll increase your monthly allowance."

"Wow?" Nacaria smiled. "Am I rich?"

"To you, based on what life was like when you left, yes. To the rest of us, no. You are merely comfortable. But you'll never have to work or want for anything within reason." Howard explained.

"I have a question?" Nacaria asked.

"Shoot."

"Are you and my sister still an item?"

Howard choked on the sip of coffee he was drinking. "Uh, no. Artemis and I ended things long ago."

"I hate that," Nacaria frowned. "I would have liked you for a brother-in-law."

. . .

Far away, in the marshlands of Charleston, amid the dangling Spanish moss from trees older than the city itself, lay the Obreiggon plantation. *Oleander* stood three stories tall like a white monument nestled beneath the canopy of oaks and pines. Inside the house, a bleak interior diminished the beauty of outside. Arielle was doing her best to elevate the moodiness of the house high on a ladder removing some of the more disconcerting gothic artwork from the darkly painted walls.

"What are you doing, Miss Obreiggon?" snarled Mrs. Chatswick, the pinched housekeeper. Her sullen face grimacing at the clutter of paintings now scattered across the floor of the drawing room.

"I am removing these morbid pictures."

"The mistress cherished these art pieces," reminded Mrs. Chatswick. "They were gifts from her father when she married the master and came to Oleander."

"Well, they are depressing. I've always hated them," Arielle replied.

"I do not believe it is appropriate to be dismantling the mistress' parlor. She will not be happy."

Arielle whirled around to face the housekeeper. "The mistress is not here anymore. I am the mistress of Oleander now, and I say these paintings are gone. My father has lived in this suffocating environment too long. It's time to let some light in here."

"I take that to mean you are the person who has been opening all of the draperies?" Mrs. Chatwick sneered. "Your mother didn't like sunlight to enter the house. It fades the tapestries."

"Yeah, well those tapestries are coming down next!" Arielle yelled as she moved the ladder over to the next painting.

The housekeeper left the room as Xander entered. He surveyed the mess on the floor and the bare walls around and rubbed his chin.

"You do know you're a telekinetic, don't you? You could simply bring all these things down with a wave of your hands."

"I find it more satisfying to do it manually," Arielle smiled. "Every painting I toss to the floor is a victory."

"I never did like this room," Xander said. "Or any of the rooms here. Your mother wanted it to look like what she grew up in."

"The House of Duquesne," Arielle shuddered. "I hate that place. I think it's evil."

"The D'Angelos seem to like it," Xander commented. "Ever since Old Emmerick D'Angelo inherited it from his grandfather, your mother acted like it was the center of the universe. I still remember the argument we had when I refused to live there. One of the only arguments I think I ever won with her."

"I think you only won because it's just three miles away. She still goes there all the time to see her brother. Or, used to I guess I should say now. Speaking of Uncle Thaddeus, I'm surprised he hasn't had anything to say about what happened to Mother."

"He has been frighteningly silent," Xander agreed. "Though I am sure we will hear from him at some point in time."

A shadow flickered across the wall, paused at the empty spaces where painting had been, then dashed in circles around the drawing room before darting off through the doors. Arielle giggled. Xander himself, chuckled in minor triumph.

"She doesn't like what you've done to her favorite room."

"Good," Arielle said.

"I'm thinking of having a tree cut and brought in tonight," Xander said. "We've never had one before. Would you like a Christmas tree, my dear?"

Arielle's face lost a little of its joy. "I'm going back to Daihmler tonight, Daddy. I planned to spend Christmas at Blanchard House. But I'll cancel my flight if—"

"No, no," Xander replied. "Don't rearrange your plans."

"It's just that we've never celebrated Christmas here, so I naturally assumed..."

"I understand," Xander said. "You should go. Go be with your brother and sister. Be part of a happy family Christmas."

"I don't know how happy it'll be, being Salem's first Christmas without her husband and little boy. But I think my being there will help," She paused a moment and added, "You know, you could always go with me. Nacaria will be there."

Xander shook his head. "No, no. Bad idea. I don't think a reunion right now is wise."

Arielle took a seat on the eggplant-colored settee and patted the cushion beside her. Her father sat down. "Daddy, don't you want to see her?"

"I do," he admitted. "But, at an appropriate time. Nacaria only recently returned. She needs time to reacquaint herself with her family. My presence would only complicate matters. In time, I am sure we will run into one another. Besides, there's your sister to consider."

"Salem?"

"Cassandra," Xander said. "I cannot leave her here alone, not now."

"I don't see why she should factor into any decision."

Xander frowned. "She is still your sister, Arielle. And my daughter—my first born. She is fragile right now. The weight of her crimes and the shame she has endured from our community has been overwhelming. She is not doing well. I feel she might need me near."

"She's never needed you for anything. Mother was her only focus."

"Your mother groomed her to be that way," Xander explained. "I believe as time passes, we will find a new Cassandra—perhaps we might even grow to like her."

Arielle shrugged. "Whatever happens," she said, "when I return to Oleander, I'd like to see this whole place redone and all Mother's macabre belongings out of here."

Xander left his daughter to her work to return downstairs. Along his way, his eyes finally adjusted, after too many years, to see the morbid décor of his ancestral family home. Dark panels, heavy stone and iron. Tapestries woven in only the darkest of threads depicting only the darkest of scenes. The heaviness of this house had been pressing him down for far too many years. He had stopped noticing its effect. It had just been part of his life. Yet now with Arielle home, scrubbing the first coats of darkness from the house, Xander Obreiggon remembered back before his marriage, when his family home had been light and bright and alive. It seemed so long ago now.

Entering the drawing room off the entry hall, he remembered when glorious thick vases, overflowing with flowers of the most vivid colors, had crowned every side table. Sunlight once shone through those windows where now the slats of the tall plantation shutters had almost grown shut. Arielle was right; this house must come back to life again now that its dark mistress was gone.

But she wasn't gone. She was there. Her wicked shadow fluttered by, barely noticeable against the garnet-colored wall. But Xander knew she was there.

"I will restore this place to its original splendor, Atheidrelle. And you will witness Oleander shed its morose cloud and come to life once more."

Atheidrelle's shadow stopped in place, looming high on the wall as if trying to intimidate one more time. Xander found himself shaking his head and laughing at it. A freeness swept him. Chains were gone from his neck. A bravado he did not possess when his wife held physical form now filled him. He regretted the years he refused to stand up to her. Yet he also understood why. Atheidrelle D'Angelo exuded power. It had almost reverberated from her. He never understood where so much power came from, but he knew it was there, and he never wanted to challenge that force inside her. Now he didn't care. Rendered powerless by the Council, Xander could say and do whatever he liked without repercussion.

"I did not always hate you, Atheidrelle," he told the thing on the wall. "I never loved you, but I did not hate you at the beginning. You built that emotion within me. Years I spent watching you and your brother run roughshod over people. Using them to your advantage and tossing them aside after they no longer proved useful, with no loyalty or gratitude for what they'd done for you. You destroyed the life of the woman I loved without a moment's guilt. Without the slightest compassion for two innocent children who were guilty of nothing."

Slowly Atheidrelle's shadow inched closer.

"You withheld affection from Arielle simply because she was nothing like you. And you molded Cassandra into another minion for you to control. You have left a wake of damage for me to repair. But I am repairing it, Atheidrelle. I am pulling out the good person inside our daughter day by day. Cassandra is shedding you from her heart and finding her soul again. You will watch all of this from these walls, and I hope it is unbearable."

CHAPTER TWENTY FIVE

'Twas the Night...

Christmas Eve. It had come to Blanchard House in full force despite the drama and chaos which had plagued them all over the last several months. Things were peaceful now. The Blanchards knew all too well that peace usually lasts a moment before being trampled by a newer chaos, so they savored this tranquility all the more.

The fire in the hearth was glowing. The heat rising from it made the stockings on the mantle sway. Olympia smiled at how many there were these days. Later, before bed, as the fire was burning low, every member of the family would sneak down and place a small present in each one for every family member. That was the tradition, one gift from each member of the family. Of course, tradition had grown over the years and now presents also spilled out from under the tree in an obscene amount.

Demitra, being a mother, always bought several things for her girls, and this year she would have Jerry as well. Artemis always took charge of Seth, Salem and Yasmine's presents. Olympia went overboard on everyone, especially Howard because the Blanchards were the only family he had left. This year Arielle would be among them, and Olympia had a little surprise news for her.

Olympia sat in her chair by the fire awaiting the call for dinner, listening to the children all upstairs talking loudly amongst one another. She liked it best when her house was full of laughter and voices. She liked to think Blanchard House liked having so much family within its walls. She hoped it would always be bursting at the seams with Blanchards, even long after she left the earth.

The house was finally settling down after a busy afternoon receiving guests. Blanchard House was known for its hospitality on Christmas Eve as several community friends and neighbors had come over the course of the day to bring presents for Olympia or her daughters in thanks for whatever help they'd provided them in spells, potions, talisman, or simply sound advice through the year. Artemis always made sure to have many jars of jellies, jams, peanut brittle, pies, cakes, and cookies on hand to offer them as they departed.

Around the dinner table, clusters of different conversations kept the entire table bustling amid the sounds of forks and knives, iced glasses, and clanking spoons delving second helpings ringing out. Nacaria sat silently eating her dinner watching the bustle of life happening around her. Jerry and Howard were discussing the politics of a new federal reserve ruling. Artemis was telling Demitra about the Cobblestone staff Christmas party. Fable, Yasmine, and Beryl were discussing the science behind prenatal vitamins. Everyone was happy. Everyone full of life. She wondered why she felt a pang of sadness. It was her first Christmas in such a long time. She should have felt on top of the world, but somehow, she felt swallowed up by it.

She felt a soft hand reach over to her own, her mother's wise hand. Olympia always knew everything. "It must be difficult to rejoin the world," Olympia said reassuringly with that all-knowing mother's smile. "In no time at all, you'll be chattering away about your life and the things you've heard or seen yourself."

"I know," Nacaria replied. "I'm fine. Just figuring out...I don't really know what I'm figuring out, actually."

"You're figuring out where your place is," Olympia comforted. "This family has been moving along at a breakneck pace for years. You are simply trying to find the best place to jump in to start running with them. You'll settle in soon."

Nacaria nodded and went back to her dinner while Olympia returned her attention to waiting for Arielle to finish a conversation with Seth about the goings on at Oleander before she called the girl's attention.

"I had a call this morning from Pastoria," Olympia called out to the table. "Arielle, you might be particularly interested. It seems my sister has decided to drive up tomorrow morning from Mobile to spend Christmas Day with us. Of course, she is too old to make the drive alone, so her grandson agreed to escort her. Pleaded might be the better word."

Arielle's attention was piqued. "Forest?"

Olympia laughed, "Yes, child. Your handsome young admirer was only too happy to drive his grandmother."

"Well, isn't he gallant?" Demitra grinned.

Arielle blushed and continued eating her roast beef. "It'll be nice to see him again. But it doesn't concern me one way or the other."

"Liar!" Fable badgered. "You know you are seriously crushing on our cousin!"

"Yeah, I don't know if your heart can take both the thrill of Santa Claus and Forest Blanchard in one day," Yasmine smiled.

"You guys lay off my little sister," Seth defended. "I haven't decided yet if I think it's a good idea for Arielle to get involved with Forest. We don't know enough about him. We haven't seen him in years except that one Consort night."

"Look who's getting all big brothery all of the sudden!" Salem teased.

"Well, Arielle is too young to get serious with anyone," Seth said. "She's only just gotten out from under her mother's thumb. Let her live a little."

Artemis sipped her wine and interjected, "I am quite certain Arielle can attend to her own affairs without any commentary or interference."

"Thank you," Arielle nodded with a smile. She then added, "Fable can I borrow that green dress in your closet tomorrow?"

"That slutty one with the low neck?!" Seth shouted. "Oh, hell no! You'll wear something else."

Olympia winked at Arielle and whispered, "You wanted to be a Blanchard. This is what you get when you are."

Arielle confessed with a grin, "I love every minute of it."

Howard wasn't saying very much, too busy refilling his plate with potatoes and gravy until a sudden smack on his hand made him put the spoon back into the bowl. "What gives?" he exclaimed to Artemis.

"Your cholesterol. Nothing on your plate but starches."

"Beryl can fix my arteries," he said. "I want more of this gravy!"

"You can't take the lazy way with your health, Howard. You are in your fifties!" Artemis scolded.

"Good thing we never got married," he teased. "I'd starve to death."

"Broccoli first, then you can have more potatoes."

"I hate broccoli," Howard scowled. "Jerry, does Demitra treat you like this?"

Jerry looked up from his plate and grinned, "Mine is cauliflower. Awful stuff."

"My Dad hated cauliflower, too!" Beryl smiled looking across the table. "That's funny."

"Well, if you get married, I guess she's already used to keeping cauliflower off the table," Howard remarked.

Beryl choked on the sip of tea she had just taken. "I think it's a little soon to be talking marriage."

Demitra gave Jerry a sidelong look, which then was expanded to Fable. The three of them looked nervous and for the briefest of moments. Demitra almost backed out from saying her next sentence, but she roused her bravery and went for it.

"Not necessarily, Beryl. As a matter of fact..." Demitra's dramatic pause met with ceasefire to the sounds of knives and forks against the plates all around. "Jerry and I have decided we are going to be married."

Artemis looked puzzled and felt apprehensive. Her instinct was to protest—to ask questions. What was the rush? But she knew her sister and her sister's quick temper when challenged. Artemis allowed herself three silent seconds to swallow her sisterly skepticism and hide her dismay for the sake of Christmas and not disrupting a pleasant family meal. "Congratulations, I suppose," she said, but was unable to resist adding, "Although Beryl's right. It is a little soon, isn't it?"

"Even sooner than you think," Demitra replied. "We are getting married on New Year's Eve."

"What?!" Beryl exclaimed.

Fable quickly overruled her sister's surprise with her own expression of excitement. "I am so happy for you guys!" She hopped up from her seat and kissed her mother's cheek, then walked over to Jerry. "You make my mother happy, Jerry. So, you have my absolute blessing!"

Beryl didn't know what to make of her sister's sudden exhilaration. Of all people on Earth, how was Fable Blanchard not hitting the ceiling over this? Beryl had always been the bigger person when it came to her and her sister. When did Fable become so reasonable? But if Fable appeared to be okay with this situation, Beryl figured she should at least pretend to be—if for no other reason than to maintain her reputation as the calm daughter. Suppressing her own misgivings, Beryl congratulated the happy couple. Everyone else followed suit; although Olympia and Artemis exchange worried glances.

"So where are you two planning to do it?" Yasmine asked.

"The courthouse will be open until noon," Demitra said. "We just want it simple. It's a second marriage for us both."

Jerry flashed a grin her way and added, "We thought it best to keep it small. We are more ready to get on with our lives than we are to make a big fuss."

"Of course, we must have some kind of celebration," Artemis replied. "I have an available banquet room at the restaurant that didn't book up that night. Downstairs we have a band playing, and the whole place will become one big party around 10 p.m. You two plan on having a celebration dinner upstairs with the family and your friends, and we can all ring the new year in together."

Demitra was pleasantly surprised by her sister's generous offer. Artemis wasn't even sure why she'd made it; it had just seemed the right thing to do. She accepted Demitra's thanks and decided to allow her sister to make her own mistakes if she was so inclined. Artemis would help her deal with the emotional fall out later if it came.

As bedtime loomed, Howard and Jerry were saying their goodbyes when Seth bounded down the stairs with the rest of the upstairs crew following in tow. Olympia was half asleep in her chair when the pounding startled her awake.

"Seth's going to do it!" Salem shouted excitedly. "He thinks he can this year!"

"Thinks he can what?" Jerry asked, putting on his coat.

"Wait!" Fable said quickly. "Jerry, you have to stay overnight. You too, Howard, otherwise you won't be able to get here in the morning."

"What on Earth are you kids talking about?" Artemis asked.

"I'm going to make it happen this year!" Seth exclaimed. "We were all upstairs when Beryl reminded me that I brought down lightning on Patric, so I should be strong enough now to do it."

"Oh, this again!" Howard laughed, continuing to put his coat on. "Seth, you won't mind if I keep my coat on. I've seen you try for five years and still never seen a flake fall."

"You're about to eat those words, boss," Yasmine smiled. "He can do it now, I know it!"

Seth opened the door and stepped out onto the front porch. Yasmine, Fable, Salem, and Arielle followed him. Looking up to the Christmas Eve sky, he focused his mind, concentrating as hard as he could. He kept his eyes closed as he sent out the energy from his mind. He did not look, didn't blink, didn't make any moves in fear of breaking his concentration. Suddenly, he heard his wife cry out.

"You did it! Honey-you did it!"

"He did!" Arielle yelled into the house for the others. "It's snowing!"

Nacaria, Demitra, Artemis, Olympia, Jerry, and Howard stepped onto the porch to see for themselves. A gentle white snow was now drifting downward. Everyone took seats on the porch in the rocking chairs or along the rails and steps to quietly view the magical sight. Christmas snow in Alabama of all places. At first the flakes melted into the warm ground, but slowly cooler winds blew in and within twenty minutes the first layer of snowfall was piling up, sticking to the now cooled ground.

Seth made it snow for Christmas.

CHAPTER TWENTY SIX

Here Comes the Bride (And Hasn't the Groom Been Dead for Ten Years?)

Daihmler County Courthouse was not anyone's ideal locale for a wedding, but Demitra and Jerry Miller seemed too impatient to wait for a more charming, at-home affair. Although Artemis tried to get them to hold off until something better could be thrown together, the happy couple wanted the marriage expedited for reasons no one else quite understood.

No one attended the wedding except Jerry's parents and Demitra's daughters. If truth be told, Beryl was not a fan of the event and only went out of daughterly duty. Fable, however, continued to confuse her sister by seeming so euphoric over the marriage. She was further confused by the conversation when she and Fable were formally introduced to Jerry's parents.

Demitra walked the elderly couple over to her daughters and proclaimed, "Mr. and Mrs. Miller, I'd like you to meet my children, Beryl and Fable."

"Nice to meet you," Beryl said, shaking hands.

"Oh, it's so good to see you!" Fable exclaimed, forgetting herself. "How is Tipton doing?"

The Millers were puzzled. After a moment of pause, Vestus Miller answered, "He's doing just fine."

Demitra gave her daughter a scathing look to which Fable quickly corrected and replied, "My friend Felicia told me all about meeting you and about what happened to Tipton."

Mrs. Miller's expression lightened, and she said beaming, "Oh, your friend Felicia was such a godsend! We haven't seen her in weeks, though. Please tell her to drop back by and visit us."

"I will," Fable said.

Beryl gave her sister a quizzical look. "Who is Felicia?"

"A friend of mine," Fable said tersely.

"You don't have a friend named Felicia."

"You don't know all my friends," Fable shot back through gritted teeth as she kept her smile for the Millers.

"I know everybody you know," Beryl insisted.

"You don't know everybody I know."

"Who else do you hang out with except Seth and Yaz?" Beryl quipped.

Fable huffed, still attempting to maintain her smile for Jerry's parents. "I have friends."

"No, you don't."

"Drop it girls," Demitra snapped.

"Oh, my goodness," Mrs. Miller said, noticing Fable's baby bump. "Are we about to become great-grandparents?"

"Yes," Fable replied nervously. "I'm having a baby."

"When are you due, sweet thing?" Mrs. Miller asked.

Sarcastically, Beryl quipped, "Six months, six weeks, tomorrow afternoon? Who can say?"

The puzzled look came back to the Millers' faces as Demitra replied, "My girls. Always making funnies with each other. Come, the Justice of the Peace appears to be ready for us now."

Guiding her soon-to-be new in-laws into the office, Demitra shot bullets from her eyes at her two daughters.

"What was that all about? Who is Felicia?"

"Don't worry about it," Fable said. "Let's just focus on Mother's big day."

Beryl did not share Fable's confusing acceptance of this event. Hoping for a moment of shared reverence between them she commented, "It's kind of strange seeing Mom married to another man, isn't it? Makes me really miss Dad."

"He's always with us, Beryl," Fable smiled. "I can feel him here now."

Beryl watched Fable through the ceremony, still uncertain why she was not raising more hell about this. It was so unlike Fable. She even appeared to cry at certain points during the ceremony. And when it was over, Jerry Miller was the first

Fable gave a hug and kiss to, even before her own mother. It was weird. Beryl could think of nothing to attribute it to but pregnancy hormones. Yet the thing that most offended her was what her mother did during the ceremony. In her vows to Jerry Miller, she uttered a sentence that Beryl had only heard her say a handful of times in her life. It was something Beryl assumed existed only between her mother and father, but Demitra gave the phrase to this new husband. Demitra told him, "I will love you forever, and three days."

Cheers rang out for the happy couple as they walked into the banquet room of The Cobblestone restaurant. Demitra, radiant in lavender silk, looked happier than anyone had seen her in years. Seth walked immediately up to her and gave his aunt a kiss as Yasmine jumped forward to give her a hug, almost knocking them both off their feet. Howard was shaking Jerry's hand as Olympia came forth and welcomed her new son-in-law to the family.

"You might see some strange things now that you are one of us," she smiled.

"I've already seen some strange things, Olympia," he grinned. "I deem it an honor."

Everyone grabbed drinks from the bar table to toast the couple as Artemis and Jerry's parents filled the guests in on how the ceremony at the courthouse went. The Millers were overjoyed to have been there to witness the ceremony for their "son" and happy to be meeting their daughter-in-law's family for the first time.

Across the room Howard and Yasmine were talking with the sheriff of Daihmler, Charlie Bennet, who was also a long-time family friend. Charlie had not seen Yasmine in years, but their subject matter had little to do with the span of time since their last interaction and more to do with an on-going investigation.

"Yeah, it doesn't look too good for me being unable to close the case on those murders earlier this year, but at least we have a named killer. All across the country, people are still looking for that Patric guy. But it's not like I can write in the report saying he was a werewolf and the Blanchard family got rid of him."

"Yes, it would be hard to explain," Yasmine said. "I'm truly sorry about all of that. I feel responsible."

"You aren't responsible for anything," Howard defended.

"Course not," Charlie agreed. "In my line of work, I see all kinds of crazies. It's never their family's fault they went off the deep end. Don't let that worry you."

"I wonder if Demitra will still have time to help out on difficult cases now that she's married?" Howard mentioned.

"Well, I expect she will," Charlie said. "Larry never minded much. This Jerry, he seems like a good guy, I guess. Reminds me a little of Larry, but I don't know him yet. Guess I should go say hello. Kind of hard for me, you know?"

"Sure, it is," Yasmine said gently. "Uncle Larry was your best friend. But Jerry is really nice. I think they will be happy."

At the buffet table, Salem was scolding her sister for the constant glancing at her phone as they piled their plates with the delicious items Artemis' staff had laid out for the party.

"Would you stop?" Salem said. "He'll get here when he gets here. Really, Ari, you met him once at the Consort and then spent time with him Christmas morning."

"I like him, Salem," Arielle replied. "I'm just anxious for him to arrive."

"What are you two arguing about?" Nacaria asked walking up.

"Who do you think?" Salem teased. "Our cousin Forest. He made a date with Arielle tonight and is driving up from Mobile."

"Ah, I see," Nacaria smiled. "Young love. I remember it well."

"Old love isn't so bad either," Arielle quipped. "It's New Year's Eve. Why don't you take my phone and go call my father? He does have the power to pop here in the blink of an eye."

Nacaria blushed a little. "I couldn't call Xander."

"Of course, you could," Arielle said. "You should."

"It's very complicated," Nacaria pointed out. "Not to mention the fact that he's still married to your mother and will be for the foreseeable future. Possibly the rest of our lives. You can't divorce a shadow on the wall."

"They are already divorced," Arielle said.

Nacaria's face betrayed her surprise. "They are?"

"It was a request Daddy made to the Council before Mother was punished. He asked to be set free. I found out when I was at Oleander."

Nacaria looked ready to burst with joy.

"Why didn't you tell me that!" she exclaimed. "Can I use your phone? Do you think he'd really come here?"

Arielle entered her password into her phone and handed it over to Nacaria.

"No," Nacaria backtracked. "I can't. I can't call him. If ever he's ready, he knows where I am. We have too much history. He is free now of Atheidrelle and of me. He can start over with no stains on his past. No, I have to let him be free."

Nacaria walked away. They watched her pass through the glass doors to the outside terrace for a little privacy with her thoughts. She stood watching the dark water of the Black Warrior River drift by. She heard voices on the balcony around the corner. She edged closer. It was the voices of her son and her sister.

"A new year is upon us," Artemis was saying. "A lot of changes headed our way—your way especially."

"Okay, okay," Seth said. "Save the introduction, Aunt Artemis. What are you leading up to?"

"Simple," she said. "You have a wife and a baby on the way. It's time you had a job."

"A job?" Seth cried. "I'm a student in college."

"And you have been for five years," Artemis pointed out. "It is time to grow up, son. Time to get out into the world. I know we all have a fine big roof over our heads, but you cannot live off your grandmother's household forever. How do you plan to support your new family?"

"Well," Seth stammered, kicking the ground. "I haven't thought about it much. Yasmine's rich, I don't think we will go without anything."

"Are you seriously telling me you would be okay living off your wife's inheritance? Are you that lazy?"

"Not live off of her, but if we get into a bind, she's got millions stored away by Grandfather Sinclair," Seth pointed out.

"Boy, grow your ass up!" Artemis said sternly. "I did not raise you to be this way. Get off your duff and find a job. I will give you one here and you can put that business management major to use. But before Spring, I expect you to be holding down a steady job and providing for your family."

Nacaria was about to step inside and make her way to the other balcony to her son's defense but was stopped in her tracks when she turned around and found Xander Obreiggon standing on the terrace behind her.

"Xander."

"What makes you think I want to be free?" he asked, moving toward her, his arms grabbing her elbows and pulling her close to him. "Arielle phoned me right after you spoke a few moments ago. I *leaped* right over the moment she told me you wished I were here."

Nacaria had half forgotten what it felt like when Xander would suddenly appear beside her. His power to leap across distances to whatever place he wanted to be had once made their being together so easy to accomplish.

"Are you divorced?" she asked.

"I am," Xander said. "The Council was kind enough to do me that favor. My marriage was dissolved."

Nacaria was at a loss for words. She simply stared into his eyes hoping he would know what should be said next between them.

Xander picked up the cue and continued. "I never want to be free of you, Nacaria. We have waited so long to begin a life together. Let us finally have our chance. Let us agree that when we are ready to begin our lives again, we will do it together."

"But that was so long ago," Nacaria said. "Maybe not for me because I have not been living, but you have, Xander. Twenty years of life without me. How can you know you still want me? You are now free of everything; me, Atheidrelle. You could start over."

"I don't want to start over," he replied. "I want to begin."

She smiled. "Are you sure? Despite what she was, Atheidrelle was your wife for a great many years. There had to be some good moments in all that time."

"You've lived in your hell. I have lived in mine. We are the same from it," Xander answered. "Know that there is no one else for me but you. Though I must focus on Cassandra for now, our time will come. It is all I live for."

...

Back in the banquet room, Jerry Miller had his arms around his new bride as the people they loved most in the world were mingling together. It felt great to be back, Larry had missed this so much. "I am the happiest dead man alive," he whispered into her ear.

"Welcome home, my love," Demitra said with her heart beaming in her eyes.

"You sure you want another round of life with me?"

"A thousand years isn't enough," Demitra smiled. She looked over his shoulder and saw her sister outside with Xander. "I see we aren't the only ones getting a second chance. I hope it works out for them, too."

"Maybe so," Larry said. "I only met Xander once all those years ago, before they took Nacaria away. He seemed kind of weak back then. I hope he is stronger now. She needs someone strong to help her."

Demitra nudged his face slightly to show him that Jerry's parents were approaching.

"Here they come. I know it's uncomfortable."

"It is," Larry whispered. "But you want to know something? I really like them."

"You know something else?" Demitra laughed. "I like them, too! I think this time, I got two really great in-laws."

"Demitra," Cally Miller said with a gleaming smile. "Your family is remarkable. I just adore every single member. Your mother is a grand lady. It was a pleasure spending some time with her. And what fine new granddaughters I have!"

"And don't forget a new baby on the way," Vestus Miller added. "You know Demitra, it was always a sad factor in our lives that Jerry here never had any children. His first wife wasn't the mothering kind. Thought me and Cally wouldn't ever have that particular kind joy, now we got us two grown up granddaughters and a new great grand on the way. A baby that can come around to visit and fill our house with joy again. I hope you won't mind if we think of your girls that way."

Demitra gave her father-in-law a kiss on the cheek. "I am overjoyed that you do think of my girls as part of your family. And I know you'll be wonderful great grandparents." She paused a moment; it occurred to her that it might not be wise for the Millers to have too much hope for Fable's child. "I do feel the need to warn you, however—and please don't bring it up to Fable—but there are some complications. We are hoping for the best, hoping we get a healthy...normal...baby. But there is a chance she might miscarry. So, don't get too excited until it's born normal."

Larry glanced at his wife then to Jerry's parents. Mrs. Miller frowned sadly but patted her daughter-in-law's hand and said quietly, "I will be praying day and night. And I'll have my prayer group do the same."

Nacaria came back inside alone. Artemis saw the absence of Xander after having seen them talking outside. She approached her younger sister with a glass of champagne in her hand for her. Nacaria looked both happy and dismayed as she took the glass.

"Everything all right?" Artemis asked.

"He had to go home. Cassandra isn't doing well, and he's looking after her," Nacaria explained with a sadness within a smile. "He only came to tell me he loves me and wants a future."

"Is that what you want?"

Artemis was in protective mode now. She knew this would naturally be what Nacaria sought out for herself, although Artemis wasn't so sure it would be the best thing for her. Nacaria's life before her curse had been dominated by her love for Xander Obreiggon. She lost half of her life for it. It might be a mistake to immediately reconnect her happiness to that man. Nacaria hadn't had time to figure out who she was as a person in this new world. To be so eager to commit to someone she had not been around in two decades felt like a mistake to Artemis.

"I want a future with him more than anything," Nacaria admitted. "It won't be easy, though. And we aren't doing anything about it immediately. His hands are pretty full at home right now."

"Cassandra?'

"Yes—he has had virtually no meaningful relationship with his daughter her entire life. She was always Atheidrelle's property. At this time when Cassandra is reexamining her own life and her own actions, it's difficult for him to know how to be there for her when they are little more than strangers. It is not the time to bring a new wife home—particularly one she has been taught to hate all her life. But he did tell me we do have a future, and we are going to start to see each other regularly. For now, that is enough."

"I think that's wise," Artemis said. "Besides, you just got back yourself. You're still getting to know your own children again."

"Speaking of my children," Nacaria replied, pursing her bottom lip and changing her tone tersely. "I overheard your conversation with Seth. Frankly, I think you were a bit rough on him."

"Do you?" Artemis remarked folding her arms into a defensive stance. "After a little while, you'll see that the only way to get through to Seth is by slapping him with a dose of reality. He tends to be lazy. And he tends to still live like he is 17. But he is a grown man with a wife, and a child on the way. It's time he grew up."

"I think he will do it in his own time," Nacaria countered. "He's under a lot of pressure. He's been through a lot."

"Everyone has been through a lot," Artemis argued with a roll of her eyes. "It is time he stood up and made something of himself. He has a family to support."

"Isn't his wife rather wealthy?"

Her comment took Artemis aback. Of course, it was her right as a mother to defend her son, but at some point reality should set in about her son's flaws.

"Nikki, do you really think it's appropriate for Yasmine to support Seth? He needs to be a man and step up."

Nacaria's hands flew up as her voice raised. "Is that your place to say?" she asked. "He's my son. I will talk to him."

Artemis was becoming irritated now. The audacity of her sister was proving too much, and she took a step forward. "Nacaria, I am perfectly within my right to tell Seth the truth about himself."

Nacaria recrossed her arms and raised her eyebrows. "I repeat, he is *my* son."

"Is he?" Artemis cried, hands now flailing at her sides. "I'm sorry, maybe I've missed something. Were you here? Were you the one who taught him how to ride a bike? Was it you up half the night when he didn't know how to do fractions? Was it you that sat in the stands cheering at all the baseball games?"

"That's not fair!"

"Really?" Artemis scoffed. "Not fair? I was there! Scraped knees. Broken collar bone. I told him about sex. I bought him his first box of condoms. I cheered at graduation. I held that heartbroken boy when his childhood sweetheart died. I have raised 'your' son. I don't think I am out of line now to tell him he needs to get a job!"

Nacaria slammed her champagne glass on the bar so hard that it broke. She turned back to her sister and—as quietly as she could to not make a scene—said, "Maybe you did raise him. But if you think he has turned out so badly, perhaps you didn't do a good job. I may not have been a good mother, but I guess you weren't either then."

"But I was here."

Nacaria walked out of the room and down the stairs to the restaurant below. Seth saw the confrontation but hadn't heard what was said. He started to walk over to his aunt, but Artemis waved him away.

"Check on her," Artemis told him. "She needs her son."

Seth went downstairs and maneuvered through the crowded dining rooms until he found his mother standing at the bar. "You okay?"

"No," Nacaria said. "I don't like the way Artemis speaks to you. I heard what she told you on the balcony."

Seth cracked a devilish smile and laughed out loud, "Oh that? That's nothing. You should hear her when I really make her mad."

"She does not have the right to speak to you like that!"

"Mom, she's just trying to get me off my butt and make something of myself."

Nacaria was surprised. "You're defending her?"

"Sure," Seth replied. "Look Mom, I know it's rough on you being back and all.

You aren't real sure where you fit in around here. But you can't take that out on Aunt Artemis, and you can't blame her for crawling my ass. She's been doing that for years. Wait till you hear how Aunt Demitra talks to Fable when she's in the doghouse."

"Demitra is Fable's mother. I am your mother."

Seth grabbed her hand and squeezed. "Of course, you are, and I love you. But you can't erase the fact that Artemis has been my mother figure for a really long time. You can't expect to come back and jump right in. She and I have a bond and that doesn't go away just because you came home."

"Where does that leave me then?"

"Mom, you'll always have a place in my life. But Aunt Artemis and Aunt Demitra have places, too—big places. Have you stopped to wonder what it must feel like to Artemis? Maybe she's feeling like you're back now trying to take *her* place? You were my mother until I was seven years old. But Mom, from that age till now Aunt Artemis has been. You and I have a special connection she can never replace, but she and I also have something only she and I can share. I'm sorry. It is the way it is. I don't think it's fair for you to resent her for that."

CHAPTER TWENTY SEVEN

Witches in the Sky

Artemis reached into the back of the freezer and removed two large bags of peas. She had shelled and blanched them the previous summer and stored for just this day. She took a pot out of the pantry and poured the peas in, adding water and seasonings from the spice rack. When she was finished, she turned to her mother and her sister, Nacaria, who were seated at the kitchen table looking through mail and magazines.

"That's that; soon we will have our black-eyed peas."

"I forgot about that," Nacaria said, speaking her first words to her sister since their fight the previous night. "Black eyed peas and cornbread on New Year's Day."

"And don't forget about the collard greens," Artemis said, offering her sister a slight smile. "You'll have a good, old-fashioned, southern New Year's Day lunch."

"I wonder what they have in the north?" Nacaria remarked.

"Probably Northern beans, avocado, and biscotti," Olympia quipped, tossing down the mail. "Where is everyone?"

"Hungover, I expect," Artemis laughed. "After we all saw Demitra and Jerry leave for their honeymoon, I came home but the kids were still partying. I think they went to a nightclub after they left The Cobblestone."

"I hope Yasmine and Fable were responsible," Olympia noted.

"I'm sure Yasmine was," Artemis said, sitting down with another cup of coffee. "Fable is anybody's guess."

"I heard Beryl leaving for work early," Nacaria said. "And the door to one of the guest rooms was closed. Did the Millers stay overnight?"

"No, that's Forest," Olympia answered. "I tried to get the Millers to stay with us, but they have a dog at home, so they drove back to Birmingham. I like them so much, very kind people."

"Much better than Larry's family was," Artemis huffed.

"Will Forest be staying a while?" Nacaria asked her mother.

"I think he'll be staying as long as Arielle is here. I believe she and Salem leave tomorrow."

Olympia left the room for a few moments, leaving an awkward silence between her two daughters. When she returned carrying a bundle of rolled up papers, the tension in the room lessened as there was something now to draw attention to.

"Mother, what is all this?" Artemis asked.

Olympia began to unroll the bound papers, revealing the floorplans to the house. "Blueprints," she said. "I've been thinking about expanding."

"Expanding?" Nacaria gasped. "Isn't our house large enough already?"

"Really?" Olympia said. "Lately I've been realizing how small it is."

"Mother, are you serious?" Artemis exclaimed. "We have 23 rooms. What is your definition of large?"

"I understand Blanchard House is spacious to some people, but most people do not have every member of their family living with them. And with Fable and Yasmine about to usher in a new generation…that's two more bedrooms we will need just there alone."

"Fable's case is still undetermined," Artemis pointed out. "But even still, we have a couple of guest rooms already. We could easily make one of those a nursery."

"But what happens once they are no longer babies? Each one will need his or her own room. And we can't very well not have a guest room or two for friends or family that come to town." Olympia said.

"Well, I did overhear Forest say last night that he may transfer to the University of Alabama," Nacaria revealed. "He was asking Seth if he thought you'd mind if he lived here."

"If he switches colleges, of course he can live here. It's his ancestral home as much as it is any of ours," Olympia said. "See? There's another bedroom we may need."

"Where would we put these three new bedrooms?" Artemis wondered.

"In the new wing," Olympia said.

"Wing?!" Artemis gasped.

"Of course!" Olympia exclaimed. "Have you forgotten how noisy it is to have small children around? If it had not been for the third floor, I don't think you or Demitra or I would have kept our heads on straight. We are about to have four generations under one roof. Not to mention Seth and Yasmine really need some privacy. I think a whole new wing is in order."

"I don't believe she's even considering this," Nacaria told her sister. "When did Mother start cutting down trees? There are trees all around this house."

"Oh, we won't be cutting any trees down," Olympia told them. "On the west end of the house there are two trees far enough apart to build a hallway between them. We can build the new wing in the west lawn just past the trees and the hall will connect it."

"Do you know how strange that will look?" Artemis asked.

"Howard will just have to hire an architect that makes it look as good as possible without harming the trees," Olympia stated. "It'll be charming."

"I have some nursing home brochures up in my room," Artemis teased. "They are pretty charming too." Nacaria snickered at her sister's joke.

"Nonsense," Olympia said. "I'll see Howard in the morning and get him to handle everything. It is a new year for the Blanchard family. Lots of new additions, returning faces, and this house has to grow to meet them. It's my job to make sure Blanchard House always has room for everyone."

After Olympia had gone back upstairs, Artemis and Nacaria were left alone again. The tension had decreased quite a bit as the two sisters shared the common ground of thinking their mother was being ridiculous. Nothing can unite siblings like the shared belief that their parent is crazy.

"Can you believe that?" Artemis giggled, touching her sister's arm. "A hall between the trees? That stretch would have to be about 20 yards long before you even get to the clear area to build."

Nacaria laughed. "Well, now that I think about it, I probably might have enjoyed having extra rooms to roam when I was stuck on the wall. Maybe it's not a bad idea."

"It's good to laugh with you again."

"It is," Nacaria said, her voice lowering. "I'm sorry about last night. I think I was a little jealous."

"I could have been more sensitive."

"Blanchard Bitches," Nacaria laughed again. "Remember our club when you, me, and Demitra were kids and we'd just learned that word?"

Artemis giggled as she recalled their childhood. "Hey, remember something else the Blanchard Bitches did? Come with me."

Artemis led her sister out of the kitchen and into the front foyer. Nacaria was not exactly sure what Artemis had in mind until she saw her big sister lift the entranceway rug from the floor and walk out the front door. Nacaria grabbed two coats from the closet, giddy with excitement as she followed Artemis to the side yard. Placing the rug on the grass and putting on their winter coats, the two witches sat on the carpet together, Artemis in front, Nacaria in back.

"Can you still do it like when we were little?" Nacaria asked. "We weigh a lot more now."

"I lifted a van last October when we were fighting Patric; I think I can."

They sat on the rug as a winter breeze chilled them, but the cold was not a deterrent. Artemis Blanchard closed her eyes and concentrated. She imagined the rug lifting a few inches off the ground. The rug began to twitch. She focused harder. The rug began to rise a few inches. Then a foot. Then four feet. All at once the rug took off forward, slowly at first, but steadily increasing velocity until it reached the speed of a fast-moving bicycle. Nacaria squealed and gripped the sides of the rug for stability while Artemis gripped the front. Over the rolling meadows of the Blanchard property, they sped along rising slightly more and more, twisting and turning to dodge trees and bushes.

"You're doing it!" Nacaria shouted.

Artemis focused her mind enough to set the speed and height into place, and then she was free to enjoy the ride, only refocusing her mind for the turns needed to avoid the tops of trees. The wind hitting their faces was stinging, but neither sister cared as they enjoyed a freedom neither had experienced since they were girls.

"Let's take this thing up!" Artemis shouted behind her as she lifted the rug higher into the sky until they were more than three stories up.

Seeing the Blanchard property line looming ahead, Nacaria cast a quick spell to make them invisible to others. They soon crossed over the property line and intersected the highway, zipping over the cars and trucks driving past. Nacaria hoped she wasn't too rusty and that the drivers below weren't able to see them flying overhead. Artemis carried them down the backroads and wooded forests of Daihmler into the suburb communities and on past into town. The sisters rode for nearly half an hour before Artemis settled the carpet atop the roof of the Daihmler Courthouse. They stood up off the carpet and walked to the edge of the rooftop, looking down over the triangular capital capping the entrance columns.

"I can't believe we did this!" Nacaria cried with amazement. "Artemis, I haven't had fun like that since I was 8 years old!"

"Remember the whipping we got from Mother for just flying to the school playground! Imagine what she'd say if she knew where we were right now!"

"She might whip us again."

"She might."

"Did Salem and Seth ever do anything like this when they were growing up?" Nacaria asked. "I saw mostly everything from the walls, but I couldn't always understand what I had drifted into when I'd enter a room."

Artemis gave it some thought with her hand on her chin before replying. "Once. Once they got into a heap of trouble. All the kids did. It was a New Year's Eve if I am not mistaken. Fable wanted to spend it at a speakeasy in New York. The girls all dressed as flappers and Seth pulled out one of Dad's old suits. We all thought they were going to a costume party—at least that's what they told us."

"What did they do?" Nacaria asked.

"Beryl and Salem actually cooked up a spell that sent them all into the 1920s!"

"No!"

"Yes," Artemis replied. "Well, you can imagine the beating they got when they got home. I think that might have been the last time I ever spanked Seth and Salem. Seth was probably 15 at the time."

"How did you get them back out of the 20s?"

"Oh, they came back on their own," Artemis informed. "That's how they got caught. Stupid kids did not realize they'd return in the exact spot they left. They had cast the spell in the downstairs living room. Mother, Demitra, and I were watching a movie on TV when suddenly the kids popped back from the past. Beryl and Salem were also drunk. Oh, that was a night! But that's about the worst thing they ever did."

"I've missed a lot," Nacaria said, beginning to become down.

"No, no, no you don't little sister!" Artemis cried. "No more focusing on what you missed. Now we are going to focus on all there is left to experience! Let's have another go on the carpet. Ready?"

"Ready!" Nacaria beamed.

It was almost noon when Artemis and Nacaria sneaked back into the house and laid the rug back in the foyer. They went back into the kitchen where they encountered the faces of their mother, Seth, Yasmine, Arielle, Forest, Fable, and Salem. No one said a word, but all were staring.

"Girls," Olympia said matter of factly. "Zelda called me earlier. She told me she saw a magic carpet flying over her house about two hours ago. I also noticed that the rug in the hall is missing. Imagine that."

Artemis and Nacaria burst into laughter.

"You're cloaking spell needs some work," Artemis grinned, elbowing Nacaria in the side.

Yasmine cleared her throat. "So, I went ahead and cooked lunch if you two nutjobs are ready to eat."

CHAPTER TWENTY EIGHT

Growing Concerns

Artemis found it rather hard to sleep that night. Lately she had been deliberating whether or not to fire a certain employee. She did not relish terminating any member of the staff, especially someone as old as the gentleman in question. Unable to decide or fall asleep, she went downstairs for a midnight snack. She thought maybe a little ice cream with sprinkles would help. The moon was bright, sending a few random beams through the windows to light her footsteps on the kitchen stairs. Staggering down to the table, she found she was not alone in the kitchen.

"Well, well," she said, clicking on the light. "It's been a while since I came down late at night and found a brother-in-law raiding the fridge."

"Hope you don't mind," said Jerry. "I couldn't sleep."

"I don't mind at all," she smiled. "It is actually ironic. I used to catch Larry down here all the time. Maybe Demitra's just the type that runs men out of the room in the night. She snores, you know."

"Yeah," he said with an amused grin. "I know."

Pulling out a cold chicken leg from the platter in the fridge, Artemis sat down beside Jerry and began eating her troubles away. She could see by the bones on his plate, he'd already polished off a thigh and a wing.

"What has you stirring so late tonight?" Jerry asked her.

"Work," she grimaced. "When I took over the restaurant the staff was already in place. Most of them are exceptional..."

"But some aren't?"

"Well, one in particular," she said pulling a shred of stray chicken out from the small gap between her back two teeth. "He goes by the name Skillet..."

"Skillet?!" Jerry laughed.

"Yep, Skillet," Artemis continued. "He's the kindest old man you've ever seen.

He's a great cook too, just slow. He's in his 70s."

"Slowing the kitchen down, is he?"

"Yes," frowned Artemis. "Plus, he thinks himself to be everyone's wise old grandfather—always doling out advice, which usually makes little sense. But everyone loves him. He's like the mascot of the Cobblestone."

Jerry thought over what she said a moment and then rubbed his chin. "Are you asking me my opinion, or are you simply venting?"

"Asking."

"Seems to me he's pretty popular with staff and probably guests. Even if he's in the way, it might do more harm than good to oust him. Efficiency at the price of morale isn't worth it. Remember—owner or not—you're the new girl. Don't sink a ship that is perfectly seaworthy."

Artemis liked his advice. And it felt correct. She liked old Skillet herself she had to admit. It was only the businesswoman side of her presenting the dilemma. She thanked her new brother-in-law for the assistance. He smiled. She watched him in the dark of the kitchen, now eating a chicken breast. He looked so much like Larry. He'd even given her the same kind of advice she knew Larry would have if he were still alive. Artemis found herself liking the fact that Demitra married Jerry, but she still couldn't help but wonder how much her sister loved Jerry or how much he just reminded her of her late husband.

...

The next morning, Olympia came downstairs as usual to find a couple of plates on the counter. Yasmine was just starting breakfast, frying bacon up in a pan while also cracking the morning eggs. Olympia bid her granddaughter good morning and poured herself a cup of coffee. She saw Artemis sitting in the dining room reading a paper and joined her daughter.

"Have you and Yasmine already eaten, dear?"

"Huh?" Artemis said looking up. "Oh, hi Mother. No, we haven't eaten yet. Yaz just came down to start breakfast. Why?"

"Oh, I just saw two plates on the counter. I assumed."

"Oh, that's from late last night," Artemis explained. "Jerry and I raided the fridge."

Olympia looked concerned. "Artemis—you and Jerry?"

"Yes, Mother. I couldn't sleep and apparently neither could he. We met in the kitchen and finished off the fried chicken."

"That's funny?" Nacaria said coming in to join them. "I remember Larry used to do that. You and he whiled away many a late hour after we'd all gone to bed."

"Larry did often do that," Olympia nodded.

"See?!" Artemis stated. "I told you months ago Demitra was falling for a man very much like Larry. But you told me to mind my own business. Do you see now that I was right? Demitra is still not over her first husband, and her poor second husband has no idea he's just a facsimile of Larry."

Olympia did not reply. Instead, she sat pondering a while. Things were starting to become clear in her mind although she hoped she was wrong. Maybe it was just one of those things that if she didn't think about it, it couldn't be true. Or maybe she realized she had been too preoccupied a few months ago to see what was happening right in front of her. She was not sure. What she was sure about was that she needed a little more time to marinate on these thoughts. It was too soon to draw conclusions.

Later that morning as Beryl and Fable left out to work, they passed Zelda coming in. Zelda seemed in a hurry to see Olympia, but as they were in their own hurry, the girls did not stop to find out why.

"I'm here, Lympy," Zelda cried coming through the front door.

"I'm in the study," Olympia called. "Come in and close the door behind you."

Zelda did as her friend asked and took a seat in one of the winged-back chairs by the corner windows next to Olympia. The two sat a moment in silence. Zelda could feel something pressing was on Olympia's mind. Fighting her own natural inclinations to force it out of her, Zelda waited until her friend was ready.

"Things aren't right around here, and I don't exactly know what's going on," Olympia said. "I have a feeling in my bones that this family could be headed toward more troubles."

"Well, when ain't it?" Zelda snarked. "You got any particular ideas on what it could be?"

"Just mild suspicions," Olympia replied. "Demitra is acting peculiarly. Fable is nervous a lot. I'm not sure."

"Well, Fable is pregnant," Zelda pointed out. "That can make anybody anxious, especially considering her specific kind of pregnancy. And Demmy's in love."

"That's what is the oddest of all," Olympia began. "She mourned Larry so long, and now suddenly she is head over heels with a man very similar in many ways to Larry."

"So, she's got a type," Zelda shrugged. "Don't mean a thing."

"You dismiss my intuition so quickly, Zelda. Time should have taught you by now to trust my instincts."

"Normally, maybe," Zelda said leaning forward, hands on knees, towards her friend. "But you forget I know you better'n anybody. And I know what's really got you feelin' out of sorts."

"You do?"

Zelda grabbed her friend's hand and placed her other hand atop it. "I know, Lympy. I *know*."

Olympia's face went white. "How could you?"

"Don't you think I don't see it coming at you, old friend? A' gallopin' like on a black horse. You know I see everything when it comes to stuff like this."

"You didn't say anything."

"Not my place to," Zelda said. "Been waitin' for you to want to tell me. It's your heart, ain't it?"

The fortress Olympia always maintained around her vulnerabilities, lifted a gate and she allowed herself to look as fragile as she felt. "I don't know how much time I have, Zelda. It frightens me to think the family might not be settled."

"Have you talked to Beryl?" Zelda asked. "She's fixed you up many times before."

"It isn't like those times," Olympia explained. "This isn't a cough, or an achy joint. I feel it in my bones; my time is drawing closed. It would be against the Natural Order to prolong my life artificially. It's just my time."

"Hell, you ain't goin' today are you?" Zelda cried.

"No," Olympia laughed. "Nothing like that. Let's just say my life and my heart are winding down. And I have a lot to reconcile before I go. The stability and leadership of my family for one thing."

"Who you plannin' to pick to take over?"

"Artemis is the most likely person. She is the oldest and honestly the more responsible of my children. Nacaria is certainly out of the running. Not just because of her past, but she has not been around the family long enough to know how to lead them. Demitra could do it, but she's weak."

"I wouldn't exactly call Demitra Blanchard weak," Zelda sneered.

"In the important ways she is. She's strong when it counts, but she always has

Artemis and myself to lean on when she isn't. I need someone who doesn't have to lean on anyone."

"Well, that's clearly Artie."

"I believe so, too."

"Then that's settled," Zelda declared. "What else you got to worry about?"

"Everything," Olympia said, her face growing pale. "What if Atheidrelle is released in this lifetime? Will her curse on Yasmine and whoever Salem might love regenerate? What about Fable's baby? If even it is born seemingly normal, life is a long road. I will not be here as the miles down the road grow. What if the baby turns out like Patric, what will the family do?"

"That'll be up to Artemis."

"And you," Olympia smiled. She placed her palms on her friend's soft shoulders and proclaimed, "Zelda, I leave my family to you when I go. You'll look out for them. You'll guide Artemis if she ever needs help when she takes over."

"Lympy, I'm as old as you. If you ain't got much time, you can bet I don't neither."

"I feel safe in betting you will be here longer than I. You'll look out for this family?"

"You ain't even gotta ask me," Zelda smiled. "You're my sister in this life, Olympia Blanchard. Always have been. This family means more to me than my own. You ain't even got to ask."

CHAPTER TWENTY NINE

The Forest and the Trees

Forest Blanchard found he liked living at Blanchard House. He had grown up similarly to his Daihmler cousins as part of a large close-knit family, although he hadn't lived with all of his relatives under the same roof. But having Artemis, Demitra, and Nacaria around more than made up for missing his mother's attention. And Seth made a good substitute for his brother, Ocean. Seth also had to admit he liked having another guy around the house. Once Forest was enrolled at college for spring semester and was all settled in, he and Seth became fast friends...after the air was cleared.

The clearing of that air came one morning at the gym. Seth insisted Forest join the gym where Seth was as much a fixture as the leg press. Forest, trim and lean, was not averse to bulking up on some muscle, and if anyone was suited to train him, it was his cousin Seth.

Seth enjoyed teaching fitness to beginners whenever possible. He strutted around the gym almost as if he owned it, showing Forest the ropes and introducing him to the staff and the daily regular clients. Forest was mid-set on a barbell bench, pressing more weight than he believed he could handle, as Seth stood over him on the ready to assist if the weight got too much for him.

Just as Forest was straining for that ninth repetition, Seth looked down into his cousin's eyes and said, "Arielle sure has popped over from Atlanta a good bit since you moved in."

Forest felt uneasy with the tone, especially with the barbell placed directly above his neck as he tried with all his might to push it back to the rack. Seth enjoyed a few seconds of the struggle before he reached down and lifted the bar clear from Forest. Forest sat up, wiping the sweat from his brow.

"I like Arielle a lot."

"She is my little sister, you know," Seth reminded.

Forest stood up to stand eye to eye, not in an intimidating way, but to show that he was not a coward. "Man, I know she's your sister. I respect that. I respect her."

Seth relaxed his stern gaze and cracked a half smile. "I know you do. I just gotta say it, you know?"

Forest nodded.

"Arielle hasn't had much life experience, hasn't had a whole lotta people really care about her before. Even her own mother. All I ask is that you take it slow, for her. Treat her well. Treat her like I treat Yaz."

Forest could not help but laugh. He did not mean to, but Seth had no idea how funny his statement had been. "Hell, Seth! I hope I can do better than that. You two bicker all the time."

Seth's serious face blushed as a grin came across it. "Yeah, I guess you're right. Treat Ari better than I do Yaz. Come on, let's hit cable flies now."

That was the end of the man-to-man talk about Arielle. Forest understood Seth's intent, and Seth recognized that his cousin was a good guy who wouldn't intentionally hurt his little sister. Forest continued to join Seth for workouts a couple of times a week. Seth couldn't comprehend why it couldn't be more, but Forest finally made him see that fitness was only a means to health for him, not the obsession it was to Seth.

Arielle Obreiggon was becoming a regular fixture at Blanchard House with Forest living there now. No longer was she too timid to visit without Salem. She didn't even knock anymore. Arielle was at home enough in Blanchard House to walk in unannounced. Olympia and rest of the family were glad of it. They understood the girl's need for family and were all too happy that she had picked theirs to cling to. Of course, once or twice Olympia had needed to remind both Arielle and Forest that he had studying to do, and her presence was a distraction. When those times came, Fable usually took her to a movie or Yasmine would enlist her to help with dinner.

Sometimes if Forest had a particularly grueling day of studying ahead Arielle would drive up to Birmingham to see her Aunt Blackie. This gave forest the day to work leaving the nights free for her.

Blackie cherished the proximity she now had to her niece with Arielle either in Atlanta or Daihmler. Birmingham was situated between both. Blackie made up for lost years taking Arielle shopping at the finest boutique stores in the prestigious Mountain Brook area of town. They would always stop for lunch at La Paz or Che

Fon Fon, although Arielle was never happier than when they simply had a messy meat sandwich at Gilchrist's Pharmacy. Blackie was not one for such simple delicacies, but if it made Arielle happy, she was happy. One afternoon Arielle convinced her aunt to drive her up Red Mountain to see up-close the statue of Vulcan which Arielle could see in the distance from Blackie's parapet at Quinlan Castle.

Vulcan sat atop a three story pedestal of stone pointing his torch skyward as his exposed buttocks mooned all of Birmingham. Arielle was fascinated to learn that the statue was the largest cast iron statue in the world.

"I really thought that was Lady Liberty?"

Blackie muffled a laugh and shook her head, "My Love, The Statue of Liberty is made of copper."

"Oh."

The women bought an ice cream from the shop inside the museum and took a seat on the terraced area overlooking downtown Birmingham. Blackie took the opportunity to use the tranquil moment for deeper conversation.

"You seem to be spending more and more time at Blanchard House lately. Is that because you've grown so fond of the Blanchards...or just one Blanchard in particular?"

Arielle rolled her eyes and licked her cone. "Smooth segue, Aunt Blackie. To answer your question, I adore the Blanchards. All of them. They've taken me in and treated me like their own. I've never had a family before. Not really." She paused and gave her aunt a wink. "And yes, Forest being there is an added bonus."

"Are things serious?"

Arielle paused before giving her reply. She appeared to be thinking on the matter. "I can't say. Not honestly. You see I've never had a boyfriend. I've never been in love. I'm not really sure I know what that feels like. Is this love? I don't know. What I do know is that I love being with him. Forest makes me feel like a person. Not a daughter. Not a niece. Not a sister. I'm simply Arielle. She's a pretty new person to me. I think I like her."

Blackie left things at that. Arielle was not only discovering romance for the first time in her life, she was also discovering herself. Blackie had not understood this before. Living such a sheltered life at Oleander had stunted the girl. She'd spent her formative years dictated to rather than nurtured. Arielle was only now finding herself and Forest appeared to be a big part of that journey. Blackie realized Arielle's time at Blanchard House was more than an idle crush on a young man, it was supplying her with independence and self-worth.

...

One Sunday morning after breakfast, Forest and Arielle took a walk, hand in hand, over some of the Blanchard property. Through the apple orchard, down the long foot-tromped path where generations of Blanchards had walked over time, they made their way to the edge of the woods. Scanning the brush and kudzu, Forest eventually spotted the trail he remembered from childhood, now obscured by thickets and vines.

"Are you sure we get through there?" Arielle asked. "It's pretty overgrown."

Forest assessed the situation. "Yeah, I guess it has been a while since anybody has gone down to the creek. But I got us covered."

Forest took his hand and swiped across his chest, as if scooping out some invisible substance. He then tossed the unseen material at Arielle before doing the same to himself. From thin air, a bubble-like field appeared around each of them. It was transparent, like a windowpane, although when Arielle looked down where it curved beneath her, the view of the foliage warped somewhat—like looking through a pair of glasses that fit another person's prescription. She could see clearly looking straight ahead however and began walking into the scruff. The bubble parted the brambly branches and thorny vines as they walked.

"You can make force-fields!" she exclaimed as she understood what was happening.

Once inside the wall of plant life, the trail widened and the need for the bubble was unnecessary. About an acre into the woods, the sound of the flowing creek became audible. Up ahead beside the path stood a rotting shed. Arielle asked what it was, and Forest told her it was the old pump house where his ancestors got their drinking water from the stream.

The creek ran through the woods, providing little embankment for them to sit on. Tall trees, vines, and shrubs ran all the way to the bank's edge; however one crookedly grown tree provided a small bench by the water for the couple to rest upon.

Arielle removed her shoes and dipped her toes into the crisp, cool water. "I forget this land is where your family comes from too. I just think of it as Olympia's property."

Forest lifted his head proudly, "This is all Blanchards' land. Aunt Olympia owns it, but she's the first to say it belongs to us all. I used to sit out here and imagine my grandmother playing in this creek. Whenever I would visit as a kid, Seth, Ocean, Sage, and I used the pump house as our clubhouse. We wouldn't let the girls in."

Arielle smiled flirtatiously at Forest, "What about now? Would you let me in your clubhouse?"

Forest gave her a raised eye and said, "Only if you knew the password."

"Which was?"

Forest pondered a moment then shook his head laughing to himself. "If I recall correctly, it was 'Girls Stink.'"

"Nice," Arielle scoffed. "And Olympia and Pastoria let you bullies keep the girls out? Doesn't sound like them."

"Well, you gotta consider...Seth was the only boy here. So, when my brother and cousin would visit, it was the only guy time Seth got. I think our grandmothers respected that. Besides, it was the same with the girls. My cousin Sydney is the only girl on our side, so whenever we were all here, she couldn't get enough of hanging out with Salem, Beryl, Fable, and Yasmine."

"Must have been fun."

Forest pressed her a little, thinking about the things Seth had told him about her past. "Did you not have a special place you could go as a kid? You and your sister? Or cousins?"

Arielle's face looked sad for a moment. "I have never been close to my sister. And I barely know my cousins. My mother's ancestral home is a frightening place. I avoided going there whenever I could."

Forest didn't ask any more. He just placed his arm around her neck and leaned in for a kiss. It pained him to think of this sweet girl having had such an unhappy life. They sat for a while in silence, holding each other's hand as the creek drifted by them. Forest thought about the future. One day he'd be finished with college, hopefully beginning a successful career in documentary filmmaking. He wondered if marriage would fall into that plan. And if it did, would it be with Arielle? It was much too soon to seriously consider such matters, but as he sneaked a side glance at that beautiful girl beside him, he couldn't help but think she would make a perfect life partner. Maybe they'd even build a little house here by this stream and start a new branch of Blanchards.

CHAPTER THIRTY

The Werewolf's Child

Demitra and Jerry were cuddled together in bed reading the same book. Being a speed reader, Demitra had to pause a minute or two for her husband to catch up at the page's end. This used to bother her years ago, and she'd routinely ask Larry to just read the book by himself after she was finished. Now, she didn't mind at all waiting for him before turning the page. Midway through the night's chapter, they were interrupted when someone began frantically pounding on their door. Within seconds a voice followed, screaming at them to get up and come out into the hall. It was Yasmine. Demitra hopped out of bed and rushed to the door.

"What's wrong?" Demitra exclaimed as she opened the bedroom door. She placed her hands on Yasmine's baby bump. "Is something wrong with the baby?"

"Yes, but not mine!" Yasmine exclaimed. "Fable is in labor!"

Yasmine rushed back upstairs to Fable's room leaving Demitra in her doorway staring at Jerry in horror. Jerry jumped out of bed and threw on his robe as he followed his wife upstairs to their daughter's room. Behind them they could hear Artemis and Olympia climbing the second-floor stairs to join them.

Demitra made haste into her daughter's bedroom and found Yasmine and Seth on either side of Fable, clutching her hands. Demitra edged Seth back and took his place. Fable's brow was sweaty, and she looked dead white. She was heaving in pain, grappling for anything to hold onto; her cousin's arm, the headboard behind her, anything she could squeeze. Olympia made it to the doorway to find her daughter holding her own daughter in her arms trying to soothe her condition.

"Hold on, baby," Demitra cried out. "It's going to be alright."

"It hurts, Momma. It hurts."

By now, Nacaria was also in the hallway as Beryl came bounding through with her medical bag. "Okay, listen up," she said. "I need everyone out of here."

"I'm not leaving her!" Yasmine exclaimed. The moment the words left her lips the two table lamps of either side of Fable's bed lifted from the nightstands and fell back down, breaking.

"Yes, you are," Beryl demanded. "The last thing I need is for your stress levels to throw you into early labor too. Or your baby's powers to swell. Seth, get her out of here." Seth dragged a reluctant Yasmine into the hall.

"Shouldn't we get her to the hospital?" Nacaria called from the door.

"No!" Fable shouted. "No, hospitals."

"We have to deliver here," Beryl said. "We have no idea what's being born."

Artemis called out to Beryl, "I'll get towels, water, scissors, and string."

Olympia looked frightened. It pained her to see one of her children in such agony. Fable was not able to disguise the amount of discomfort she was in. Olympia had born three children herself and been present for most of the births of the grandchildren. She had been there when Zelda had her two daughters. She had been present when Pastoria gave birth to Seneca and Drake. She had seen childbirth before. Whatever Fable was going through appeared to be far worse than anything she had ever witnessed. Beryl must have noticed the expression on her face.

"She'll be all right, Hecate. Go downstairs, and I will tell you when the baby is born. This is just a home birth, that's all."

Olympia nodded in compliance to her granddaughter's request, knowing she was only being placated. This was not simply an at-home birth. All the births Olympia had ever seen except for Seth, Fable, and Drake had been at-home births. As she turned to go downstairs, she saw Jerry standing in Fable's bedroom by the door, with his back against the wall, watching. She found it strange that he would have even come into the room. Olympia reached out to take his hand to bring him downstairs with her. Suddenly Fable cried out.

"No, stay!" she said. "Jerry and Mother stay."

"No one is staying but you and me, little sister," Beryl ordered, waving everyone out.

Jerry waited for everyone else to clear out. He approached Fable's bed. "Do what your sister says. Your mother and I will be right downstairs."

"Please stay with me," Fable begged him. "I need you."

Beryl was completely confused by the situation taking place and adamant that she needed total cooperation if she were to bring her sister and her sister's baby safely through this intense labor. She was losing patience with her new stepfather and everyone else for that matter. She looked down at Fable's twitching stomach. It moved with a sporadic and violent jolt—like a heart zapped with electricity. Beryl laid her phone atop Fable's stomach, just to test the magnitude of the force trying to escape. Within a couple of seconds Beryl's phone was kicked off. It did not slide off, or lightly bounce off. It jumped off from the pressure within. Childbirth should not cause such pulsation. This was not human.

Beryl was beginning to become frightened. She had no idea what was about to happen. Was the baby about to burst its way through her sister's abdomen? Was it going to be a monster and try to kill the first person it laid evil eyes upon? Beryl had no way of knowing. She needed everyone out of the room.

"Jerry, please get out of here," she requested. "And take Mother with you. Fable and I have to get this baby out now."

"Don't leave me!" Fable pleaded.

"I won't leave you," Jerry said, darting around Beryl and taking hold of Fable's hand.

Beryl was exasperated. "Jerry, we have known you for four months. You are not part of this. For your own safety, I need you to get the hell out of here."

Fable grabbed Beryl's wrist and pulled her close, "Beryl, I want him here."

Beryl did not understand, nor did she have time to try. Whatever was trying to be born right now was trying to get out with a fervor. Fable was now doubled over, pressing her hands into her abdomen in attempt to block the blows being waged on the inside.

There was not much time...

Downstairs in the living room as the sun was beginning to rise outside, Olympia and the others could hear Fable's screams two floors above them. Yasmine leaned into her husband's chest, frightened for her best friend and a little apprehensive that she would be in the same situation in a few months. Nacaria sat beside her mother, trying to comfort the old woman as best she could. Artemis was in the kitchen brewing coffee for everyone. Forest helped her bring the tray. He lifted a cup and took to Olympia.

"Aunt Olympia, drink this. It'll help."

Olympia patted his hand and took the cup and saucer and sat on the table beside her. She didn't feel like having it but was glad it was there. Something about a cup of coffee calmed her nerves, even if it went untouched.

...

Upstairs, Fable let out a glass-shattering cry. Beryl stared unblinking at Fable's heaving chest as she saw what appeared to be a tiny black point begin to emerge through the skin. Trickles of blood immediately flowed around the rising point—that now was hook shaped, like a talon.

"The baby's crowning!" Demitra screamed.

Beryl took her place between Fable's legs to see a small head expelling. It was flesh colored and had hair. It looked to be human...so far. But just above her line of sight, another talon had pierced through Fable's belly, followed by a third. Blood was rushing over her stomach and down onto the sheets.

Demitra continually chanted "Oh no, oh no," as Jerry tried to pull her back out of Beryl's way so that Beryl could get the baby pulled free. Fable was screaming with the agony of a woman literally being ripped to shreds from the inside.

Beryl kept her hands in place between Fable's legs where the head was now fully out and the shoulders were coming. Above, the abdomen had several tiny claws now poking through the blood and flesh. Beryl pulled the baby free from the birth canal and lifted him up for Demitra to take. In the flash of the second she removed him he appeared to be human. Beryl quickly looked to her sister's stomach. The claws were gone. Only the holes they sliced remained.

"Check the hands," Beryl shouted behind her. "Does it have claws Mother?"

Demitra was now wiping the baby with clean towels, removing the mucus and birth fluids from its chest and face. She looked him over thoroughly. Smiling proudly, she cried, "No! He is perfect! Perfect. Toes and fingers only!"

"I don't understand," Beryl began to say but was interrupted by her sister releasing another fevered cry into the quiet of the room.

Beryl looked down and saw another child being born. Beryl was struck with instant fear and panic. Emerging from Fable's cervix came a blackish, shiny snout.

"Push, Fable, push! Quickly!!!"

Fable leaned forward with the help of Jerry and gave a final push. The snout protruded enough for Beryl to grasp and pull, followed by a long mouth and furry face. Its ears were pointed and covered in brown wiry fur. Beryl reached in and grabbed the shoulders of the creature and yanked it free. Its arms and legs—haunches actually—were all covered in fur.

There was no time to spare examining the creature, Fable was dying. Her chest was sliced, and her lower body was eviscerated from the final birth. Beryl handed Jerry the animal and began immediately healing her sister's mortal wounds. It took longer than usual and for a few seconds she worried that she'd be unable to. Last year when she had tried to heal one of Patric's victims, Lana Leighton, she'd been unable to because Lana was a werewolf. There was a second there at Fable's side when Beryl feared her healing power may not work on Fable now. But it did. Fable's wounds began to repair themselves beneath the bright glow of Beryl's regenerative power. Fable was human and she was going to survive.

"I want to see my babies." Fable whispered, half exhausted after the ordeal.

Demitra handed her the boy, shiny and clean. He was beautiful. Fable took him in her arms and smiled. She thought he smiled at her, even though she knew babies do not smile so young. She kissed his cheek and nestled him down into her left arm.

"Give me my other one."

Jerry still had hold of the creature, who was now attempting to lick himself clean, but much too little to understand the way. "It's a wolf," Jerry said. "A male."

"Hand me my other son please," Fable asked.

Beryl and Demitra exchanged nervous glances as Jerry gently laid the small cub into Fable's right arm. The baby wolf seemed to know who she was. He licked her forearm and nuzzled close.

Looking down at her sons, Fable asked to be alone. Unsure what to say or how to handle the situation, Demitra and Jerry complied, stepping out into the hallway. Beryl didn't budge. She was on guard. The wolf might attack. She couldn't be sure. Fable did not seem to share this concern. Beryl looked on in disbelief as Fable removed her breasts and began to feed her children, both of them.

CHAPTER THIRTY ONE

Baby and the Beast

Fable waited in her bedroom, physically and emotionally drained from childbirth. With the question of what kind of baby she might give birth to behind her, there was a new situation looming. What would the family decide should happen next? The family was downstairs, all except her father, who was sitting beside her bed rubbing her hand. The Blanchards were meeting down below to decide the fate of her babies as Fable lay in her bed wondering what they might be saying down there.

"What will happen?" Fable asked her father.

Larry was reticent to say. He truly had no idea what the others would decide. He shrugged—the only thing he knew to do. Then he simply reached over and stroked his daughter's cheek before moving down and caressing the *extremely unidentical* twins in her arms.

Fable yawned as her father leaned back into the chair by her bed. She felt so comfortable between her clean sheets with her two boys resting quietly in her arms. One boy was wrapped in a fresh blanket, snoring softly against her chest. The other boy was snuggled up to her, also snoring, his heavy coat of fur the only blanket he required to keep warm. Every so often, he would open his eyes to look up at her in mild confusion. He was like a small puppy with all its precious exploratory cuteness. She looked at this creature she had just given birth to, and thought to herself, *he's going to be my favorite.* He was going to need her more than the other, that was certainly for sure. She smiled lovingly upon both her children and finally knew that mysterious emotion she had heard about...a mother's love.

"What are we going to do?" Artemis asked Olympia after Demitra and Beryl caught the family up on the events of the birth.

"I'm not certain yet," a shaken Olympia admitted, pacing the living room floor.

Nacaria spoke up from a chair beside the fireplace, "I realize I haven't been back long, but am I the only person concerned that those children's father killed a bunch of people?"

"Nacaria, those babies are innocent," Yasmine defended. "And those babies are my nephews."

"One of those babies is an animal," Nacaria pointed out.

"It's a lot to take in," Seth admitted.

Before anyone else had a chance to weigh in, the front door opened, and Zelda bounded inside. She saw the family gathered in the living room as she passed through the foyer to the stairs. She said nothing to them, only offering a quick wave of acknowledgement before she marched, heavy footed up to Fable's room.

"What is Zelda doing?" Seth asked.

"I called her," Artemis announced. "I want her to examine Fable's babies."

"Excellent idea," Olympia said, clapping her hands together. "I am embarrassed to say *that* perfectly obvious idea failed to occur to me."

"I don't understand," Yasmine replied.

"Don't you see?" Olympia explained, facing the family from the fireplace. "Zelda can look into people's minds better than anyone I've ever known. Artemis was right to call her in. Zelda can look into those babies and see what's lying under the surface."

"Beryl?" Seth asked. "What're your thoughts on the babies? You delivered them."

Beryl stared at her cousin's waiting face, then to everyone else, all looking at her for answers. "I am at a loss for words. This is something my scientific mind cannot fathom."

The family waited for Zelda's report. It did not take long. Within 15 minutes she was back downstairs telling the family everything she had been able to read with the children.

"I don't see nothing that makes me think these kids are a threat."

"But the human child?" Olympia asked. "Will he turn into a werewolf when the moon is full?"

"Are they wolves or witches?" Seth asked. "Do they have powers?"

"Look ya'll," Zelda said. "I don't know all that. You know as well as me that powers show up whenever they show up. All I can tell you is that I used every bit of my psychic senses to read those two babies up there. I can't find anything evil in either one of 'em. That human one seems normal and that baby wolf...well, he's a baby wolf."

"What is your opinion on whether or not we should destroy them?" Artemis asked.

Demitra jumped to her feet from the sofa, "We are not destroying Fable's children!"

"I am speaking to Zelda," Artemis snapped. "I am asking her opinion."

"You aren't the leader of this coven," Demitra said

"Neither are you," Artemis pointed out. "But I am the one who asked Zelda to come here this morning and give us her opinion, and I mean to hear that opinion."

Zelda plopped down in a nearby chair and sighed, "I'd leave things be. I think Fable got herself pregnant by a werewolf and out of some cosmic fluke, instead of having a baby that'd turn into a wolf, the curse split itself separating the man and the beast. Call yourselves lucky and leave it be."

Everyone looked around at each other, unsure how to process Zelda's opinion. Zelda appeared to be very satisfied with her findings and began pouring herself a glass of iced tea from the pitcher on the coffee table. She then cut herself a double portion sized piece of the strawberry rhubarb pie lying beside the pitcher.

"It still is worth addressing that we have an actual wolf in the house," Nacaria said. "He's a wild animal and even run-of-the-mill wolves can be very dangerous."

"Grandmother," Yasmine began. "Killing those babies would be wrong. Zelda just said she felt no evil in them. Maybe we got lucky. I say we let my nephews live. Maybe one day they'll be like their father—maybe they won't. But if we destroy them now, we aren't even giving them a chance."

Fable appeared at the bottom of the stairs. She was wobbly, but thanks to her sister's healing, she was healthy and strong. "I have something to say."

"Where are the babies?" Beryl asked.

"Jerry is with them," Fable said then paused while she and her mother shared a few seconds of silence only the two of them understood. "First of all, I am profoundly sorry that I have placed this dilemma on the family. But I want to assure all of you that my sons are no threats to anyone. I am not going to allow anyone to harm them."

"You cannot make assurances for the wolf," Nacaria said. "His instincts do not have to be of an evil nature to make him want to hunt and kill. It is part of his makeup as a wolf."

"He is not a danger, nor will he be."

"How can you be sure?" Seth asked.

"Because I have the power to communicate and control any animal there is. Have you all forgotten that?"

"So, he will remain here as a pet?" Nacaria asked.

"He is not a pet," Fable said with a clipped tone. "He is my son just as much as the other one. Just as much as Seth is your son."

"Honey, Nacaria didn't mean that the way it sounded. But her point is valid," Artemis replied. "Do you really believe you can bring that animal up the same way as his brother?"

"No," Fable frowned. "I guess to the outside world he'll be considered a dog, or a pet or what have you. But we know. He is a Blanchard. A Blanchard, just like the rest of us. I love him. I can teach him. I have the power.

"It is like Hecate has said before, *the Natural Order of things always works itself out*. The Order solved my problem. Instead of a boy who would turn into a wolf, nature divided it into two babies. And with my power to communicate with animals, it almost feels like a kind of destiny."

Olympia called an end to the debate. She had made her decision. "As head of this coven, I am declaring that Fable's sons be awarded the chance Yasmine argued for." Yasmine and Fable ran to each other and hugged. Olympia waved a finger of caution to them, "However, if at any time one or both of these children exhibit murderous tendencies, I will destroy them myself."

"Understood," Fable smiled, wiping tears.

Fable returned upstairs to be with her sons. Her father was walking them both around the room in his arms. Her heart felt so full seeing him holding his grandsons and seeing him not discriminating between them. He handed the boys off to her and let her be alone with them.

It was only a few moments before a knock came to the door. It was Olympia coming in to see her great grandchildren. Fable was laying in the bed holding them in her arms. Olympia strolled over to look down upon the three of them.

"Now I can look at these two knowing they will be here from now on," she explained. "You'll understand that I couldn't bring myself to view them before I'd made my decision."

"I understand."

As Olympia stared down at the two infants, the human one had his finger wrapped around one of Fable's curls. The little cub was staring up at Olympia with deep, emotional eyes. He was the one she held first.

"He has my father's eyes I believe," she smiled. "They are almost human. So blue, almost crystal."

"It's all going to work out fine, Hecate. You'll see."

"Child, I am happy to see you so happy, but please do not mislead yourself into believing your life will be easy. It will not be. You have damned yourself to quite a difficult journey."

"How so?"

"My sweet naive Fable," Olympia whispered, stroking her granddaughter's hair. "You will watch one son grow into boyhood, and later manhood, while the other son will always walk on all fours, always frighten those he encounters. He will always be dismissed as a well-trained companion and never be regarded with the dignity and respect of his brother. You will never hear him laugh or sing. He is doomed to walk with beasts. That will break your heart as a mother."

"But I will love him enough to compensate."

"There isn't enough love to compensate him for what he has been deprived," Olympia cautioned. "But you will love him, probably the most. I suspect I will love him best too, for the same reasons. I do not fault you, child. You gave in to the wrong man, and now that man has marked your life forever as the father of your children. But I have every confidence that you will do the absolute best you can for these children."

"Thank you, Hecate."

Olympia sat on the edge of the bed and handed the cub over so that she could hold the human infant. "Have you given any thoughts as to what to call these boys?"

"Yasmine wants me to name one Oliver, but I already know their names," Fable said. "The boy you are holding is named Constantinople."

"After my father," Olympia smiled. "He would be pleased to know his name lives on."

"And this one," Fable said, kissing the cub on the head. "His name is Romulus."

"Constantinople and Romulus Blanchard," Olympia repeated. "I like it. The next generation certainly is off to an intriguing beginning."

CHAPTER THIRTY TWO

Parents and Children

The smell of country ham sizzling in the cast iron skillet brought many feet running down the stairs. Yasmine was cooking a big, fine, Blanchard-style Saturday morning breakfast while the other members of the family—minus Beryl, who was on a jog—gathered their yawning faces around the table. Fable came down the stairs last, with both babies in her arms. Her mother took the boy from her while Jerry took the cub. Fable poured herself a cup of coffee and settled down in a chair.

"Sleeping any better?" Jerry asked.

"A little," she smiled scooping up some of the eggs on the plate in front of her. "Believe it or not, Rom sleeps all night. It's Con that keeps waking me up. I think the last time mother got up with him. I was so tired I barely remember. I just remember her coming in and telling me to go back to sleep."

"I did," Demitra said. "I took him in with your—with Jerry and me. I put him back in your room once he was asleep again."

"Your Mother is loving it," Jerry laughed. "These last two months, I think she's lapsed back into Mama mode with Con and Rom."

"I hate those names," Seth groused as he chomped down on a piece of ham, talking with his mouth full. "Rom and Con."

"I love them," Olympia declared, sipping her coffee. "We almost named you Constantinople, but your mother read one of those romance novels and named you Seth after the—what was he Nacaria? A beefy lighthouse keeper?"

Nacaria blushed, "Yes."

Forest ribbed Seth in the side, "You're named for a cheesy Harlequin lighthouse keeper!"

"Shut up, man!"

"Oh my God!" Yasmine yelled from the stove, slamming the spatula down dramatically. "My husband is named after a character from a trashy romance novel. Fitting."

"I don't hear you complaining, babe!" Seth grinned.

"No, you don't," she winked, tossing more piping hot ham onto the platter at the table.

Seth grabbed himself another piece and lifted his plate toward Forest who had the bowl of eggs. Once Forest spooned Seth another helping, Seth announced, "We're naming our son Titan."

"No, we are not," Yasmine corrected as she took her seat at the table now that everyone had everything. "If it is a boy, we are naming him Oliver."

"The hell we are!" Seth barked. "We are not naming my son after the maniac that tried to kill us."

"Hush up, Seth," Demitra scolded. "He was her brother."

"Still not happening," Seth affirmed, shooting his wife a stern look.

Nacaria, curious now about the baby names, turned to her mother. "Where did the name Michael come from?" Nacaria asked her mother.

"Oh, that was David's father's name," Olympia answered. "Salem wanted to name her son Bayne, but David wanted to honor his father."

"I wish I could have known my grandson," Nacaria frowned. "That's why I am so excited about Seth and Yasmine's baby."

"I just realized," Demitra said, clapping her hands together in glee. "We will be grandmothers together! Oh, the fun we will have spoiling these children and laughing at everything they put our own little demons through."

"Demons?!" Seth cried in playful outrage.

"Yes, demons!" Demitra repeated. "You and Fable were a mess. Seth, you used to fall off the stairs practically every day trying to climb the outer rail. Fable used to take her finger paints and smear all over the walls. And you were always getting Yasmine caught up in your schemes. She was never a problem until you two roped her into something."

"And I suppose precious Beryl and Salem never did anything wrong?" Fable bantered.

Beryl heard the conversation as she rounded the corner, coming in from a morning run. "We knew how to behave."

Nacaria chuckled. "I heard about the 1920s flapper trip. I'd say that was pretty bad."

"Oh, my word," Demitra exclaimed. "I forgot about that! You kids really put us through it."

The kitchen door flung open as Zelda bounded in. Her presence was startling initially because the family had only seen her once since she colored her hair bright copper. She was wearing a deep purple dress and looked like someone stuck a freshly minted penny atop an eggplant. She grabbed herself a cup of coffee and a biscuit. Scooting in between Artemis and Demitra, she reached over the table and grabbed the jar of Golden Eagle syrup from Fable and poured over the biscuit. She took her first bite and asked, "What's the morning chatter about today?"

"Just reminiscing about the children's exploits growing up," Olympia explained.

Zelda didn't miss a beat before responding through a mouthful of biscuit and syrup, "Oh yeah, you girls were terrible. Not as bad as my two, but lordy you were some weird little kids."

"We meant the grandchildren," Demitra corrected.

Zelda dabbed a napkin to her chin to catch the syrup and answered, "Oh, them too. But you three girls!"

"Tell us what they did, Zelda?" Yasmine asked.

"Throw me on a piece of that ham and I'll tell you," Zelda ordered. "Artie used to come in this kitchen and drag ever' pot and pan out she could find and throw out the back door. Every time Lympy went to cook supper, she'd have to go out in the yard and get her skillets."

Demitra laughed.

"Oh, and Demmy," Zelda continued. "She used to eat rocks."

"What?" Jerry chuckled. "You ate rocks, Demitra?"

"She didn't eat them exactly," Olympia clarified. "She just liked to store them in her cheeks for some odd reason.

"That's insane!" Nacaria laughed. "My sister, the chipmunk."

"It was better than what you used to do," Demitra teased.

"What did I do?" Nacaria asked. "I don't recall doing anything especially strange."

"Used to pick your nose constantly," Zelda offered. "Ever' time we turned around you were digging in your nose. We called the wall your bed was on the *booger wall.* Lympy had to wrap your hands in towels to keep your fingers out of your nose."

Nacaria turned beet red as the younger generation rolled in laughter. She was always so poised and ladylike, the thought of her as a nose picker was a riot.

"The point of all this," Olympia said, redirecting the conversation, "is that children do outlandish and sometimes wondrous things, and we are excited to see you as new parents go through it, too."

Finished with her breakfast, Fable stood up to leave the table. "Speaking of children, I need to get mine back upstairs for their next feeding."

Fable and Demitra took the babies back upstairs. Olympia and Zelda had a park restoration committee meeting with the mayor's wife and a few other prominent Daihmler women. Seth and Yasmine left out to go do some baby shopping. Forest was driving over to Atlanta to see Arielle for the weekend, and Artemis had to go into work. This left Beryl and Jerry alone together in the kitchen, each volunteering to load the dishwasher and clean up the breakfast mess.

"I don't believe in pre-rinsing," Beryl told her new stepfather. "Just toss everything in the dishwasher, and I'll start scrubbing the pans."

Jerry stacked the dirty plates from the table and placed them in a neat upright line on the rack of the dishwasher. Next, he grabbed all the utensils from the table in both fists and carried them over to drop into the utensil bin. Releasing one grip of forks, spoons, and knives, a single carving knife fell through—with the sharp edge facing into his hand—and sliced his palm open with a two-inch gash.

"Damn!" he cried.

Beryl whirled around and saw the cut. Blood was coming out pretty fast. She rushed over to him with a dishtowel. "Here, Jerry. Hold this firmly." She paused to think but remembered he had seen her heal Fable, so he knew all about their magic. "Would you like me to bandage this, or...I can just heal the wound."

Jerry did not seem afraid of the offer. He tilted his head and gave a sly grin, "Just heal it, please."

Beryl placed her hands on his arm, allowing that deep inner light that lived within her to begin its swell. Rapidly it grew bigger and bigger, emanating throughout her entire being. This gift bestowed to her began doing its thing, and with it always came the visions. She could see his worth, see his life as the power surged through and began healing his small wound. His love for his wife. His love for his children. *Children?* she thought. *Jerry has no children.* Daughters. Two of them. She could see him playing with them as girls. Tucking them in at night. Teaching them how to drive when they turned 16. Only the man in her vision did not have Jerry's face. And the girls in her vision were she and Fable. The wound was healed, and the power shut off. Beryl took an involuntary step backward away from the man. He was puzzled by the expression on her face. She looked aghast. In shock.

"Beryl? You all right?"

"You're not Jerry Miller," she choked on the words. "Oh, dear heavenly God, what is happening? Your memories are my father's memories."

Jerry walked quickly to the door between the kitchen and dining room and closed it. He turned back to Beryl, tears in his eyes, and opened his arms. "Yes, Princess, it's me. It's Daddy."

Beryl's eyes watered. She believed him—she had to. She had seen it with her own power. "How?" she stuttered.

Larry Mariner attempted to clasp his eldest's hands, but she pulled back, still unsure, still in shock. "Your mother brought me back and put me in this body."

"That isn't possible," Beryl cried, knowing very well as she said it that in their world almost anything was possible. "Who does this body belong to? Is Jerry Miller a real person? I met his parents. Are they fake too?"

"No, no, Jerry was real and so are his parents. They believe I am Jerry."

Beryl could not believe what she was hearing. She asked the question she didn't actually want the answer to. "Where is Jerry now?"

Her father answered as gingerly as he could. "He's here, inside. Pushed way down. Eventually he will disappear."

"You mean die!" Beryl shouted. "How can you be so caviler about this? You or Mother?! This is not the Dad that I remember. My father would never take another man's life."

Demitra was now on the stairs, hearing everything. She bounded down and confronted her daughter. She was furious and, without thinking, she slapped her daughter across the face.

Instantly Larry jumped between them. "Demitra?!" He turned to Beryl, "Princess are you alright?"

"Don't you ever speak to your father like that," Demitra raged. "You know what a good man he is."

"What about you, Mother?" Beryl asked. "Are you a good woman? Haven't you essentially killed a man?"

"Jerry Miller had nothing worthwhile in his life," Demitra argued. "He had virtually no friends. His marriage was over. His job was lackluster. He had withdrawn from his parents. Now his parents have us. A family. A daughter-in-law they adore and new step granddaughters. Everyone is better off this way."

"Except the man who is dying inside this body!" Beryl snapped tapping Larry's chest.

Demitra paced the kitchen frantically. She never dreamed Beryl would have this reaction. Fable had been overjoyed. Why did Beryl always have to take the high road? Larry reached out to grab her hand on one of her laps, but Demitra rejected it as she continued to shake her head and try to think of some way to appease her daughter's conscience.

"Beryl," Demitra said softly. "Your father is back. And we can all go back to living our lives together now."

"It's not right, Mother. Dad lived his life and died. You have stolen another man's life journey. It's against everything we believe."

Larry didn't want to be harsh with his daughter, although it was hurting his feelings that she wasn't the least bit joyful he was back. After her last statement, he ruptured like a dam. "What do you want Beryl? Do you want me to be dead again? Do you want me to come clean and tell the world that my wife is a witch and by supernatural means resurrected me? Do you want your mother being tried and convicted by the witch's council?"

"I don't know what I want!" Beryl cried. "I think things should have remained the way they naturally were. Don't get me wrong, I am so happy you're here. But this is not right. You have stolen another man's body—his life!"

"It was no life," Demitra restated coolly. "Jerry Miller had nothing in his life going for him. He was virtually all alone."

"Does that give you the right to steal it from him?" Beryl shot back. "There is something wicked about this. Deceitful. It isn't fair that I should get my father back when everyone else in the world must suffer through their loss of loved ones. Think of Salem. Why is it fair for you to do this yet she lost David and Michael? The Natural Order has been defiled."

"Beryl, I don't think this is harming anyone," Larry told his eldest. "It's just one person, me."

"When you break a natural law, you set up an imbalance in the world," Beryl said. "Mother, you know that. You have set off a chain of events none of us can fathom. You cannot defy death!"

"I think I already have," Demitra said imperiously.

Beryl started for the door, but paused before walking out and said, "You are not God."

CHAPTER THIRTY THREE

Sisters

Fable was in her room with the babies. Con was sleeping soundly in the bassinet beside her bed. Romulus was curled up in a ball on the settee on the wall. As Beryl went inside, she found her sister dressing for work in her veterinarian scrubs with little doggy bones and kitten whiskers covering a lavender cotton.

Startled by Beryl's entry, Fable said, "Oh, I thought you were Mother. She going to watch the boys while I go into work. Is something wrong?"

The boys, Beryl thought. A human infant and a baby wolf. This was her family now. And a father resurrected from the dead. It was almost too much for her logical mind to comprehend. Beryl sat down at the edge of the bed.

"Fable, do know about Jerry?"

Fable froze. She had one of those looks about her like a character in a daytime soap opera being caught in a lie right before the commercial break.

"I see that you do," Beryl remarked. "How long have you known Jerry is actually our father?"

Fable did not want to answer. She knew her sister would be furious. But she answered anyway. "Since before Christmas."

"Christmas!" Beryl exclaimed. "It's Spring now! Why did you not tell me? I deserved to know."

"I didn't think you could handle it," Fable said. "You know how you are."

Beryl angrily threw a pillow across the room before blowing a stray blonde curl from her eyes. "And how exactly am I?"

Fable continued adding mascara to her lashes. The very act during such a serious conversation seemed flippant and only succeeded in angering Beryl more. "Everything with you is so black and white, good or bad. With you there are no shades of gray. No spectrum. Something is just right or wrong"

"That's because things are either right or they are wrong, Fable."

"I don't agree," Fable argued, facing her sister. "I don't see the big deal here, Beryl. It's a miracle."

"Miracles are the creations of God, not us. This is *our miracle*. Not God's."

"God." Fable said rolling her eyes. "But let's just say there is a God..."

"There is."

Fable sent another eye roll her sister's way. "Okay, say there is...He gave us powers then. If He made everyone the way He wanted them, then He gave us this ability."

"Not to do this!" Beryl exclaimed. "We are meant to help people. To protect the earth. Not resurrect the dead."

"But if we can, why shouldn't we?"

Beryl took another frustrated huff at her curly bangs until they fluttered out of her eye. "Because it is unfair, Fable. Why do we get to have our own private miracle when everyone else in the world in grief doesn't? It is not right, or fair."

Fable could see her point but still didn't feel compelled by it, "True, not everyone gets this gift we have been given, but why should that keep us from being thankful for it?"

"Because it isn't a gift, Fable. It's a theft. It is stealing a life."

"Don't you even care that our father is here?" Fable challenged. "Have you even spent three minutes just embracing that fact? Have you hugged him? Talked with him? Told him the things you've wished all these years you could say to him?"

"I just found out."

"The second I found out I almost suffocated him with my hug," Fable admonished. "I'd think you might be just a tinsy bit happy over it."

Beryl stood defiantly, "Don't you dare question my love for our father."

"Then show some."

CHAPTER THIRTY FOUR

Fathers

Demitra and Larry took the boys out for a short walk on the property. Demitra held baby Con in her arms, wrapped snugly in a warm blanket while Jerry watched Romulus hopping and running across the yard on their way to the apple orchard. Romulus was mesmerized by the outdoors. The brown grass was just beginning to turn green, and a few clumps of dandelions were sprouting up in places. The cub scurried toward one and yowled at it, snapping his little teeth at the stalk and shaking the weed. The little white speckles of seed shook off, a couple fluttering onto his nose. He sneezed and blew them off. In the distance a squirrel scampered across the ground near a tree, and Romulus took off after him. The squirrel fled for his life up the trunk of the tree as the baby wolf tried with all his might to jump high enough to reach. Once he figured out that was impossible, he took a chance at climbing. Inserting his razor claws into the bark, he made some progress but only got about a foot or two from the ground when he toppled off backward and landed on his back. He gave a shrill little yelp, and Larry picked him up.

"Buddy you can't chase other creatures around. We give you plenty of food. You must learn to control your instincts and not harm any other living things."

Romulus licked Larry's chin as a means to acknowledge the guidance or perhaps to appear so cute that his grandfather wouldn't be angry. Larry put him back down on the ground and let him return to running freely across the meadow.

Romulus had to be walked several times a day, but at so young an age, his exploratory nature was kicking in and he was eager to cover as much terrain as his little legs allowed. Fortunately for Demitra and Larry, those little legs exhausted quickly, so he didn't get very far.

As they rounded the chicken houses, Larry picked Rom up and carried him. The little wolf was tuckered out from the run across the field, and Larry wanted to keep him from pestering the chickens. He was still too young to understand he could not attack the birds. It was a surprise when they saw Beryl at the chicken house, basket in hand, collecting the eggs. At first, they considered going a different direction to avoid her, respectful that she needed time to herself to process things. But Beryl saw them and went to them.

"I want to clarify something," she said rather woodenly when she approached. She looked into her father's eyes and continued. "I am genuinely happy to have you back." Beryl gave Larry a hug. A real hug. She lingered, allowing herself to push past the stranger's body she held and feel the father she loved within it. Tears came to her eyes, as well as his.

"Princess."

Beryl placed her hands on his face and told him, "Dad, I am glad you're here. The fact that I get to hold you again and tell you how much I love you is everything to me. I have missed you so much."

Demitra broke in on the moment, "Does that mean you will keep our secret, Beryl?"

"I can't promise that." Beryl admitted. "Even though I am happy to have you back in our lives Dad, it does not undo the fact that this whole situation is wrong. And Mother, you know it is. Hecate has always taught us the dangers of breaking the Order. Aunt Nacaria broke the Order, and you know what happened to her. Fable made a mistake, and now her children have to pay for it. There is always a price to pay."

"I don't believe any of this!" Demitra said resentfully, trying not to wake Con with her raised voice. Rom, uncomfortable with the tension, jumped down from Larry's arms and curled behind Demitra's legs. "Your father is back in our lives, and all you can do is protest that it is wrong."

"It is wrong," Beryl said flatly. She turned to Larry, "I love my father. I have missed you more than my heart can express. But you are not my father. Oh, I believe you are Larry Mariner. But when I look at you, I see the man I held in the highest esteem, hijacking a stranger's body. I realize this is not your fault. Mother did this. And I get that you, she and Fable—and even me—would love nothing more than for you to stay. But that basically means killing an innocent man who didn't deserve to have his life commandeered just because my mother missed her husband."

"I guess you wouldn't be our Beryl if you didn't see it that way," Larry said.

She turned to her mother, "A witch is supposed to protect the Natural Order of things. Supposed to help look after those who cannot protect themselves. What you have done is trample on the life of someone else just to get what you want. I'm so disappointed in you."

"Beryl," Demitra pleaded. "You don't understand what it has been like for me without your father. He is my soulmate."

"Forever and three days," Beryl said. "When I heard you say those words at the wedding—words you and Dad always said to each other—I should have known then what you have done."

"Beryl, please don't tell this to Mother or Artemis."

"Larry Mariner," Beryl explained. "He lived a fantastic life and was fantastically loved. But he had his time. Jerry Miller has been murdered simply because you wanted more. There is *nothing* you can say that erases that fact."

"If you won't understand," Demitra requested. "At least do not reveal us."

"I won't, for now," Beryl said. "I am holding out hope that you, Dad, and Fable will come to your senses and do the right thing."

...

Seth was picking the most ridiculous combinations for the nursery. Yasmine was going behind him and deleting his selections from the handheld scanner at the baby store. Blue gingham bedding mixed with yellow and light green giraffe curtains and a bright red chest of drawers were not the vision she had in mind.

"Why do you keep vetoing everything I pick?"

Yasmine rolled her eyes to another expectant mother on the aisle with them who was witnessing Seth's selections. The woman gave a sly wink in solidarity. "Because you have terrible taste," Yasmine replied.

"I picked you," Seth flirted, pushing the cart farther down the aisle.

"After years of me waiting," Yasmine scoffed.

"Well hell, Yaz, you were my cousin," Seth replied.

The woman on the aisle who had been squarely in Yasmine's corner with Seth's lackluster baby selections overheard this exchange too. Immediately the solidarity with Yasmine faded and a look of abject disgust came over her face. Yasmine noticed right away.

"It's Alabama, lady!" she blurted out to the woman as she and Seth turned the cart onto the next aisle.

"Yaz why don't we buy everything in blue in case it's a boy and everything in pink in case it's a girl, then we have all the bases covered," Seth suggested.

Yasmine looked at the price tag of the baby carrier on the shelf and gasped. "Do you know how much that would cost?"

"You're rich!" Seth exclaimed. "What did Howard say you were worth when he did the taxes in April, like $20 million?"

"We are not throwing good money away, Seth," Yasmine insisted. "We will pick things that suit either a boy or a girl. Besides, it's a gender fluid time. Our baby may not even know what sex it identifies with."

Now it was Seth's time to roll his eyes. "Well, boy or girl, gay or straight, gender fluid or not, we gotta pick something."

Yasmine scanned the medium-priced baby carrier and continued on her way. Seth snatched the scanner from her and scanned the more expensive one. When she turned around to argue, he simply stuck his phone in her face where he had Googled the safety ratings for the one she picked. She scanned the comments from other buyers and pressed delete on her selection.

"There. You got to pick something," she told him.

A few minutes later they passed through an aisle of stuffed animals. Yasmine was having fun picking cute little fuzzy bears and penguins and rabbits. It was more difficult than she imagined—picking neutral toys that would fit any sex. It caused her to think more about what they'd talked about earlier.

"Seth?" she asked. "Would it bother you if our child was gay?"

"Lord, Yaz, let the kid get born before you throw curveballs at us."

"No, seriously, honey," she pushed. "How would you feel if our little boy or girl turned out to be gay?"

Seth gave the thought a roll around in his head a moment and answered, "I don't guess it would matter much really. I mean, I'd prefer it to not be only because some people out there are still cruel as fuck to people different than they are. But for me personally, I don't guess it'd matter. It's still my kid."

"That's how I feel too!" she beamed. "I'm glad to know we're on the same page."

Seth then looked as if he were considering something in his mind. He grabbed her hand to stop her from continuing down the aisle and said, "But you know I will have rules."

"Rules?"

"Yeah, when my daughter starts dating guys, I have a bunch of restrictions and rules. And if we have a boy that ends up being gay, those same rules apply to him."

"What if we have a straight son?"

Seth grinned and said, "Then that's the problem for the father of whatever girl he dates."

"That's sexist, Seth!"

"I don't care."

Yasmine was appalled. "So our straight son can go out and do whatever he wants. But our daughter, or our gay son has a set of rules they have to follow when they date?"

"Yes."

"Why?"

"Because guys are awful," Seth replied. "And no daughter of mine or gay son of mine is going to go out with any guy I don't okay first."

Yasmine didn't understand. "But if we have a straight boy he can do whatever he wants?"

"Yeah."

"What if we have a gay daughter?" Yasmine asked, thinking she'd trip him up on his logic.

Her attempt didn't work, as Seth responded, "She can do whatever she wants too."

Yasmine whacked him with the large stuffed ostrich in her hand. "Seth Blanchard you are a neanderthal!"

CHAPTER THIRTY FIVE

The Secret is Out

For the last couple of weeks, Olympia sensed something was wrong within the family. Beryl seemed distant—both emotionally and physically. She rarely came home for dinner much anymore. When she was around the family, Olympia took notice that her interactions with Demitra and Jerry were very limited. Olympia tried to question Demitra on the matter once, but it was quickly dismissed as nothing to be concerned about. Olympia let it go at that. She had more on her mind anyway than Beryl's slow adjustment to her mother's new husband.

Olympia had already begun construction on the new addition to the house. It was an unsettling endeavor to her nerves having the crews pounding and hammering and beep beep beeping their yellow excavating vehicles all day. But she was doing her best to not complain. The house needed enlarging. The family was growing, and the house must grow with it. She had to make sure Blanchard House was settled before her time came. And it was coming closer. She could feel it. Her heart felt so fragile now. The least bit of excitement or exertion was a strain. She let her garden be her medicine. Tending to her flowers always supplied her with peace.

She was in her garden, tying the snapdragon blooms to twigs she stuck upright beside the plants, hoping to keep the stems reinforced from the weight of the heavy flowers. She loved the month of May. It was the end of Spring. Spring was typically her least favorite season. The blooms all around in the trees and the flower garden were beautiful in spring, but the unpredictability of Alabama springtime usually made her joints ache. Warm one day, bitterly cold the next, Spring was far too impulsive for her tastes. May typically offered fewer surprises. She liked the weather to know what it was doing. It never occurred to her until summer every year, that she could have asked Seth to warm at least their yard with his powers. But then again, she usually refused to utilize Beryl's healing powers unless it was something relatively minor. A cut. A headache. A slight cold. Olympia felt no qualms in being healed from such ailments but the biggies—it wasn't fair in her eyes to defy death, or aging. This was also why she was keeping the secret about her heart issue. She'd lived a life protecting the Natural Order of things, she was not about to turn her back on those convictions now that it was inconvenient for her.

The roaring noise from the construction going on at the other end of the house was disrupting the tranquility she usually felt in her garden. But it had to be done, so she would find a way to adjust to it.

Jerry was getting out of his car in the driveway and saw Olympia piddling in the garden. He walked over to her and said, "Are those the same plants you had out in the greenhouse two months ago?"

"Same ones," she smiled. "They are quite the growers this year. How was work? Still liking your new job?"

"I do," Jerry said.

He was about to say something about his day when he saw Olympia suddenly bristle, like a disturbed cat. He followed the trail of her eyes and saw a construction worker lifting a chainsaw from the back of his pick-up truck.

"Hey!' she shouted, reaching her hand out for Jerry to assist her from the ground. "What is that saw for?"

The man walked over to Olympia's garden with the chainsaw in hand and tipped his hat to the elderly lady. "Afternoon, ma'am. It's nothing really, just a pesky tree limb in our way. Whole tree is in the way really. We should cut it down."

"No tree is ever in someone's way," Olympia declared. "If a tree is in your way, find another way."

"But ma'am we're trying to build you an addition here. It's just a sweet gum—more of an eyesore than a tree really."

"Young man," Olympia said mightily. "That tree is your brother. Go around it."

"But Miss Blanchard, that would mean that hallway is gonna have to turn in three different directions before it even connects to the first room."

"Then we will have an exciting walk to that part of the house. No trees are to be cut down. Work around them."

The worker eyed Jerry as if awaiting some indicating nod that the old woman had a screw loose. Jerry offered no such indictment. He simply told the man, "You are never going to win this argument. Please just do as my mother-in-law asks."

The man wandered off back to his workers, muttering to himself as he went, stopping to place his chainsaw back into his truck before he returned to work. Olympia returned to her snapdragons, and Jerry took a seat on the garden bench.

"You know Olympia, I had a look at those sketches of yours for the addition and if you don't mind my saying so, you didn't think it out very well."

Olympia looked up at him in surprise. "Jerry, you have been a part of this family for four months now, time enough for you to have learned how I feel about nature and cutting it down."

"Oh, I don't mean that," he clarified. "What I mean is there's really not much difference in building the hallway under the trees or jutting out a few feet from them, either way you are going to have one long dark corridor when the rest of the house is so bright. I was thinking you've made a mistake with building the hallway out of reconstituted lumber."

"I only use repurposed materials in building," Olympia noted.

"Yeah, I know, but why make the hall out of wood at all? There are no rooms to connect with until it clears the trees, so no need for conventional walls at all. Just run a glass hallway through the tree line and allow natural light in. Plus, you'll get to see the lawn and gardens on that side of the house as you make your way to the new wing."

"What a splendid idea, Jerry!" Olympia exclaimed. "I can't believe that notion never occurred to me before. It's brilliant! I'm going to go inside and call the contractor right now." She paused and said, "Oh would you be a dear and wait out here for the pool maintenance man? He's supposed to be here any time now to install a new pump."

"I'd be glad to," Jerry said, then he gave a deep chuckle and added. "I still can't believe you allowed Sinclair to put in that pool. That was quite a battle back then."

"Yes, it was," Olympia replied, eyeing Jerry suspiciously. He was not paying attention to her, too lost in what appeared to be his own memories to catch his mistake.

"You came home, and he'd already had the hole excavated. Boy that was a doozy of a fight! We thought for sure you'd fill it back in, but you gave in and let him pour the concrete."

Olympia continued with the conversation, her eyes inspecting him closely as he stood reflecting. "I knew the kids wanted a pool so badly. You did too, although you let them do all the arguing. But I knew you wanted the pool just as much as the grandchildren did...didn't you Larry?"

"I really did," Larry laughed. "I put Seth up to bringing it up every night until finally—" he stopped. "No, Olympia, it's me, Jerry. Remember, Larry is dead. He was Demitra's first husband. Maybe you are overheated out here."

"Lawrence Mariner do not stand here and try to make me think I am senile. You know me far too well to think I'd fall for that."

Larry looked into his mother-in-law's eyes. His own were swelling with tears, as were hers. He grabbed her in his arms and gave her the hug he had been longing to give the old woman since he had first been introduced as Jerry Miller. He loved this woman, always had. He had missed being able to be himself with her. They had been so close.

"Olympia! Olympia!" he said crying as he squeezed her in his arms.

Forgetting her morals for a moment, she gave into her emotions as she felt his arms around her. "Larry, oh Larry, I have missed you so much. You cannot know how deeply I mourned you. You were like my very own son." She pulled away from him. She regained her composure and was quite serious now. "But Larry this is wrong! This is an abomination."

"I know," he said. "We both know, Dee and me. But Olympia, I have my life back! My girls! You, Seth, Yaz! I have grandbabies now! Olympia, please don't send me back. I've come home."

Olympia wiped her eyes with her soft aged fingers, then she wiped his. She clasped his hand and brought it to her cheek as another tear strolled down and over it. "But Larry, this is another man's body. I cannot believe Demitra did this. She must have used one of Nacaria's old spells. When they were girls and their cat died, they brought it back in the body of a stray we found. It took me a while to figure out it was our old cat. I thought I'd made them understand way back then, why this is wrong."

"What will you do, Olympia?"

"I must think, Larry," the old woman replied. "My heart is so full of happiness and yet it's breaking all over again."

"Please, just remember how much I love your daughter," Larry begged. "How much I love this whole family."

"That's all I can think about. And remembering how much this family loves you."

CHAPTER THIRTY SIX

Guess Who's Not Dead Anymore?

Olympia took a long stroll over her property. The last time she had walked as far and for as long, her legs had been much younger. The breeze blowing over the meadows used to always clear her mind. It was not working the same now. All the walks in the world could not tackle this problem. Larry was back. Her precious son-in-law whom she had cared about so very much. What should she do? She knew what ought to be done, yet it was almost too terrible to consider. She loved Larry. From the moment Demitra brought him into their lives all those years ago, everyone loved Larry.

Olympia could still recall the night decades ago when Demitra brought him to dinner. Olympia was married to Martin then. Martin was already sick with the cancer growing inside him, but he still insisted upon coming down to meet Demitra's beau. Everyone was taken with Larry. Handsome and friendly, he made them all laugh a lot. After that first dinner came many. Within time Larry was a regular face at their dinner table every Friday and Saturday night. When Martin died, Larry took over completely for the Blanchard women. He arranged the funeral, contacted Martin's son and friends. He aided Olympia in any way he could. The following summer he married Demitra.

Olympia laughed to herself recalling the day he asked for Demitra's hand. Olympia had been in the greenhouse, trimming some of her plants. He'd wandered in and within a second, she knew why he was there, although she allowed him the time to work up his courage to say it. He tried to soothe his nerves by helping her trim a boxwood. He spoke of love and life. He compared nurturing love to trimming the boxwood. It was a hilariously incoherent speech which at the end both Olympia and Larry looked down to the boxwood to find he had trimmed it to the trunk. The look on his face was priceless.

But that was a long time ago. Things were different now. Larry was supposed to be dead. The Blanchards made their peace with that long ago. Olympia was happy when Demitra had spoken of being in love again after such a long period of mourning. Jerry Miller was a welcome presence which Olympia celebrated. Now to discover it was all a lie. Demitra had not recovered from her grief, she had only found a way to resurrect the dead. And this was a crime against nature.

The old woman journeyed back to the house after her walk. The fresh spring air accomplished nothing in sorting her thoughts. Instead, they were far more jumbled than ever. Demitra was waiting on the porch when Olympia came up the steps.

"Mother, I—"

"Don't," Olympia cut her off. "I need to be alone for a while."

"Let me explain," Demitra urged.

"There is nothing to say," her mother replied. "I know why you did it. That does not excuse it. You have hurt us all, all over again." Olympia went upstairs to her room.

Alone in her room, Olympia Blanchard sat on the bed and knew what had to be done. She picked up her telephone and called Atlanta. She instructed Salem and Arielle to come to Blanchard House the following morning for a coven meeting. Next, she phoned Artemis at the restaurant and asked her to take the following day off. Then Beryl. She walked down the hallway to her grandnephew Forest's room. Since he'd been living at Blanchard House while attending spring semester at the University of Alabama, she only really saw him at meals and weekends—if he wasn't visiting Arielle. She knocked on the door, then opened it.

"Hi, Aunt Olympia," Forest said, setting aside his theology book.

"I need you to skip classes tomorrow. You're going to have your first coven meeting here."

A nervous look crossed his face. He spun around in his chair to face her. "Is this about the speeding ticket I got yesterday?" he asked. "Honestly, Aunt Olympia, I didn't even know I was speeding. The sign said 40 but then just a mile down the road it went to 25 and I didn't know. Yeah, I was driving 50, but you're supposed to get 10 miles over the limit forgiveness. At least that's what I've always heard."

Olympia shook her head at the boy.

"But you don't have to call a coven meeting about it." Forest continued. "I'll pay the fine; I just have to tell my Dad first, and he's going to be furious."

The self-absorption of the young always tickled her. Olympia mused a gentle smile before replying, "We don't hold coven meetings over traffic violations, Forest. Put the ticket on my desk in the study, and I will send out a check to cover it. No need in upsetting your father. But if you get any more, I will call him myself. Just be home tomorrow for the coven meeting."

Olympia went to Seth and Yasmine's room, followed by Nacaria's, then Fable's. She ordered them all to be present the following day.

. . .

The next morning at Blanchard House anxiety filled every nook and cranny, clinging to the timbers and creeping under the doors. Demitra was nauseous with it. Larry felt his share as well. Never under their roof had so much conflict and chaos reigned. It was too much for Demitra to handle. She never thought the secret would come out when she reconstituted Larry. She should have known it could not be hidden forever. Larry had always been far too much of a member of the Blanchard family for it to have gone unnoticed or unsuspected. He wasn't simply a son-in-law; he was the same as blood. How could she have expected people would not figure it out? Jerry may have a different face but underneath he was pure Larry.

"I can't stand this waiting," Demitra said to Larry up in their room, waiting for the meeting to be called down below. "Let's run away. You and I can go far from here and be together the rest of our lives."

Larry sat beside his wife and stroked her shiny black hair. "Think clearly, Dee. That's not an option."

"Sure, it is!" she cried. "We can go as far away from Daihmler as we can get. We can stay together."

"You and your family are far too close to do that. Besides the whole point in bringing me back was to have our family restored. You, me, the girls, everyone. You didn't bring me back just to become severed from everyone else."

"I can't lose you again, Larry," she sobbed. "My heart can't survive that again."

He did not want to lose her either. He loved her so much, always had. Her alabaster chiseled face, her soft black hair which always seemed to smell of gardenias. Those violet eyes. She was his entire world. Would the Blanchards really insist on returning him to the nothingness of death?

A car door slammed outside. Larry got up and looked out from their window. "Salem is here with her sister."

"That's not good."

Olympia called the coven meeting to order. Demitra and Larry came down the stairs and took a seat on two of the dining room chairs brought in for the meeting. The room was abuzz with chatter, family members curious to know what it was all about and why everyone had been summoned. Nacaria could tell it had something to do with Demitra by the way Demitra sat clutching Jerry's hands with Fable seated at her feet on the floor, almost as if guarding them. Romulus was curled at his mother's side, his head in her lap. Baby Con lay sleeping in the bassinet in the corner.

"What is all this about Hecate?" Salem asked.

Olympia cleared her throat and called the family to attention before she began. "I just discovered something which must be handled immediately. It's a serious matter for this family."

"You aren't going to send him back!" Fable cried, interrupting her grandmother with what sounded more like an order, which was something no Blanchard ever thought they would dare hear anyone give Olympia.

"So, you have known all this time," Olympia said.

"Not the entire time," Demitra replied. "But she does know."

"In all disclosure," Beryl said. "I found out myself recently. I have been waiting for one of them to come clean. I realize I should have done so myself."

"What is this all about?" Salem cried.

A silence covered the room. No one spoke. Perhaps those who knew the reason were waiting for Olympia to speak it. Perhaps Olympia was waiting for the guilty to confess. But not a sound resonated from the walls beyond that of the grandfather clock in the foyer.

Jerry looked at the faces around the room—faces he loved. They had to be told. "I'm not Jerry Miller."

Seth turned to Yasmine. She shrugged. He didn't understand. "Then who are you?"

"I'm the man that coached you in Little League. The man who taught Salem to drive. I am the one who gave Yasmine the nickname Yazzy."

"That wasn't you," Seth said. "That was our Uncle L—"

"He is Larry," Olympia announced.

Salem, Seth, and Yasmine were shell shocked by the revelation. Forest, Arielle, and Nacaria were just as in the dark, but their relationships with Larry Mariner, when he was alive, had been either nonexistent or brief. Seth eyed Jerry suspiciously for a long time before turning back to his grandmother. She reconfirmed her statement. A gentle nod told him it was the truth.

"That isn't possible!" Yasmine exclaimed.

"Demitra infused Jerry Miller's body with Larry's spirit," Olympia explained.

"I don't believe it," Nacaria gasped. "Larry? It's really you?"

"Hey, Nikki," he smiled.

Seth walked closer to him and stared into his eyes, "You're Uncle Larry?"

Larry looked lovingly back at his nephew. "Yes, son. I am."

Seth stood before him, scanning his face, his eyes, his aura for any semblance of the man who'd meant so much to his life. A flicker in Jerry's eyes told him what he needed. Seth threw his arms around him. Larry gripped Seth tightly and patted his back as they embraced. Seth was crying.

"Larry, damn I've missed you!" Seth said, brushing the tears away with his wrist. "I have so much to tell you. I'm having a baby soon! Yaz and I are married—"

Stating the obvious, Salem told her brother, "He's been here through all of that, Seth," She was glaring at her aunt and uncle now. "I'm guessing we have never actually met the real Jerry Miller."

"No, you haven't," Larry said. "It's been me the whole time."

Suddenly Salem's face lit up with a new comprehension of the facts. "That means it is possible!" She turned to Artemis. "We can bring David and Michael back!"

This was exactly the kind of repercussion Olympia feared most. The fallout from Demitra's selfishness would hurt far more people than Demitra ever considered. Olympia had been there with Salem in that terrible moment when she learned her husband and son were killed in a car accident. Salem had broken. Unable to accept reality, she tried to change it, sending herself backward in time to stop their deaths. It was a fruitless effort, and Salem grieved hard. She was only now finally coming to terms with her losses. This development with Larry was certain to set her back now.

It was Artemis who stepped in to try to explain to Salem, saving Olympia the pain. "No, Salem," Artemis answered. "You don't understand. If Larry is here, then Demitra killed Jerry Miller."

"I did not kill anyone!" Demitra defended herself. "He's just asleep."

Artemis shot her sister a look of disapproval. "That's semantics, Dee."

"You have essentially killed him, daughter," Olympia professed. "Softening the deed by calling it sleep does not alter the deed."

"So what?" Seth cried. "The point is we have Uncle Larry back!"

"That's what I say too!" Fable agreed. "It's something to rejoice over, not be upset about."

Salem stood up and walked over to her aunt Demitra. "Then why can't we bring back my husband and son?" she asked. "If this is possible, you can bring them back too, Aunt Demitra. Please. Give me my David and Michael back."

Arielle rushed to Salem and wrapped her arms around her waist. Laying her head on Salem's back she whispered, "No, Salem. No. It's dark—this is dark witchcraft. The stuff my mother's family deals in."

"Even so?" Salem said.

Artemis was incensed. She rose from her chair and confronted Demitra, pulling Salem out of her way. Arielle directed her sister back to a chair. "This is what you have done by this, Dee," Artemis said. "Look at what this puts Salem through now."

Forest turned to Arielle and whispered, "I am so confused."

"I'll explain later," she told him.

Nacaria faced her sister and said, "Demitra, this is bad. This is akin to what I did way back then. This is Council stuff, Dredmore stuff. This is really bad."

"Not if we keep this within the family," Fable pleaded. "We've already bent the rules for Rom and Con. What's one more?"

"We bent nothing for your children," Olympia explained. "They are witches being given the chance to prove they are not dangerous. Larry's situation is on a different level. A crime has been committed."

"We just deal with it," Seth said waving his arms. "It's not like we can undo it now."

"It is precisely like we can undo it now," Olympia corrected her grandson. "Jerry Miller can be restored."

"As he should be," Nacaria added.

Demitra was furious, furious at everything, but she directed her fury the safest place she could, to her younger sister. "You're just jealous because I have my man and you never could have yours. Even now, you've seen Xander maybe twice since New Year's. He's probably never going to come back for you, and you hate me because I have Larry back!"

"Why would I hate you?" Nacaria yelled. "I loved Larry, too. Why would I find pleasure in your losing him?"

"Because Artemis and I raised your children, and you hate us for that and sending Larry away would be your way to punish me!"

Nacaria slapped Demitra across the face. Suddenly all hell broke loose as Fable jumped to her mother's defense and shoved Nacaria backwards. Seth caught his mother before she fell and charged forward. Salem raised her hands and froze everyone in the room. Her entire family stood stone still in the living room as she began to cry. She cried from the shock of what she had just heard. She cried from the tension her normally close-knit family was demonstrating. She cried because she knew now it was possible she might restore David, yet probably wouldn't ever be able to.

Olympia allowed her to cry. She remained as still as possible, allowing her granddaughter to believe she had privacy. But old bones do not stand still long, especially if that witch also has the power to freeze. After a few minutes, Olympia began to move.

"Hecate?" Salem gasped. "You're not—"

"You can't freeze me, child. We share the same gift. Besides, I am a great deal more powerful than you kids have ever realized. But it seemed like you needed a moment."

"Hecate, it is possible. Demitra has proven it," Salem said with a look of hope on her face that broke her grandmother's heart. "Can't we try? Can't we just this once do something for ourselves? After all we have been through, aren't we owed it?"

"Salem..."

"Don't give me that look, Hecate," Salem told her. "You have no idea what it's like for me. Every day of my life I drive that highway. I see that shiny new steel guard rail on the side of the road marking where my husband crashed. It is grey and bright against the rusty worn pieces on either side. That is where they died. That shiny, bright beacon I pass every day."

Olympia placed her frail hand on Salem's cheek, "Oh my sweetheart, don't do this to yourself. I beg you."

Salem fell to her knees before the old woman. "No, Hecate, I beg you! As head of this coven please give me this. I'll do anything. Every day I see that crash sight. Every day I pass mothers with their children. I see moms so tired and worn out; they act like their child is a nuisance. I want to shake them and remind them how blessed and lucky they are. People ask me if I'm married. Do I have kids? I lie now, Hecate. It hurts too much to have to explain every time. I just lie now. Please Hecate, help me to not have to lie anymore. Give me my family back."

Olympia pulled Salem to her feet. Pushing her nose to Salem's, she stood eye to eye with her granddaughter. "We do not murder people, Salem. To do what you wish would mean taking some other wife's husband from her. Some other mother's baby. Think of those women. Their pain would be the same as yours. Think of that man and that child. Do you really want to kill those innocent creatures? It is murder Salem. We do not kill people."

Salem got it. She didn't like it, but it registered. She nodded her head a few times and wiped the tears from her eyes. She regained composure and understood.

When she could speak again, she asked, "You're going to send him back, aren't you?"

"This is bigger than me," Olympia said. "I think you need to release everyone, and let's get on with this meeting."

Salem relinquished everyone from her spell and the commotion resumed until Olympia waved her arm across the room, sending everyone hurdling back to their original seats when the meeting had begun.

"I caution this family to cease their quarreling before words are spoken which can never be taken back," she said. "We must remember we are a family that loves one another. We are not going to turn on each other now."

"Olympia," Larry said. "I am sorry. I wouldn't want to hurt you for the world."

Olympia placed a reassuring hand on her son-in-law's shoulder, "This isn't your fault, Larry. You simply woke up alive. You didn't cast the spell."

"How can you stand here, Mother, and consider ripping my husband from me?" Demitra screamed, jumping to her feet.

Artemis stood and placed herself between her mother and sister. "Your husband was ripped from you a long time ago. That was not Mother's fault. This isn't either. This now is on you, Demitra. You have defied the Natural Order."

"I don't see what the big difference is for the universe if Larry stays!" Demitra cried.

"Then I've taught you nothing," Olympia said sadly.

Yasmine intervened. "Grandmother, I realize what Aunt Demitra did was wrong. But it *is* done now. Can't we allow this one time to pass?"

"Yazzy," Artemis said as calmly as she could find the patience for, "What if every witch brought back a deceased loved one? What would that do to the world? Ignore the population growth and the physical repercussions, wouldn't it be saying that a witch has supreme rights over everyone else? That our loved ones are somehow more important than those of a regular person? We don't have the right to end a person's life just so we can reconstitute someone we'd rather have."

"What good is being a witch then if we can't make our lives better from it?" Fable asked.

"The point of being a witch is to protect the Order," Artemis explained. "Witches are the chosen ones to defend the helpless and protect the equilibrium. There is a harmony to the universe and if that balance is upturned, it ripples further than we can fathom. The most infinitesimal misdeed can catapult into catastrophe. And your mother is supposed to know this."

Demitra, tears streaming, eyes red, clasped her hands together and begged at her mother's feet. "Please don't take Larry away from me. I know I was wrong. I'll take whatever consequences there are, but I cannot lose him again."

Olympia looked down at her pitiful daughter and placed her hand atop her head, smoothing her soft hair with her fingers. "If I could offer my life for his I would, but even that would be wrong. I know what loss is, child. I have lost three husbands. But my dear, we do not have the right to cheat death."

"Mother, what happens next?" Nacaria asked.

"The ultimate decision lies with me," Olympia acknowledged. "But I would like to hold a coven vote to see where the family falls in this matter. I will say that if the family persuades me to allow Larry to remain, I will turn the matter over to the Council and let them make the final decision."

"I will go before the Council now!" Demitra cried. "I'll argue the case."

"And they will send you to Dredmore, Demitra," Nacaria warned. "Do not change places with me and suffer what I have suffered."

"If the family votes for Daddy to stay, why do you have to say anything to the Council?" Fable asked.

Olympia sighed and told them, "Because your vote would not absolve my conscience. And let us not forget we have a Council member in our own coven. It would not be fair to Salem to ask her to hold this secret."

"Well, I vote Daddy gets to stay," Fable cried.

"I do as well," Demitra added.

Olympia turned to Artemis, "You, daughter?"

Artemis stroked Larry's face and frowned. "I don't think I ever told you that you were my best friend in this house. I have missed our midnight kitchen raids, our mutual love for detective stories, and all our glorious talks about everything and nothing under the sun. I love you, brother, very much. But I cannot in good conscience vote for you to remain."

"Nacaria?"

Nacaria looked at her sister's broken face. "I cast my vote no—not out of jealousy, nor because I don't love Larry. I cast my vote against because I do not want to see my sister put before the Council. I love her too much to see her damn herself."

"Aunt Olympia?" Forest muttered. "I didn't know Larry well. I think I should sit this vote out."

"Both you and Arielle will cast votes today," Olympia demanded. "You are both members of this coven now, and this is a coven matter. Whether you knew him or not is meaningless. The question before you is whether you feel Demitra's actions were right or wrong."

Forest looked at Seth beside him, "I'm sorry, man. But I don't think it's right. I have to vote no."

Seth nodded, he understood.

"I have to agree," Arielle said apologetically. "I'm so sorry."

"Beryl?" Olympia said. "You have been very quiet. What do you vote?"

Beryl walked to the sofa where her father was looking lovingly into her eyes. Beryl lowered herself to the floor and wrapped her arms around his knees. She laid her head on them and closed her eyes as he gently stroked her curly honey hair. Just like when she was little. "You are the only man I've ever loved. But I must let you go. I am sworn to save lives. Jerry Miller's life counts whether Mother understands that or not. He was a living man, and he didn't deserve this."

"Salem?"

Salem faced her Aunt Demitra. "I love you so much. I love both of you so much. I want Uncle Larry to stay because I am also a widow, and I know now what pain you suffered when he died the first time. Yet, I can't help but think of the pain of all the widows out there who do not have the power to bring their husbands back. Someone has to stand for them. I think that someone has to be me. I have to vote no."

"Yasmine," Olympia said. "You are in this family as well."

"I know it is wrong," Yasmine stated. "I am not saying I agree with what she did. But I cannot send Uncle Larry back to the grave. I vote yes. He should stay."

Olympia turned to Seth. "Does it matter?" Seth said. "The vote is already decided."

"I think the family would still appreciate your word on the matter," Olympia said.

"I can't?" Seth sniveled. "It's Uncle Larry? The only real dad I ever knew." He looked at his uncle and said, "I can't imagine ever standing against you. I owe you too much to ever do that."

"Vote your conscience, son," Larry said, absolving him of duty. "You are a man now. And what a man you're turning out to be! Forget who I am. Vote with your convictions."

Seth began to cry. "I have to vote no. I'm so, so sorry."

"I am proud of who you are, Seth Blanchard. Never apologize for being true to your principals."

All fell silent in Blanchard House. No one moved. No one spoke. The harsh reality of what had to occur next was settling in. Demitra laid her head in her husband's lap and wailed just as agonizingly as she had the night he died. Fable slowly sank against the cold brick of the fireplace hearth, her son Romulus pulling up on his back legs to lick her tears. Beryl walked out of the room, Nacaria behind her with a sympathetic hand on her back.

Every Blanchard heart was breaking.

CHAPTER THIRTY SEVEN

Say Goodbye

That night would not end for the people living in Blanchard House, no matter how often anyone rolled over and checked the time. With so much tension and raw emotion surging through the house, the family only retired to bed from habit, not sleepiness. Everyone knew what was to happen by morning. They would awaken and Larry would be gone.

Fable clung to her children in bed as she cried harder than she ever had before. This was even worse than when she had lost her father the first time. That had been abrupt, unexpected. They'd all had to face it together. But now she better understood how difficult the years without her father had been. That old sadness swept over her once more. She had so little time with him this time. She knew she should be grateful to have even had that, but she was greedy and wanted more. She didn't care how wrong it was. She needed her father now more than ever, and by morning he would disappear. At least she was able to say goodbye. Larry went to her room before going to his own and said all the things she would need to carry her through life. It wasn't enough, but it was at least something.

He did that for them all. Yasmine. Seth. Salem. It was Beryl who was the hardest to face because she was the most disappointed in him for coming back in the first place. But that was Beryl. Moral. Good. Loyal to the definitions of right and wrong. Larry loved this about her. He could tell she was devastated by losing him again and by her own inability to embrace his return. She sat quietly on her bed while he said his goodbyes and told her how proud he was of her. Once he left her room, Salem stepped into the hall and tapped lightly on Beryl's door. Beryl did not answer. Salem twisted the knob and walked inside. Her cousin was laying on her side facing the wall. She was not sleeping, but Salem didn't try to speak. She simply covered Beryl lovingly with the blanket at the foot of the bed, kissed her cheek, and clicked the light off as she went back to her own room.

Demitra and Larry held each other in their bed, fighting the urge to sleep, squeezing out every priceless moment together. Demitra cried like a child through most of the night. It was one of those cries that reaches down from the stomach, stealing breath, and sending prickly fingers through the extremities. Larry wept too, but for other reasons. Returning to death was not painful, nor particularly frightening. He wept for the pain his wife and daughters would feel from dawn until the end of their lives.

The potion Artemis gave him was beginning to become too powerful to compete with much longer. His eyes were heavy, and his body ached for sleep. Demitra clung to him, begging him to fight the effects and stay with her just a little longer. He knew time was running out. He could already feel himself beginning to drift away.

"I have many things to say to you," he whispered into her ear as she lay against the pillow, soggy from where her tears landed. "You have always been a perfect wife. I have never loved anyone but you, Demitra. It has been a great gift to have been able to love you twice."

"I'll never regret bringing you back, Larry," she said to him. "Even though this is ripping me apart, I have no regrets. At least we have had ten more months together. That alone has been worth everything."

"I need for you to promise me something, Dee," he asked. "I never had the chance to say this to you the first time I died. I want you to hold on—don't fall apart after I am gone. You must be there for our daughters and our grandsons. I have connected with Rom; he's already quite a pup. But Con will never remember me. I need you to tell him how much I loved him. Let him know that even though his grandfather was dead, he was able to be there at his birth. Tell him it meant everything to me."

"I can't go on without you," she cried.

"Don't say that to me," Larry warned. "I can only die with peace if I know you will stay together and keep living. Sacrificing your life to grief doesn't prove you loved me. You've already proven that every day of our lives."

"You don't know what it's like," she whispered, half to herself. "The pain never stops. Each day is worse than the day before because it is that much further from when I last held you. Days go by. They turn into years. Every one of them is fractured, incomplete because we are not together. When good things happen, they seem trivial because the only person I want to share them with is gone. And when bad things happen, I can hardly bear it because my rock is not there to lean against. Every breath I take mocks my broken heart."

"Don't do this, Dee. Do not drive yourself mad. We have been given a wondrous gift. More time. And a proper goodbye. We didn't have that last time."

"What do I do when it is all over?" Demitra asked. "How do I go on?"

"You already faced that once," Larry said. "Your mistake was trying to rebuild the old life rather than construct a new one. I need you to open yourself up and love again."

Demitra twisted around to face him, her red eyes and pale empty face broke his heart. "I couldn't love another man."

"You can if you try. Like I said, Demitra, I already know you love me. Loving someone else doesn't undo what we had together. I love you too much to let you condemn yourself to loneliness." He stopped talking and leaned back against the billowy pillows on the bed. "I'm so tired now, Demitra. I don't think I can stay much longer."

"Please," she begged.

"It has been my honor to have been your husband."

Demitra clutched his shirt in her hands, desperately trying to shake him back into consciousness. He was fading fast. "Larry, I will love you for forever...and three days."

Demitra realized as he closed his eyes, he was gone.

...

There was a knock at Artemis' door. Demitra walked in. She made it only a few steps before collapsing. Artemis caught her before she hit the ground. She carried her sister to the bed and laid down with her, holding her as she cried.

Footsteps echoed across the floor. Artemis glanced up to see Nacaria standing in the room. She motioned for their baby sister to join them, lifting the blanket for Nacaria to crawl in. Demitra lay between her sisters, their loving arms wrapped around her. No one said a word. No one needed to. There was nothing to say. Demitra's heart was broken and that was enough to break the hearts of Artemis and Nacaria. The three Blanchard sisters fell asleep together, in each other's arms.

CHAPTER THIRTY EIGHT

The Stranger She Wed

Forest leaned Jerry Miller's body over the steering wheel of the car. At first it slid off into the floorboard. On the second attempt, Forest repositioned it, propping one arm over the wheel. That seemed to hold the body upright, although slumped somewhat, but when Forest let go of his shoulders it slid to the side again and fell into the passenger seat.

"Tie him to the wheel," Seth said from beside the car.

"How would we explain that?" Forest called behind him. "Think, dude."

On the third try, Forest successfully balanced Jerry against the wheel, placing the right arm over the console and the left on the door rest as he gingerly closed the driver's side door without it falling. He backed away softly as if his very footsteps might dislodge the body somehow. He looked around the secluded road just off the Blanchard property and saw no cars coming. Forest then swept his right hand across his own chest, cupping his hand to collect the invisible material he'd swiped from his body. He tossed the unseen byproduct toward Jerry's unconscious form. The faint translucent covering glistened around him, like an imperceptible armor.

"Okay, your turn," he told his cousin.

Seth looked above their heads at the great poplar tree, to the limb which stretched out over the road. Focusing his mind on the limb, Seth sent a bolt of lightning crashing onto it from above, snapping the limb and sending it hurdling down atop the car. The top of the car, as well as the hood, smashed inward around Jerry, yet left Jerry unharmed thanks to Forest's forcefield. The two young men gave each other a fist bump and hopped back into Seth's car to head back to the house for breakfast.

Back at Blanchard House, the morning was finding the family not well rested after the events the previous day. Olympia was seated at the breakfast table sipping her morning coffee but had touched none of the food on her plate. No one was eating. This did not stop Yasmine from continuing to prepare meals for the other family members waiting on their breakfast. The act of cooking itself was soothing her, and it mattered little if anyone ate what she served them.

Demitra looked as if she had died along with her husband. She'd wanted to remain in her room after the boys had lifted Jerry Miller from the bed and taken him away, but her mother insisted she come downstairs with the family.

"There is much to discuss," Olympia declared

"I don't care," Demitra sobbed. "I just want to be left alone."

Olympia possessed neither the patience nor the understanding to be gentle now. "I'm afraid you aren't going to be," her mother explained. "This is your mess we are having to clean up, and you will play your part in it."

"Where is Daddy now?" a red-eyed Fable asked, clutching baby Con to her chest as baby Rom was curled at her feet.

Pulling her long dark hair behind her back and rubbing her tired eyes, Artemis explained, "Larry has returned to the unknown." She looked out the window, off in the distance to where the dirt road stretched out beyond the acreage of the property line. "Jerry, however, is being carried by Seth and Forest down the road a ways in his car. They are arranging a little accident to explain why he will not have any memory of any of us when he wakes up."

"I'm supposed to find him on my way in to work," Yasmine recited. "I will call the ambulance, then notify the family."

Olympia gave an approving nod before adding, "Demitra and I will go to the hospital. We will contact Vestus and Cally from there. We will all be present when Beryl wakes him up. He will of course be confused."

"I can't do it," Demitra fought the plan. "It's too soon, and I am barely holding on. I can't go to the hospital and see a total stranger where my husband used to be."

"You can, and you will," declared Olympia without much sympathy for her daughter's feelings. "Again, this is your mess."

Yasmine exchanged a secretive glance with Fable. Neither girls had ever seen their grandmother so terse. Olympia was in no mood for insubordination. Her aggressive demeanor was a little disturbing.

"I don't understand why anyone has to be there?" Arielle asked crunching a piece of crisp bacon. "Can't the hospital phone his parents and that be that?"

"Jerry Miller is legally Demitra's husband," Artemis explained. "His parents know our family and saw them get married. There is a legal marriage certificate with both of their names on it. Jerry Miller is Demitra's husband whether she likes it or not. She must be there when he wakes up."

"What is going to happen after that?" Fable wondered.

"I suspect he will be very upset," Olympia acknowledged. "What happens afterward will be Jerry's decision. Will he want to try to learn about his new wife or will he want an annulment? We will have to wait and see."

"I can't stay married to him," Demitra said. "I won't stay married to him."

Salem, who had remained silent up until this point in the conversation, could remain silent no longer. The sympathy she'd felt for her aunt the night before had waned, replaced now with a twinge of resentment. "Aunt Demitra, you got the privilege of running around for ten months reunited with the love of your life. You got to say and do all the things others like us only dream about. Now you have to deal with the consequences of that amazing privilege."

Demitra appeared both wounded and shocked by Salem's interjection. Fable, Yasmine, and Arielle looked down to their plates to avoid the tension.

"You'll do as you're told," Olympia said to Demitra. "You married that man's body, and now his spirit has been reunited with it. You'll deal with whatever comes from that."

...

Vestus and Cally drove as fast as traffic would allow from Birmingham to Daihmler Hospital. The first thing they did as they entered the sixth-floor patient room was embrace their daughter-in-law. Demitra appeared disheveled, shaken, on the verge of breakdown.

"Demitra, honey, Momma is here," Cally Miller exclaimed as she hugged her tightly. "We will see him through this."

Vestus Miller looked over to the bed his son was in and saw the arrangement of wires and clips to his fingertips. Jerry was unconscious, but surprisingly unmarred in appearance after having a tree limb fall on his car driving to work.

"Beryl says he has quite a bump on the head," Olympia told them. "Otherwise, he was very lucky."

"I'll say," Cally said, approaching. "Not a scratch on him. Any broken bones?"

"Not that they can tell," Olympia said.

Demitra was not talking. She was barely moving. She looked simply devastated as she stood watching the stranger in the bed and his parents. She thought it interesting that she felt more affection and connection to this man's mother and father than she did to him. Of course, she had known him a little. She had been on a couple of dates with him months ago. That was how she had selected him for Larry's vessel. Standing above him looking down on his unconscious form, she could not remember anything about either of their meetings. She only saw where Larry had been yesterday.

Beryl came into the room with her clipboard. "Hi," she said, greeting the Millers. "I have some information from the tests we ran earlier. The accident caused a severe trauma to his brain. We will have to wait until he wakes up to see how severe it is."

She hated putting this sweet couple through all of this. Staging an entire accident scenario just to explain their son's imminent odd behavior. She was angry at her mother for this. She was also doing her best to shelve her grief for her father and her regret for not having spent time with him once she had learned who he really was.

An hour or so passed with Olympia, Demitra, and the Millers holding vigil at Jerry's bedside. He began to stir a little before noon. Olympia called Beryl's cell. Beryl came in almost immediately.

"Jerry," she asked him, shining a tiny light into his pupils. "Can you understand what I am saying to you?"

"Huh?" he muttered. "Uh, yeah. I guess. Mom? Is that you over there?"

Cally stepped closer while still respectfully keeping out of Beryl's way. "Hey, son. Dad is here too. And Demitra. Beryl says you're gonna be fine."

"Who's Barrel?" Jerry asked. His question made both Beryl and Demitra tense up, even though they both knew to expect this reaction. Jerry turned and saw Olympia sitting nearby. "Who are you?"

Beryl stepped into his line of sight and asked him, "Jerry, do you know who I am?"

"No. No, I don't."

Olympia nudged Demitra forward toward the bed. Demitra stammered as she asked, "D-D-Do you know m-me?"

"No," Jerry answered. "Wait. Yes—sort of. Didn't we go out a couple of times? Your name is Demitra."

"This is your wife, son," Vestus said.

Jerry's eyes widened, hearing this for the very first time. He glanced at his mother for confirmation. She nodded her head. He knew she would never joke about something like this. But he had never spent more than four or five hours with Demitra. How could he be married to her?

"I didn't get married to her," he told his mother. "We only went out a couple of times." He looked at Demitra and asked, "What are you pulling? Why did you tell my folks we got married?"

Demitra said nothing. She stood voiceless, tears welling up, her nerves raw. It was all too much for her so soon after Larry. Cally grabbed Demitra's hand and squeezed it and raised it to show her son the ring he had placed on her finger. All Demitra could see was the wedding band she'd worn when she married Larry so many years ago. Now she had to pretend it was Jerry who'd placed it there.

"She is your wife, Jerry."

"Look, I don't know what she told you guys," Jerry said, trying to sit up, "but I didn't marry her."

"Son, Dad and I were at your wedding," Cally informed him. "We were the witnesses. We watched it happen."

Jerry looked to his father who nodded in agreement. "Son, what's the last thing you remember?"

Jerry thought a moment and looked at Demitra. "You. You and I were on a date. But it goes blank after that. Did I have a wreck last night after our date?"

"That was almost a year ago," Demitra finally found words to say. "It's May now."

"May?"

"You were married New Year's Eve!" Cally gushed proudly. "Oh, Jerry, she's a wonderful wife. Her whole family is wonderful. You'll remember soon. I just know you will." Cally linked arms with Demitra. "We love her very much, son. You did good."

Olympia brought the Millers back to stay at Blanchard House so they could be nearer to the hospital. The couple was overwrought by their son's amnesia, but Beryl assured them it wasn't completely abnormal after an accident. That was not at all true but thanks to Hollywood and years of medically incorrect films, the Millers accepted her statement.

"It is awfully kind of you to take us into your home," Cally thanked Olympia.

"Not at all, we are family."

"I wish our boy could remember that." Vestus grunted.

"The two of you are going to have to face the possibility that Jerry may never regain his memory," Olympia warned. "I've had to tell this to Demitra as well. Beryl thinks that part of his brain may be damaged irreparably."

"Poor Demitra," Cally sniffed. "You could plainly see how upset she was at the hospital. Looked like she'd lost everything."

"She really loves him, that's for sure," Vestus said. "Imagine having a year knocked out of your head like that. Beats all I ever seen."

Vestus was curious about the new wing to the house. He had noticed it from the car and the odd angles it seemed to make. When Olympia explained the reasons were to avoid chopping down the trees, Cally cheered at the idea. Olympia gave her a brief tour of the construction before helping them upstairs to lie down. Cally was tired but still wanted to see Fable's baby before taking a rest. Fable wasn't in her room, but the children were.

Olympia led her upstairs to the third floor to Fable's room. Upon entering, Cally saw two cribs at the foot of Fable's bed. "I didn't know she had twins!" Cally exclaimed. As her eyes peered into the cribs and caught sight of the sleeping babies within, she jumped backward. "Oh my! What is that?"

"Looks like some kind of... dog?" Vestus said.

"You know Fable," Olympia offered. "It is a rescue from her clinic. She brought him home around the same time she had the baby. So, she has them both in a crib. I think she thinks of him as a second child."

"Well, I can certainly understand that," Vestus laughed. "Our Tipton is just like a kid to us. But I don't think I've ever seen a dog like that before. Looks like a coyote."

Cally lifted baby Con out of the crib and held him close to her, kissing his head. "Vestus, our own great grandson. Just look at this boy."

Olympia enjoyed seeing the happiness on the couple's faces as they tickled and cooed with baby Con. Baby Rom lifted his head from his bed to watch, administering a slight growl of protection for his brother. Olympia placed a reassuring hand on his back and stroked him lovingly. Her heart fluttered again. It was doing that more and more often these days. *I won't see you fully grown, my sweet great grandson. I won't be here to help you through the trials you are doomed to suffer.*

...

It was around 11 o'clock that night, after everyone in the house had gone to bed, when Madame Zelda showed up at the back door and came quietly inside. Olympia met her by the door and, as cautiously as they could, the two old women raised the secret door in the kitchen stairs to the vault below. Only a few minor creaks rang out, but they weren't loud enough to raise attention. With the kitchen stair treads hinged open in the air above them, the lifelong friends made their way down the steps into the cellar room, steadying each other as they descended. Clicking on the light, the two witches gathered around a small round table near the shelves of ingredients. Olympia realized the severity of what she was about to do and paused, rethinking her motivation and questioning the correctness of the plan she and Zelda forged that morning.

"Stop thinking so much," Zelda advised as she began sprinkling powders and herbs from jars into a bowl. "There ain't nothin' wrong with what we're doin'."

"I wish I could be sure," Olympia responded. "Free will and all."

"We ain't hinderin' anybody's free will. This ain't a love spell," Zelda reminded her. "All we are doing is helping things along. We are gonna suppress some of Demitra's grief and open Jerry up to the possibility of love. It's up to them whether they fall in love or not. We ain't causing them to. Just clearin' the obstacles out of the way in their minds."

"So, we are not manipulating events?" Olympia asked.

"Hell, no!" Zelda said. "I ain't about to defy the Natural Order this late in life. We're just getting rid of their fear or guilt about connecting with somebody new."

"I hope it works," Olympia admitted. "I don't have much time left, and I need to know that Demitra can be happy."

"I done told you to stop talkin' like that."

"Zelda, I am old. And I am not completely unconnected to the synergy of this world. I know my time is nearing. I feel it, like something walking closer and closer to me every day. I know what that something is. Death. We have met before, and I recognize the feeling. I must have this family settled before it comes."

"Don't worry, Lympy," Zelda said, lifting the potion. "This will work. And that'll be one problem solved."

CHAPTER THIRTY NINE

Life Goes On

Demitra had not gone home in two days. She did not understand it herself why she stayed. Something inside her would not let her leave Jerry's bedside. She owed him a little more than that; an air of responsibility tied her to him. He was there because of her. Because of her selfishness. The slippery vinyl chair with the pull-out ottoman had not been giving her a decent night's rest. Or perhaps it was the hideous harvest orange color. She hated that color. Demitra was all too happy to leave when Beryl came in and released Jerry to go home.

"Mother, have you been here all night again?" Beryl asked her as she was signing his release forms.

"She has," Jerry said. "I told her it wasn't necessary, but she wouldn't go. I guess that's what a wife does. I wouldn't know—I still don't remember anything."

"You may not ever," Beryl told him. "You'll have to resign yourself to starting fresh."

"I guess," Jerry moaned. "I don't know what I'm going to do. Apparently, I quit my old job and moved out of my apartment. I don't know anything about my new job or those people. Your mother says my boss is being understanding and giving me a couple of weeks. If my Mom and Dad are still at your house, I'll go back to Birmingham with them."

"You don't have to do that," Demitra said. "You are welcome to stay with us. All your things are there anyway."

Jerry looked at her face. He could not get over how beautiful she was. He wished he could remember something, anything, about her. "I'm sorry I can't remember you. Must be hard on you."

"I think it is hard on the both of you," Beryl said. "Go home. Don't worry about going to your parents for a couple of days. They are still at our house and will be there a few more days. You can figure out what you want to do then."

On the drive back to Blanchard House, Jerry Miller remained quiet for most of the way, staring out the window and trying to jog his memory with landmarks and scenery. As Demitra turned onto the main road to Blanchard House, Jerry looked at her again.

"Were we happy?"

Demitra felt the tears swelling in her eyes. "I was very happy."

"And we are legally married." He said it more as a statement than anything else, as if he were trying to convince himself.

"That's what they tell me," Demitra replied.

"A man would have to be in some pretty bad shape to not remember you, Demitra."

She gave him a sweet smile as she steered onto the property. "Thank you...Jerry."

As they came into the house, Olympia and the Millers were there to greet him on the porch. Cally Miller fussed and mothered over him, and Vestus continually told her to give him some breathing room. They settled him down on the living room sofa with his legs propped up.

"My legs aren't broken," Jerry remarked. "And I'm not tired."

"Well, are you hungry?" Olympia asked. "Your mother has fixed a huge lunch for everyone whenever you feel like eating."

"Yes, son, let me get you a plate. I made all your favorites," Cally said, running off to the kitchen. She returned and thrust a plate of fried pork chops and vegetables at him. Jerry looked as if he were becoming agitated by all the attention.

Demitra lifted the plate from his hand and set it aside. She announced, "I think Jerry might need a little space. He's been through quite a bit, and the last thing he needs is all of us suffocating him."

Jerry gave her a wink of appreciation.

"I know you don't remember it," Demitra told him. "But our property is pretty large and has quite a nice walking trail right beyond the meadow off the backyard. Maybe you would like to take a walk and clear your head. You've been cooped up for a couple of days in a hospital bed."

"That sounds pretty great," Jerry replied. He stood up and looked around. "How do I get—"

"Go through the kitchen—just there beyond the dining room—and there's a back door," Demitra said pointing.

Jerry started to go, then paused before turning back around. He made eye contact with Demitra and asked, "I don't suppose you'd care to join me?"

Olympia had no idea how her daughter might reply to this statement and was pleasantly surprised to hear Demitra answer, "I think that would be lovely."

After the two had disappeared outside, Cally turned to Olympia and smiled brightly. "I think they are gonna be all right. He may not remember the last year, but I think we may soon be seeing him falling in love with her all over again."

"Grandmother!!!!!"

The scream came from upstairs. Olympia went as fast as a woman nearing 90 could go up the two flights of stairs. Her heart was pounding in her chest, and she prayed it would not give out on her just yet. Cally and Vestus were right behind her. They made their way to Seth and Yasmine's room. Yasmine was lying on the bed panting heavily, a terrified look on her face.

"Yasmine, is it the baby?"

"Yes! I think it's coming!" her granddaughter shouted.

"Oh, my goodness!" Cally exclaimed, rushing to Yasmine's side.

Yasmine winced in pain again. "I called Beryl!" she exclaimed. "She's on her way, but I don't know if she's gonna get here in time!"

"It's all right, sweetheart," Olympia said reassuringly. "We will manage until she does."

"Where's Fable?" Yasmine asked. "She may just be a vet, but at least that's some kind of doctor."

"She is at work," Olympia answered. "She went back to work this morning and took Rom and Com with her."

"Demitra? Nacaria?"

"Not home."

"Grandmother!" Yasmine was really afraid now as the contractions intensified.

Olympia joined her on the edge of the bed and placed a calming hand on her shoulder. "My Darling, relax," Olympia said quietly. "I have delivered babies before. And Cally is here to help as well. Everything will be fine."

Vestus looked around nervously, "What can I do?"

"Try to find Demitra and Jerry. Also, my phone is downstairs on the coffee table. I don't have a password to it. If you would telephone Seth and then Artemis."

Vestus rushed out to do what he could. Olympia and Cally flanked Yasmine and tried to keep her calm. It wasn't easy, the girl was frantic. Beads of sweat were already forming on her brow, and her hair was becoming stringy and damp. She puffed sharp breaths and began to lift her knees up to her chest.

"It's too early," Yasmine cried.

"Only by a month, nothing to be upset over," Olympia calmed. "Cally, I think it's coming."

"This quickly?" Cally gasped.

"My offspring tend to come fast and furiously," Olympia said, attempting humor. "Yasmine, I am going to deliver your baby; do everything I tell you to do."

CHAPTER FORTY

Another New Blanchard

Hecate!" Seth shouted bursting through the door! "Hecate! Where is she?"

Seth took the stairs three at a time on his way to his room. He met Olympia coming down the second-floor staircase with Mrs. Miller. He was running so fast that as he stopped suddenly to keep from knocking them down, he slipped backward two steps and smacked into the railing.

"Slow down, slow down," Olympia said. "Everyone is fine. Beryl is here now, and Yasmine and the baby are perfectly fine."

"Beryl got here in time?"

"No, I delivered it," Olympia said.

"You?" Seth gasped.

"Now don't be so surprised," his grandmother laughed. "I have lived a long time and done a great many things. Delivering your daughter was not even in the top ten most difficult things I've managed to do."

"My *daughter*?" Seth looked as if he were going to cry.

"Yes. A girl."

"Oh, Seth, she's just beautiful—like her mother," Cally congratulated. "Your grandmother was spectacular in there! I was amazed."

"I have a little girl," Seth whispered.

Olympia had not bothered to consider which sex he might have preferred the baby to be until that exact moment. It was possible he'd wanted a boy; he had seemed to habitually speak of the baby in the masculine whenever the subject came up—but watching his face on the stairs just then, Olympia marveled at the genuine joy in his eyes.

Seth passed them on the stairs and went in to see his wife and child. Beryl was sitting on the side of the bed with Yasmine while the new mother was holding her little girl in her arms. Nacaria was standing a few feet away, saturated with pride watching her new granddaughter. Seth stood in the doorway a moment, taking it all in. It was in that moment when everything Aunt Artemis had been trying to tell him New Year's Eve sunk in. He had a family now. Responsibilities.

Looking up, Beryl saw her cousin in the doorframe. "Come in, *Daddy*. Come meet your little girl."

Seth stumbled closer to the bed and looked first at Yasmine—his beautiful, sweet Yasmine—then down to the little girl in her arms. "Are you okay?" he asked his wife.

"We both are," Yasmine replied with the brightest smile he had ever seen on her face.

"The baby was a few weeks early, but nothing is wrong," Beryl informed him. "I healed her lungs, so she won't have any need to go to the NICU and be on a ventilator. Your wife and child are perfectly fine, Seth."

"She's magnificent, Seth," Nacaria said, stepping forward. "None of us can stop staring at her. But now it's your turn. Come be alone with your family, son." Nacaria tugged Beryl's elbow and tilted her head toward the door. They closed the door behind them.

"I can't believe it," Seth grinned. "We have a daughter."

"Grandmother delivered her!" Yasmine exclaimed excitedly. "Can you believe that?"

"She told me—lucky she was here. I'm so sorry I wasn't. I was in class."

"I know," Yasmine smiled, reaching her hand up to his face. "It's all right, Seth."

"I wanted to be here for it."

She laughed. "No, you really didn't. It was not pretty, and it was not magical like on TV. I wish *I* could have skipped it, but Grandmother and Cally were awesome. And Beryl got here just in time to make sure she's all right."

Seth stared awestruck down to his baby girl. "What should we call her?"

"I want it to be strong like Grandmother's name."

"Why not call her Olympia then?" Seth suggested.

"I would," Yasmine replied. "But there's only one Olympia Blanchard. That's too much pressure on one little baby girl."

Seth tilted his head thinking over some of the powerful women and witches he'd known or learned about over the years. One name kept rising to the forefront of his mind.

"Hera," Seth said. "How about Hera?"

"I like it."

Seth looked down to his daughter and lifted her out of Yasmine's arms. He walked across the room with her, bouncing her slightly in his arms as he moved. "Hello, little girl. You're going to be something pretty special one day. Like your momma, and like your great-grandmother. Welcome to the world, Hera Blanchard. It's quite a place."

. . .

The moment Fable came home, she thrust Con into Demitra's arms and bolted upstairs to see Yasmine and the baby. Romulus pounced after her, and when she went into the room, he jumped on the bed and began licking baby Hera's head. Yasmine outstretched her hand and stroked the baby wolf's soft fur.

"This is your cousin, Rom. Her name is Hera."

"I just can't believe it, Yaz!" Fable exclaimed plopping down on the bed beside them. "You're a mother now, too!"

"I know!" Yasmine squealed. "Our kids are going to grow up together just like we did."

"Another Blanchard witch added to the family," Fable said. "We are getting to be a pretty large bunch. I'm glad Hecate is adding on to the house."

The door to Yasmine's room swung open again interrupting Fable and Yasmine's private moment, but neither minded once they saw it was Arielle and Salem. Salem rushed the bed and started snapping pictures with her phone. Arielle wasted no time taking the baby into her arms and cuddling it to her cheek.

"I have a niece!" she shrieked as she smothered Hera's head with kisses.

"As do I," Salem announced. "Don't get too attached to that baby because I'm holding her myself in a second." Salem looked down at Yasmine. "I cannot believe it. Little Yaz is a mother. Hell, what I really cannot believe is my brother is a father!"

"I didn't know ya'll were coming," Fable said to her cousin.

"Are you kidding?" Salem gasped. "The second Seth texted me, I rushed home from work and grabbed Ari, and we flew down the interstate from Atlanta. I was not about to miss the first day of my niece's life."

"What's her name?" Arielle asked.

"Hera."

"I love that!" Fable cried. "I didn't even stop to ask. Good name!"

Salem took her turn holding her newborn niece before handing her back to her mother so that she and Arielle could retrieve their overnight bags from the car. Demitra passed them on the stairs, bringing baby Con, who was crying for his mother, up to Fable. Fable took her son in her arms and settled onto the bed beside her cousin. Romulus snuggled between the two babies and licked the sides of their heads. Yasmine rested her head on Fable's shoulder and closed her eyes.

"This is nice," Yasmine sighed.

"It really is," agreed Fable.

"You know what's really cool about it though?" Yasmine asked.

"What?"

"This is my family," Yasmine softly whispered. "I don't mean it the way it sounds. I love the Blanchards, and I am a Blanchard through and through. But sometimes over the years...it was just kind of hard being the only cousin in the house not related by blood. But this," she said looking down at the children, "This is *my* family. The same blood coursing through them courses through me. My daughter and my nephews."

Romulus, as if understanding what she had said, tilted his little head up and began licking the underside of Yasmine's chin. Fable looked down and patted his belly as he rolled on his back.

"I've never considered that before," she replied. "But you're right. Our kids share your blood as well as Blanchard. These babies are all Sinclairs. Wouldn't Grandfather be thrilled!"

Yasmine smiled, "He would absolutely be over the moon right now."

CHAPTER FORTY ONE

Happier Times

Raised voices echoed through the hall and down the stairs from the third-floor den. Laughter. Giddiness. Excited voices. Then more laughter. It was a sound Olympia relished hearing again in the house, so much so that she wanted to be a part of it. She wanted to experience her family in a blissful state. It took her a while to make it up the stairs. Her body was getting weaker with every passing day. She had been able to shield this fact from the family so far but had anyone witnessed her climb—witnessed the numerous pauses made on the stair to catch her breath—they would have become worried at first sight. She didn't mind the pauses. Each one gave her a moment face to face with the photographs of her family hanging on the staircase wall. Snapshots of a life well lived and memories not even death could steal from her. Olympia reached the den door and went inside.

"That is a joyous sight for these ancient eyes," she said, taking a seat on one of the sofas to better observe Fable and Yasmine sitting on the floor with their children. The rest of the grandchildren were there as well except for Arielle, who had gone out on a date with Forest.

"We were loud," Yasmine recognized. "Sorry."

"Do not apologize, my dear. Never apologize for happiness when it comes; it is too great a gift."

"Romulus keeps licking Con and Hera's heads and growling at anyone besides their mothers who try to hold them," Salem explained. "It's really funny."

"He's very protective of his brother," Fable said. "And now his cousin. I think he knows they are related."

"Of course, he does," Olympia stated. "I realize he appears to be an animal, but Fable you mustn't lose sight of the fact that he is also part human. I'm certain he understands their familial connection, and he probably considers himself their protector—leader of the pack, so to speak."

"Hera keeps laughing; it's adorable," Yasmine said proudly.

"Babies don't laugh this early," Beryl corrected. "She's just smiling, and that is gas."

"Michael used to laugh all the time and I thought he was the happiest baby, until I changed the diaper and saw what that laugh really was," Salem giggled.

Seth put his hand on her shoulder and said, "That's really the first time you've talked about Michael without tearing up."

"Having these new babies around helps me feel better."

Fable smiled at her cousin and told everyone, "Last night I laid Con in his crib and Rom in his, but when I was going to bed and looked over to check on them, Rom had jumped out of his bed and curled up next to his brother. It made me cry; it was so sweet."

"I got up early today," Seth started his own tale. "I laid Hera in bed with Yaz while I took a shower. When I got out and was drying off, I saw my two girls just lying there in bed and...I never felt anything like it before in my life."

Salem winked at her grandmother. "They joined the club, Hecate."

"The club?" Fable asked.

"You have become *those people*," Salem laughed. "*Parents*. You will never view anything the same way again."

"I am going to miss Hera's powers, though," Yasmine noted. "I kind of liked being able to do things."

"It won't be too many years before Hecate has the children in the magic room," Beryl grinned. "I remember my first day up there."

Olympia did not respond to Beryl's statement. But it saddened her to realize she would not be the Hecate teaching these new babies in the future. That privilege would belong to the next generation. She had spent so many years teaching her own children and grandchildren. It would be someone else's turn now. Then she looked at Salem and Beryl. She would never know the children they might one day have. Or any that might come later for Seth, Yasmine, and Fable. To live your life to the end is a great accomplishment, yet to think of what will come after you pass which you will miss is hard to take.

"Salem, do you think you'll ever have any more children?" Fable asked as if she heard Olympia's thoughts.

"I think so," Salem thought aloud. "I certainly don't want any right now. I want more time to grieve the child I lost. Besides, the Witches Council position is a lot more work than I anticipated. Witches be crazy!" she laughed.

"I wonder who you'll meet and marry?" Yasmine said dreamily.

"Uh-no one," Salem coughed. "I have no interest in marrying. I had the best husband I could ever have wanted. I don't think there's another David out there."

"You know, Salem," Olympia began. "Don't tell your mother or aunts I said this, but you could always be artificially inseminated and have a child on your own."

"Hecate! I can't believe I heard you say that!" Fable laughed.

"There's nothing wrong with using science to make things easier," Olympia elaborated. "And if Salem does not happen to find a man she wants, that is no reason for her to never have a baby. Time tends to run out when you least expect it."

"Did you guys just hear what I heard?" Salem guffawed. "Hecate just told me my biological clock is running out."

"Nonsense," Olympia laughed. "I just don't want you to wait as long as I did for children. I was nearing 40 when I had Artemis."

Beryl had not really thought about it before, how old her grandmother had actually been when she began her family. "Why did you wait so long before starting a family, Hecate?"

Olympia mused a moment, smiling secretively to herself before she continued. Thoughts from a life these children knew nothing about. Sometimes it even slipped Olympia's own mind just how much she'd experienced before beginning a family. "I went through a series of ill-fated relationships before I met John Windham. Then after we were married, witch affairs and not a small number of adventures got in the way before I became a mother."

"You really don't share much about those days," Beryl said. "When we were rescuing Nacaria from Dredmore, we ran across a cell housing a vampire. I read the case file and it said that you, Pastoria, and Zelda were the ones who captured him! We were amazed."

"Tell us, Grandmother," Yasmine urged. "Tell us about when you were young."

Olympia reflected a few seconds as to whether she should fill their heads with tales of her glory days or not. She would not want to misstep and say something they ought to not know. But she'd had so many adventures in her day, it would be a shame to leave this life without giving them something to remember her youth by.

"When I was your age," she began. "I was tasked by the Council as a sort of watchperson for the Order. If word came to the association of something mankind was not equipped to handle—supernatural elements, you understand—it was my job to take care of it."

"Your job?" Seth repeated. "Were you like some kind of superhero or something?"

"*Something*," Olympia said, flashing a mischievous smile. "I, your Aunt Pastoria, and Zelda, we had a few escapades in our day. Of course, we worked with others as well. But most things we could handle on our own."

Her grandchildren listened intently, enthralled by whatever she was about to reveal. Olympia felt the way she did when they were all little and she'd read them a bedtime story from Aesop or the Grimm brothers—only this time her tales were true and had happened to her.

"When we were fighting Patric you said he wasn't the first werewolf you'd come across," Fable recalled. "There was another one?"

"Two other ones," Olympia remembered. "Your grandfather and I actually battled one together in Europe on our honeymoon! It was a spectacular fight. John didn't like encountering the supernatural world. I did my best to shield him from that part of my life. But that fight was quite unavoidable. He was magnificent. I had the power, but he had the brawn, and he fought valiantly. I was never more turned on by a man in my life!"

"Hecate!" Fable squealed. "I've never heard you talk like that!"

Olympia ignored the comment, now caught up in her memories. She hadn't thought of those days in a very long time. It was nice to free those memories and share them with her children.

"And then there was another werewolf in New Orleans," Olympia went on. Her face brightened as she made a verbal footnote for the children. "That's actually how Zelda met Fred by the way! He turned the corner just as she chopped the monster's head off."

"What?!" Seth exclaimed. "How have we never heard this story? You've been holding out on us all these years Hecate. Sounds like you were pretty badass in your day."

The astonishment on everyone's faces tickled Olympia. "Goodness, children. I wasn't born an old woman, you know." She glowed with pride as she recalled the lost years of her life. The grandchildren sat glued to her every word; they had never seen her so exhilarated.

"Are there creatures worse than werewolves?" Yasmine asked.

"Oh, my yes!" Olympia cried. "There is an entire other world out there none of you have ever had to encounter."

The others looked around at each other, each observing that everyone else was equally captivated with this conversation. And all were shocked to hear how adventurous their matronly—and always so proper—grandmother had once been.

"Why don't we hear about it?" Seth asked.

"Well, there isn't much of it left thanks to the Council and the groups like I used to belong to. We eradicated the evils for the most part."

"Grandmother, you talk like you saved the world or something?" Yasmine giggled.

"Not just me," Olympia surprised them by saying. "Generations of witches went to a lot of trouble and sacrificed many of their lives so that you kids can live in the relatively peaceful world that you have now."

"I cannot believe we are only just hearing about this!" Fable gasped. "Hecate, why haven't you ever told us this stuff before?"

"Oh, your mothers didn't want you kids growing up afraid the way they did," Olympia explained.

Seth was as excited as a little boy watching a monster movie. He was eager for more. "What is the worst monster you ever faced down?"

Olympia had to think on the question a moment before answering. Her very pause captivated the grandchildren more than anything else. The fact that she had to stop and think about it was further evidence that she'd lived a remarkable life before they came along. "I'd say the Rain People are the worst I ever ran across."

"Rain People?" Beryl asked. "What are they?"

"Similar to vampires but far more deadly," Olympia recalled. "Instead of drinking your blood, they suck the water from your body—you die of dehydration. They were a vicious lot. But there are not any more of them, thank Heaven."

"Did you stop them?" Seth asked.

"Oh no, that was in my father's time. I did see them myself a couple of times, though, when they tried to attack us. But my father handled them. He went away for a while to work with another witch, and the two of them ended the tribe. I never met that witch, but I grew up hearing about her. If you ask me, they might have had a fling during that time."

"Mother!" Artemis exclaimed from the hallway. "I thought we talked about filling the kids' heads with your old stories."

"We aren't kids anymore!" Fable exclaimed. "And Hecate's life before us sounds fascinating."

"And dangerous," Artemis added. "Which is why it is best left where it belongs, in the past."

Olympia took the cue and left the children alone again to walk back downstairs with Artemis. Doing her best to keep pace with her daughter, Olympia winced here and there as she descended the stairs. She was not very skilled at concealing it. Artemis noticed right away.

"Something is going on with you."

Olympia raised a brow and lied, "I don't believe so."

"I've noticed it happening with more frequency," Artemis remarked. "And now I find you waxing sentimental with the kids about glory days long forgotten. What's going on?"

Olympia knew it was time to prepare the next in line for what was approaching. "Walk with me, Artemis. You and I need to discuss some things."

CHAPTER FORTY TWO

The New Hecate

The sun was high overhead and the smooth breeze had cooled the unusually warm late spring day. The grape vines were sprouting new tendrils to run along the small arbors lining the path just past the vegetable garden. In a couple of months, they would be heavy with grapes. Artemis felt her mother's frail hand on her shoulder as they moved between the vines toward the open meadow where dandelions and tick seed flowers supplied a field of yellow before them. Artemis could not tell if the hand gripped her shoulder as a loving gesture or more for stability. She linked her arm with Olympia's to supply both for her mother.

"Everything renews," Olympia said as they walked on. "Spring is earth's proof of that." She touched the green off-shoot from one of the older grape vines. "See—this new vine came from the older one. Next year one will sprout from this. Family is like that, isn't it? A well-tended vine will go on and on. That is a matriarch's purpose... to tend the vine."

Artemis stopped walking and looked into her mother's eyes. She didn't know why tears were beginning to form in her own eyes as she stared into her mother's ancient ones, but they were. "Mother-"

"Sshhh," Olympia commanded, pulling her forward to resume their walk. Facing straight forward, head high, Olympia said, "I leave my share of the vine to you."

"No," Artemis grimaced. "We are not discussing this."

Artemis stopped walking, only to be pulled forcibly forward by her mother. It was easier for Olympia to have this talk if the two did not face each other. Walking with the breeze in their faces looking out onto Blanchard land somehow lessened the severity.

"You knew I couldn't live forever, Artemis. None of us can. But I will remain inside you and your sisters. I am inside Beryl. I am inside Salem. I am inside Seth—

somewhere down deep, but I'm there. Fable, Yasmine, the new babies. I am there. Now I ask you to lead them, to tend them."

"Me?" Artemis asked.

"Of course, you," Olympia laughed as if the very question were ridiculous. "Only you. You are the only person I would trust this family to besides Zelda. Since you were born, I could always count on you. You have never let me down."

You have always followed the covenants of the Natural Order. You are the one, Artemis. You will be the new Hecate."

"Momma, don't."

She hadn't called her Momma in years. Not since she was a little girl. Something about the word and the way she said it nearly broke Olympia's already compromised heart. Despite their ages, somewhere inside Artemis still dwelled a girl clinging to her mother's hand and somewhere within Olympia was always the mother guiding her girls through life.

"Always face the truth, child," Olympia told her as the cool breeze wafted over her silky white hair. "Always face the truth. I cannot live forever. My time is drawing near. A Hecate must be prepared for what looms ahead. You are the head of this family now. Or, rather, you will be very soon."

They paused in the meadow among the yellow blooms and the many bumblebees flying around. Olympia appeared drained. Her coloring was pale, her breaths a struggle. Artemis sent her powers forth, visualizing a bench for her mother to sit upon. Within moments the garden bench came drifting across the field, grazing the tops of tall spring grasses as it came forward. The bench righted itself behind Olympia, and the two witches sat down together.

"Thank you, daughter. I must admit I am quite tired these days."

"I understand why you wouldn't use Beryl," Artemis said. "It'd be selfish to borrow time. But could she help ease your pain."

"The sheer fact that you comprehend why it would be wrong to utilize Beryl to give me more years, is further evidence of why you are my successor. But I have no real measurable pain," Olympia reassured. "I'm only tired. So very tired, daughter."

"Let's go back to the house so you can rest."

"Not yet. We have much to discuss."

Olympia looked around the meadow and beyond to the woods, then back behind them past the gardens and arbors to where the great house stood with its new addition almost complete. She breathed in the fragrant air and exhaled slowly, wiping a stray tear from her eye.

"I really will miss this place," Olympia sighed. "This land has been a part of this family for more than two hundred years. I know you will never part with it."

"Never."

"This must always be open to all Blanchards. It is our home, our haven. It is as much yours as Demitra's, as much Nacaria's as Hera's, as much Pastoria's as mine. You will own it, but it belongs to everyone."

"I understand."

"Now, I must share with you some things only you may know. Things you will need to understand how to guide this family," Olympia presaged.

"I'm listening, Mother."

Olympia faced her eldest, her serious face already in place, ready to bestow the secrets of the job. "There is another vault in the house. It can only be accessed in the magic room."

"Another vault?" Artemis gasped. The news was a shock. She had lived in that house her entire life. "How? The magic room has windows on all sides; there's no space for another door."

"Under the floor," Olympia explained. "The hardwood planks of the floor have to be removed."

"But there are bedrooms underneath."

"There is a space on the third floor, between the walls of Seth and Fable's bathrooms. Between those walls lies a secret staircase leading all the way through the center of the house, behind the living room wall. It leads to a second Vault under the house."

"Why is it secret?" Artemis asked.

"It is the place where the most powerful things are kept."

"But your forbidden shelves in the vault, we all use—"

"Those are dangerous and forbidden," Olympia smiled. "But not earth shattering. No, the things in the coven leader's vault should never be messed with unless there is no other way."

"May I ask why? We've had a few close scrapes with death and some pretty powerful problems in this family over the years. Why didn't we access that vault?"

Olympia had never appeared more serious in her life, not as far as Artemis could recall, when she answered, "Because nothing we've been through—nothing—warranted that room. Not Nacaria's trouble, Demitra's resurrection of Larry, or even the dangers Patric posed. That room is for when the world is in peril, and everything used in that room comes with a price."

"I don't understand."

"I hope you never have to. I have never had to access that room, but I was told its whereabouts when my father died and made me coven leader. Artemis, there is an underside to our world where people do not seek to protect the Natural Order, but to bend it to their will."

"What do we do?"

"For a hundred years, we haven't had to do anything. Peace exists, but there are factions to watch. Atheidrelle Obreiggon was always one of those. Her family is dark. I have suspicions that they know things people should not know."

"What kinds of things?"

"I have no idea," Olympia chuckled. "I am one of those people that should not know."

"Do you believe Atheidrelle will come back?"

"Who knows how long her sentence was set to be? By chance she should return to life in this lifetime, you will need to protect Yasmine. You will need to prepare Hera and any child which comes to Seth and Salem. Atheidrelle's curse is dormant now, but should she ever return, so will the curse."

Artemis tried to smile, but it did not come off just right. "Being Hecate is more responsibility than I thought."

"A Blanchard Hecate, definitely."

"Is that everything you wanted to share with me, Mother?" Artemis said squeezing her hand. "I really think we need to get you back to the house now."

Her mother took a long, deep breath and faced her. "There is one more thing I must confide." Olympia removed a small 4x7 picture frame from the pocket of her house dress. She handed it to Artemis.

"I've seen this before, many times," Artemis smiled. "It's the picture from your dressing table in your room. You were so young. What are you, twenty?"

"Nearly thirty," Olympia answered.

"And that's Aunt Pastoria and Zelda with you. God, you three were really something back then."

"There are four of us in this picture," Olympia informed her.

"I only see the three of you."

Olympia turned the frame over and removed the black backing with the stand attached. Carefully she lifted the photograph out and handed it to her daughter. It was folded on the end. Artemis righted the folded edge and revealed the fourth woman in the photograph.

She gasped, "I don't understand? How?"

"I cannot say more on the matter, but very soon you will understand."

"Mother, I need something more than that. You were thirty! That makes Pastoria somewhere around twenty-five. And Zelda—she would be around thirty as well! How can *she* possibly be in this picture with you? She wasn't even born! How has she never said anything to us before?"

"Because it hasn't happened yet," Olympia replied. "But it will happen. When it does her life is going to be devastated. She will need your support and your understanding. More than one person's life will be changed forever. And I am not going to be here when it happens."

Artemis looked deeply into her Mother's eyes and saw the light behind them flickering dimmer than she ever remembered. "How much time do you have?"

"I fear not very much."

CHAPTER FORTY THREE

Xander

Nacaria liked telephones, at least the new, modern ones. In her day, a phone was something that hung on a wall or sat on a tabletop. Now phones were so small and fit into your pocket, but the best thing about them was everything else they could do. Since the time she had been back home she'd taken nearly 1,000 pictures with the phone Salem gave her, and Yasmine had signed her up to something called Spotify and now all the songs Nacaria had once loved in her youth could fit in the palm of her hand.

Collecting the eggs from the chicken houses each day was fun now with her headphones in, listening to her music. She had attempted listening to some of the new music Spotify suggested for her, but she didn't connect so well with the new artists—well maybe Taylor Swift. Nacaria's wicker basket was brimming with eggs when she was startled by Arielle at the last chicken house.

"I have a surprise for you," Arielle smiled, grabbing Nacaria's elbow and leading her back around to the other side of the chicken house.

Standing in the grass by the weathered wooden structure was Xander. Xander Obreiggon at Blanchard House. Nacaria could not believe it. Though she had communicated with him once or twice over the text thing, she had not seen him since New Year's Eve.

"Xander!"

"Nacaria," he smiled. "You are just as beautiful as ever."

Suddenly Nacaria realized she wasn't. Her sundress was old with faded turquoise and yellow flowers and her hair was so windblown it could not possibly look good. *And did I even put my makeup on this morning?* Gently, Arielle lifted the basket from her hand and sent her off with a gentle nudge to walk with her father. Xander took it from there, linking his arm with Nacaria's and proceeding down the path to the apple orchard.

"I can't believe you're here," Nacaria said.

"I literally popped over," Xander grinned. "I've missed you."

"I've missed you too," she said. "Are things better now with Cassandra?"

"Yes, much," Xander replied. "Her depression has eased a bit and she seems ready to rejoin the world again, slowly. And she wants to meet you, Nacaria. Officially. She asked if I would bring you to Oleander for a visit. She wants to get to know you. Would you be amenable to that? I know she put you through quite an ordeal."

"I have long forgiven her for that," Nacaria smiled. "I think it might be nice for us to meet. For her to see that I am not what she has been led to believe I am. And Xander, you and I could have some time together—to see if perhaps there is a future."

Xander took her in his arms and kissed her softly. "I've already told you we definitely have a future."

The Blanchard family enjoyed a hearty Sunday afternoon lunch. Upon hearing that her niece was in town, as well as Xander, Blackie drove down from Birmingham to join the family. Everyone was in good spirits although Artemis seemed preoccupied by something she would not say, so Yasmine stepped in to assist her in preparing the lunch. As Yasmine marched the fried chicken to the table, everyone's faces lit up.

"And who do we have to thank for this treat? You or Artemis?" Howard asked.

"Me," Yasmine answered proudly.

"You?" Seth gasped. "This looks like Aunt Artemis' chicken.

"Well, she did teach me how to make it. But why is it so surprising that I cooked this, Seth Blanchard?!"

"Cause you burn everything," Fable said, grabbing a piece of the still hot chicken.

"You guys lay off, Yaz," Artemis ordered bringing in the biscuits. "I'm a little off my game today, and she really stepped up."

"Anything wrong?" Demitra asked.

Artemis exchanged looks with her mother but said nothing.

"I think Artemis has been working too hard at the restaurant lately," Olympia offered.

"I hope my dropping in was no trouble," Blackie stated as she took a piece of the perfectly fried chicken. "Then again, with a meal such as this, I really don't care."

Nacaria laughed and patted her friend's hand. "As many times as you've taken me out since I've been home, we owe you many more meals like this."

"Have you and Blackie rekindled your old friendship?" Xander asked.

"As if we didn't even pause for two decades," Blackie smiled. "I've taken Nacaria out and shown her everything she needs to know about where to have her hair done, her nails done, and we've replenished her wardrobe with modern clothes, although why she's wearing that old sundress I do not know."

"I always loved this dress," Nacaria smirked. "And I also didn't know Xander was going to show up."

"My little surprise," Arielle laughed. "I think I am going to go back to Oleander with you for a few days."

"You are?" Xander asked excitedly. "That'll be so nice."

"I figure if Cassandra is attempting to become a better person, I might as well test the waters with her," Arielle explained. "Besides, I want to finish clearing out that awful art Mother had—perk up the place. I left a message for Uncle Thaddeuss telling him he could send someone from the House of Duquense to collect whatever we discard. Most of that junk came from there anyway."

Xander made a troubled face. He never did feel comfortable around Atheidrelle's relatives—except Blackie—and the idea of her brother coming to Oleander after everything that had transpired made him uneasy. "Maybe it isn't a good time for your uncle to come to Oleander, not while Nacaria is there," Xander pointed out. "I wouldn't want her visit to be unpleasant."

"I'm sure he'll just send someone," Arielle said. "I doubt he will come himself."

"He won't disturb me," Nacaria smiled. "I'm not afraid of a confrontation with Atheidrelle's brother."

Blackie grimaced. "Perhaps you should be," she warned. "My brother is rather sinister. Arielle, perhaps you should put off his coming to collect Atheidrelle's things until after Nacaria's visit."

"It's all right," Salem said. "I'll be there as well."

"You're going?" Beryl asked.

"Yes," she said, turning to her father. "If that's alright with you? I would like to see Michael's burial place again."

The smile on Xander's face was answer enough to her question. He exchanged proud glances with Nacaria and then looked back to Salem.

"My dear, it is your home," Xander said graciously. "Seth, the same goes for you and Yasmine and my precious granddaughter. Though you have never been there before, you are Obreiggons and Oleander is your ancestral home. All of you are welcome at any time."

"Maybe next visit," Seth said. "I don't think Hera would do too well in a strange environment yet."

Olympia looked around the table at her family. It pleased her very much to see everyone so content. She had never seen Nacaria so happy. No one could have ever guessed years ago that a day would come when Xander Obreiggon would be sitting alongside Nacaria sharing a family meal with his children. And Demitra and Jerry appeared to be coexisting well together. Perhaps their budding romance was not as rich in depth as what she had with Larry, but something was definitely developing there. Artemis was on edge, however, but that was understandable. Olympia had handed her quite a burden to carry, and soon the family would have to be told about the new choice for Hecate. Every so often, Olympia would spy Artemis staring at the face of the one she had seen in Olympia's photograph. Olympia could feel her wondering—she wished she could tell Artemis more, but that could change too much history. It would all need to play out on its own.

"How long do you plan to be gone, Arielle?" Forest asked. He looked a little deflated.

"Aw, can you not live without her too long?" Seth teased. Forest shot him the finger behind his napkin.

"I'll be gone two or three days at the most," Arielle reassured him.

"You could come along too, young man," Xander invited, stunning his daughter. "If you'd like that is. We have plenty of room."

Forest was clearly at a loss for words. He was not even certain Arielle wanted him to go. But he hoped so. He did not like the idea of her being seven hours away. Atlanta was far enough, but Charleston was much too distant. Arielle was excited by the idea and thanked her father for suggesting it. She told Forest she would love to show him where she grew up and take him all around Charleston.

"What about your classes, Forest?" Olympia reminded him. "I assured your grandmother I would see you excelled at this school. I do not want you missing classes."

"I'd only miss a day or two, Aunt Olympia," he said. "And I can get the notes from a buddy of mine."

"I don't know," Olympia frowned.

"Let him go, Mother," Demitra winked. "Love is in the air." Fable and Beryl watched as Jerry Miller appeared to squeeze her hand under the table. The sisters looked at each other in confusion.

Yasmine broke the moment as she addressed Xander, "I have a weird question.

Why does Atheidrelle's family call their home the House of Duquesne?"

Before Xander could answer, Blackie closed her eyes and rather morosely began reciting something,

"Blood on the wealth, blood on the name.
Too many secrets
In the House of Duquense."

"Well, that's disturbing," Fable remarked. "Is that some kind of poem?"

"It once was. A long time ago," Blackie said. "There's more I can't recall. The house I grew up in is rather twisted, diabolical. I got away from it as soon as I could and at quite a price."

Blackie and Xander exchanged glances. Olympia noticed. There was a secret there.

"I've heard the story," Olympia interjected. "The Duquesne family was rather a wicked clan. They're all gone now I believe."

"Yes," Blackie sighed. "The D'Angelo's inherited the house a couple generations ago."

"I'm intrigued," Salem admitted.

"It's a tale for another time, say some scary night by a fire," Blackie laughed. "Thaddeus owns the house now. I'm sure he will want all of Atheidrelle's precious pieces restored back to the House of Duquense."

"I am only too happy to get rid of them," Xander said, winking at Arielle. "My daughter has already begun purging the house when she was visiting at Christmas. It'll be nice taking my family's home back to the grand house it used to be before Atheidrelle tried to force it into a reminder of her family mausoleum."

CHAPTER FORTY FOUR

Nacaria at Oleander

It was even more beautiful than she had ever imagined. Even with Atheidrelle's decorative touches still darkening the place, Nacaria could envision what it must have been like back in antebellum times when Oleander was a thriving tea plantation. The tall, floor-to-ceiling windows with their open wooden shutters would have looked out to the groves keeping a concerned eye on the delicate plants forced to weather storm, draught, and predators. The exterior of the grand house was breathtaking. Inside, however, Nacaria's breath was stolen for more dismal reasons. Atheidrelle's presence lurked everywhere. Though she had never seen the D'Angelo's ancestral home, one look at Oleander's insides told her all she needed to know of the dark and sinister House of Duquense located only a few miles away. But now Xander had the shutters of Oleander open where sunlight washed inward making the overly gothic furnished rooms less uninviting.

Salem enjoyed seeing the place in the daytime. Her only other experience with the house last year was hurried so as to not be caught by the staff when Arielle sneaked her in to meet their father. Forest was equally amazed. His mouth hung open from the moment the car made its way through the streets of Charleston until they entered the Oleander gates on Wadmalaw Island. Oleander was unlike anything he had ever seen before.

"I thought Blanchard House was something," he whispered to his cousin Salem. She giggled.

Forest's branch of the Blanchard family lived quite normally in less austere housing like any other middle-class American. Three bedrooms and one and a half baths meant luxury during his upbringing. Moving into Olympia's country mansion was like moving into a hotel. Plenty of bedrooms, baths, living space—even a swimming pool. But Blanchard House was at its core an inflated farmhouse with plank board walls and minimal architecture. Now faced with something as ornate as Oleander, Forest indeed felt like the poor relative.

"This place *is* impressive," Salem agreed.

Overhearing them, Arielle sneered, "It will be once we repaint and restore it to what it used to be before mother took it over."

Nacaria and Xander did not linger long in the foyer. Xander led her upstairs to his daughter's bedroom. He rapped at the door, then opened it without waiting for a response. Cassandra was sitting demurely on a settee at the foot of her large over plumped bed. She was dressed in light green, and it occurred to Nacaria that she had never seen her out of a nurse's uniform before.

"Nacaria," Cassandra said, nervously rising with her hand formally outstretched. It shook slightly, unsure as to whether it would be accepted. Nacaria shook it politely and smiled.

"Please don't be anxious with me," Nacaria said. "I want to become your friend. I realize we started out badly, but I forgive you all that. And I hope you've learned that I was never what you were taught to believe of me."

Cassandra exhaled some of the tension she was holding. She had expected a cordial reserve from Nacaria, but not warmth. Not after everything she had done to her in Dredmore. When she thought back to those interactions, she flushed with regret and shame. She was grateful Nacaria was being so generous with her.

"I'd like to try, Nacaria," Cassandra replied. "I'd really like to. It is difficult for me now. I have lived my life thinking you were the enemy, and my father was a traitor. In these last months, I have come to learn my father has a caring heart—even to those like me who do not deserve it."

Nacaria felt pity for the girl. Cassandra Obreiggon faced a challenging road ahead of her as she readjusted her view of the world and reevaluated every preconceived idea she had ever held. It couldn't be easy for Xander either. He too was having to reevaluate. Not only his relationship with his eldest child but his own participation in the emasculation of his life and the role he had played in it. With Atheidrelle gone, he was navigating new territory where all decisions fell to him, and he did not want to make wrong choices.

A shadow passed across the wall and paused in the white space between two paintings. Though it was only a shadow, Nacaria could feel the hatred it bore her. No one spoke until it departed the room.

"It is strange," Nacaria noted. "Seeing one of those after having been one."

"She's always around," Cassandra whispered shakily. "She's trying to drive me crazy."

Nacaria instinctively clasped Cassandra's hand and gave it a squeeze. "She can't. She cannot do anything to you now. Not as long as you hold on to yourself."

"I'm not sure who that is. I don't think I've ever actually met me before."

Xander took his daughter into his arms and gave her a reassuring embrace. Nacaria noticed the look on Cassandra's face as he did. It was one of relief, almost restoration. Nacaria could see now how fragile Xander's daughter was. She understood why it had been so important for him to remain at Oleander with her after the Consort. Just the two days without him had left Cassandra unnerved.

As Xander led Nacaria to one of the guest rooms, Nacaria asked him, "Do you think it is wise for Atheidrelle's spirit to be here?"

"I don't understand?"

"Why did you consent to have her soul imprisoned in this house, Xander? You could have asked the Council to send it someplace else."

"My dear, the Council doesn't take requests. It was actually rather shocking they let me give Salem my seat. Besides, I think on some selfish level I wanted her here."

Nacaria gave him a concerning look.

"No," he said, shaking his head softly. "Not like that. You see after you went away, I really felt as if I had nothing to live for. I only existed here. On some level I think I enjoy her being imprisoned at Oleander. She is forced to watch me live again after so many years. And she she's you here, in this house—where you should have been at my side all this time. It is a petty triumph I realize, and perhaps a cruel one. But I believe after all I have lived through with that woman, I have earned the privilege to enjoy something so petty."

"I suppose," Nacaria replied, not certain how healthy his reasoning was.

"Nacaria, I plan to marry you," Xander confessed. "She will see us here and see us happy for the rest of our lives. That is a perfect hell for someone like Atheidrelle."

Nacaria was taken by surprise at his pointedness. She indeed held hope that the two of them might one day end up together as man and wife, but until now she had questioned the probability of that fate. She smiled and gave him a gentle kiss. But her mind was still concerned with Cassandra.

"I worry about Cassandra's well-being," Nacaria admitted. "Atheidrelle's shadow is always around to frighten her."

"Are you frightened?"

"No. I lived her specific doom. I know her form has no power. But my children were disturbed by my presence for a long time. Keep an eye out on Cassandra. She may need to leave here for a while. Perhaps she could go back to Atlanta with Salem and Arielle?"

Xander made a face. "I think we have already received about all the luck we can expect. I don't place too much stock in a closeness developing between Cassandra and Salem. Let us leave well enough alone for now."

. . .

Outside, across the lawns, near the old pavilion, Salem walked silently to the gravesite of her little boy. As she approached, she was taken aback by what she found. A lovely garden now covered the place where baby Michael was cremated last year. Summer flowers grew around a new statue which had been added. It was the archangel, Michael. She smiled at the thoughtful gesture. She knew her father had done this for his baby grandson.

She sat on the green grass beside the grave, deadheading the spent blooms around the spot. She reflected on the brief life of the child laid to rest here and what magnificent joy that brief life had given her. She thought of David and her years with him and how much had changed in only a year's time. She was a widow now. Childless. Her mother was back. She had a new sister. Two technically. She had a new sister-in-law. A niece. And of all things David would have laughed at, she was now a Councilwoman on a board of witches. So much was so different now. If Michael were alive, he would be running all around the house now, getting into all sorts of mischief, magical and otherwise. She wondered if she would ever have another child. She wanted one. Perhaps she should consider Hecate's advice and simply have one on her own. She was considering the matter when a shadow fell over Michael's grave. It startled her and for a second she thought it might be Atheidrelle's. *But she can't leave the house.*

"You're one of the bastards," growled a throaty voice.

Salem turned around to see a great man towering over her. He was dark in appearance, with brown hair clipped short on the sides and top. His sideburns trailed into a thinly defined beard and mustache. If ever anyone looked sinister, it was this man. It did not require much deducing to figure out who he was.

"You're Thaddeuss D'Angelo," she said, rising.

"I am indeed."

Salem sensed this man was accustomed to people fearing him. It delighted her to stand face to face, a half step too close, encroaching into his personal space. Salem Blanchard feared nothing about this man, and she enjoyed his understanding this.

"I was told you'd never come to Oleander now that your sister is banished."

"But she isn't banished," he corrected. "She is, in fact, prisoner here."

Salem gave a smile of vindication, "By her own doing."

"Or yours."

Salem shot him a dirty look and took yet another half step closer towards him. "I suspect you are accustomed to people revering your family. Perhaps even being afraid of you," she said coldly. "I assure you I am not one of those people."

"Perhaps you should be," Thaddeuss warned.

"I wasn't afraid of your sister. I doubt I'd be afraid of the likes of you or any other D'Angelo."

Thaddeuss almost smiled, as if he were in on something she wasn't. "It was foolish of you to not fear Atheidrelle. Youthful mistake."

"Yet I'm standing here at Oleander, and she is not," Salem smiled.

"For the moment," Thaddeuss replied with a nod of concession. "Things do tend to change. And now I will leave you to your dead son. I have only come for my sister's personal effects. The housekeeper alerted me Xander had returned."

"You'll find him at the house. With my mother."

Thaddeuss did not wince when she gave him that bit of information. Obviously, the housekeeper had imparted that tidbit as well. Probably a spy for him or a loyalist to her old mistress. Salem would be sure to divulge this vital information to her father or Arielle.

Xander was both surprised and also not surprised at all when he found his ex-brother-in-law standing in the front parlor. With Thaddeuss were two men, probably staff at the House of Duquesne, on site to collect the boxes and objects Arielle had set aside at Christmas, along with boxes the staff at Oleander had been packing up since.

"I rather expected you'd have collected these sooner," Xander said as he entered the room.

"I have been away," Thaddeuss responded. "Had I not, I would have come to your little Council meeting and advocated for my sister."

"I was under the assumption you were not a member of the Witches Association," Xander replied.

"Not that one."

Xander knew what he meant. He was about to comment when Arielle entered with Nacaria. Xander noticed how Arielle flinched ever so mildly as she caught sight of her uncle. Recovering quickly, she forced a gracious smile to her face.

"Uncle Thaddeuss," she greeted politely. "Thank you for coming to retrieve Mother's things. I figured you'd prefer to have them returned to the House of Duquesne rather than my throwing them out."

"I suppose I owe you thanks for the consideration," Thaddeuss nodded. "Although your complete betrayal of your mother forces me to regret the civility."

Arielle retained the smile, and it now looked almost playful. If he were going to take the gloves off, she might finally enjoy sparring with this man she had never liked. "Now Uncle Thaddeuss, you know as well as I do that I mattered very little to Mother. I doubt my *betrayal,* as you call it, requires that much indignation."

Ignoring his niece's statement, Thaddeuss turned his attentions to the exquisite woman standing behind her. He inspected her from head to toe, from her long, cascading blonde hair to the pastel blue dress covering her trim figure.

"And you must be the infamous Nacaria Blanchard," he said approaching. Nacaria took a step backward from him, although she did not know why she had. "I see you live up to the reputation. You are as beautiful as you are destructive."

"Destructive?'

"You did destroy my sister's family, her happiness, and now her life. I wonder how you will be rewarded for what you've done."

"If you are threatening Nacaria, Thaddeuss," Xander said, stepping forward.

"My, my, my, look who has acquired a backbone," Thaddeuss mused. "She's not worth my time. I only want to collect my sister's things."

"Everything is here," Xander said.

Thaddeuss directed his men to begin hauling the pile of boxes and various art pieces strewn around them to a van parked out front. He glanced around, investigating his sister's objects. Rubbing his chin, he made a quizzical face.

"Is there something missing?" Arielle asked.

"There is a portrait of Atheidrelle I would like to have. The one which hangs in her bedroom."

Arielle knew the portrait well. She turned to Xander, "Daddy?"

"He may have it," Xander agreed.

"I'll get it for you," Arielle said.

"Never mind," Thaddeuss said. "I will retrieve it myself."

He disappeared up the staircase to the second floor. Nacaria moved closer to Xander, allowing his reassuring arm to ease her nervousness. Arielle watched as the men finished loading the van with her mother's baubles and trinkets. Some of these things had been collected over the years, but the vast majority Atheidrelle had brought with her from her childhood home when she had married. Xander. Arielle was thrilled to have these morose items returned to the D'Angelo family.

Upstairs in Atheidrelle's grand gothic style bedroom, heavy with tapestries and darkly stained wood panels, Thaddeuss stood before the life-size portrait hanging on the wall. Atheidrelle's presence still dominated the room by method of the painting. It captured her essence entirely. Her undeniable beauty—golden hair, piercing eyes, almost marbleized skin. It also captured her wickedness. Her conceit. Her condescension toward anyone looking up at it. Where an average person might feel jolted by the image, Thaddeuss felt pride. His sister and he were the last of the D'Angelos who understood what that name meant.

"I have come Atheidrelle," he told the painting. "I am returning everything which belongs to the House of Duquesne."

The shadow, Atheidrelle's shadow, darted into the bedroom and hovered momentarily across the fireplace mantle and hearth. Thaddeuss gave a wicked smile in its direction and scratched his beard at the strange sight. This was his sister's soul left to haunt the walls of a house she no longer controlled. He would spare her that indignity.

"As I said, sister, I am here to return *everything* that belongs to the House of Duquesne."

The shadow, understanding his meaning, moved slowly toward the painting on the wall. It situated itself into the perimeters of the frame. Thaddeuss walked to the portrait and lifted it from its location. As the portrait lifted, the shadow detached with it, clinging to the canvas. Thaddeuss D'Angelo smiled demonically as he carefully covered the portrait with the silk sheet from the bed. When he reached the bottom of the stairs, he passed the cloaked portrait to his men and watched as they carried it from the house—as they carried Atheidrelle out of Oleander.

"Again, I extend my gratitude for this kindness," Thaddeuss said, bowing to Arielle and Xander. "My family will be pleased to have everything restored to us."

CHAPTER FORTY FIVE

New Relationships

Cassandra didn't expect a knock on her door so late in the evening. After a quiet dinner in her room, she was sitting in bed reading, unable to fall asleep. Her nerves were unsteady, and the knock jolted her for a moment. She called out to the visitor to come inside. When Salem walked into her room, it was the last person she expected to see.

"I saw the light under your door," Salem explained. "I thought I might say hello. I haven't seen much of you these last couple of days. We leave tomorrow. I thought perhaps you and I could use a moment together."

Cassandra's anxiety was building. She was not sure how to respond or what Salem's intent might be for this late hour visit. "Come in," Cassandra welcomed although she didn't feel like extending the invitation.

Salem walked in and made a brief inspection of her half-sister's room. It was not as darkly designed as the rest of the house, but it wasn't the cheeriest bedroom Salem had ever seen either.

"You are up late," Salem noted. "Anything the matter?"

Cassandra eyed her suspiciously and replied, "The same can be said for you."

Salem broke the tension with a playful chuckle which Cassandra did not expect. "It's really silly. Arielle and Forest are not back yet from their date in town, and I never can go to sleep until Ari is home."

Cassandra felt her face smile as she replied, "Is that so?"

Suddenly the defenses seemed to fall slightly as Salem rather boldly and quite familiarly took a seat at the foot of Cassandra's bed. "You know how Arielle is. She is so naive at times. At home in Atlanta, I can never sleep unless I know she is home safely."

"Naïve?"

"You know," Salem continued. "She trusts way too easily. There have been a couple of times she put herself in the company of the wrong person, and I had to come to the rescue. I've had to teach her a little about not making friends with *everybody* she meets."

Cassandra looked down to her lap and frowned a little. "I'm afraid you know more about our sister than I. I regret that very much."

Salem leaned forward and patted Cassandra's hand. "It's never too late to change that."

Cassandra nodded and returned her gaze toward Salem. "You don't think she's at any risk with her friend, do you?"

Salem shook her head, "Oh, no Forest is a good guy. I'm just awake out of habit. I don't sleep till she's home."

Cassandra looked down to her lap again, fiddling with the book in her hand. Her hands were jittery, nervous. Salem noticed how the spine of the book had little worn lines from being opened and closed quite often, yet from the placemark in the book, Cassandra was not even a quarter of the way through it. Obviously, she spent many nights simply bending the cover back and forth.

"I don't sleep much anymore."

Salem inched closer, placing her hand on Cassandra's covered legs. "I know what you are feeling. I had a mother on a wall too, for a long time. When I was a little girl, her shadow frightened me so much I couldn't sleep either. Took a long time to stop being afraid of it."

Cassandra appreciated the commiseration, but it didn't help. "Yes, but you were a little girl, and your mother didn't hate you for betraying her."

"Fear is still fear," Salem pointed out. "I was a little girl afraid of something strange I didn't understand. You are a woman afraid of something menacing that is purposefully trying to frighten you. Fear is fear. I understand why you can't sleep anymore."

Cassandra reached out and clasped Salem's hand in some sort of strange solidarity she never imagined they would share. "I haven't seen it tonight. Usually she's in here, hovering, looming. Emitting her hatred at me."

Salem laughed. "She's probably in my room. Maybe my being here takes her off your hands for the night."

Cassandra shared the laugh and enjoyed the feeling it gave her. They said nothing more. Salem simply pulled the covers up around Cassandra's shoulders and lifted the book from her hands. She clicked the light off on her way out the door. As Salem went back to her own room, she imagined one day she and Cassandra Obreiggon might call themselves sisters.

. . .

On the floor above, Nacaria was also awake but for vastly different reasons. She had just made love to Xander for the first time in over two decades. Laying her cheek upon his chest she listened to his heart beating. Listened to his lungs breathing. It felt so good to be in his arms again. She never dreamed this would be a possibility back when the men from the Consort dragged her off to Dredmore. Yet here she was. Resting against the chest of the man she loved in a bedroom inside Oleander.

"I am so unbelievably happy Nacaria," Xander said, kissing her softly. "I have never been truly happy in my life, until now."

She rolled over to face him, resting her chin on his chest. "We have missed so many years. We deserve this happiness."

"Yes, but you look the same as you did back then. I'm afraid I haven't weathered the test of time as well."

"You are still the handsomest man I've ever laid eyes on," she assured him. "The only man I have ever, or could ever, love."

"I wish you would stay."

Nacaria closed her eyes and smiled brightly. "Wouldn't that be wonderful? But not right now, Xander. Cassandra still needs your full attention. Besides, I am not ready to leave my family yet. I just returned to them. And of course, Hera. I really enjoy being there with her every day. For now, I don't want to miss any of it."

Xander kissed her soft lips once more and replied, "We will have our time, when it is time."

CHAPTER FORTY SIX

Driving Home

Demitra and Jerry spent the evening in Birmingham with Jerry's parents. Cally and Vestus Miller were pleased that their son had come to visit and brought his wife. They initially feared he may end the marriage to such a wonderful woman due to his amnesia. But all throughout the evening, the Millers got the feeling that Jerry and Demitra may be rediscovering one another again. Things weren't as they were before—there still appeared to be a barrier between them—almost as if they were strangers still, yet that barrier looked to be cracking. They witnessed Jerry laughing with his wife, and once or twice Demitra even caressed his hand without him pulling it away from her. It was progress.

On the drive home, Jerry himself appeared to notice how things were becoming easier with Demitra. They were just minutes out of the city when he made a comment about it.

"Tonight was nice," he said. "Honestly, I didn't know what to expect. I guess I think since you're unknown to me, you are unknown to them. But my folks and you have a relationship already, one I'm not in on, and it was nice to see. They really love you."

"I love them," Demitra replied and meant it. "Your parents are the salt of the earth."

"I enjoyed myself with you tonight too, Demitra."

"Surprise you?"

Jerry chuckled. "Not exactly surprised. I remember liking you a lot on our initial dates. And these last couple of weeks we've had some nice times on our daily walks and our dinners out. I guess what I'm saying is even though I don't exactly feel comfortable in our relationship yet, I am beginning to see why we are together. Why I married you. I could very easily fall for you."

"I think I feel the same about you."

He laughed again, "Well, I should hope so. You're not the one with amnesia. I haven't changed."

But you have. Demitra thought to herself. Jerry Miller was no Larry Mariner. Her heart would always belong to Larry. Yet she did feel something for Jerry. She could not explain how or why, but something was emerging. Larry said he wanted her to love again, perhaps she was beginning to. Or perhaps she could not bear the loneliness anymore and Jerry was a perfect runner up.

"You've changed," she said. "You aren't the Jerry I married. But like you said, I am starting to feel some feelings. I think I might one day be able love the Jerry you are now. We'll see."

"Yeah, let's just let it play out a while longer."

...

Far away on another interstate, Salem, Nacaria, Arielle, and Forest were driving home to Daihmler. Their stay at Oleander had only been a couple of days, but it was time enough for everyone to come to conclusions about their own futures.

Nacaria spent her days in Charleston getting to know the man she loved again. It was a good feeling to know that no matter how many years had divided them, their love was intact. She rejoiced at the thought of having a future with him. He made it abundantly clear it was something he wanted. She leaned her head onto the cool glass of the passenger window and stared out at the darkness, daydreaming about her future.

"Look at her smiling up here," Salem said using the rear-view mirror to catch Arielle and Forest's attention from the back seat. "I'd say someone is still in love."

"Why shouldn't I be?" Nacaria smiled to her daughter. "He's still as kind and wonderful as ever."

"Daddy told me he plans to marry you soon," Arielle replied. "Salem won't that be cool! Your mother marrying our father; it'll almost be like we are whole sisters!"

Salem gave her sister a wink through the mirror as she continued driving.

"It's really a pretty powerful love story," Forest noted. "Hell, I remember as a kid hearing my grandmother talk about the tragic love of Nacaria and Xander, and now to think it's going to get a happy ending after all."

"Daddy deserves to have love," Arielle said. "I've watched him all of my life be so withdrawn, so sad. As if he'd lost some part of himself. I think he's found it again now."

Arielle stopped talking. Her body shuddered. Forest thought it was sweet, to care about her father that much that she could become overtaken by the emotion of his pain.

"You are the cutest thing," he said.

"Love is powerful," Arielle said. Her voice seemed changed somehow. Robotic. "Love can't be denied, and it can't be stolen. Even by a whore."

Forest looked at her, surprised by what she had said. Something was off. Arielle was tense, almost pulsing with something...anger maybe. He thought for a moment she might be having a mild seizure, yet she continued talking and people in mid seizure do not usually speak.

"I have watched this play out and it sickens me. I can't pretend for another second."

Salem's eyes darted to the mirror. She did not know what was happening. Arielle seemed uncharacteristically vicious suddenly. From the reflection in the mirror her eyes were dark, hostile, furious. Salem split her attention between the road ahead and whatever episode her sister was having in the back seat.

"You tried to destroy my parents' marriage!" Arielle told Nacaria, who was now turning around in the passenger seat to face her. "You think you're so beautiful, so enticing. You could never satisfy him the way my mother could. You are the one barrier to my family's happiness. Well, my sister may not have ended you, but I sure as Hell will!"

Thrusting her hands forward, Arielle sent forth a burst of energy pounding into the passenger seat like a cannon. The force bursting from her hands was so powerful that suddenly the seat, Nacaria, and the passenger side door ripped from the car, hurdling out into the night. Salem and Forest looked on in horror as they witnessed the seat, door, and Nacaria herself tumbling across the pavement of the lane beside them.

Salem slammed on the brakes as Forest tackled Arielle in the backseat. She clawed his face and rearmed herself to send another burst his way. Salem swung around in the seat and instinctively froze her sister as still as a piece of stone in the backseat, before she leapt from the car to rush to her mother's aide. Nacaria's battered body, ripped by the pavement, lay bloodied and unconscious, flecks of skin hung in tatters from her face and arms. Forest jumped from the car, dodging other motorists now honking and swerving to evade them. He ran to Salem's side. Salem was in shock, doing nothing but staring at the pile of flesh, bone, and blood which had been her mother. *Just like David.* She did not know what to do.

"Freeze her, Salem!" Forest shouted. "Freeze her before she dies!"

Forest's words knocked Salem back to reality and she obeyed. Forest scooped Nacaria up in his arms and carried her back to the car, placing her in the seat with Arielle. Salem stood horrified, unable to move. Forest ran back and grabbed her arm, pulling her back to the car. Other drivers were stopping now, exiting their own vehicles to offer assistance. Forest ignored them all and shoved Salem through the doorless entrance to the passenger seat. He ran around to the driver's side and hopped in, flooring the gas pedal and sending the car zooming down the interstate.

"What just happened?" Salem stuttered. "What did she do?"

"I have no idea," Forest panted as he violently weaved in and out of traffic in an attempt to reach Daihmler as soon as possible. "Keep them both frozen, Salem. I'll call ahead and make sure Beryl is home when we get there."

"I need to call Xander," she muttered. "He needs to know what Arielle's done. And about Mother."

...

Olympia Blanchard stood on the front porch, staring out into the devious night. Something was wrong. She could feel it in her old bones. From all appearances, the early summer evening was beautiful. The sounds of crickets chirping in the grass mixed with the cries of birds, calling for companionship in the trees. The fragrance of juniper berries and confederate jasmine trickled across the air as stars glowed above. Her heart faltered a moment. She grabbed the railing, unsteady.

Artemis, something is wrong.

Artemis came outside, the screen door slamming behind her. She saw her mother swaying slightly at the porch rail. She came to her side and steadied her with her strong hands.

"Mother?"

"I don't feel well, Artemis."

"What's wrong?"

"I don't know," Olympia whispered to the air. "Something has happened. I can feel it. And something is wrong with me as well. I think it's my heart."

"I'll get Beryl," Artemis said, turning to go inside.

"No," Olympia grabbed her arm. "I told you my time was drawing near. I have these moments now and then. It will pass. Just help me to my chair."

Fable ran outside, slamming the screen door behind her. "Aunt Artemis, Hecate! Forest called. There's been some trouble. They'll be home in an hour."

CHAPTER FORTY SEVEN

Arielle's Wrath

The Blanchards were in shock as they huddled together in the living room awaiting news from upstairs where Beryl was with Nacaria. When they heard footsteps on the staircase, all attention turned to the foyer.

"Aunt Nacaria will be fine," Beryl said as she came into the Blanchard living room. "Xander is with her. She'll be down as soon as she changes clothes. I was able to heal all of her injuries. It was really a good thing you froze her, Salem. Otherwise, she would not have survived the car ride home."

"How did Xander get here?" Demitra asked.

"I called him on the way," Salem answered. "You know he has the power to zap anywhere. He was already here when we pulled up."

"I don't really understand what's going on?" Jerry exclaimed. "What did we pull up into when we came home? How exactly did you *heal* Nacaria? And why is Arielle catatonic like that? She looks like a statue!"

Demitra placed her finger to his lips to quieten him then she gently clasped his hand with her own, leading him outside to explain about her family. It was a conversation she had not expected to have to have so soon.

Salem walked over to the sofa where Arielle had been placed, still in her frozen mid-lurch toward Forest. Forest and Seth sat beside her, waiting. Yasmine stood beside her husband, staring at the crazed expression on her lifeless sister-in-law's face.

"I have no idea what has happened tonight myself," Salem said to Seth. "Could Arielle have been playing us this entire time? How could I have been so wrong about her?"

"We," Seth corrected. "We all believed her, believed she cared for us."

"I think she did," Yasmine replied. "I think she still does. I just can't believe she would have been manipulating us this whole time."

"You weren't there," Forest said. "The way she went after Nacaria. The things she was saying. I thought I knew her, too. It was insane. So much hate spewing out of her. That wasn't my Arielle."

"The same thing happened with Patric," Fable recalled. "None of us saw it coming until he was attacking us."

Artemis walked over to Arielle's still form on the sofa and examined her closely. "I find it strange that we would all be fooled so long by her."

"What do you mean?" Salem asked.

"Simple," Artemis answered. "We have seen Arielle care about us all—genuinely care. The way she was there for you after David and Michael. The way she turned on her mother and left her coven for ours."

"She was faking all of it," Seth said. "She was just trying to get inside our family for her bigger plan."

Artemis paced the floor in front of the fireplace. Her long black hair swinging behind her with every giant step. "That's exactly my point," she declared. "What bigger plan? So that one night she could throw Nacaria out of a moving vehicle? That is a pretty clumsy revenge plan. She has had a thousand opportunities to do harm to us and hasn't. Why tonight? What changed?"

Olympia sighed from her chair by the fireplace. "Artemis is correct. I cannot explain why Arielle changed tonight, but I trust her. I trust that she has not been deceiving us this last year."

The front door swung open as Zelda came barreling inside. She did not say anything to anyone. Her first order of business was Arielle. She walked over to the sofa and stared into her vacant eyes. Zelda placed a hand on the top of Arielle's head and zoned out into a brief trance. When she came out of it, she scratched her head and turned around to face Olympia.

"That's not Arielle."

"We know," Salem said. "She isn't the Arielle we know. Something has happened to her tonight. Either she's shown her true colors, or something has ignited some force inside her."

"No, Salem," Zelda repeated. "That ain't Arielle. It ain't her aura. Not her spirit neither. Somethin' is in her body."

"Possession," Olympia said as if it were now obvious. "Why didn't I pick up on that?"

"Cause you ain't psychic," Zelda scoffed.

"Could it be..."

Xander and Nacaria now appeared at the bottom of the stairs. "It's Atheidrelle," Xander said. "It's the only explanation. I know how much my daughter loves this family. She truly does. She would never harm Nacaria or any one of you."

"How could Atheidrelle manage this?" Nacaria asked. "When I was in her condition, I was powerless."

"You are not Atheidrelle," Xander said. He shook his head in confusion. "I can't explain how because even I do not know, but she is terribly strong. Stronger than anyone I have ever known. Even I don't know the extent of her powers."

Demitra came back inside with Jerry. He looked ashen, pale, shaken by whatever she had told him. He said nothing but took a seat on the bottom stair and observed. The poor amnesiac man had enough to contend with on his own. Now he had just learned that witches are real and his wife and her family—whom he lived with—were among them. It was a lot to process.

Back in the living room, Salem had a suggestion as the real problem pressing the family at the moment was still going on. "We can unfreeze Arielle and find out who or what she is."

"Not yet," Artemis said. "We have to be ready for her. And we have to protect those who can't protect themselves."

"I don't understand?" Seth said.

Artemis explained. "Jerry?" She looked into the entrance hall at her frazzled brother-in-law on the steps. "Jerry? Are you okay? Can you understand me?"

Jerry glanced up from the floor and looked back into the living room. "I can hear you. I'm okay."

"Good," Artemis smiled, walking to him. Placing a reassuring hand on his shoulder, she knelt down before him. "We need your help. I need for you to drive yourself, Yasmine, and all three of the children to Howard's. Stay there until you hear from us."

Yasmine cried out in protest, "I'm not leaving Seth!"

"You are a mother now," Artemis said sternly.

Beryl placed a gentle hand on her cousin's arm, adding, "And you are not a witch, Yaz. If this goes badly, you and the children need to be in a safe place."

"I disagree," Yasmine argued. "When we battled Patric I was very useful. My place is alongside this family and my husband when trouble comes. Not running to hide at Howard's."

Artemis clearly did not appreciate being challenged on the matter. She shot her niece an angry look the likes Yasmine had never been the recipient of. Seth and Fable had seen that look on their aunt's face a few times growing up, but never Yasmine.

"I am not asking you or arguing with you over this," Artemis announced. "You are a mother now and your job is to ensure the safety of the children. Go get the babies and go with Jerry."

Yasmine argued no further. It took only a few minutes for she and Jerry to gather the children and the things they would need. It also came as quite a surprise to Jerry that the strange puppy in the house was also considered one of the three children. Demitra had apparently forgotten to reveal that piece of information to him during their brief discussion on the porch. Artemis alerted Howard he would have guests. Demitra and Seth said goodbye to their spouses in the driveway.

"I still don't understand what's about to happen here," Jerry said. "Are you in danger?"

"We all are."

"I don't understand why we aren't calling the police," Jerry said.

"The police would be powerless in this situation," Demitra explained.

"But if you are in real danger, Demitra."

She smiled at her new husband and gave him a soft kiss on the lips. "I've faced dangers like this before. I see no reason to believe I won't face this one down unharmed as well. I will call you later. You take care of my grandchildren and nieces. That's how you can help me tonight."

On the other side of Jerry's car, Yasmine clung to her husband while holding their daughter. "I'm afraid Seth. If this is Atheidrelle, you are not safe. She hates you and Salem enough to kill you."

"Which is why you have to leave, Yaz. The worst thing she can do to me is to hurt you or Hera. You need to go, now. I love you Baby, remember that. Just in case."

"Seth! Don't say things like that!" She kissed him harder than she had ever kissed him before. "I'm coming back in the morning. You had better be alive and unharmed, or I will kill you myself."

Once Jerry pulled away and everyone was gathered in the living room, Salem outstretched her hands and unfroze her sister. Arielle lurched forward and fell off the sofa—the momentum from the car was still perpetuating its velocity. Quickly, she righted herself and looked around.

"I see," she said. "You have brought me to the Blanchard clan in all its entirety."

She laughed as though the idea amused her. "You have done me quite the favor. I will have the pleasure of killing all of you in one evening."

Forest stepped forward and grabbed her arm. "Arielle, can you hear me?"

Arielle closed her eyes and sent Forest sailing backward high into the air. His back hit the spot in the wall where the ceiling and wall met. The family heard the snap of his spine from the impact and then watched dumbstruck as his body fell to the floor.

"Forest!" Seth screamed rushing toward his cousin.

Arielle clapped her hands and sent all the furniture in the room hurdling toward Forest. Olympia was knocked off her feet by a wingback chair as it flew forward. Forest, paralyzed and unable to run, saw his great-aunt stumble. Instead of cloaking himself in a forcefield only his power could manifest, he tossed the defensive shield toward the elderly woman, wrapping her in protection as her frail, aged body crashed to the ground. She was unharmed. The sofa caught Demitra by the legs and propelled her over it, knocking her to the floor as the coffee table hurdled toward Seth. Seth, as if remembering his high school glory days in sports, dropped to his knees, and slid, baseball style, under the legs of the coffee table to safety. The furniture crashed into the spot where Forest's body had lain.

The Blanchards were about to charge forward to rescue him when they noticed Xander standing by the stairs in the entrance hall, clutching Forest's hand as the boy struggled for breath. In the blink of an eye, he had zapped forward and zapped back taking Forest with him out of the path of flying furniture.

"Hello, Daddy," Arielle sneered. "I see you've come to save your precious Nacaria."

"You can drop the Daddy nonsense, Atheidrelle. I'd know you anywhere."

Arielle's face grimaced as her darkened eyes widened. Gone was Arielle's sweet innocence. Gone was the gentleness she so often displayed. Her mother was inside of her now, and the viciousness of Atheidrelle was undeniable. "My love. You do know me, don't you?"

"What have you done with Arielle?" Salem demanded.

"Oh, she's in here with me," Atheidrelle laughed. "Shrinking minute by minute. Soon there will only be me. And I will live as her long after all of you are dead."

"You're forgetting one thing, aren't you?" Artemis stated. "There are far more of us than there are of you."

"Perhaps. But even all of you are no match for me."

Atheidrelle waved her hand and suddenly Artemis fell to the ground as the bones in her legs shattered beneath the flesh. She screamed a blood curdling scream. Beryl, who had just finished healing Forest, rushed forward toward her aunt.

"Oh, no you don't!" Atheidrelle laughed.

She waved her other hand toward Beryl. All at once, Beryl was sent vaulting across the room with such a force that she crashed into...and through... the living room wall out onto the lawn beyond. Dust and debris filled the room as the Blanchards looked at the human-sized hole in the wall where the broken wood splintered at the edges outlining where she had crashed through.

"Beryl!" Fable screamed rushing toward the hole in the wall. There was no way anyone could have survived such a strike. The wooden walls of Blanchard House were too thick. A body sent hard enough to smash through would surely be eviscerated. But Fable did not make it to the hole in time to investigate, before she could look out to the lawn the overhead chandelier crashed down atop her. Fable was pinned to the floor by it, blood spewing from her mouth with the impact, spraying across Olympia's face.

Demitra rushed to her daughter, trying to lift the heavy chandelier from her crushed body. Seth joined her and together they pulled Fable out from under. Fable couldn't speak, she could only cough more blood onto her chest as her eyes tried to hold focus and not lose consciousness. All the while she fought for consciousness, her only thought was of Beryl. What was Beryl's condition outside? Someone had to manage to escape Atheidrelle long enough to check on Beryl.

"Where did you get this kind of power?" Zelda shrieked. The brave old woman began walking toward Atheidrelle, pausing only to assist Olympia to her feet before continuing to confront their enemy. "It ain't right for one witch to have this much power. What are you?"

Atheidrelle watched the aged woman coming closer and released an amused laugh. She then swiped her arm and sent out an energy burst which toppled Zelda and propelled her through the front window out onto the porch.

"Atheidrelle," Nacaria said calmly. "This fight is with me. Leave my family alone." Nacaria approached her bravely. Xander grabbed her arm and tried to pull her behind him, but Nacaria shook him loose.

"I've waited years for this moment, Nacaria," Atheidrelle sneered. "I have lived every moment of my life knowing one day I would kill you for coming between my husband and me."

"I never loved you, Atheidrelle!" Xander cried. "And you certainly won't win my love this way. I hate you. I have always hated you."

Perhaps he had thought the truth might give her pause—make her understand she would never win him back. Perhaps she would end this senseless fight. His words had no effect. It changed nothing for her.

"My dear Xander. Love and hate are not that far removed from one another. You belong to me, and you will never escape me as long as you live. Marriage is forever."

Fable was still conscious, but barely. Laying on the floor, she fought back the dizziness to focus her mind—her power--on anything out in the night which might help. Seconds later, a stream of blackbirds flew like bullets through the broken window and the Beryl-shaped hole in the wall. The birds directed their sharp beaks towards Atheidrelle and attacked. With the wave of Atheidrelle's hand each bird exploded into pieces before even one left a mark on her.

"Where does your power come from?" Xander demanded. "I've never seen you this strong."

"There is much you do not know about me, Husband."

Atheidrelle recentered her focus onto Nacaria. "Let me see if I can split you in two pieces," she laughed. "One for each of your bastards to cling to as they die with you."

Another surge of energy swept forward from within her. Nacaria closed her eyes, anticipating what was coming. But Xander had already blinked himself from where he stood to where Nacaria was standing. He grabbed her hand and zapped her away before the fatal blow reached her. Nacaria opened her eyes to find the two of them standing safely in the kitchen.

"Forest!!!"

Nacaria and Xander heard the scream from the other room. Salem's scream. The spell which had been aimed at Nacaria hit Forest directly after Xander zapped her from its path. Rushing back to the foyer, Nacaria and Xander saw the body of Forest Blanchard, ripped down the center from head to groin. Blood, entrails, muscle, and organs spilled from the opening onto the floor around him.

"NO!!!" Seth shrieked, crawling over to his cousin, hysterically attempting to push his body back together as if reassembling his two halves were all that was needed.

The front door flung open, taking everyone by surprise. Beryl stood in the threshold unbloodied and alive, heaving breathlessly as she looked down to her disemboweled cousin.

"Back for more!" Atheidrelle cackled.

Without a moment's hesitation, Atheidrelle sent the same curse which had ripped Forest apart toward Beryl Blanchard. The remaining Blanchards watched helplessly in horror. Demitra screamed for her daughter. Beryl stood, as shocked as everyone else who was watching as the force hurled at her from the evil witch hit. Her body shook for a moment, then stopped as the spell passed through. It left not a mark on her, passing through to hit the foyer wall. The wall ripped, tearing a massive hole to the room beyond it. Faint moonlight through the study window revealed the room, now visible through the hole. But Beryl was intact.

From behind Arielle's eyes, Atheidrelle looked out in utter disbelief. "How? How did you--?"

Beryl was as surprised as Atheidrelle. She looked at her mother in disbelief, Demitra—relieved and thankful—simply shrugged, she had no answers. Atheidrelle tried again, she flapped her hand sideways and sent the chandelier, which had crushed Fable, catapulting toward Beryl. Instinctively, Beryl lifted one hand to shield herself... and caught it. Olympia, Demitra, Artemis, Seth, Nacaria, Xander, and Fable looked on in bewilderment. Beryl had not a scratch on her as she clutched the heavy fixture effortlessly in one hand, as if it were made of cardboard. She dropped the chandelier at her feet. The sound of the crash reminded everyone of its true weight and mass.

Atheidrelle was dumbfounded. She stood silently staring onward at Beryl, trying to understand. Her piercing eyes squinting as if attempting to scan her or hone in somehow on what had changed.

"Salem!" Xander shouted. "Freeze her."

Salem froze Atheidrelle once again. Arielle's body stood motionless. For seconds no one said anything. Then the Blanchards rushed into action. Beryl darted to her sister's crushed form and began healing her as Fable clung to life. Then she focused on healing Artemis and then Olympia.

"Heal Forest!" Seth screamed, holding, as hard as he could, his cousin's blood covered divided sections together.

Beryl looked in his direction with anguished eyes. "I can't," she sobbed. "I can't heal the dead."

"He may still be alive," Seth said hysterically.

Olympia could feel her heart fluttering. It was too much for her. She looked down to her sister's grandson on the floor, his body eviscerated, ending his young beautiful life. She saw Seth still trying to reassemble Forest. Seth's hands covered in blood, body fluid and muck no living person should see. His mind unable to fully accept. Olympia's heart was beating dangerously hard now, almost painfully so. *I think this is my end.* No one noticed her clutching her chest, everyone's eyes on Seth and his reluctance to come to terms with what happened to Forest.

Artemis went slowly to her nephew. Kneeling down to him and cradling him in her arms, she whispered softly, "He's not alive, Seth. He's gone." She turned to Salem. "How can Atheidrelle be this strong and you still be able to freeze her?"

"The ability to stop time and people is one of the most powerful magics there is," Olympia said. "I think Salem is the only person equipped to take Atheidrelle down. And perhaps Beryl."

"Hecate," Beryl gasped. "What's happening to me? I don't have invincibility."

"Maybe you do," coughed Zelda in the doorway, coming in from outside. "Powers can grow. And you are a healer. You healed me out there, didn't you?"

"Zelda!" Demitra gasped hugging their old friend.

"We have to kill Atheidrelle before she fights Salem's powers off," Seth cried.

"But we can't kill her," Salem said. "This is Arielle's body. If we kill Atheidrelle, we kill Arielle."

"How did she get inside Arielle?" Nacaria asked aloud. "Did she use a spell? If so, maybe I can reverse it. Maybe it's a *mother's tie* kind of magic."

"No," Xander said suddenly, as if realizing something. "A blood tie, maybe. But not a mother's tie."

"Why not?" Nacaria asked.

"Because Atheidrelle is not Arielle's mother."

CHAPTER FORTY EIGHT

The Truth

The Blanchards waited while Xander was gone. A questioning silence fell over them all as they evaluated the havoc dropped upon them that night. Forest's blood covered the floor, separating into little riverlets which seeped into the wood grain, leaving what looked like veins across the old, cracked hardwoods. The smell in the air was putrid, helped only by the breeze blowing through the broken window, the front door, and the hole in the wall which had mysteriously caused absolutely no harm to Beryl. Seth covered his cousin's body with a bedspread, unable to stand the sight of what Atheidrelle Obreiggon had done to poor Forest.

"How do I tell my sister about her grandson?" Olympia said, wiping the tears from her eyes.

"Mother, you have to keep yourself calm," Artemis warned. "Your heart."

"I'm afraid it's too late for that," Olympia panted. "My heart is going now. I can feel it. I don't have much time."

Artemis started toward Beryl, but her mother gripped her arm. Olympia shook her head in refusal. She would not accept a healing. Artemis wanted to argue. Wanted to explain to her mother that this was not the time for her to die. She didn't know exactly when the proper time to die might be, but this was absolutely not it. But something in Olympia's eyes told her that her wise old mother knew more than she did, and her wishes were to be honored. Artemis steeled herself and said nothing.

Demitra and Nacaria were sitting on the sofa which they had righted to its feet. Nacaria was visibly upset, blaming herself for everything which had taken place. Demitra was repeatedly reassuring her that none of it had been her fault. Atheidrelle was the only one to blame.

"I thought we were done with that woman," Nacaria cried. "I really thought all of the past was behind us."

"What I don't understand is what Xander meant before he left," Demitra remarked. "If Atheidrelle isn't Arielle's mother…Nacaria, did you by chance give birth to twins when you had Seth?"

"Of course not."

"What if you did? What if Atheidrelle did something then, stole one without you even knowing. It would explain Arielle's emotional connection to this family."

"I think I'd know if I gave birth to twins," Nacaria said incredulously. Secretly she wondered, however. She clearly recalled Seth's birth, but now seeing just how unfathomably powerful Atheidrelle Obreiggon's magic was, perhaps no theory was off the table.

Xander zapped back into the living room holding Blackie D'Angelo by the hand. Blackie looked perplexed and shaken. She stared at the site of Arielle frozen in place in the living room as the Blanchards swarmed around she and Xander.

"I've filled Blackie in," Xander informed the Blanchards. He took a deep breath, gave a nod of solidarity towards his sister-in-law and announced, "Blackie is not Arielle's aunt. She is Arielle's mother."

No one expected to hear those words, yet as they hit the air, things began to make a little more sense in the larger scheme of things. The revelation explained quite a lot, from Atheidrelle's disdain for Arielle to Blackie's special closeness with her niece. It also explained Arielle's innate kindness which was hard to reconcile if Atheidrelle was her mother.

Nacaria was shaken by the news. Her immediate reaction was to feel betrayed. Her best friend and the man she had loved all her life—they shared a child? Blackie could see it in her eyes and knew what she was thinking.

"It's not like that Nikky," she reassured her friend as she took hold of Nacaria's hand. "It was that spell Atheidrelle cast all those years ago, the one we told was how Arielle was born."

"I remember," Nacaria said. "Atheidrelle cast a spell to make Xander fall in love with her, but it backfired. Instead of seeing her and falling in love with her, he only saw the woman he loved…me. He made love to her that night believing it was me. Atheidrelle got pregnant with Arielle."

"Only it was me he saw that night. Not Atheidrelle," Blackie revealed. "Atheidrelle was furious. He was meant for her, but he saw me before she could get to him. He thought I was you."

Nacaria needed a few minutes to soak it all in. The revelation did not make her feel any better. "I can understand the spell on him," she told Blackie. "He was under magical influence. He made love to who he thought was the woman he loved...me. But you, Blackie? Atheidrelle did not cast a spell over you. Why did you make love with Xander?"

"My reasons aren't important," Blackie said. "Not right now."

"I think they are," Nacaria snapped. "You were my best friend."

"It wasn't Blackie's fault," Xander said, taking hold of Nacaria's hand. He took a deep breath and gave her the rest of the painful story. "I raped her."

Nacaria gasped.

Blackie was still clutching Nacaria's other hand, which she now shook up and down in desperation as she tried to diminish the gravity of Xander's statement. "He did not rape me, Nacaria. He did not think it was me. Her spell was meant to ensure they made love. He was compelled to carry it out. It was not Xander operating with Xander's compass. Once I realized he was not in control of his impulses, I stopped fighting him and let it happen. Xander, you did not rape me. You would never do that to a woman. None of what occurred that night was your fault."

Nacaria walked away for a moment back to the sofa. Her sisters wanted to console her but gave her space. She sat on the couch and contemplated what she had been told.

Artemis had questions now which she directed to Blackie. "And so you became pregnant that night?"

Blackie nodded. "Atheidrelle's spell also carried a fertilization component to it. She wanted to ensure Xander would impregnate her. But he ran into me first."

No one had yet noticed how out of breath Olympia was, or perhaps they had only attributed it to the mayhem they had been through. But she managed to push through her shortness of breath long enough to ask Blackie a question, "And you gave your sister your child? May I ask why?"

"To be free," Blackie stated. "She and Thaddeuss agreed I could leave the House of Duquesne and be awarded financial freedom, in exchange for the baby. I asked to remain in its life, as its aunt, but to never have to step foot in that house again."

"I do not understand," Artemis replied. "You could have left on your own at any time."

"No, I couldn't," Blackie answered mysteriously. "There is much you do not know about that house or the D'Angelo family. Just trust that I did what I had to do, otherwise Arielle and I both would have been damned all of our lives."

Demitra was astounded. No matter the reason, how could Blackie abandon her own child? Much less leave it in the care of someone as vile as Atheidrelle? She wanted to know the reason. Blackie had no answer. Xander chimed in at her defense.

"The child grew up at Oleander, free from the D'Angelo's control," Xander added. "Atheidrelle saved face in the public eye, and Arielle and I were all we had."

It was all rather sad and mind blowing but Salem was tired of the distraction. She looked at the older generation of the room and announced, "This history lesson is all very interesting, but can we please get back to saving my sister?"

Blackie snapped back to the present moment, pushing the past back where it belonged. Looking toward her immobilized daughter, now able to freely claim her as such, she said, "I can pull Arielle from wherever Atheidrelle has pushed her down inside. I am not as strong as my sister, but strong enough to reach my daughter and push Atheidrelle out."

"Where will Atheidrelle go?" Salem asked. "Will her spirit become a shadow here at Blanchard House?"

"We can't kill a shadow," Seth replied.

"We aren't going to," Olympia announced. "We are going to kill a body. My body."

CHAPTER FORTY NINE

Olympia's Sacrifice

Blanchard House had stood for 150 years. During its life it rarely stood silent. That night, after the words everyone had just heard its matriarch utter, Blanchard House was as silent as the grave while the family looked on to Olympia Blanchard in disbelief.

She met their gazes and said it again, "We are going to kill my body. We will draw Atheidrelle out of Arielle and into me, and I will be the one who dies. And I'll take Atheidrelle with me."

All at once the other Blanchards rang out in protest, their voices shouting over one another to the point none of what they were saying was clear or coherent. Only Artemis remained quiet. Olympia locked eyes with her eldest and gave a nod of reassurance. Artemis understood. Nodding back, she closed her eyes, squeezing a lone tear from the corner of one before reopening.

"Mother!" Demitra exclaimed. "What are you talking about? You are not sacrificing yourself."

"It's what has to happen," Olympia asserted. There was nothing faltering in her decision. Never before had Olympia Blanchard been more sure of herself.

Zelda still argued the point. Grabbing her friend's wrist and shaking it she said, "Lympy, surely we can think of somethin' else."

"No, old friend," Olympia replied with a pat to Zelda's hand. "You and I both know we haven't time to come up with another plan."

"I don't understand what anyone is saying," Fable cried.

Artemis took charge of the chaotic scene. "It is simple," she explained. "Blackie will draw Arielle forward, Arielle will push Atheidrelle out of her body, and we will steer Atheidrelle into Mother."

"And then," Olympia finished. "You children will kill me."

"No!" Seth shouted. "No, this is insane."

Salem pulled her hair up into her hands and wringed it frantically as she paced the blood-stained floor. She could not face this prospect. She had lost too much already. She could not lose her grandmother now. She wanted to shout at Olympia. She wanted to beseech her to find another alternative. But Salem could not find adequate words nor the strength to say them. She simply paced the floor, wringing her hair, occasionally looking at the blood-soaked sheet now covering her dead cousin's body as she contemplated what life was going to be like if she lost her grandmother tonight as well.

Fable found words—which was never a problem for her. "Hecate, we can pull Atheidrelle out of Ari and she can just go back to shadow form. We'll stop her another day."

Olympia's voice turned authoritarian, "There is no other day. No other way. This is it."

Seth, not considering his own strength or the height of his anxiety, grabbed his grandmother by the arms. She winced at the pressure of his grip. "Then we'll choose somebody else," he demanded.

"Who else would we choose?" Olympia responded incredulously. "I have lived my life, Seth. You all still have years to go."

"This is ridiculous, mother," Nacaria said teary eyed. "I just got you back. I'm not going to let you sacrifice yourself to solve yet another one of my problems."

"Atheidrelle isn't just your problem, Momma," Salem noted. "This isn't your fault."

"Regardless, this isn't happening this way," Demitra insisted.

"It has to be me," Olympia informed them. "And we must hurry."

"Why does it have to be you?" Demitra said.

Olympia looked at Artemis for help. The baton always passes from one generation to the next and now it was Artemis' time to take it. All of her life, her mother had been the personification of strength and fortitude. Now those ancient eyes looked frail, frightened, and at a loss for how to handle a situation. Artemis Blanchard clasped both Demitra and Nacaria's shaky hands and proclaimed, "Because Mother is dying anyway."

"What?" Beryl exclaimed.

"I'm dying, children," Olympia said meekly. "I have felt it coming closer every day. I am afraid tonight has been too much for me. Even as I speak my heart is giving out. I am struggling even to stand. It is my time. I did not realize it would come this way, but it has arrived, and it has come with a purpose."

Demitra turned on Artemis, "You knew?"

"Mother told me the other day."

"Why you? Why didn't she tell all of us?" Nacaria asked.

"Because Artemis is the new Hecate," Olympia announced. "She will take my place."

As this announcement registered with the others, Beryl approached her grandmother and lovingly stroked her cheek. "Hecate, you don't have to die. You know I can heal you."

"But it would be wrong to let you," Olympia smiled. "All of us have a time to die. This one is mine. This very situation proves it. Even if you were to heal all my frailties, I would still have to be the one to die tonight to save the family. It is the final honor life has bestowed upon me. I get the privilege of saving your lives."

"But Atheidrelle's body," Seth reminded everyone. "Her body is in Dredmore."

"The body lying in Dredmore ceased to be her body the moment she possessed Arielle," Xander explained. "I expect the body in Dredmore has already passed away. The moment she enters Olympia, Olympia's form becomes Atheidrelle's physical form. That is the danger when you can jump bodies. The moment Olympia dies, Atheidrelle dies."

Olympia was growing weaker by the minute, a pain now emanated down her arm as her struggle for breath grew. The family had to act quickly, but she steeled herself with the last vestige strength within her to say her goodbyes to those she loved.

Resting against the soft cushions of the sofa, she clutched Salem's hand as Salem knelt on the floor beside her. "Salem, restart your life. Reclaim everything you have lost by building again. Find love. Have a child. And use your Council seat to lead the association into a new age. You are the new generation of the Consort. Reign in honor."

Beryl came to her side next as Seth helped Salem away with an arm of comfort around her waist. "Beryl, your path is only beginning. Great things await you as well as many tribulations. Lean on Artemis when you need strength; look to your mother when you need love. Remember I will be with you when you need me."

"I love you, Hecate."

Seth came over next. He was struggling to hold it together. He wanted to be strong for his sister, his mother, and himself, but it was proving more difficult an endeavor to achieve. Tears swelled in his eyes as he squatted down before his grandmother.

"Seth, you have it in you to be a great man. Lead your little family well. Protect my precious Yasmine. Tell her how much I have loved and cherished her. Raise your children with the dignity and pride I have instilled in you."

As Seth staggered away from the sofa, Fable passed him to take her turn. They squeezed one another's hands as they switched places.

"Fable, your path will be rough at times and joyous at times. Love your boys well and equally. Traverse the hurdles ahead using your strength and your beautiful spirit. Do great things and teach your boys the same."

Nacaria came next, wiping her eyes and struggling to not hyperventilate herself as she sat down on the edge of the sofa by her mother's legs. She looked deep into Olympia's eyes as she gently held her hands in her own.

"Nacaria, my precious baby. Begin your new life in wisdom. Helm your family with love and encouragement. I believe in you. You will make a remarkable life. It is your time to live."

Demitra followed, lowering herself to both knees as she stroked her sweet mother's forehead. "Demitra, face the mistakes you have made and twist them into triumphs. Do not be afraid of your weaknesses because your strengths outweigh them tenfold."

Once Demitra walked away, Artemis approached. She could see this was taxing her mother and felt everything that ever needed to be said between them had been. But Olympia persisted, desiring to give her eldest one last moment. "Artemis, lead this family your way. Not mine. Do not try to replicate me. Be your own Hecate. You are the wisest person I know. I wouldn't have left my family in your hands if that were not the case."

Xander and Blackie had remained back, giving the family their time. Now they stepped forward to assist the old woman to stand. The family gathered around her for one massive family hug, the last they would ever experience with their precious Olympia. Olympia looked over to Zelda. Zelda grinned at her dearest friend and told her with her mind, *I already know. And you know I've got them...always.*

Demitra, Beryl, and Nacaria went down to the vault and gathered the few items Olympia instructed them to bring up. Seth and Fable went upstairs and retrieved other items Olympia told them to get. While they were gone, Olympia took the opportunity to pull Artemis aside for one final embrace while Blackie and Xander stood by Arielle's motionless body.

"You were my first great love," Olympia told her daughter. "I'm going to miss you."

Artemis sobbed on her mother's shoulder. "Mother, I will never stop missing you for the rest of my life. I love you so much."

"One more thing," Olympia said, glancing around to make sure no one could hear her. "Beryl."

"What about Beryl?"

"Tonight, her invincibility. I never thought I would see it. I've heard of it, but never imagined...It is called *The God Strain*."

Artemis looked confused. She was about to ask when Olympia shook her head and placed a finger to her lips. Demitra and Nacaria returned from the vault with a potion they had made and a golden cord with frayed edges.

Artemis dipped the cord into the liquid potion before tying one end to Olympia's wrist and the other to Arielle's. Blackie stood before Arielle's body and placed her hands on both sides of her daughter's head. She concentrated as hard as she had ever concentrated before until she reached Arielle's spirit inside. She urged her to wake up, to come forth, to push Atheidrelle out. Blackie felt Arielle growing stronger and stronger beneath the surface.

"Now!" Blackie cried stepping out of the way.

Salem unfroze Atheidrelle. Atheidrelle lifted Arielle's arms to attack but couldn't. The arms were unsteady, Atheidrelle was losing control of the body. She began to sway, then slightly vibrate.

"Get...out...of me!" Arielle shrieked.

Suddenly Arielle fell backward, the loose cording falling free from her arm as she hit the floor with a thud. Olympia stood in the center of the room, her chest heaving as if gathering large breaths after a long deprivation of air. She turned to look at the Blanchards standing in front of her. Her blue eyes enlarged and slowly went black as Atheidrelle realized she now possessed the body of Olympia Blanchard.

"Now!" Seth screamed, withdrawing a shotgun from behind his back and firing it directly into Olympia's chest.

Fable followed suit firing a pistol at her grandmother's heart. As the cousins fired repeating rounds into the old woman, their tears made it almost impossible to see clearly. But they did not miss, unloading several rounds of ammunition into the form of their precious grandmother. Olympia's body shook from the impact as bullets riddled her. The sounds of each blast echoed and reverberated off the walls causing Nacaria to jump into Xander's arms. Likewise, Artemis pulled Demitra close, the sisters squeezing each other in their embrace as they watched the terrible sight of their mother's blood and flesh being ripped away by the blasts. Zelda placed a reassuring hand on both their backs, steadying them. Olympia's punctured body stood rigid, Atheidrelle's black eyes staring forward, focused on the last sight she would ever see...Nacaria in Xander's arms.

Salem bounded forward next, brandishing the same family heirloom sword with which they had battled Patric the year before. Olympia's father's sword. With one sharp swing, Salem sliced her grandmother's head off. Blood spurted from the severed neck as Olympia Blanchard's head hit the floor and rolled onto its side. Atheidrelle's black eyes stared blankly forward from their sideways stare on the hardwood planks. Slowly, Olympia's lifeless torso crumpled to the floor, landing beside it with a thud. Atheidrelle Obreiggon was vanquished.

And Olympia Blanchard was dead.

CHAPTER FIFTY

Steaks, Cakes, and Memories

Hummingbirds had finally found the feeder Artemis hung for them on the corner of the house. Or perhaps Fable told them it was there. However, they found it, their addition provided a component of peace which had been lacking for a long time. Artemis stood back on the lawn and admired the life all around. The pots lining the railing of the porch were brimming over with petunias, lantana, dahlias, and Gerber daisies. The rose bushes around the house and in the flower garden bloomed in brilliant golds, reds, and corals. The morning glories streaming across the eaves of the porch were in high blue blossom. In the distance, near the chicken houses, two deer were grazing in the meadow. Summer was back at Blanchard House in full force, and it was spectacular. This time Artemis welcomed it.

She hadn't welcomed it so much last year. That had marked the one-year anniversary of Olympia's death. She had not felt much like gardening then. Artemis felt terribly guilty about allowing the porch and the rose garden to go untended last year, especially considering how much her mother had loved her flowers. But it was too emotional for her. This year was different. This year she felt like honoring her mother and bringing life back to the grounds.

Fable had finally broken Romulus of pestering the birds and squirrels around the property, although he still had quite a problem letting a rabbit hop past without a good high-speed chase. He wasn't a cub any longer. He was three years old now, a fully-grown wolf even though his brother had only recently graduated out of diapers. Romulus was something to see. As a result of Fable's genes, his brown coat was silky and long. His teeth were pointy and his claws sharp when protracted. Despite these frightening characteristics, Rom was the most affectionate—and popular—creature in Daihmler County. Town tongues loved to wag to newcomers in the area about the large wolf that lives with the witches on the property at the edge of town. Of course, those same gossipy women also were vehement to clarify that the Blanchards' pet wolf was docile and domesticated. Fable didn't know how many times townspeople had called over the last couple years to ask her to bring Rom over to solve a rat problem. Even Charlie Bennet would ask Demitra to bring him to cases on occasion if a scent needed tracking. Romulus Blanchard had become the token town pet.

Artemis was clipping flowers for an arrangement when she looked across the yard to see Rom playing chase with his brother. Little Hera was riding him, clutching his fur in her hands, squealing in delight as they sailed over the grass after Con. Over the wall of the pool area, Artemis saw black smoke swirling, letting her know Seth and Jerry were most likely burning the steaks. Probably because Howard was mixing the drinks extra strong in the kitchen.

Demitra was seated on a bench outside the gazebo, keeping an eye on the children while she flipped through police files for a particularly difficult case she was currently helping with. The rest of the children were playing badminton in the side yard. Beryl and Fable against Salem and Arielle. Fable was continuously swinging wide and hitting Beryl in the back of the head with the birdie. Yasmine was feeding baby Titan a bottle on the porch as she laughed with Zelda over something. She'd given Seth a son last November, completing their little family.

Down the road, the sound of crunching gravel under tire wheels met with swirling dust rising around Nacaria's car as she drove onto the Blanchard property. Artemis was excited everyone would be home this weekend. She didn't see much of Xander and Nacaria these days. Being the mistress of Oleander took up a lot of her sister's time. Charleston was offering Nacaria quite a whirlwind of parties and activities. As they pulled into the parking area in front of the porch, Artemis was happy to see Cassandra, as well as Blackie in the back seat. Having been shed of her mother's influence for the last two years, Cassandra was developing into quite a nice person. She had even started to develop relationships with Seth and Salem, as well as repairing the one she had with Arielle. It took Arielle a few months to work past discovering Blackie had been her mother all along, but in the years since that revelation their relationship was developing into quite a close one.

Seth, Yasmine, Salem, and Arielle ran out to meet the car. Artemis hung back a few minutes giving the Obreiggon family a moment to greet each other. Xander immediately began rubbing Salem's stomach. In all fairness everyone did. She was due very soon now. She had already named her little boy Olympus, partly to honor her grandmother's legacy and partly because the baby had been Olympia's idea in the first place. Seth and Fable still made artificial insemination jokes, but Salem knew it was just good family teasing. Once she had been made president of the advertising firm after Travis Dandridge retired, she knew it was time to begin a family of her own again.

The barbeque steaks were not burned as badly as Artemis thought they would be. Jerry was a terrible griller, notorious for burning everything, which meant Seth had to have done the lion's share of the cooking. Howard and Xander pushed the three large picnic tables together on the lawn and the family gathered with their plates to dine.

Lympy would love this, Zelda told Artemis with her mind.

Yes, she would.

Artemis surveyed the family with pride. *Her* family. It was her family now. And what a family they had turned out to be. Fable's practice was booming. Beryl was as successful a physician as ever. Yasmine was now quite the businesswoman, taking over Sinclair Industries and continuing her grandmother's philanthropy. Seth, never much for ambition, had become quite the proficient stay-at-home dad. Between the kiddie birthday parties, playdates, and general daily responsibilities he had become quite the father for Hera, Con, Rom, and little Titan. Arielle was now Howard's assistant, living full time in Blanchard House. Olympia would truly be proud.

Sitting at the head of the picnic table, Artemis dug into her steak and potato salad and joined into the nonsensical conversations swirling around. After a little while she felt tiny feet climbing up the back of her chair. Two little arms wrapped around her neck.

"Hi there, baby girl!" she said, pulling Hera into her lap. "Did you finish your lunch?"

"Uh huh," the beautiful little girl said. "Hecate, I think it is time for the cake."

"What cake?" Artemis teased.

"The cake you made this morning, silly," Hera laughed. "Con, don't you think it's time for cake?"

"Yeah!"

"All right, children," Artemis smiled. "We will cut the cake in just a minute."

"These kids are sugar-crazy!" Yasmine remarked.

"These kids?" Demitra laughed. "All of you were at that age too."

"Same thing with you and your sisters, Demmy," Zelda chuckled. "Kids is kids no matter what generation."

"And there have been quite a few generations on this land," Artemis smiled looking out over her large family.

"How long has the Blanchard family lived here?" Jerry asked his wife.

"Oh, a very long time. Even before we were Blanchards."

"It's fun to think about it, isn't it?" Salem began. "All the many ancestors who walked these same paths, maybe even sat right here on this same patch of lawn. It's nice to belong to a homeplace that spans the generations."

"We are pretty lucky," Seth added. "We have Blanchard House and now Oleander. I really do want to spend some more time in Charleston and get to know Dad's side of our family tree."

"Nothing would please your mother and I more," Xander grinned.

"Oh, do!" Cassandra exclaimed. "If you and Yasmine plan a trip out to see us, I'll show you everything there is to see."

Hera whined again behind Artemis' ear. "The cake, Hecate. The cake."

"I'll go get the cake, Aunt Artemis," Beryl offered.

"Thank you, Beryl," Artemis said. "It's on the counter. A big sheet cake, you can't miss it."

Beryl stood up and gathered the few empty plates from those around her who had finished eating. Fable rose to help her and together they started for the house to put the dishes in the sink and grab dessert.

Everyone went back to their chattering when suddenly the sound of crashing dishes brought everyone to attention. Fable stood alone, horrified, as she stared to the empty space on the lawn beside her where Beryl no longer stood. Only a heap of broken dishes in the grass marked where her sister had been moments before. Fable looked back to the picnic table.

"What happened? Where did she go?"

"Beryl?!" Demitra cried jumping from the table.

"She just vanished!" Fable cried.

Zelda glanced at Artemis. "This is it. I know 'xactly where she is."

Artemis lowered her voice and replied, "Do you mean...."

"Yep," Zelda nodded. "You still got that picture your momma gave you? Everything is 'bout to change."

ABOUT THE AUTHOR

Micah House lives in Birmingham, Alabama with his husband and son. He is a former columnist and has published two short stories, Thursie and The Three Mrs. Rogers. His first novel, *The Blanchard Witches of Daihmler County*, was the first in the Blanchard Witches series. This novel, *Prodigal Daughters*, is the second book in the ongoing series.

BOOK 3 SYNOPSIS

THE BLANCHARD WITCHES : STITCHES IN TIME

Things are not always easy for the Blanchard family of Daihmler, Alabama. Over the last few years, they've experienced more than their share of tribulations even for a family of witches. Through the many ups and downs they have always had each other. The world seemed to be settline down for the coven, but everything changed at the family picnic, when Beryl Blanchard suddenly vanished before their eyes without a trace.

In the third book of the Blanchard Witches series, the family must search the past to find their beloved Beryl. They'll encounter relatives they have only heard about through family lore. Facing new challenges in unfamiliar worlds, dangers will arise as the family timeline might change forever. Join your favoutite Alabama witches for their next adventure as they battle one of the greatest foes they've come up against... time.

Milton Keynes UK
Ingram Content Group UK Ltd.
UKHW020639310723
426074UK00019B/1442